Two Hearts

When I Said I Do, I Meant Forever

Two Hearts

When I Said I Do, I Meant Forever

James Eric Richey

This book is a work of fiction. Names, characters, places, and incidents are the product of the author's imagination or are used fictitiously. Any resemblance to actual events, locales, or persons, living or dead, is coincidental. The publisher is not responsible for websites (or their content) that are not owned by the publisher.

All rights reserved. In accordance with the U.S. Copyright Act of 1976, the scanning, uploading, and electronic sharing of any part of this book without the permission of the publisher is unlawful piracy and theft of the author's intellectual property. If you would like to use material from the book (other than for review purposes), prior written permission must be obtained by contacting the publisher at james@jerbooks.com. Thank you for your support of the author's rights.

Printed in the United State of America.

Copyright © 2014 James Eric Richey
All rights reserved.

ISBN: 0990918106
ISBN 13: 9780990918103
Library of Congress Control Number: 2014915690
JER Books – Cheyenne, Wyoming

*This one is for my dear
sweet wife, Heather Richey,
for her patience with me as
I struggled to write my first book.
I will ever be grateful for
your love and support.*

Chapter 1

Jaxon

The Find

As Jax tilted his head back, the beam of light from his headlamp cut through the darkness, illuminating the top of the mine wall. A gaping crack, weaving its way from the ceiling to the ground, meandered like a river, widening in some places and narrowing in others.

Two hundred feet deep into the mine, he could still see where sunlight filled the railroad-tie framed entrance, but he was too far away for the light to reach him. He breathed deeply; the air was cool this far down into the shaft.

The beam of light, a natural extension of his eyes, focused on a spot on the wall at the edge of the crack, marking his target. He lowered his safety goggles into position and gripped the wooden handle of the rock pick. He raised it overhead. With a loud clang, the pick struck, its single fang bouncing off the solid surface. He scanned the light over his victim. Nothing. Not even a scratch.

His fingers brushed against the rough carving at the end of the wooden handle as he let the rock pick slip through his hand and drop to the ground. JTT. The initials he'd carved into the handle stood for Jaxon Thomas Tagget. That was a mouthful. Only his mother pronounced every syllable, and usually it was when she was hot around the collar. Everyone else, including Mrs. Bradshaw, his twelfth-grade English teacher, called him Jax, and that's the way he liked it.

He removed his safety goggles and placed his left hand high on the wall over the crack. The rock wall was cool like the air.

He closed his eyes as he slowly moved his hand down the wall, following the jagged edge of the crack. He slowed his pace in a few places, and twice he stopped, his skin connecting with the rough surface. He opened his eyes and examined the crack, but, neither seeing nor feeling anything, he continued on.

He'd heard somewhere that a miner could sense where gold was from just the touch of the skin—a miner's sixth sense.

He reached the bottom and sat back, leaning on the old iron rails of the tracks that led out of the mine. Nothing. He looked toward the entrance and to the last five places he'd dug. At each spot he'd employed the same technique: touch the rock, feel for the gold, and strike. He smiled. Who was he kidding? He wasn't a miner—not yet, anyway.

Jax returned his focus to the wall in front of him. He put on his goggles and picked up the rock pick. His strategy hadn't worked before, but maybe it would this time. He swung the pick, aiming just below his last target. His aim slightly off, the pick struck four inches from the edge of the crack.

He must have hit a weak spot, because a three-foot section of wall crumbled to the ground, sending up a cloud of dust. A century of neglect rose from the floor of the mine, filtering through the air, making it difficult for Jax to see or breathe. The musty smell made Jax gag and cough. He yanked the blue bandana tied around his neck over his mouth and nose and held his breath.

Just as he turned to head toward the entrance, his headlamp flashed across something shiny in the crumbled wall at his feet. His eyes bulged. He dropped his pick, wildly scooped up a double handful of rock, and ran, his lungs starting to burn. After fifteen feet he cleared the cloud of dust and stopped. His body convulsed as he bent, gasping. He breathed deeply, fresh air filling his lungs to capacity. He exhaled and inhaled again.

Jax dropped to his knees. Opening both hands, he dumped the rocks on the ground. His light found it first, a gold nugget a bit larger than a shooter marble, partially buried at the top edge of the pile of rocks. He carefully brushed off the gravel fragments that covered it and reached down to pick it up.

"Whoa!" Jax roared.

It was huge.

His horse neighed, startled by his yell. Jax watched his horse dance across the sunlit entrance, still tethered to the left support beam.

"Bullet? Oh, shoot," Jax said.

Bullet was a Morgan horse with a creamy tan coat and matching points of black mane, black tail, and four black socks—a sharply dressed buckskin. Bullet had one blemish: a small black clump of hair the size of a silver dollar on his right rump, an island in a sea of cream. Jax's oldest brother, Tommy, had said it looked like a bullet hole, and that's how Jax's horse got his name.

Jax pulled out his cell phone and hit the power button to wake it up: 6:45. It would be getting dark soon. He'd tethered Bullet at the entrance just over three hours ago, and in his excitement to start digging he'd forgotten all about him.

He glanced back down the mine shaft. The billowing cloud of airborne particles slowly started to settle, but it was still too thick to see anything. It would be another ten minutes before he could thoroughly sift through the crumbled rock.

But looking down at the gold nugget in his hand, he realized he'd found what he'd been looking for. A rush of excitement flooded through his veins as he jumped up and raced to the entrance.

Outside, the air was fresh and warm, filled with the powerful but beautiful scent of wild flowers and—moisture. He glanced around. Everything, including his saddle, had a sheer covering of water. He shouldn't be surprised. It was Saturday, May 4, and typical of spring in Dillon, Montana, there had been an afternoon rain shower.

Jax stopped and stared, taking in the whole scene before him.

The Western Pleasure Mine, perched on a hillside of the Hogback Mountain, had a commanding view of Trapper's Valley, with its lush green grass spreading out to the west below him. A rainbow, in its full spectrum of color from red all the way to violet, stretched from one side of the valley to the other. The fire yellow was especially vibrant. The Big Hole River, shrouded in willow and cottonwood trees, made its way northeast. A world-class trout fishery, the Big Hole crossed the Double T. The setting sun reflected off its rippling surface like a golden seam cutting through the vale. The river passed under the high-arching rainbow, a gateway to a magical world beyond.

Off in the distance Jax could see the Pioneer Mountains rising in the west, minutes away from hiding the descending sun. Just to the north, Trapper's Valley was flanked by the McCartney Mountains. Jax leveled his gaze to see the Pioneer Mountains reflected from the mirror-like surface of Jenny Lake. It wasn't any lake you'd find on a map or a fishing guide book. It was more of a watering hole for the cattle on the ranch, but it was big enough to swim in, something Jax and his friends had done every summer for the past twelve years.

Movement caught his eye. A red-tailed hawk with wings stretched wide soared through the sky on a current of air, scanning the ground for dinner.

The view was majestic. And to think, one day this could all be his.

From where he stood and as far as the eye could see was the Double T. Just over fifteen thousand acres—twenty-four sections, to be exact—the Double T was currently the largest privately held cattle ranch in Southwestern Montana.

The ranch, named after Jax's sixth great-grandfather, Thomas Tagget, was owned and run by Jax's father, Tru Tagget, and like any proud father, Tru wanted to pass it on to one of his children to make it six generations deep.

First came Tommy, the oldest, then Maddie in the middle, and finally Jax, who brought up the rear. Tommy, now an orthopedic surgeon, lived in Denver with his wife and two children. He'd made it clear he wasn't coming back to work the family ranch. Maddie had been married for only one year. Her husband had just finished law school at the University of Montana and had recently secured an associate position with a ten-partner firm in Billings. They wouldn't be coming back to the ranch either.

That left Jax.

He loved the ranch; it was all he'd ever known. But he wasn't sure if he wanted to stay. The memories were endless, and living in Montana on the Double T was heaven. But Jax wanted more. He was capable of something bigger, something grander than this small town. He wanted to see the world.

Jax took out his cell phone and activated the camera. This was what posters were made of. He took several pictures, making sure he captured every angle, but he knew his little digital device couldn't adequately capture the true beauty of the scene before him.

Bullet nickered, bringing him back.

The horse came up to him, but when Jax reached out his empty hand to touch Bullet's nose, the horse shook his head and stepped away, letting Jax know he wasn't pleased.

"I know. I've been gone a long time." Jax stepped closer to Bullet and reached out again. "I'm sorry, boy." Jax opened his other hand to show Bullet the gold nugget. "Look what I found."

This time Bullet nodded his head as if he understood and stepped toward Jax, seeming to accept his apology.

Two Hearts

Jax held the gold piece in his hand for Bullet to smell, but not finding anything edible the horse pulled away. Jax placed the nugget in a small leather pouch with a few other flakes of gold he'd found in the last three months.

He pulled out an apple from his saddle bag and held it in his hand beneath the horse's nose. Bullet sniffed it a couple of times, blew hot air on Jax's cold hand, and took a bite. Apology accepted, all things forgotten, Jax rubbed Bullet's muzzle as he ate.

"Well, big fella," Jax said, "we'd better be getting home."

※

It was dark when Jax and Bullet rode up to the barn. Bullet neighed as they stopped at the hitching rail in front of the barn, happy to finally be home.

At the sound of the horse, Jax's father stepped out from the side door of the barn.

"Been up to Western Pleasure?" Mr. Tagget asked, starting the same conversation he'd had with his son every Saturday since March, except this time Jax's answer was different. Jax slid off his saddle, a cheesy grin lighting up his face.

"Yup."

"And? Did you strike out again?"

"Nope, not this time."

Mr. Tagget's eyes grew large in the fading light. "You found something?"

"The mine is abandoned, but not completely barren." Jax pulled out the leather pouch from his saddle bag. He loosened the throng around the top and dumped out the nugget into his palm. The overhead fluorescent light hanging from the side of the barn reflected off the gold, making it sparkle.

"Wow," his father said. "It's huge!"

"Mount Everest huge!"

"No kidding!"

Jax slipped the nugget back into the leather pouch and put it into the front pocket of his pants. He turned and started stripping his saddle and gear off Bullet.

"You know . . . you don't have to do this," Mr. Tagget said over Jax's shoulder. He could hear his father's feet shuffling in the dirt behind him. "You know, your mom and I are happy to help you buy Annie a ring. You could use the gold to make something else."

Jax didn't answer. He grunted as he pulled the saddle from Bullet's back, and then he disappeared through the open door into the tack room.

He'd been through this before with his mother and father, and he knew where it was going. In fact, his father had come to him several times alone offering his help, but Jax had turned him down then, as he was going to do now.

"Thanks for the offer," Jax said as he stepped back out of the tack room, "but I want to do this on my own." He picked up the saddle bags and the reins and headed back to the tack room.

"Jaxon," his father said, using his full name.

Jax stopped and turned to face him.

"That is truly honorable," Mr. Tagget said. "Really, it's very noble of you, but you're going about this the wrong way."

Two Hearts

He cleared his throat. "Your mother wanted me to tell you this. When you give a girl an engagement ring, it makes a value statement. It tells her and the world what you think her true worth is—do you see her as your queen or as someone common and ordinary?"

"I treat Annie as my queen and she knows it."

"But, it's not just how you treat her. When a girl receives a ring, she wants it to be perfect. Shiny. Big. Fancy. She wants it to sparkle. A girl wants something she can show off to her girlfriends—something she can brag about."

"Annie's not like that."

"I know she's not, son, but making her a ring in shop class won't let her know she is your queen."

His father extended his hand. In it was a Visa Credit Card.

"Your mother and I want to help. Take Annie shopping. Let her pick out something big and flashy. Whatever she wants. Make her feel special."

Jax turned, strode into the tack room, and dropped the gear on the work bench. He shook his head just once. It wasn't that his parents couldn't help; they could afford any ring Annie would pick out. It was just the way they wanted to help. Their way was the easy way—go buy her a ring, any one she wanted.

But Jax had sacrificed every Saturday for the past three months going to the abandoned mine, and today he'd finally found what he was looking for—enough gold to make Annie a ring.

When Jax returned, the credit card had disappeared.

"I appreciate the offer, but I don't want to buy Annie just *any* ring. I want to give her a part of me. It's more than just the ring; it's the sacrifice, the effort. That's what I'm giving her."

"Is it enough?"

"I hope so."

"Will she say yes?"

Jax paused and shrugged, squinching up his face.

"Her mother?" Tru asked.

"Yeah," Jax whispered.

"Just remember this: when you marry a girl, you marry the entire family—including the mother—and all her baggage. Are you ready for that? Are you sure you want to do this?"

"I've never been more sure about anything in my life. Annie is worth any extra baggage she may have."

His father's hand came out again, empty this time, and Jax took it. "I'm proud of you, son. You're a good man, and I know you'll do the right thing. If you want some help, just let me know."

"Thanks, Dad."

His father drew him in, and they embraced. "So, when are you going to pop the question?"

Chapter 2

Annie

Broken Promise

Friday, June 9, twelve noon. Annie Bradley would remember this day forever. She was seventeen years old. Young in comparison to the ninety-seven other seniors graduating with her.

As the outgoing student body president of Beaverhead County High School, it was her responsibility to speak at the graduation ceremony. Fortunately, she wasn't alone on the stand. Sitting next to her was Susanna Rimes, the valedictorian. She would speak before Annie.

Annie had been sitting in the same seat for the past half hour, and her backside was numb. A tingle went down her leg, so she moved ever so slightly to a new position in her chair, easing the pressure. She wanted to get up so badly and stretch, but she couldn't.

Seated before her, the entire Town of Dillon, Montana, filled the B. W. Lodge Gymnasium to capacity to celebrate with that year's graduates. It was the largest group she'd ever spoken in front of. She was nervous.

The high school band performed first, playing the theme song from the popular movie *The Hobbit*.

The graduating class, occupying the first four rows of chairs in front of the stand, looked stunning in their blue and gold caps and gowns. Jax sat in the back of the group, his last name starting with the letter T. Fortunately, from Annie's place on the stand, Jax was practically straight out in front of her. He had his cap on with the gold tassel hanging on his right side, his dark hair visible around the edges and out the back. He looked good.

They locked eyes. He gave her a smile and a wink. He made a funny face. She smiled discreetly, fighting desperately to control the giggles that wanted to burst out.

Annie glanced toward her mother. She was sitting as close as she could get—fifth row, sixth seat in from Annie's right. She was alone. Typical.

Annie's grandparents on her mother's side lived in Denver, Colorado. They'd made arrangements to come, but last week her grandmother had fallen down two flights of stairs and broken her hip. She and Grandpa were at home recuperating. They hadn't come.

Being on the stand in front of everyone, Annie didn't want to look like a spectacle with her head shifting down the rows like a typewriter, reaching the end of the line and making a hard return. So, with a smile set firm on her face, Annie's eyes gently moved back and forth over the faces of the people, scanning the crowd for her father. Row by row, section by section, she studied each face separately, carefully.

A handful of men stood behind the chairs at the back of the gymnasium. They'd come in late and didn't want to make a scene by crossing over people to get to a seat, so they chose to stand in the back. She didn't see her father back there. He wasn't sitting in any of the sections on the floor, nor was he standing in the back.

She double-checked until she had studied every person in the gymnasium twice.

He hadn't come.

Her facade faltered, her smile dipping just a bit. Annie looked to Jax. He raised his eyebrows in question. She gave a slight shake of her head.

Her left hand rose from off her lap and found the familiar scar on the side of her head, the tip of the scar just barely protruding from her hair line at her temple. The tip of her index finger moved back and forth over the blemish.

She began studying the faces one more time in case she'd missed him in the first two passes.

The choral group finished their second piece, and then her name was announced.

No more time; it was her turn.

Annie stood and stumbled to the podium. Her voice cracked with the first word out of her mouth, but she quickly recovered.

She encouraged the graduating class to set their goals high and not let fear stop them from achieving those goals. She told them to never give up, that the only way to fail was to stop trying. She finished with a quote from Winston Churchill, "Success is the ability to go from failure to failure without losing your enthusiasm." That was the main theme of her speech, which took her just under fifteen minutes to give.

She finished and then took her seat. Jax and her mother clapped the loudest of everyone.

The keynote speaker, Cheryl Thompson, a prominent businesswoman from Dillon, addressed the graduating class next. She spoke for thirty minutes straight, making jokes, giving sound advice, and sharing several experiences of lessons she had learned the hard way. It was good, but ten minutes too long.

Ron Lovegood, the school board chairman, and Kay Reynolds and Tami Peterson, the trustees, handed out the diplomas.

It was done.

The band started playing. The graduates yelled and screamed and threw their caps in the air. Annie had officially graduated from high school.

When Annie saw Jax on the gymnasium floor at the edge of the stand, she raced to him and jumped into his arms, burying her face into his chest.

"He didn't come," she said, the muscles in her jaw tightening.

"I'm sorry."

"But he'd promised," she said through gritted teeth.

Jax, always the optimist, said, "Something must've come up, or else he would've been here."

Annie had called and invited her father last week. She'd told him she was speaking. He'd sounded interested. He'd promised to come and even sent her a text saying he would be there. But he still hadn't showed.

Annie's mother found them.

"Congratulations," she said as she placed her arms around both of them.

"Thanks, Mrs. Bradley," Jax said.

Annie stepped back and looked away. She kept her eyes from her mother.

"What was that for?" Mrs. Bradley said. She stepped in front of Annie and looked her in the eyes. "What's with the long face? This is a day of celebration."

"He didn't come," Annie said.

"I tried to tell you."

"But he promised."

"When was the last time you saw your father?" Mrs. Bradley asked.

Annie was silent.

"When?"

Annie shrugged.

"Exactly. How many of your birthday parties has he come to in the last nine years, even though he'd promised?" Annie's mother began getting riled up, her voice rising slightly. "None. And, what about Christmas? In the past nine years, has he ever come to see you? Not once. Even though he'd promised."

"But this time I talked to him; he told me he would come hear me speak."

"He promised me, straight to my face, he would pay child support, but has he done it? Not once. Promises, promises. Easy for him to make, and even easier for him to break."

Annie stepped in front of Jax as if her body would shield him from her mother's tirade that she knew was coming. Over the years Annie had heard it all before, and she knew what was coming next. She didn't want Jax to see her family's dirty laundry. "Mother, not here," Annie whispered.

"Excuse us for a moment, will you, Jax?" Mrs. Bradley said. She didn't wait for a response. She placed her arm around Annie's waist and guided her ten feet away.

"Your father is a no-good, low-down, lying dirtbag," Mrs. Bradley said. "He is the scum of the earth."

"Mother!"

"It's true. He's the biggest loser on the planet. I'm sorry to have to tell you this, but your father is a man, and like all men, he only thinks of one thing—"

"Mother, please, not here," Annie said, effectively cutting off her mother before she could embarrass her any further.

"He only thinks of one thing and one thing only: himself. I've told you this over and over again. You can't trust men, especially your father. I'm sorry he let you down, but I've tried to warn you."

She gave Annie a hug. She kissed her on the forehead and gave her a squeeze—her mother's way of saying good-bye.

Mrs. Bradley broke her embrace with Annie and then stepped back. She reached out her hand toward Jax. He came over and took it.

"Congratulations again," Mrs. Bradley said. "I'll see each of you later." She turned and left.

Her mother had been right. It wasn't the first time her father had let her down. But this time was different. She had spoken to him, and he'd promised her he would come. She reached her arms around Jax's waist and drew him in close, placing her head against his chest. She hurt deep inside. She needed to be held.

After a moment, Jax asked, "You still on for tonight?"

"I don't know. I'd rather be alone with you, but we made plans, and . . . we can't leave our friends hanging."

Graduation parties. Friends. End-of-the-school-year good-byes. They had to do it.

She knew Jax was thinking the same thing.

"Well," Jax said, "I better get going if I'm going to make it to the party by the time it starts," Jax said. He bent and kissed her gently on the lips.

When he tried to pull back, Annie held tight for one more second and said, "He promised me."

"I'm so sorry, Annie. I'm sure he had a good reason."

Annie, practically half a foot shorter than Jax, glanced up into his eyes.

"Jaxon Tagget, don't you ever make me a promise you can't keep."

Chapter 3

Jaxon
The Ring

Jax gave Annie a hug and went to his truck. It was a four-year-old Ford F-150 extended cab. The off-white exterior paint was scratched here and there, and the inside was a little worn. It was fairly new in regard to years, but it already had 155,000 miles, most of which were freeway and ranch miles. It was a hand-me-down, his father's old truck. Without fail, every three years his dad purchased a new one. This year Jax had been the lucky one in the family to inherit the old one.

He stripped off his cap and gown, throwing them into the back seat. Jax pulled his cell phone from his pocket: 3:43. The graduation ceremonies had taken longer than he'd planned. If he didn't hustle, he'd be late to the party.

Jax jumped into the front seat and started the truck. He left the parking lot, turned right, and headed toward the school.

His shop teacher, Ray Stevens, had given him permission to work after school so he could finish the ring by graduation. For the past three weeks, Jax had sacrificed every night in order to complete it, but it still wasn't quite finished.

Jax wiped his brow and tucked a loose strand of wavy black hair behind his ear. After tonight, a haircut was next on the list. He raised the gold ring to the high-speed polishing machine one last time, then held it out in front of him for inspection. What once was a gold nugget from the Western Pleasure Mine now was a wide gold band with a half-karat solitaire diamond perched on top, held in place by four gold prongs.

Perfect. Annie was going to love it.

He hit the power button on the machine. The high whine of the spinning wheel died away. The shop grew still. He turned out the lights and locked the door behind him. He held up the ring to the afternoon sunlight as he walked from the shop. Light reflected off its smooth surface. It was brilliant. The extra time had been worth it.

Annie was worth it.

Annie had been Jax's girlfriend for the past ten months. Last summer, at the beginning of his senior year, Beaverhead County High School won their season-opening football game, and the entire student body had gone to Sparky's Garage to celebrate.

Sparky's, often mistaken for an actual mechanic's shop because of its rundown appearance and automotive theme, was a restaurant. Napkins were oil rags, the Hubcap Nachos were served on Baby Moon hubcaps, and it even had a green 1949 Chevrolet flatbed pickup truck parked right inside. Old-fashioned oil signs, among other things, decorated the place, and there were several gas pumps strategically placed throughout the inside. It looked like a garage, but it didn't smell like one. It smelled like burgers grilling on the barbecue.

After the game, Sparky's was packed. Annie had been sitting with a group of cheerleaders in a booth. Jax knew who she was. Beside the fact that she was the prettiest girl in the school, she was also the captain of the cheerleading squad and the student body president. Everyone knew Annie.

But did she know him? That's what he was dying to know that night.

"Tonight's the night," Jax had said as he slid out of the booth and stood. "I'm going over to say hi to Annie."

"Dude, you're nuts," Zeren Carr said. "That girl's poison."

"You can't believe everything you hear," Jax replied.

"Dude, everyone knows she's a man-hater. She'll chew you up and spit you out. Remember what happened to Johnny Wilcox in tenth grade?"

"None of that's true," Jax shot back. "And, even if it were, that was over two years ago."

"It's true," Charlie Downs said, siding with Zeren. "It's all true."

Jax hadn't taken his eyes off Annie the whole time. Now he turned and looked back at Zeren sitting in the booth with Thomas and Charlie, his other two friends.

Jaxon, Thomas, Zeren, and Charlie, or Easy, as everyone called him, had been best friends since first grade. The four were inseparable. He loved each one of them like a brother, actually more than that. There wasn't anything he wouldn't do for any one of them. But it was the start of his senior year, and he didn't want to waste the year on these three guys. Jax was tired of always just talking about girls. He was tired of staring at them from across the room.

Jax glanced over to the girls' booth. The booth normally sat six, but right now eight dainties were crammed in together. Guys wouldn't do that, not the ones he knew. He smiled. Just like girls. They had to all be together, no matter how uncomfortable it might be.

"Yeah?" Jax asked, challenging his friends. "Rumors are rumors. I'm sure 80 percent are made up, and the other 20 are embellished for the sake of the story."

"It's her mother," Easy said. "The mother's messed up. Jilted by her old man, she's pure evil, and she's poisoned Annie. Believe me, you don't want to get messed up in that."

"Speaking from experience?" Jax asked. He knew what had happened to Easy last year—everybody did. Easy had tried to put the moves on Annie, but she, without saying anything, had simply gotten up and walked away.

Maybe Easy was still embarrassed after Annie's blatant rejection.

Jax looked to Thomas for support. Jax nodded, but typically shy Thomas, cheeks coloring slightly, looked away, not saying anything. Jax shouldn't have done that; he knew better. He knew Thomas wouldn't have opened his mouth, and now Jax felt bad for putting Thomas on the spot.

"Believe what you want." Jax turned to face the girls. "I'm going over there."

"Dude, you're crazy," Zeren said. "Don't expect us to stick around and pick up the pieces. We've warned you."

"True friends, right, through thick and thin?" Jax asked.

"Friendship only goes so far," Zeren said. Laden with sarcasm, the words dripped of his lips like Mrs. Butterworth's maple syrup off a stack of pancakes. Jax knew Zeren was only messing around.

"Crazy—yeah, maybe just a bit," Jax said, "but, I'm not sitting in this booth all year with you smelly doofuses and wondering what if."

"What if what?" Easy asked.

"What if I had the guts to go over there and talk to her—would she be my girlfriend?" Jax didn't wait for a response, he just headed to Annie's booth. He wasn't shy—never had been. Nothing was going to stop him.

Surprised by Jax's audacity, or maybe by his insanity, the mouths of the three remaining boys dropped open.

Jax, shoulders half-cocked, sauntered over to the girls' booth as if he owned the world.

As he approached, all the girls stopped talking. Even the girls in the booths on either side of Annie seemed to hold their breath, waiting to hear what he wanted.

Looking right at Annie, he thrust out his hand. "Hi, I'm Jax." All the girls giggled, but he wasn't to be put off. To them it must've seemed kind of silly for a boy to want to sit with the girls.

"Where's the rest of your gang?" one girl taunted.

"They're all chickens," he said, gesturing with his head over his shoulder.

Annie took Jax's outstretched hand, her blue eyes sparkling.

"Hi, I'm Annie." They locked eyes for a moment, neither turning away. He could feel the calluses on his hard-worked palms against her perfectly soft skin. She didn't remove her hand. He was embarrassed, yet she still didn't pull away. This was good.

Now, onto what he'd come here to do, before he lost his nerve. "May I join you?" he asked.

There was an audible gasp, not from Annie, but from those sitting around her. She hesitated.

It came out so formal. The way he'd said it seemed to get to her. He felt sure she was laughing inside, and he knew it was only a matter of seconds before she burst into giggles and said no. Maybe she'd just get up and walk away.

Jax maintained eye contact. Her smile, which never seemed to disappear, grew bigger and bigger. Annie slid over and gave his arm a little tug, pulling him to the bench.

From that moment, they'd never been apart. It had only been ten months, but it seemed as if he and Annie had been together their whole lives—it felt so right.

It was a storybook romance. High school sweethearts. They were voted by the entire student body and the faculty and documented in the yearbook as the cutest couple.

Homecoming, Winter Formal, Sadie Hawkins, Spring Fling, and the coveted Prom were all landmarks in their budding romance.

But, one thing was still missing.

Jax placed the ring in a little black jewelry box and slipped it into his pocket.

Chapter 4

Annie

The Party

Annie's Toyota Corolla appeared to be at least a hundred years old, evident by the fading blue paint and the numerous rust spots over the wheel wells. After a lifetime of driving the snow-packed roads of Montana and picking up the salt from the streets, it amazed her the car hadn't fallen apart.

Annie didn't really care what it looked like. It started every morning without fail, it drove her where she needed to go, it had a heater, and it had a radio. Old Faithful, she called it.

Her mother wanted to buy Annie a newer car but didn't have the money. It was just the two of them, but no matter how much Annie's mother worked, there never seemed to be enough for the extras.

Annie wanted to help, so she'd taken a part-time job waiting tables at Harlan's Creamery, a small mom-and-pop ice cream shop straight out of the fifties: a checkered, black-and-white floor, servers wearing poodle skirts, and a miniature jukebox on each table. Fortunately, the owners didn't require the employees to wear roller skates.

Annie made a couple hundred dollars a week, which she knew could help around the house, but her mother wanted Annie to keep it. She'd told Annie over and over again that she would need it for college. So Annie saved it.

Annie pulled Old Faithful into her driveway, keeping to the right, positioning it over the small oil spot that frequently dripped from its oil pan. She put it in park. The space to the left, where her mother usually parked, stood empty. She'd gone shopping after the graduation ceremonies and had told Annie she wouldn't be home until later.

Annie had the house almost to herself for a couple of hours.

"Thanks for inviting me over," Tayla Olsen said. She sat in the passenger's seat with her hands resting in her lap.

"I'm glad you could come," Annie said, but she couldn't keep her eyes off Tayla's hair. Annie's mother had taught her to keep eye contact while speaking to others, but it was all Annie could do to not gag, the bile rising in the back of her throat.

Tayla's hair, straight and brown and just past her shoulders, was lifeless. It was greasy in spots, causing its brown color to appear almost black. It looked like it hadn't been washed in months. Tayla didn't have any makeup on either. She looked pale and ghostly. And those glasses. Kids at school called her Tadpole behind her back because of the way her glasses made her eyes pop. Tayla the Tadpole.

Annie had known Tayla since grade school. They were friends, but they weren't close friends. They didn't run in the same circles, but Annie would say hi to her when they passed in the halls at school.

Annie would normally have spent the evening with Jax before the party, but he'd said he had to work on "the project," which he still hadn't shown her. He'd meet her at the party later. With Jax busy, Annie probably would have spent the evening getting ready for the party with her girlfriends from the cheer team. But tonight, Annie and Jax had a different plan. They wanted to make tonight the best night ever for Tayla Olsen.

"You know there's going to be lots of boys at the party tonight," Annie said.

"Which one are we going to?" Tayla asked. The school hallways were decorated with colorful poster boards announcing at least half a dozen graduation parties. Annie and Jax had thought about making an appearance at several of them, but ultimately decided on just one.

"We're going to Carla's party. It should be the biggest, and the one with the most boys."

"Lots of boys?" Tayla stammered.

"Tons."

"Do you think . . ." Tayla looked down at her hands fidgeting with the strap on her purse.

"Yes?" Annie asked, trying to encourage her. She thought she knew what Tayla had intended to say, but Annie waited.

Tayla looked up, opened her mouth, and then closed it. Nothing came out. She looked down. "Do you think . . . Thomas will be there?"

Just what Annie had wanted to hear. She knew that Tayla had had a secret crush on Thomas Edison, one of Jax's friends, since ninth grade.

"Maybe."

Annie pulled out her cell phone—five o'clock. "But, there really is only one way to find out. We only have three hours before the party starts, and we have so much to do to get ready." Annie opened her door and stepped out. Tayla followed.

"You look ready to go, you're so beautiful," Tayla said. "I'm the one that needs help."

Annie fluffed her hair. The curls in her shoulder-length blonde hair were flat after wearing her cap all day. Without having to look in the mirror, she also knew her eyes needed some help.

"You're so sweet," Annie said. She'd wanted to say that they only had three hours to perform a miracle, but she stuck with, "We better get going if we plan to make it on time."

"What do you have in mind for tonight?"

"Oh, lots of things. Nails, makeup, hair, and clothes, for starters." When Annie said *nails*, Tayla held up her right hand and inspected her own nails. Annie caught a glimpse, and what she saw turned her stomach. The ends were jagged from biting. Tayla slid her hand to her side and out of sight. Her head tilted down slightly, away from Annie.

Annie sensed Tayla's embarrassment. She put her arm around Tayla's waist. "Come on," Annie whispered. She held out her own hand for Tayla to inspect. "See, my nails need some work too. Let's go see what we can do about them." They walked into Annie's house arm-in-arm like they'd been best friends forever.

Two Hearts

Annie and Tayla arrived at Carla's twenty minutes after eight. Carla's house faced east on the south side of town on Washington Street. The quintessential Victorian home, it had a large wrap-around covered porch, decorative trim, and octagonal tower to the left side. With its low-rise white picket fence around the perimeter of the property, the home looked like a child's playhouse.

According to county records, the home had been built in 1905; but after the Watsons had purchased the home, they remodeled it, leaving nothing untouched. If something old of the house couldn't be repaired to look new, something new that looked old replaced it.

The yard was no different. The house sat toward the front edge of a half-acre city lot, creating a spacious backyard. Rumor had it that Dr. Watson, Carla's father, had spent a hundred thousand dollars just on the backyard. A waterfall dropped into a lazy river feeding a Koi pond. A gazebo stood to one side toward the back of the lot, covered in hanging ivy. Stamped and stained patios and walkways led through the yard. Landscape lights, strategically placed, illuminated the trees and the shrubs. The Watsons had their own private park—their own Garden of Eden.

Annie and Tayla pulled up to the house but couldn't find a parking place—cars lined the curb. They drove down the street. Annie scanned the road as she drove, hoping to see Jax's truck, but she didn't. They parked and made their way back to the house.

People were everywhere—standing and sitting on the porch, on the grass, and inside the home. Annie and Tayla followed the lighted sidewalk around the side of the home to the backyard. A DJ stood behind a table full of his equipment, just to the right of the back door, a set of earphones covering his head. "Clarity" by Zedd blasted from the speakers. The DJ bounced with the beat. People danced on the back patio and on the grass. Annie liked the song. She started snapping her fingers.

"Hey," Annie said, "Let's go inside and get a drink."

"Okay." Tayla followed Annie to the back door like a lost puppy.

"Annie?" someone called just as they stepped into the house. Annie and Tayla turned.

Beth Allen approached from off the dance floor with her boyfriend, Ronnie Gilbert, the captain of the football team.

"Beth."

"Annie."

Annie didn't want to, but they embraced. Beth pulled back and noticed Tayla next to Annie.

"Who's your friend?" Beth asked.

"Tayla Olsen, you remember her."

Shock registered in Beth's eyes. Her mouth gaped open.

Just then "I Need Your Love" by Ellie Goulding, started playing and Ronnie saved the day.

"Come on, Beth," he said. "I've been waiting for this song all night." He dragged Beth toward the patio.

"What was that all about?" Tayla asked.

"She didn't recognize you."

Tayla's face squinched. "Totally weird, she's known me her whole life."

Annie smiled. She had performed a miracle. She grabbed Tayla's hand and stepped into the house.

Two Hearts

No more stops. Annie and Tayla, hand-in-hand, went straight to the kitchen.

The kitchen had state-of-the-art, stainless steel appliances, mahogany cabinets, marble floors, and granite countertops. The kitchen had nothing old in it, nor did anything look old. The house was beautiful, but the kitchen was a masterpiece.

They found a large plastic bucket stuffed with soda pop and ice. Annie grabbed a grape, and Tayla picked out an orange. Dr. Watson, standing next to his wife and leaning against the center island, popped the tops off their drinks.

Annie still hadn't seen Jax yet, so she made her way to the front room. The room had a large picture window that looked out over the front yard—and the street.

Just as she and Tayla entered, Annie saw Jax's truck pull into a spot in front of the house. *Lucky, front-row parking.* Both doors opened. Jax got out of the driver's side, and Thomas got out of the passenger's.

The plan was coming together perfectly.

Chapter 5

Jaxon

Keys

With Thomas in tow, Jax entered the crowded living room through the front door. Music from the backyard bounced off the walls, mixing with the low roar of people talking inside the house. Red, blue, yellow, and green dance lights flashed from the backyard through the windows. Jax could see close to a hundred kids dancing in the backyard.

He knew most everyone in the room. He waved and nodded as he passed through, heading for the kitchen. He scanned the faces, but didn't see Annie.

Suddenly, Zeren Carr intentionally threw his shoulder into him, smashing him up against the door frame between the living room and kitchen.

"Dude, sorry. I didn't see you standing there," Zeren said, playfully. He slammed his shoulder into Jax one more time, smashing him against the door frame again. "Hey Thomas," Zeren said with a nod in Thomas's direction.

"Dude, glad you two finally showed up," Zeren said, throwing a couple of fake punches at Jax's chest and stomach. "Easy's in the backyard dancing. I'm headed in the kitchen for a drink; come get one with me."

Jax and Thomas followed Zeren. The kitchen had a square table to the left side and a large granite covered island to the right. Dark mahogany cabinets, forming a horseshoe around the island, drew Jax's attention as he walked into the room. *Classy*, he thought as he studied the rich wood. Classmates clustered in groups of two's and three's were everywhere.

"Have you seen Annie?" Jax asked as he grabbed a root beer from an ice-filled bucket.

"She was just heading out back when I came in. Don't worry about it though. By now, since you're so late, she's probably already found someone new to hang on to."

"Real funny," Jax said.

Jax excused himself and went to look for her. Thomas stayed in the kitchen with Zeren.

Jax spotted Easy on the dance floor. A slow song was playing, and he had a girl wearing a leather mini-skirt, white blouse, and black pumps wrapped up in his arms.

His three best friends were accounted for, Zeren and Thomas in the kitchen and Easy outside on the dance floor. Tonight could be the last time he ever saw these guys.

As long as he could remember, since kindergarten at least, the four of them had been best friends. It hurt to think that after tonight, everyone would head in their own direction. He scanned the crowd, trying to chase the depressing thoughts from his mind.

He found Annie quickly. She sat alone at a small round table, positioned to the side of the large stained and stamped patio that served as the dance floor.

Jax approached her table. She raised her voice slightly to be heard over the music. "Jaxon Thomas Tagget," Annie said using his full name. "You took long enough!"

"Sorry. But I . . ."

"Don't tell me, your project?"

"Yes, but I . . ."

"You've been working on that thing for months. I haven't seen you after school for three straight weeks. You won't tell me what it is, and you chose tonight to work on your mysterious project?"

Playfulness sounded in her voice. Annie rarely got upset. But tonight, he noticed a slight edge in her delivery.

As she stopped to catch her breath, Jax said, "It's done."

"You're finished?"

"Yeah, totally finished."

"Sweet, show me," Annie said

"Not here."

"Where?"

"Somewhere else."

"When?"

"Soon."

He set his root beer down on the table next to Annie's grape soda and then pulled out the chair next to her and sat. They were now both on the same side of the table, facing the patio filled with dancers.

"How'd it go with Tayla?" he asked.

"See for yourself." She raised her arm, pointing to a couple on the dance floor. "That's her."

Jax looked at the pair. A slow song was playing, and the boy's back was to him and Annie. He couldn't quite see Tayla. The couple turned and Tayla came into full view.

Jax gasped. He didn't recognize her. Gone was her straight brown hair, replaced by large bouncy curls that fell off her shoulders. She wore a bright blue cotton dress that only went down about mid-shin. The dress fit like a body glove, showing her curves—nice curves at that—all in the right spots. She wore blue sparkling heels to match the dress. Jax had seen that outfit before, because Annie had worn it on several occasions.

And, no glasses.

"That's Tayla?" Jax asked. "What happened to the glasses?"

"She has contacts, but doesn't like to wear them."

"Oh my goodness, she's beautiful."

Annie playfully punched Jax in the shoulder. "Hey, don't stare too hard."

Jax turned back to Annie. "You're amazing."

"Thank you."

"Let's dance." Jax stood, moved his chair in, and held out his hand. Before she could stand up, the song ended. "Maybe the next one," he said.

Jax grabbed the back of the chair, ready to pull it out, when Tayla, escorted by her last dance partner, showed up at the edge of the table. Jax recognized Tayla's escort as a boy from school but couldn't remember his name. Jax gave him a nod. The boy responded with his own nod and then disappeared.

"Hi Jax," Tayla said.

"Hey Tayla," Jax said. "You look great."

Tayla, a bit sheepishly, ducked her head. "Thanks."

"Tayla, come and sit by me," Annie said. The chair Jax had just set against the table magically slid out, with a little help from Annie's foot. Jax pulled it out further for Tayla to sit.

"Oh no, I couldn't. That's Jax's chair."

"Jax was just leaving, weren't you Jax?" Annie gave him a stern expression, trying to send him a message, but Jax couldn't quite figure it out.

"I was just leaving," he said, following her cue, not quite sure where she was going with it. She mouthed the name Thomas. He got the message. The plan.

"Right, I was just . . . going." He helped Tayla sit. "You take this chair. I forgot something in the kitchen," he said.

Jax dashed off.

He found Thomas, still in the kitchen with Zeren. Zeren, pulling out all the stops, was trying to flirt with three girls at once. He made the girls laugh, which kept them there, but that was about it. From the expressions and body language of the girls, it didn't look like Zeren would score with these three beauties.

Typical Thomas stood back watching the show. Jax went up behind him and whispered over his shoulder, "Hey, come outside with me for a minute."

Thomas gave a slight nod, turned, and quietly followed Jax from the house.

Two Hearts

Annie saw Jax and Thomas approach. She stood, Tayla following her.

"Hey Thomas," Annie said. "This is Tayla."

Silence. Jax watched Thomas's face for any reaction. His eyebrows rose ever so slightly, almost imperceptibly. But Jax saw it. And then he saw something else—a twitch, or maybe a muscle spasm—on the left side of his face. He saw it again. The muscle around his left eye twitched.

"Hi Tayla," Thomas stuttered. His voice quivered three times pronouncing her name. He held strong, though, never breaking eye contact. *Thomas, you're the man.*

Jax pulled up two more chairs, and they all sat, Jax next to Annie and Thomas next to Tayla. Probably the closest thing to an actual date Thomas had ever been on.

Thomas, athletic and halfway decent-looking, as Annie described him, could carry on a conversation, if he ever got one started. Looking at Thomas sitting there quietly, Jax knew his problem—Thomas was shy. Every girl that started to like him quickly lost interest when he wouldn't talk to them.

※

An hour went by. Jax and Annie danced. Thomas and Tayla danced. Jax and Annie talked. They asked questions to Tayla and Thomas, who answered but didn't elaborate.

Zeren showed up to their table empty handed—no girl had taken the bait. Zeren couldn't have caught a girl even if she accidently landed in his lap. Jax knew Zeren's problem—his looks.

With his goofy-looking face and his daily wardrobe of tattered jeans and a T-shirt, Zeren wouldn't be out of place gracing the cover of *Mad Magazine*.

Zeren had a slightly pugged nose that made him look like a bulldog. It didn't help that he had acne that never seemed to clear. He had blond hair that he wore crew cut, so short you could see little red dots on his scalp. Yuck. Zeren's father, a retired army drill sergeant, still kept his hair high and tight, regulation style, like he was still on active duty. Like his old man, Zeren had to wear his hair the same way.

Jax got him a chair, and he sat down.

Easy showed up. He had a girl draped over his shoulders, the same one in the black leather mini. Easy's father owned one of two insurance companies in town. They sold every type of insurance: health, home, auto, and life insurance. His parents had money, and it showed.

Easy wore a dark blue sports jacket over a pair of pleated white cotton slacks. A gold chain was visible at the opened collar of his soft blue button-down shirt. A silver watch could barely be seen at the end of his cuff. He wore brown, suede saddleback shoes. Maybe a bit dressy, but that was Easy. He looked good.

Easy never had a problem finding someone to hold on to. Jax glanced at the girl; he didn't recognize her, which didn't surprise him—new weekend, new girl. That's the way it was with Easy. Jax got two more chairs. The gang had finally gathered.

Jax stood and held up his can of root beer in salute. "We did it." Everyone raised their drinks and clashed their cans together. "We survived high school."

Two Hearts

"Here, here," Zeren roared.

Jax pointed to Thomas. "So, Thomas, where will you be in three months, when the summer's over?"

Thomas shrugged. "I don't know. Maybe . . ."

Zeren didn't let him finish. "Dude, I'm out of here," he announced. "I'm not even waiting 'till the end of the summer. Once tonight is over, I'm gone."

"What about your dad?" Thomas asked, his voice so low that Jax had a hard time hearing him.

"Aren't you enlisting?" Jax asked.

"Dude, eighteen, baby." Zeren pumped the air with his fist a couple of times. "My old man's made it clear the moment I get my diploma, I'll be enlisting in the corps. But I got plans. There are things I want to do and places I want to see, and the corps isn't on that list. Now that I'm eighteen, he can't tell me what to do."

"You running?" Easy asked.

"Totally," Zeren said. "Early tomorrow morning, before my old man wakes up, I'm taking off. My car is already packed. I could leave right now if I wanted."

"So, where're you headed?" Easy asked.

"I don't know yet, but I'm leaving Dillon, and I'm never coming back."

"You headed up north to Canada?" Annie asked.

"Nah, South for sure, somewhere warm. What about you?" With a can of soda in his hand, Zeren gestured to Easy.

"Pretty simple. I'm headed to MSU. I'll get a master's in business, then I'm coming back to work with my father in his insurance business." No surprise there. He'd been bragging about his plans for the past year.

"Jax?" Easy turned to him. "What about you?"

"Mining. I'm headed to MSU to get a master's in mining engineering, then I'm off to see the world."

Everyone seemed to start talking at once, with college as the hot topic. Jobs came second on the list. Jax watched as everyone added their thoughts and ideas about the future. Thomas and Tayla both added their two bits, and even the girl hanging on Easy's arm contributed to the conversation. Jax never got her name, which was just as well. As was typical with Easy, Jax would probably never see the girl again after tonight.

With the talk of graduation, college, and jobs, Jax felt a little sad. Just as he'd been afraid of. Everyone seemed to be scattering in their own direction. His life, the world that he'd known for the past four years, with its sense of security, seemed to be crumbling around him. He wanted to reach out with both hands, grab ahold of it, and never let go.

He and Annie had talked about this very thing last Saturday. They both had agreed that even though it was hard, it was the natural course of events to grow up and move on—college, jobs, marriage, and family. It scared him to talk about it, though, especially marriage and family.

He hoped they would all stay close and keep in touch.

He looked at Annie; a smile crossed his face. She had been talking to the girl with no name, and from what he could hear and see of their body language, they were having a deep conversation about dating after high school.

Jax hated to interrupt, but he wanted to show Annie the little box in his pocket.

He stood, and without disturbing anyone, he got Thomas's attention. Jax gestured for Thomas to follow him. Thomas excused himself from the table. Jax and Thomas stopped about twenty feet from the group.

"Hey buddy," Jax said, "I need to ask a favor."

"Okay." Thomas had always been willing to lend a helping hand, which Jax counted on tonight.

"Tayla needs a ride home."

"I don't mind. There's plenty of room in your truck for all of us."

"No, you're not following me. Tayla came with Annie." Jax slipped the little black box out of his pocket and secretly showed it to Thomas. His eyes widened.

"Annie and I are leaving right now, so Tayla's going to need a ride home."

"Okay?" A puzzled look crossed Thomas's face.

Jax took out his keys and placed them in Thomas's hand. "Do you think you could give Tayla a ride home in my truck?"

The muscle twitched at the edge of Thomas's left eye. He smiled but didn't hesitate. "Sure."

Jax and Thomas returned to the table. Jax got Annie's attention.

"I'm ready to go," he mouthed.

Annie quickly turned back to the girl so as not to seem rude, while at the same time giving a couple nods to acknowledge she'd received Jax's message. After a few moments of conversation, Annie embraced the girl. They hugged and then Annie leaned back and said goodbye. Annie leaned to her other side and gave Tayla a hug good-bye. Annie whispered in Tayla's ear. It must have been something exciting because Tayla's lips parted with a radiant smile. She nodded several times enthusiastically. *Thank you*, Tayla mouthed over and over again as Annie stood to leave.

Annie slipped her hand into Jax's. "Ready," she said.

"Thanks for the stimulating conversation," Jax announced to everyone, "but Annie and I are taking off."

Chapter 6

Jaxon

Proposal

Jax stepped around the table, giving high-fives to Easy, Zeren, and Thomas. Annie waved good-bye to everyone around the table. The night was still young, but no one tried to stop them from leaving.

"Where are we going?" Annie asked as they turned toward the house.

"For a little drive."

They first stopped by the closet to grab Annie's coat. Jax politely helped her put it on, standing quietly. He kept glancing back over his shoulder through the open back door toward his friends.

Without Annie noticing, he caught Easy's eye, gave him a wink, and rolled his shoulders. Taking a deep breath, he followed Annie out.

After walking a little ways down the street and past all the parked cars, Annie's car came into view.

"Where did you say we were going?" Annie asked.

"Too many questions." He needed to keep her interested, so he added, "But, I have a surprise for you."

"Is it your project?"

"No more questions, or I can't show you."

"Bugger."

Annie grabbed Jax's hand with both of hers and drew him close as they reached her car. Jax felt a shiver run through her; the June nights in Dillon could still be chilly. He drew his hand from hers and placed his arm around her shoulders. Her arms snaked around his waist, inside his jacket. She gave him a squeeze. A half-foot shorter than Jax's six feet two inches, her head rested easily against his chest. He held her close.

They were finally alone. His plan was working.

They climbed into Annie's car. Jax drove. They headed north on the highway, toward the town of Twin Bridges. Jax was sure Annie knew this stretch of interstate, it being the same road she'd taken practically every night on her way to the Double T.

"We headed to the ranch?" Annie asked.

"That's for me to know and you to find out."

Annie pouted, her lower lip sticking out. A laugh slipped between Jax's pursed lips. He tried to hold it in. Seeing him, Annie began laughing, too. She punched him in the shoulder.

"It won't be much longer," he said. Jax turned on the radio to help pass the time.

They spun off the interstate and onto the Double T Ranch road, crossing a black cattle guard. The car vibrated as it bounced over the twelve pipes of the guard. A short distance later, they turned right, off the ranch road and onto another dirt road.

Jax knew Annie was familiar with this road as well. After five miles and a dozen switchbacks, this second road would stop on top of a tabletop mountain known by the locals as Lover's Flat. The west face of the butte was a sheer cliff with a two-hundred-foot drop to the valley floor. The east side sloped away from the top, allowing for access to the surface through a series of switchbacks. Lover's Flat had been a part of the Double T ever since Jax's family had settled on the ranch, but the Taggets allowed public access. It was a favorite place to park, for the younger crowd.

A jackrabbit darted across the road. Jax slowed.

Jax had brought Annie to Lover's Flat on their fourth date. He'd spread out a blanket, brought a picnic basket from the back of his truck, and served dinner by candlelight. It had been one of the most romantic dates they'd ever been on. It was also the first night Jax had kissed Annie. They'd held hands several times before, but until that point, he'd never made a move on her. Not that she'd complained.

They'd become best friends, which was the way Jax had wanted it to be. Jax had been a true gentleman; he hadn't wanted to make a wrong move, or move too quickly. But, from that moment on, for Jax anyway, their friendship had become something more.

"Lover's Flat?" Annie asked.

"I thought it appropriate, since that's where it all started . . . for me."

"Me too." She took his hand, giving it a little squeeze. Her skin felt soft and warm.

They made their way over the road and through all of the switchbacks until they reached the top of the butte.

Normally for a Friday night the place would be packed with cars, but tonight, graduation night, everyone seemed to be someplace else. Lover's Flat was empty. They were alone. He pulled up near the edge, but not too close, facing west. He turned off the car, keeping the key on accessory power to leave the radio on.

The sun had disappeared behind the Pioneer Mountains, but fire red, lemon yellow, and tangerine-orange sunlight filled the cloudless sky. His timing couldn't have been better. It was magical.

He looked at Annie. She was perfect. Her golden hair shimmered in the fading light of the evening. Her dazzling blue sapphire eyes sparkled.

He watched her as she swallowed a mouth full of air and sealed her lips, holding her breath, as the last rays of light faded.

Annie let out her breath. "Isn't it beautiful," she said, as the last of the light disappeared.

He leaned toward her. Their eyes met. She filled in the gap, leaning toward him. Gently, they kissed. Her lips, moist and warm, pressed against his. They were soft and silky. This was not the time to rush. They held their lips together for a second longer.

Jax pulled back and cleared his throat. "I've been dreading this moment for a long time."

"That bad, huh," a frown drained all the happiness from her face, "being up here alone with me?"

"No, I meant I've been dreading graduation night, when we would all be free to choose our own paths, when we all head off into the world to discover who we are."

"Zeren's running away," Annie said, her eyes growing wide in the darkening night. "Might be the last time we see him."

"So you believe him, too?"

"Sure. Why not? He's capable of doing something that stupid."

"Yeah, it sounded dumb to me," Jax said. "He's actually going to do it. Got to be the stupidest idea he's ever come up with. I give him a year. He'll run out of money and then come crawling home."

"You're too generous. I give him six months, then he'll be back." Annie looked out over the valley floor. The city twinkled like a field full of fireflies.

"Scary," Annie whispered, not taking her eyes from the view.

"Totally scary," Jax said. "Tonight might be the last time we see him or any of those guys. That's what saddens me the most."

"We don't know what the future holds," Annie said, turning to face Jax.

"Tonight at the party, you never said what you'd be doing after the summer," Jax said.

"We've talked about this, right? College and then . . . we see what happens," Annie offered.

Jax shifted in his seat, crossing and then uncrossing his legs. He stretched them out in front of him and cleared his throat again.

Annie must have sensed his nervousness. "Are you okay, Jax?" She placed her hand on his arm. He hoped she didn't feel it trembling.

He took out his cell phone, pushed a couple of buttons, and then set it on the dashboard. The power-off chime sounded.

"No interruptions," he said.

Annie took the hint and turned off her phone as well.

"Excuse me, excuse me," a voice interrupted the song on the radio.

"Is that Easy?" Annie asked. Jax turned up the volume.

Jax understood her confusion. When they'd left the party, Easy had still been cuddled up with that no-name girl, and now he was on the radio.

"Excuse me, Mr. DJ, this is Easy on the mic." Easy burst out laughing at the sound of his nickname. "I just received a special request, and I'm wondering if you could change the song."

"Okay, Easy. What song do you have in mind?" the DJ asked. A new song began to play.

Annie gasped. "That's our song."

"I'd like to dedicate this song, "Two Hearts", to Jax and Annie," Easy said. He paused. When he spoke again, it was as if he were sitting in the car between them. "Jax, you're the luckiest man in the world. I can honestly say I wish it were me sitting where you are. Congratulations, you two."

"What's he talking about?" Annie asked.

"Annie," Jax said. Annie turned. In Jax's outstretched hand was a small black jewelry box. The lid was down.

Annie's voice trembled. "Did you just request that song with your phone?"

"Yes."

With a trembling hand, she took the box.

"Oh, Jax."

Annie lifted the lid and peeked inside. She turned the opened box toward what little light was coming through the front window. Inside rested a gold necklace with a shiny gold pendant hanging at the end.

"Oh Jax, it's beautiful."

"I've been working on this project for the past three months." Jax pointed at the chain hanging from the edge of the box. "I purchased the chain in Butte, but the pendant is pure twenty-four karat gold, mined from the Western Pleasure Mine on the Double T. I dug it out myself. It took me two months to find enough gold to make it. But, once I had enough, with the help of Mr. Stevens, I created the pendant's mold in shop. I melted the gold and poured it into the mold. For the past three weeks I've been working on smoothing out the edges to make it worthy of your beauty."

Annie's cheeks reddened, she turned away. "It's beautiful." She hesitated, staring at the pendant. "I hate to ask, but what is it?"

"I didn't think you would know." He pulled her hand close to him, the box still in her open palm. With his index finger he traced along the edges of the pendant as he explained its meaning.

"In the center is a figure eight, which represents eternity—never-ending—just like our love. The figure eight is made of two hearts lying next to each other. This represents our two hearts, just like the song, joined together, beating as one for eternity."

"Oh Jax, it's amazing." Annie liked it, but Jax could tell from her delivery that her initial excitement had disappeared.

"You don't seem as excited, now that you've opened the box . . ."

"I am, but. . ."

"But what? Were you expecting something else?"

"Well . . . yes, to be completely honest. It's not that I don't love the necklace." She looked down, tracing the two hearts. "It's just that I . . ."

"Expected this?" In his hand Jax held another small black box with the lid up. Sitting elegantly in the middle was a wide gold band with a diamond perched in the center. Annie gasped. Her hands came to her mouth. She started to cry.

"I don't want to wait and see what happens," Jax said. He reached into his pocket. He withdrew a couple of crumpled dollar bills and a few coins. "This represents all the money I have in the world, two dollars and sixty-three cents. I gladly and willingly give you all the money I have. I know it isn't much." He closed his fist around the money and raised his hand to his chest, just over his heart. "But, what I do offer you is every beat of my heart, today and every day, from now until forever. I'm yours, and I promise I will always be yours. I love you, Annie Bradley. Will you marry me?"

Chapter 7

Annie

No

The following morning Annie woke with a smile. Sunlight cut through the blinds covering her window, illuminating the microscopic dust particles floating in the air. She gazed at the clock on her night stand, but the red digital numbers were blurry. She gently rubbed her eyes. The haze cleared and she peered at the clock again: 10:33. She had never slept in so late in her life.

She and Jax had stayed up till just past two in the morning talking and planning and talking some more. The night had turned out to be one of the most beautiful nights she'd ever had. She'd never wanted it to end.

She held up her left hand. The diamond sparkled in the sunlight. She was getting married to Jax. He had asked, and in the excitement of the moment, without talking to her mother, Annie had said yes.

She slid out of bed, pulled on some sweats, and a worn-out, comfortable hoodie.

Noises were coming from the kitchen. Her mother, always an early riser, bustled about the kitchen, keeping herself busy. Cupboards opened and closed. Drawers opened and closed. Loose utensils slid around. Her mother was trying to find something—probably a favorite spatula or one of those bright plastic orange peelers.

Annie's smile dropped.

It had been late when she'd gotten home last night—she hadn't checked in with her mother. She hadn't wanted to wake her. If she only knew how her mother would react to her news. Her good news. Would her mother see it that way? Would her mother be happy for her?

Annie opened the door, peering down the hallway.

She stepped out of her room. The door to her mother's bedroom, directly across the hall, stood open. The bedspread had been pulled up and tucked in tight. The house had only three bedrooms, two on the main floor and one in the basement. It had two bathrooms, one on each floor. Guests entering the house stepped right into a small living room. The kitchen occupied the southwest corner of the main floor, just behind the living room. Their television was in the basement family room.

They had a fenced backyard and an attached two-car garage on the north side of the home.

It was a small home, nine hundred square feet on each level. They didn't need much more, it being only the two of them. It had been this way for the past nine years, ever since her mom and dad had gotten divorced. Her mother never remarried. She had had many chances over the years. Several men had proposed, but Annie's mother had turned them down.

It was better this way, her mother had said. They needed to stick together. But Annie knew the real reason: her mother didn't want to get remarried. It didn't mean Annie had to go through life being single, Annie's mother promised. Mrs. Bradley liked men—at least she said so. And she said she liked Jax. But Annie had always questioned her sincerity. Though Annie wondered what there was to *not* like.

Jax had muscles and broad shoulders, weighing in at one hundred and eighty pounds. She liked the way he smelled. She liked how he ran his hand through his long and dark, wavy hair.

Jax was a man.

Annie's lips parted. Her body relaxed as she sagged against the frame of her bedroom door. Her face flushed, and her heart pounded. He was her man. Suddenly, starting in her chest, she felt the burn—warmth spread over her body. Her eyes drooped slightly as she was caught away in a daydream. She shook her head, not allowing her imagination to take her too far. Not right now, anyway. The warm sensation faded.

Annie loved Jax. He made her happy. She looked at the ring again. She knew he loved her. The hall light caught the diamond, sending tiny triangular bits of light shooting against the far wall. Brilliant. She would marry him, no matter what her mother said.

She moved down the hall. As she neared the kitchen, she took a deep breath. She let it out slowly before stepping around the corner.

Her mother stood at the sink peeling an orange, the plastic yellow peeler held tightly in her hand working its magic. Annie grinned.

"Hi, Mom."

Her mother turned. "Sleeping Beauty has awakened." She placed the orange and the plastic peeler on the counter and held open her arms. Annie didn't hesitate. She stepped forward, and her mother's arms closed around her.

"How is my high school graduate this morning?"

Annie pulled back. "Fine." Then, without thinking, she held up her left hand, showing the ring to her mother. "Actually, I'm better than fine. Jax proposed last night."

Annie placed her hand in her mother's outstretched hand. Her mother's eyes shifted quickly from Annie's face to the ring. Her brow furrowed. She dropped Annie's hand, turned back to the orange on the counter, and said, "It looks homemade."

Annie stepped back. "Really? That's it? That's the first thing you're going to say?"

"Well, it does." Her mother turned back around and rolled her eyes. "Did he make it himself?" she asked

"Yes." Annie took another step back. "He made the ring from gold he dug out of the Western Pleasure Mine on his ranch."

Mrs. Bradley turned back. She looked at the ring again. "It's shiny, but a little uneven around the edges. It definitely doesn't look professionally made."

"He made it with love," Annie said. "That's what's important." The hurt was evident in her voice.

"Right. That's all that matters." Sarcasm dripped from her lips. "You keep telling yourself that."

"Mother, seriously."

"Don't get mad at me. I'm sorry if I've offended you by pointing out the obvious," Mrs. Bradley said. "But, it's him you should be mad at. He's the one that gave you that homemade thing."

"Ring, Mother, he gave me a ring."

"And, it appears you said yes," she gestured to Annie's hand, "or else you wouldn't be wearing his homemade thing."

"I did say yes, and stop calling it a homemade thing. It's a ring."

"The guy has money, and he went cheap on you—he made you a ring. Really, Annie, you disappoint me." Mrs. Bradley shook her head.

"Jax doesn't have any money, and even if he did, that wouldn't matter," Annie squealed, her voice rising a pitch.

"That's just what a silly little school girl, one who is so in love, would say. Don't be fooled. His old man, Tru Tagget, is loaded. He's got the biggest ranch in the county, and it's been in the family for generations. Probably doesn't owe a penny on the place. Runs a thousand or more head of cattle every year. Buys himself a new truck practically every month. He just finished adding on and remodeling the old ranch house, and he built himself a spanking new two-hundred-and-fifty-thousand-dollar barn." She wagged her finger for emphasis. "You can't tell me Jax doesn't have any money. His old man has it leaking out of his joints like tree sap."

"Mother, really, is money all you think about?"

Her mother didn't even acknowledge that Annie had spoken. "Well, you can't marry him. You're only seventeen and still a minor. I won't give you permission."

Her mother sat down at the table to eat her orange. Annie took the seat next to her. This wasn't over. Oh no, it had just begun.

Annie opened her mouth to protest, but her mother raised her hand, cutting Annie off. "It's final. You're not marrying him." Annie clamped her mouth shut, holding back the obscenities that raced through her mind. She took a deep breath and held it. Her insides boiled like a tea kettle ready to blow its top. She screamed inside her head.

Annie had been seeing Jax for the past year. Whenever he'd come over, her mother acted kind and civil, but never warm and loving. When Jax came over for Thanksgiving dinner, he offered to bring pie. She'd turned him down. When he arrived at the house, he offered to help set the table, but she said she could do it. He offered to carve the turkey. She said it didn't need to be done. She lied. She acted as if he hadn't even come. She liked him? More like she tolerated him. To Mrs. Bradley, Jax was just another man, no different from the rest of them.

Annie rubbed the scar on her temple. She let out her breath and calmly said, "I'm going to marry Jax, whether you like him or not."

"You're a minor and . . ."

Annie held her left hand up showing the ring, effectively cutting her mother off. "Right now we are engaged, but as soon as I'm of legal age, I will marry him. You can't stop me."

Her mother didn't respond. Annie could see the gears turning inside her mother's head. She was working on something.

Annie gave her a look.

"Annie, maybe you're right, maybe you should marry him."

"Really?"

Two Hearts

"Sure, why not. Just remember, I tried to warn you. He's a man, and just like your father, he only thinks of himself, and the homemade thing is proof. He is cheap. He can't even spend a few bucks to buy his future wife a real ring." Her voice was calm. "Just remember I tried to warn you."

Annie's mouth dropped opened. She couldn't speak. She sat in shock, staring at her mother.

Her eyes darkened and her voice subdued, Mrs. Bradley continued. "Just don't sign any prenuptial agreements; that way, when he leaves you for another woman, you will get half the ranch and half of everything else he owns. It's an excellent idea, actually. Why didn't I think of it earlier? Marry him, and in five years, *we* could be living on the ranch."

Annie stood, and without saying a word, she walked to the front door. She had to leave. She wouldn't sit there and take any more abuse from her mother. She opened the door, but before she stepped outside, she turned. She had to say the last word.

"Jax loves me and I love him. And just because Dad cheated on you doesn't mean Jax will do the same to me. I feel sorry for you because you're living your life in the past." Annie stopped, took a breath, and squared her shoulders, waiting for a cutting response from her mother. But none came.

"What Dad did was wrong. He should've stayed true to you, but he didn't. But it happened nine years ago, and ever since then, all you've ever told me over and over again is that all men are cheaters and think only of themselves."

Annie's voice had raised an octave. "I don't believe you anymore. Jax is a good man. He loves me. He will take care of me." Annie got control of herself, her voice lowering. "Maybe it's time you got over your pain and moved on. Stop being the victim and quit being so bitter. Find love. Be happy."

With that, Annie turned and stormed out of the house, slamming the door behind her. Annie heard her mother yell as she reached the bottom of the front porch steps.

"Don't forget, I tried to warn you."

Chapter 8

Annie

Good-bye Montana

For the rest of the summer, things stayed quiet at home. Annie and her mother didn't talk much. Civility, that's how Annie saw it. "Pass the butter." "Pick up a gallon of milk." "Start the laundry." "Turn on the oven at four." That was the extent of their conversations ever since Annie had shown her mother the ring.

She worked as much as she could at the ice cream parlor, picking up any extra shifts that came available. She needed the money for college, but the extra shifts also got her out of the house.

The extra work also meant she didn't see Jax that much. But that was okay. He was busy on the ranch anyway. They would have plenty of time to make up for the lost summer when they got to school in the fall.

June, July, and most of August dragged on. Annie counted down the days, which only made it worse.

Finally, summer ended. They packed Jax's truck with both of their belongings and carpooled to Montana State

University in Bozeman, Montana. From Dillon, it was only a two-and-half-hour drive—close enough to come home on the weekends if they needed to, but far enough to be an excuse to stay.

Annie and Jax got married the summer of her nineteenth year. The June wedding, with trees and flowers in full bloom, was held in a little white chapel on the prairie, next to the Big Hole River. The colors, teal with black and white accents, were stunning in the summer outdoor setting. Jax and his best men wore solid black tuxedos with teal ties and matching cummerbunds. The cake, a five-story masterpiece with teal-colored fondant and black and white icing that was as fancy as lace, was the centerpiece. The whole thing was a dream. After the formal ceremonies, they had a grand reception on the Double T.

All of their friends and half the town of Dillon came. Zeren never showed up, though. His parents didn't have a current address for him, so Annie couldn't send him an invitation.

For their honeymoon, Jax's parents surprised them with a week-long trip to Mexico.

Everything moved so quickly, the wedding, the honeymoon, and the summer. Before either of them knew it, they were headed back to MSU. Everything they did was fun because they did it together. Being married, they found it easier to endure the last two years of college. Annie couldn't have been happier. They were living a dream.

After four years, Jax finished his mining engineering degree. Then, before the ink had dried on his diploma, they took off to see the world. Jax had applied to fifteen international mining companies. He'd received fourteen rejections and one acceptance.

VMI, Venezuela Mining Industries, offered Jax a position as a foreman in a thriving open-pit mineral mine outside of Ciudad Bolivar.

"So you're really packing up and headed to Venezuela?" Jax's father had asked at their graduation. "But, that's so far away." Jax knew his father's dream was for Jax to take over the Double T, but Jax had other plans.

"We want to see the world; plus, good money and a warm climate, what else do we need?" Jax said with a smile.

His father put his arm around Jax's shoulder. "Well, you know you're always welcome back here on the Double T, son."

"Thanks, Dad. We won't be gone forever. You keep up the Double T until I get back. We just want to see what life is like outside of Montana; we need to see that great big world out there. It'll be good for Annie and me."

"Are you sure you're ready for it?"

"Couldn't be more ready," Jax said, squeezing Annie's hand.

Standing next to Jax, Annie whispered in his ear, "Are we really ready for it, Jax? We've never been that far away from home."

"We can go anywhere we want, Annie. As long as we have each other, we'll be alright. Two hearts in one, remember?"

Annie smiled and ran her fingers over the pendant she wore around her neck. "Two hearts," she said.

Chapter 9

Jaxon
Mariana Delfino

The headquarters of Venezuela Mining Industries was located in Ciudad Bolivar, Venezuela, which had a population bordering half a million—large compared to Dillon, Montana. But that wasn't where Jax would be working. He was hired as a foreman, a field position. He wouldn't wear a suit and tie. His daily uniform would consist of a pair of blue coveralls with reinforced knees and elbows and two large orange reflective strips that ran across the chest of the jumpsuit. He'd wear a pair of work boots and a bright yellow hard hat and oversee the day-to-day operations in the field. He'd get dirty. And he was going to love it.

Jax would be working at the Pit, as the company called it, which was an open-pit mine carved out of the jungle approximately forty-six miles outside of Ciudad Bolivar. He and Annie set up their home in a one-bedroom apartment in a small town near the Pit.

Time flew by quickly, and before Annie or Jax knew it, three years had passed.

"You're gonna do great, Jax," Annie told Jax before he left for work one day. In the last three years that he'd worked for VMI, he'd only been to the headquarters twice, both times to deliver the monthly reports at the request of Jose, the general foreman and Jax's direct boss.

The night before, Jose stopped Jax as he left the Pit for home. "Mr. Flores wants to see you at headquarters first thing tomorrow morning," he grunted. "So don't show up at the Pit, and don't be late."

Things were going well. Jax liked his job as foreman. He managed a small crew, and he had found a comfortable routine. He could think of no logical reason why Mr. Flores would want to see him.

"I hope so," Jax had told Annie. He knew he couldn't hide his nerves from her.

She moved in and squeezed him tight. "Don't worry. Everything will be fine. Just remember, I love you."

Jax arrived at Venezuela Mining Industries' headquarters early. He was to meet with Mr. Julio Flores, the chief executive officer, and the other department heads. The corporate office was quite a sight compared to the Pit.

Constructed of red brick, concrete, and lots of glass, the office loomed in front of him. It was a large square building with five stories. The owner's office, the chief executive's office, and the four directors' offices occupied the fifth floor. The chief financial officer and the entire financial department occupied the fourth floor. The rest of the company filled in the remaining three floors.

Two Hearts

Jax pushed through the front door, found the stairwell, and, taking the stairs two at a time, climbed to the fifth floor. The elevator would have been faster. It took him five extra minutes to take the stairs, but he wanted to walk.

As he stepped out of the stairwell and onto the fifth floor, Jax saw a woman standing at the open end of a lounge just outside the executive suites. The lounge contained three brown leather couches set in a perfect three-sided horseshoe that faced a large oval coffee table, the surface of which was covered by numerous copies of the most popular international mining magazines and journals. Jax recognized most of the titles.

As he approached the secretary's desk, the woman approached him. She stood five feet six inches tall and weighed one hundred and fifteen pounds. She had straight, long, black hair that hung to the middle of her back, light olive skin, and brown eyes, encased with eyelashes that fluttered like butterflies.

Mariana Delfino went to the gym religiously, rain or shine, and worked out for three hours every day. She hired a personal trainer with one job description, keep age at bay. He excelled at his job. She had rock-hard abs and sinewy muscles, both accentuated by her 2 percent body fat. Her birth certificate held the only remaining proof of her actual age—forty-two. Her face and body looked like that of a twenty-one year old.

She was personal friends with Dr. Raul Jimenez, a plastic surgeon, with his number on speed dial. A little tuck here, a little tuck there never hurt anyone.

She had on an expensive, cream-colored, two-piece business suit that complemented her olive skin. The suit didn't hide her athletic body. Under her business jacket, she wore a black satin blouse that lay generously open, revealing a red ruby sapphire that hung suspended at the end of a gold chain. Jax saw the ruby and diverted his eyes, glancing at the coffee table.

"Hello," Mariana said, extending her hand and taking a step toward him. "You must be the new general foreman, Mr. Tagget." She spoke impeccable English, with only a slight hint of a Venezuelan accent.

New general foreman? Could that be why Mr. Flores wants to see me?

"I'm Mr. Tagget." Jax took her hand, moving his eyes straight from the table to her face and bypassing everything in between. She returned the eye contact. Two pumps, no more. Strong grip. Professional. He let go and nonchalantly took a half step back.

"And, you are?" Jax asked.

"Mariana." She smiled. White teeth. Straight. An inviting, happy smile. A secretary, perhaps.

"American, right?" she asked as her eyes scanned him from head to toe.

"Yes."

"Tasty."

"Excuse me?" Jax asked.

"Let me guess, New York? No, no, California? Florida maybe?"

"Montana."

"Never heard of it." She extended her hand again and Tagget took it. "It's nice to meet you," Mariana said. They shook, but she didn't pull away. He could feel her hands—warm and soft, but strong at the same time.

Two Hearts

"It's nice to meet you." Jax pulled his hand back. He smiled, fighting to keep his eyes up. He thought of Annie. What was she wearing this morning? Red and white polka dot pajamas? He tried to focus on her outfit. He turned with Mariana as she walked past him, her eyes thoroughly going over him like an MRI scanner.

"Well, aren't you big and strong," she smiled, nodding several times, agreeing with her own verbal assessment. "You will do well here. Very well indeed." She batted her giant butterfly eyelashes at him. "Welcome to the team. I hope you enjoy your new position. I know I will." The eyes. The smile. The tone of voice. Was she flirting?

Help.

"My wife and I are having the time of our lives." He spat out the first two words so quickly, they practically shot out of his mouth like a heat-seeking missile bent on destruction.

She said nothing, just smiled as if she hadn't heard him. She batted her eyes a couple more times, fanning the air. She stepped in closer to him, narrowing the gap. He tried to back up, but he had nowhere to go, the couch was behind him. He could smell her perfume, a sweet, gentle, splash of roses. It teased his senses.

"May I call you Jaxon? That is your name isn't it?"

"Yes. Sure. Jaxon is my name."

"Perfect," she placed her hand on his forearm. "I will see you again then, Jaxon." She placed heavy emphasis on his name drawing it out. "Soon, very soon, if I'm lucky." She winked and glided away.

"Great," a high-pitched squeak came from his throat. *Stupid idiot.* He clenched his teeth, the muscles tightening in his jaw.

Mr. Flores came out of his office followed by three of the four top executives. They spread out, forming a half circle around him. One by one they all shook hands with Jax.

"Thank you for coming to the office this morning," Mr. Flores said. "This is a little on the informal side," he gestured with his left hand in the general direction of the lobby area, "but, as you might not be aware, we've recently added an additional position, a general foreman over the Pit. You've been with VMI now for three years, we like your work, and we would like to offer you the job."

"General foreman?" Jax said, surprised. "Thank you, but does that mean I will be replacing Jose?"

"No," Mr. Flores said. "As you are aware, VMI is expanding, and with that expansion, there is greater need. You will be working side-by-side with Jose. We need two general foremen to oversee the mine properly."

"Well, I'd be honored, sir," Jax said humbly. "Thank you."

They discussed the technicalities of his promotion, and soon Jax left the offices and headed back to the Pit. He immediately called Annie and told her the good news.

"General foreman overseeing the mine? That is incredible!" Annie screamed. Their dreams were coming true. Jax was finally taking a step up the corporate ladder.

But with the move came trouble, by the name of Mariana Delfino.

Mariana, Jax quickly learned, wasn't a secretary. He mentioned the encounter to one of the crew managers the following day at lunch. Jax didn't want to be overheard talking about a female employee, so he waited until practically everyone had left the lunch room. The crew manager had worked for VMI for five years. He knew everyone that worked there, both the day and night shifts.

He tried to describe the woman discreetly, choosing his words with care.

"Hey, Diego, do you know a secretary by the name of Mariana?"

Diego shrugged. "Secretary? No, never heard of her. Describe her for me."

"Very skinny, olive skin, and long dark hair to the middle of her back."

"You just described half the woman in Venezuela. Specifics, please. Give me details."

Be careful, Jax.

"She has big eyelashes and was very well dressed for the office. Her body, well. . . She must spend most of her time in the gym."

"Mariana Delfino?" Diego asked.

"I don't know. She never said her last name."

"Well, from your description, you're talking about Mariana Delfino, the owner's wife."

"Not a secretary?"

"No. She's the owner's wife. Where did you meet her?" Diego took the last bite of his sandwich.

"Yesterday morning in the lobby, just outside the executive offices. I thought she might be a secretary."

"Mrs. Mariana Delfino." Diego glanced side to side to make sure no one was listening or watching. He shook his head. "Be careful with that one. She's a viper." Diego scanned the lunchroom one more time. No one stood within earshot. He raised his right hand, his first two fingers bent like fangs, and hissed. "Viper. But you didn't hear it from me." The crew manager stood, gathered the remainder of his lunch, and left.

Her last name, Delfino, which she had failed to mention when they first met, was the same as Juan Felipe Delfino, the owner of VMI—Jax's boss. Juan Felipe wasn't her father, although with the age gap, some twenty-five plus years, he technically could have been. Husband and wife, not father and daughter.

Tasty, she'd called him. His boss's wife had been making eyes at him.

Jax didn't tell Annie about his encounter with Mariana, nor did he share with her the insightful news from the crew manager. He didn't want her to worry. He liked his job with VMI. He and Annie liked Venezuela and wanted to stay. He didn't want either one of these incidents to jeopardize his work. He decided to do nothing about it. As work picked up and he got into his new routine, he hoped Mariana would forget about him.

※

Jax worked hard, losing himself in the labor. He continued expanding VMI's mining systems, seeing where they could be improved. With Jax as general foreman, the mine showed even more progress. Though it was functioning efficiently before he was in charge, the mine had improved production output by an impressive three percent. It was progress, not monumental, but progress.

It wasn't until the start of his second month as general foreman that trouble started. Jax's office, a portable work trailer, had been parked at the edge of The Pit. The trailer could be moved, but it hadn't for the past ten years. The wheels and the hitch had been removed. The trailer wouldn't be going anywhere anytime soon.

Jax sat at the desk in his office, studying a mineral content report that Diego had just brought in. The crew manager sat across from him.

"Nice work, Diego. Bauxite production is up. Same with alumina. Bath Material and Cryolite productions are stable from last month. Aluminum fluoride is up also. Very good. Overall production levels are up. We should have a solid report at the end of the month."

"The morale of the crews have changed. They are working harder, more efficiently, taking shorter breaks."

"Excellent," Jax said.

"You've been general foreman just over a month, but everyone likes you."

Jax waved off the statement. He didn't like compliments.

"No, really. The men like working for you, and it shows. You are a good man. You are fair, you work hard, and you aren't afraid to stand next to the men, getting your own hands dirty. You are one of them, and they appreciate that. They will work for—"

One of the two telephones on Jax's desk rang, stopping Diego mid-sentence. The telephone that rang was connected directly to the corporate offices of VMI. When it rang, everyone knew who would be on the other end—someone higher up.

"Excuse me," Jax said, as he picked up the phone. "Tagget," he answered. Jax listened for a second. "Yes, sir, I'll be right there." Jax hung up the phone. He peered at Diego. "That was Mr. Flores," Jax said.

"The chief?"

"He wants to see me, immediately."

"Headquarters?" Diego asked.

"Headquarters, right now."

Diego raised his right hand, his two fingers bent as fangs. He hissed. "Something smells bad."

"I'm just going to see Mr. Flores." Jax picked up the production report as he stood. He flashed it at the crew manager. "I'm sure he just wants to see this."

Chapter 10

Jaxon

Corporate Office

Jax had his coveralls on. He was dirty, having spent the morning down in the Pit with his crew. But Mr. Flores had told him to come dressed in his reinforced gear, dirt and all.

Jax grabbed a company truck and headed to town.

After five miles, the dirt road dumped into a double-lane paved road. He turned onto the paved road and stayed on it for ten miles, until he caught the freeway, heading straight for Ciudad Bolivar, the location of the corporate offices. Forty-six miles total from the Pit to the offices. It took him just over an hour.

Before he left the mine, he'd phoned Annie to let her know he would be late for dinner.

"Hey baby, Mr. Flores asked me to come see him at the office," Jax had told her.

"At the office? Again? That's all the way into Bolivar. Why?" She sounded surprised, just like Diego had.

"I'm sure he wants to see this month's production reports."

"It's only the beginning of the month, and you were just there."

"I know, but what else could it be?"

"You're not getting fired, are you?" Annie said. Jax could hear the smile on her face.

"No, it can't be that."

"Let me know what happens as soon as you hear," Annie said.

"Will do. Love you."

They clicked off at the same time.

It was late afternoon, the sun already well into its descent for the day, when he drove into the parking lot. He found an empty space and adjusted the rearview mirror, scanning his hair. A compressed ring, like a halo, circled his head. He had a severe case of hard-hat hair. He ran his fingers through the tangled mess several times. Improvement, but the indention in his hair could still be seen. He rubbed his face, feeling the stubble on his chin. He had a two-day growth.

He glanced at his dirty coveralls, then back at his face and hair. He looked rough. What did they expect? He ran his fingers through his hair one more time, grabbed the file folders containing the monthly reports, and got out of the truck, heading for the front door.

He took the stairs to the top floor. As he opened the door to the fifth floor, Jax saw a secretary in the lobby. She sat facing a computer and typed on an ergonomically correct keyboard. A name plaque, angled at the corner of her desk, read Elisa Vega. She sat with her back straight as she typed. She appeared about Jax's age and like most of the Venezuelans he knew, she had dark hair and olive skin. She turned and smiled when Jax approached.

"Mr. Tagget to see Mr. Flores," Jax said.

"I'll let him know you're here," she said in broken English. She had a heavy accent and stumbled over the words. She stood and stepped to Mr. Flores's office. She knocked, opened the door without waiting for a response, and poked her head in. She said something in Spanish that Jax didn't understand.

The secretary returned. "Mr. Flores will see you now."

Jax crossed the lobby. He followed the example of the secretary—he knocked and went in.

Being chief executive officer of a large company had its perks. Tinted windows filled the entire north wall from floor to ceiling, creating a breathtaking view of the Angostura Bridge that spanned the Orinoco River. On the west wall stood an eight-foot-tall black walnut bookcase that served as Mr. Flores's credenza. A matching desk sat directly in front of the bookcase. It had the typical desk items: a computer in the middle, a stapler in one corner, and a fancy cup that held pencils, pens, and paperclips next to it. An antique desk lamp sat at the other corner. The desk didn't seem cluttered, partially due to its size. Jax figured he could've parked his truck on top, and maybe even his horse trailer.

In front of the desk sat three overly stuffed leather office chairs. To the side of the desk and next to the wall of windows, Mr. Flores had an electronic putting green, the kind with a twenty-five-foot strip of fake grass. The fake grass, stretched tight, ran parallel to the wall of windows and gave the golfer a sense of being outside as he putted. At the corner of the bookcase near the windows, five putters leaned up against the wall. A pile of golf balls lay bunched together on the floor.

To Jax's right, Mr. Flores had his own rectangular conference table with eight executive office chairs placed around it. Light reflected off the glass.

Mr. Flores stood from behind his desk with his hand extended.

"Mr. Tagget, thank you for coming." Unlike the receptionists, Mr. Flores spoke perfect English, only a small accent. They shook hands.

"Sorry about the way I'm dressed." Jax glanced down the front of his coveralls. "Had I known we'd be having a meeting, I would have worn a suit."

"No problem." Mr. Flores waved off Jax's comment. "It's what you wear at the Pit. You didn't know I would be calling you today."

Mr. Flores pulled out two chairs from the conference table, inviting Jax to sit down. Jax placed the folder on the table, taking the offered seat.

"How is the work?" Flores asked. Small talk, before business. He could do that.

"It's good."

"And Venezuela, do you like it here?"

"Yes, we love it."

"Excellent, excellent." Mr. Flores leaned back in his chair, draping his right arm over the empty chair next to him. The small talk had ended quickly.

"We've been watching you. We like what we see. You've only been general foreman for a short time, but already you've made improvements. The processes you've initiated are effective, and, as a result, production levels are up."

Jax picked up the file folder and pulled out a stack of papers. "I brought this month's reports for your review."

Mr. Flores waved it off. "I didn't invite you here to talk about that. We already know the progress you've made is wonderful. Your work with the men is stellar. They like you. They respect you. It shows. What we would like is for you to bring your talents into the office, here. We'd like to offer you a new position as the director of business operations."

The muscles in Jax's jaw slackened and his mouth slipped open noticeably. He blinked a couple of times, turned toward the windows, and stared blankly at the city landscape. He said nothing. He cleared his throat and swallowed hard.

He turned back. "Director of . . ."

"Of Business Operations. You will be responsible for financial reports, a sales division, and a small team of managers. Business operation development. We want your golden touch to be felt throughout the company, not just with the Pit crews."

A smile spread across Jax's face. "Really?"

"Really."

"Thank you."

"No, thank you. You've earned it."

"When would I start?"

Mr. Flores stood. He stepped back from the table. "Well, if you accept the position, we'd like you to start right now."

"Now?"

Mr. Flores stood. "Yes, follow me. There is something I'd like to show you."

Jax followed Mr. Flores out the door. They walked across the lobby to the other side of the building. Mr. Flores stopped in front of an office. Jax came up to his side. They both stared at the door. A gold nameplate shone brightly, reflecting the light of the fixture in the hallway. Mr. Flores just stared at the door.

Jax didn't know what to do. He just kept staring in disbelief. It took him a nanosecond before it hit him. The nameplate read *Jaxon Tagget*.

"That . . . that has my name on it."

"This is your office," Mr. Flores said, speaking in present tense as if Jax had already accepted his offer. Mr. Flores opened the door, and they stepped in.

The CEO's office was huge and open. But this one was small and cramped. It had a normal office window from which could be seen the busy Via Puente Angostura Freeway on the south side of the building. An oak desk, positioned in the center, occupied most of the space. The desk had a computer and a business telephone with hundreds of buttons, which would only be useful for interoffice conferences, placing angry customers on hold, or taking ten different calls on ten different lines. Nothing else.

A desk chair rested against the back wall. Two guest chairs rested against the opposite wall. Visitors would have to shuffle past a two-shelf bookcase to sit down.

A clean and bright space. Natural light from the window flooded the room. It smelled fresh; the cleaning lady had probable come earlier that morning.

"Thank you," Jax said.

"So, is that a yes? Are you accepting the offer?"

"May I speak with my wife first?"

"Do you need to?" Mr. Flores asked.

He didn't need to. He could make the decision himself. But he wanted to. Ever since he and Annie had been married, they had always discussed big decisions together before they moved forward. They were a team. But he already knew she would flip with excitement.

"I want to." He bit his lip, anxiously waiting for Mr. Flores's response.

"Excellent. That's what I like to hear, a team player." Mr. Flores stepped back through the door. Before he closed it, he said, "Take all the time you need. When you're ready, I'll be in my office."

"Thank you." The door closed. Jax was alone. He sat in the desk chair. Comfortable. Soft. It felt good. He spun around in a complete circle.

Amazing, he thought. Three years ago, he and Annie were in the green pastures of Montana, where they had spent their whole lives. They'd left their home of over twenty years and traveled thousands of miles to seek a new adventure, never expecting an opportunity like this one.

He cracked a smile and slipped his cell phone out of his pocket to dial Annie. She picked up after the first ring as if she'd been waiting for his call.

"You got fired," she said.

"Worse."

"What's worse than being fired?"

"Just kidding," Jax said. "I got promoted again."

He heard her gasp, then scream.

"Promoted? Really? What, are you the president of the company now?"

"Close. I'm the new director of business operations. There are four directors, total. I'm now one of them."

"You're kidding?"

"Nope."

"Seriously?" Annie asked.

"Yep. Should I take the offer?"

"What? You haven't accepted it yet?"

"I waited to call you first."

"Take it, take it," she yelled into the phone.

"Done."

"Hurry home so you can tell me the details."

They hung up together as they always did.

He crossed the lobby, knocked, and entered Mr. Flores's office once again. They shook hands, officially sealing the deal. There would be an increase in pay, a meal package, covered travel expenses, extended paid vacations, and a company vehicle. He and Annie would need to move to Ciudad Bolivar, closer to the offices, instead of living in the small town near the Pit. Annie would like that.

They concluded their discussion, and Jax excused himself. He walked back to his office, stepped in, and closed the door behind him. Sitting in the desk chair again, he leaned back.

Things were happening so quickly. Last month general foreman and now director of business operations. Was he ready for the big step? He'd always planned on working up the corporate ladder. With this new move he'd bypassed several rungs, maybe even a hundred. He was now close to the top.

Could this be real?

A knock at his door interrupted his thoughts. *Mr. Flores with one last comment before leaving*, Jax thought. But it wasn't him.

"Come in," Jax said as he stood.

Mariana stepped in, her rosy perfume instantly tickling his nose. Dressed to kill, she wore a black satin cocktail dress with spaghetti straps and a dangerously low sweetheart neckline. The gold chain with the ruby red sapphire still hung around her neck. The hem of the dress stopped just above mid-thigh.

"May I?" she asked, motioning to the guest chairs.

"Uhm, sure."

She passed the first chair, choosing to sit in the further one, the one next to the window. The hem of her dress slid two inches up her thigh. She slowly crossed her long, tan, fit legs. Jax stood at the corner of the desk, staring. The empty guest chair right next to her was only two feet away. Four feet behind him stood his chair. Keeping the desk between them, he opted to sit in his chair.

"Congratulations," she said. "You're a shooting star."

"Thanks?" Jax said, surprise sounding in his voice.

She seemed to sense his confusion. "Word travels fast."

"It must. I only accepted the offer five minutes ago."

"It was bound to happen, sooner or later. Look at you, you're big, strong, handsome, intelligent, and you're capable. Pointed in the right direction, you could probably conquer the world."

"Thank you, again." Jax felt the heat rush to his face. He didn't like compliments, especially coming from someone like Mariana, a gorgeous woman—and his boss's wife.

Jax stared out the window, trying to hide his embarrassment. She stood, gliding to the door.

"Climbing the ladder of success isn't always about what you know," she said. "It's who you know." She lifted her hand higher than necessary to push open the door. "It still amazes me what a cleverly placed word to the right person can do." She winked, then turned and walked out.

※

Jax opened the door to the apartment slowly. He didn't know why he felt so nervous. He hadn't said anything inappropriate to Mariana, and he'd tried to stay focused on Annie while Mariana spoke to him. But he felt dirty, and he didn't know what to do about it. *I should just tell her*, he thought.

"Hey babe," Annie said when she saw him come through the door. She was wearing an apron and setting dishes on the dinner table. She put down the last dish, walked up to Jax, and kissed him on the lips.

"Annie?" Jax said quickly.

"Yeah?" Annie drew back her head and looked into his eyes, trying to read his thoughts.

He pulled her close and hid his face in her hair. "I— I— I love you," he finally said, squeezing her tight. "Let's eat."

Chapter 11

Jaxon

Errand Boy

Jax arrived at his office early the next morning before the sun had a chance to rise in the east. He had kissed Annie on the cheek before leaving, but she hadn't even flinched. He let her sleep.

As the new director, he arrived early every morning for a full week to get a jump start on his new responsibilities. Corporate executive. Big-time responsibility. He wanted to make a good impression. Also, he felt safe working that early in the morning when no one was around. He was relieved Mariana hadn't been in the office for a few days.

When he walked into his office on his fifth day as director, a stack of reports was still piled high on his desk. He didn't hesitate but rolled up his sleeves and dove in.

After an hour, the sun began to poke its head over the eastern horizon, the darkness fading. Brilliant red and orange rays lit up the horizon, like it had every morning he'd spent in his new office.

A knock sounded. He stood, crossing the few feet to the door. When he opened it, he found Mariana standing in the entrance holding a plate overflowing with blueberry, strawberry, and cherry pastries. In her other hand she held an insulated cup. Steam rose from it, filling the air with the strong aroma of coffee. At the sight of the food, Jax's stomach grumbled.

"Good morning, Jaxon," she said with her exotic accent.

"Good morning, Mrs. Delfino."

"Please, call me Mariana. I feel old when people call me by my last name."

"Okay," replied Jax, knowing he wouldn't. She was the owner's wife. He couldn't call her by her first name. That was too informal—too personal.

"May I come in?" Mariana still stood outside in the hallway.

"Oh, sure, I'm sorry." He clumsily stepped back.

She moved past him effortlessly, like a graceful swan floating on a calm lake. Her flowery perfume played games with his senses as she glided by.

He followed her with his eyes.

She had on a two-piece spandex exercise outfit: black, low-cut yoga pants and a dark red sports bra, with at least eight inches of skin between them. Sealed to her body. Every curve, every angle, every muscle of her body accentuated under her second layer of skin. She had tight abs, and seeing them started his heart pumping double-time. He pulled at his collar. *Think of Annie. Think of Annie.*

"Is it hot in here?" he asked.

"No, I'm fine, thank you."

Two Hearts

She took the far seat again, the one next to the window. As she sat, sunlight from the window flooded over her. Something flashed in the room, coming from her mid-section.

She leaned forward to set the coffee and pastries on the desk. As she did, Jax quickly glanced down at her stomach. Her belly button was pierced with a large two-carat, princess-cut diamond. With the sunlight streaming through the window, the stone winked at him. She sat back, the vision disappearing.

"Early riser, I see," she said. "Just like me."

Jax took his seat behind the desk. "The early bird catches the worm," he said. "I'm just getting started as the new director, and already I feel behind." He put his hand on top of the stack of reports on his desk. "I've got a lot of catching up to do. Every minute counts."

Mariana nudged the plate of pastries and cup of coffee closer to Jax.

"You're probably wondering what I'm doing here."

Jax said nothing.

"Well, on my way to the gym, I passed your office and saw your light on." She gestured to the food. "I figured, this early in the morning, you probably hadn't eaten breakfast yet. A big, strong guy like you shouldn't miss a meal. So I brought you something to eat."

"Thank you," he stammered. "But really, Mrs. Delfino, you shouldn't have."

"Please, call me Mariana."

He hesitated. "Fine, Mariana. Please, you shouldn't bring me food . . ." He knew it wasn't right, he just couldn't say it. He was too afraid of offending the owner's wife.

She waved off his comment. "It's just one of the many perks of being at the top. I hope you enjoy the pastries." She floated to the door. "See you soon, Jaxon." She stepped out, shutting the door behind her.

Jax laid his head on the desk. With his eyes closed, he reached out, fingers extended, and slammed his hand on the desk. The cup of coffee didn't move, but the plate of pastries bounced once, sending the food shooting off the plate.

"Idiot," Jax whispered.

※

Every day for the next three months Jax saw Mariana. She seemed to know where he was at all times, like she'd slipped a tracking device in his coffee that first day. He'd take the stairs from the fifth floor, heading to the ground floor. When he'd open the door at the bottom, she'd be standing there. Once, he'd gone to the supply room for more paper, and she was standing outside the door when he came out, waiting.

Another time, Jax had been called to the fourth floor to go over some numbers on the monthly budget with the chief financial officer. Jax spent over an hour in the man's office. When he came out, Mariana stepped in right on cue, bumping into him.

Two or three times a week she'd bring him food, either early in the morning or just before lunch time. *Perks of being at the top*, she'd say. He was one of four directors, so he casually watched the others throughout the days and weeks that followed. He wasn't stupid. He knew he was the only recipient of her gifts, but he wanted to be certain.

Just as he'd thought, the other directors never received food from Mariana, or from anyone else.

Several times, while he'd been sitting in his office digesting a financial report laid out on a spreadsheet, the phone on his desk would ring. The first time Ms. Vega, the receptionist in the lobby on the fifth floor, had called.

"Mr. Tagget?"

"Yes."

"Mrs. Delfino is on the first floor. She is requesting your assistance."

"Okay," Jax answered.

"She says it's urgent."

"Thank you, I'm on my way." Urgent, Ms. Vega had said, so he'd taken the elevator, not the stairs. Jax shot out of the elevator when the doors slid open. Mariana, wearing a tight black mini-skirt and a white tank top under a sheer, black chiffon blouse, stood in the front lobby waiting for him.

"Thank you for coming so quickly," she said.

"Ms. Vega said it was urgent."

"Yes, I have three potted plants in the back of my car that I need you to carry to Mr. Delfino's office." She hadn't said her husband's office. She'd said Mr. Delfino's office as though she were just one of his employees.

He bit his lip and followed her to her car. It took him three trips, and during each one Mariana followed him close behind. His being Mariana's errand boy happened on other occasions, until he finally started turning her down; it was making him too uncomfortable.

"I— I'm sorry, Mrs. Delfino," he said after one of her errand requests. "I've got too much work to do."

"Oh, that's too bad," she pouted. "Maybe next time."

For a while, Jax thought about approaching Mr. Flores, but he didn't want to bother him or make him question Jax's integrity. So, he said nothing, though his heart was screaming inside.

Over the next few weeks, Mr. Flores had nothing but good to say of him. His monthly assessments from Mr. Flores were glowing with praise, and in the past three months he'd received the company's bonus twice for achieving the monthly performance goals.

But where was Mr. Delfino? Jax couldn't figure it out. Mariana came to the office every day, making it a point to run into Jax. Yet, in the last three months since he'd been promoted to director, Jax had only seen Mr. Delfino three times, always briefly in passing and always in the lobby on the fifth floor.

After the third month as the director, and after a noticeable increase in the personal errands he'd been doing for Mariana, Jax decided to ask Ms. Vega about Mr. Delfino.

"Ms. Vega?" Jax said, as he approached her desk.

She turned. "Yes, Mr. Tagget?"

"Have you seen Mr. Delfino?"

"He is not in right now."

"When will he be in?"

"He's out of the country on business, but he's planning on stopping by the office next week."

"I've noticed he doesn't come in very often."

"No, he travels almost every week—always for business. Sometimes he will be gone for three weeks at a time. When he does come back, he sometimes stops by the office for a day or two. But other times he won't even come to the office. He is usually home for a week only until he leaves again."

"Wow, he travels a lot."

"Yes, he is a busy man," Ms. Vega said.

Jax returned to his office.

Now he understood. Mr. Delfino traveled for business, which meant Mariana was here alone—all by herself, all the time. She came and went as she pleased. Did whatever she wanted. Visited whomever she wanted. As the owner's wife, no one could stop her. No one would question her presence at the office either.

The next week, Jax saw Mr. Delfino in the lobby. Mr. Delfino had just stepped out of Mr. Flores's office when Jax entered the lobby through the stairwell. Mr. Delfino had broad shoulders and was four inches taller than Jax. Jax felt small and a little intimidated standing next to him. Mr. Delfino had silver hair, which he kept short and parted on the side. He wore round wire-rimmed glasses that looked good with his blue, three-piece, pinstriped suit. Stylish, professional, and very impressive.

"Mr. Delfino," Jax said as he extended his hand. "I'm Jaxon Tagget, one of your newest directors."

"Yes, Mr. Tagget. I remember meeting you when you first came to work for us." Mr. Delfino's voice sounded strong, but not overbearing. It wasn't an authoritarian kind of voice. Jax remembered their first meeting as well. "If I remember correctly," Mr. Delfino continued, "you looked ghostly white, a little overwhelmed with all of the changes.

I mean, a new job, a new country, and a new language. I would have felt the same way."

That was exactly how Jax had felt. If Annie hadn't been standing at his side during the whole transition, he probably would have packed it all up and gone back to Montana.

Mr. Delfino impressed him. Their first meeting had taken place over three years ago, yet Mr. Delfino still remembered it.

Mr. Delfino held up a stack of papers that Jax recognized as production reports. "Mr. Flores and I have just finished going over the mine's reports for the last several months. Production levels are up, way up. I must say, Mr. Tagget, your work is outstanding. Well done."

"Thank you, sir."

Mr. Delfino clapped Jax on the back. "Keep up the good work." He then excused himself.

Jax floated back to his office, never once feeling his feet touch the floor. He gently lowered himself in his chair, a big smile crossing his face. His boss, the owner of the company, had liked his work.

Jax pulled out his cell phone, keying in Annie's number. She picked up on the second ring, and he told her his good news.

"Your hard work is paying off, Jax!" she squealed with joy. "And just think what the future holds with this company. We may be here longer than we thought."

The thought made Jax anxious, despite his excitement. "Thanks, Babe," he said, trying to sound calm. "I've gotta stay late again tonight to finish some work due tomorrow. I'll be home by eight."

Two Hearts

"Dinner will be waiting for you, as always," she said.

Jax, a little slower than his wife in shutting off his phone, heard Annie scream with joy one more time. He smiled, wishing he could share in her excitement.

Chapter 12

Jaxon

Viper

Every day without fail as soon as the clock hit five, everyone left the building—the work day had ended. On a rare occasion, one of the directors or sometimes Mr. Flores would stay until five thirty, but never later. For Jax, after hours, when the place was quiet, proved to be the best time to work—as long as Mariana didn't hang around the office after hours. He hoped she hadn't.

By seven thirty the sun had already been set for over an hour. It was dark outside. Jax cleaned up his desk and organized his work, getting it ready for tomorrow. He would be in early, as usual, to finish the last details on the financial report he'd been working on. He shut down his computer, picked up his jacket, and stepped through the door. He locked it behind him.

The lights in the lobby were still on, but the place was empty and quiet. Before Ms. Vega had quit for the day, she'd asked Jax to turn off the lights when he left. He walked across the lobby, heading for the corner where the panel of light switches lay hidden behind a big green office plant. He had to walk past Mr. Delfino's office to reach the panel of light switches, and as he did so, he noticed the lights were still on in the owner's office. Work piles up on your desk when you leave the office for an extended period of time, even if you're the owner. Mr. Delfino had probably stayed late to catch up on things. At least Jax hoped.

Jax had taken two steps past Mr. Delfino's door when he heard it open behind him.

"Oh, Jaxon," Mariana said, as she stepped out behind the door. "I'm so glad you're still here. I need your help." She reached out a hand, beckoning to him as if she could draw him into the office just by sheer willpower.

Earlier in the day, when Mr. Delfino had been in the office, Mariana had been wearing an expensive business suit. Now, after hours, she wore faded jeans, tennis shoes, and a loose-fitting T-shirt. Comfortable and casual.

"Okay, I guess so," Jax said. She turned, opened the door all the way, and gestured for him to go inside. He did. She followed, closing the door behind her.

He'd been in the owner's office three times before, each time when he'd helped deliver plants with Mariana. Just as he'd seen it before, it was elaborately decorated with a mahogany desk and matching credenza. Their color and stain treatment gave them an antique look. The space for a conference table and chairs instead contained a black leather couch and two chairs, which formed a half a square around an oval-shaped coffee table.

Flanking the couch, one on each side, stood two tall mahogany bookcases. Books, that look liked they'd never been opened, lined the shelves. Several of the shelves contained little knickknacks, strategically placed for aesthetic appeal.

On top of the right bookcase, a beautiful green plant draped over the side, its branches almost reaching the ground. Jax didn't recognize the type of plant. He'd seen its kind before, but didn't know its name. He glanced to the left bookcase. That was when he understood Mariana's problem.

The top of the left bookcase sat empty. A three-step ladder stood in front of the left bookcase, right at the corner of the couch. A green plant, identical to the plant on top of the right bookcase, sat on the floor next to the ladder, waiting to be lifted up.

Mariana pointed to the plant. "Can you put this on top of the bookcase?"

"Oh yeah, no problem."

Jax set his suit coat down on the chair closest him. He stepped over and stretched his arms out to pick up the plant. As he reached down, the shirt on his back drew tight.

Suddenly, Mariana placed her hand on his back. The warmth of her hand penetrated his shirt, sending a shiver up his spine. His heart raced a little faster.

"Thank you so much for your help, Jaxon." Her hand noticeably moved back and forth over his back, caressing him.

He stood, her hand dropping from his back. He held the plant cradled in his left arm and stepped up the ladder. With both feet securely planted on the second step, he raised the plant in both hands high above his head. While stretching out to his full length, he set the plant on top of the bookcase. The instant he let go of the plant, Mariana stepped in front of him and wrapped her arms tightly around his legs, pressing herself against him.

"Mrs. Delfino, please," Jax said. "You're going to make me fall."

"Jaxon, I want you. I need you."

"Mrs. Delfino."

"Mariana, please call me Mariana. I love it when you say my name."

"Please let go, or I'm going to fall." Jax tried to brace himself by gripping the top of the bookcase.

Mariana held his legs tight, he couldn't move. He tried to wiggle from her grasp, but it only made things worse. He started to lose his balance, so he stopped moving.

"Jaxon, please, I know how you look at me. I know you want me just as much as I want you. It's only natural that we express our love. Please Jaxon, let's not fight our feelings anymore."

He gazed down at her. Her big, beautiful, brown eyes stared back. Heat flooded his cheeks. He knew they were bright red, as red as a ripe tomato. He hesitated and turned away. She seemed to sense his hesitation, and she pushed her body against his legs.

He lost his balance and fell, his arms flailing wildly.

He wanted to twist and land on his side, but he couldn't, Mariana still held his legs tight. She let go just before he hit. He landed directly on his back on the couch.

Like a rattlesnake posed to strike, the second he touched down, she leaped with lightning speed, climbing on top of him, body to body. She peered up at him with those big, beautiful brown eyes. She moved, her body sliding up his. She stopped with her face inches from his.

He wanted nothing more than to push her off, but his body was frozen, his heart pounding like a steel drum in his chest.

"Please, Jaxon, here I am. I'm yours. Take me, right here, right now."

Chapter 13

Annie

Fired

Annie sat at her little desk typing on the computer keyboard. She had been responding to a few emails from friends in Montana while she waited for Jax to get home from work.

One of the perks of Jax's promotion was their apartment in Bolivar, a big city in Venezuela. With his previous position as the general foreman, he needed to be close to the mine. They had lived in a one-bedroom apartment in a small town five minutes from his office, the portable trailer parked at the edge of the Pit.

With Jax's office located in the corporate headquarters, they now lived in an apartment twice the size of their previous one. Their new place had a large living room and a combination kitchen–dining room. It had a laundry room, a master bathroom, and a main bathroom off the hallway. It also had two big bedrooms for guests—or for little ones.

She would paint the walls a soft pink or maybe blue, depending on what they had first. She imagined white lacey curtains over the windows. There would be a white oak crib with fancy scroll work and a matching changing table filled with baby supplies. A rocking chair would sit in the corner for those late nights when the baby couldn't sleep.

That's what she'd wanted.

The last year of college, Jax and Annie figured the time had come to start a family. They knew they would probably end up overseas, but they considered it an adventure. Their little ones would spend the first years of their lives living in a foreign country. They would grow up culturally well rounded.

That was the idea, anyway.

They'd been trying to have a baby for the past year, but Annie still hadn't gotten pregnant. Annie wanted to see a doctor, but Jax thought they needed more time. Annie went along for a while, thinking she needed to be more patient. But after a year, she began to wonder if something might be wrong.

So, the extra bedroom, with its plain white walls and empty floor, became their home office, where the computer sat on a little desk.

She glanced at the clock at the bottom right corner of her computer monitor: 8:25. Jax said he'd be home by eight, and he was late. What could be keeping him?

She scanned her inbox and saw an email from her mother. A sad feeling flooded through her. Her mother had sent the email from her home in Denver, Colorado. She'd moved from Dillon to Denver to help take care of her own mother after her father had passed away just before Annie and Jax had left the country.

Dillon held so many fond memories for Annie, memories with Jax and memories with her mother. It had been the only place she and her mother had ever lived—the place they had called home. It was hard to think that her mother didn't live there anymore. Even sadder, though, was that Annie didn't even live there anymore either. Time seemed to keep on moving, separating her from her beloved hometown.

Annie scanned through her inbox again. She hadn't received one from her father, though she really hadn't expected to. But, she had hoped. She opened the Sent folder. Her letter to him occupied the top slot of yesterday's emails. Annie never received any emails from her father, although she diligently wrote to him. Maybe she had the wrong address. She'd expected the emails to have bounced back, but none of them ever did. Her father just never took the time to respond. Probably just too busy.

Living internationally had its drawbacks. It required effort and lots of emails to stay connected to family and friends. She couldn't just pick up the telephone and call—it was too expensive.

Annie heard the front door open. Jax was home.

"Hey Jax," she yelled from the extra bedroom. "I'm back in the office."

"Hey." His voice sounded flat—toneless. He must be tired and hungry after his long day of work.

She closed her email and turned off the computer for the night. Walking through the living room, she found Jax standing in the kitchen. With its vaulted ceiling, the combination kitchen–dining room was an open area.

Jax stood, rocking slightly from side to side with his back to Annie, facing the open refrigerator. His arms hung straight down.

She snuck up behind him. "Gotcha," she yelled, throwing her arms around his waist and pinning her body against his.

He flinched, jerking his arms free, and pushed her arms from his waist. "Gee, you scared me half to death," he said, turning to face her. He shut the refrigerator door and took a step back, trapped against the counter.

"Sorry," she smiled. She stepped in and put her arms around his waist. His arms stayed at his side.

Roses. She smelled roses.

A faint scent of flowers came from Jax's shoulder. Had he brought her flowers? Did he have them hidden behind his back?

Jax twisted, causing Annie to let go. There were no flowers behind him. She scanned the room. No flowers anywhere. Jax left the kitchen and went into the living room. Annie watched him slump down onto the couch in the center of the room.

She left the kitchen and leaned against the framed archway that connected the kitchen with the living room. She stared at him. His shoulders were hunched, and his head drooped slightly. His eyes stared at his outstretched feet. He didn't move. She hadn't noticed it earlier, but he looked pale, his skin ashen white.

"You okay?" she asked.

"Fine."

"You sick?"

"No."

"You look sick."

"I'm fine."

"Tough day at work?" she asked.

"Tough day."

"Want to talk about it?"

"No."

"Are you hungry? Can I get you something to eat?" she asked.

"No."

Something had happened at work. Whatever it was, it bothered him. Annie sat down on the ground at his feet, gazing into his face. He turned, diverting his eyes. The air swirled as he turned. She smelled the faint scent of roses again. She put her hand on his leg. Heat pulsed through his pants. He was on fire.

"Oh my gosh, you're burning up." She got on her knees, and kneeling at his side, she placed the back of her hand on his forehead. Initially it was cold and wet—clammy with sweat. Through the initial wet, she could feel the heat. He had a fever.

"I think you have a fever," she said. He pulled her hand down.

"I'm fine." He glanced at her, reassurance in his eyes, then turned away.

"Jaxon," she said with a firm voice. She placed a hand on his leg. "Jaxon, please, what is——"

Pounding on the front door cut her off. "Policia, abre la puerta." The pounding grew louder. "Policia, abre la puerta." *Police, open the door.*

Having spent six months in Venezuela, Annie knew exactly what it meant.

Jax jumped up, knocking her to the ground. He ran into the kitchen and back, wringing his hands together. "Don't open the door," he whispered, fearfully. He ran into the bedroom and poked his head out from the hallway. "Pretend we're not here," he stammered.

Annie stood, hands on her hips. "Jaxon Thomas Tagget, what is going on?"

The police had heard Annie's raised voice. "Mr. Tagget, we know you're in there. Open the door, or we will break it down," the officer yelled in English.

Annie walked to the front door. Jax stepped into the room. He reached out. "Annie, no."

The instant the lock clicked open, four police officers pushed their way in, forcing Annie back.

"Arrestalo, arrestalo!" Three officers rushed Jax, grabbed him by the arms, and restrained him.

"Mr. Tagget, you're under arrest," the officer giving commands said.

Annie rushed to Jax's side, turning to face the officer in charge. "Why?" she pleaded.

The officer turned to the open door. Mr. Delfino stepped in, his wife trailing behind.

"Because, Mrs. Tagget," Mr. Delfino said, "your husband has been a naughty boy. Tonight after everyone left the office, he sexually assaulted my wife. She fought back, but not before he left his mark."

"Jax?" Annie implored, her face in shock. She dug her eyes into Jax's soul. "This can't be true," she said to Mr. Delfino, clinging to what little hope she had. She dreaded the idea that her mother might be right, that Jax was just like any other man. She turned back to Jax. "Jax? Is it true?" Annie asked.

Jax gave a slight, almost imperceptible shake of his head.

Mr. Delfino stepped back, exposing his wife, who stood in the open doorway visible to everyone in the room. A soft breeze nipped at her long flowing hair. Annie smelled roses, this time much stronger. Her brow furrowed. *Roses?*

Mrs. Delfino turned slightly so the light from the living room chandelier fell on her right cheek.

Annie gasped. A vicious scratch, blood red, cut across Mrs. Delfino's cheek from the corner of her lip to the back of her jaw. It took everything Annie had to take her eyes off Mrs. Delfino's wound. For no apparent reason, Annie's left hand immediately started rubbing the scar on her left temple.

Jax slipped his left hand behind his back.

"I trusted you, Jaxon," Mr. Delfino said. "I brought you up—made you a director. Your work performance amazed me. You were my shining star—my ace in the whole. You were unstoppable. You were on top of the world." Mr. Delfino pointed to the scratch on his wife's face. "And this is how you repay me."

Jax stood with his head down and his mouth shut, not speaking.

Mr. Delfino said something in Spanish to the officer standing on Jax's left side. He spoke so quickly that Annie couldn't make out what he had said. But the officer had understood.

He grabbed Jax's left arm, forcing it around to the front.

They struggled. The officer on Jax's right clubbed Jax in the stomach with his baton. Jax slumped, but he didn't go down. He stopped struggling.

The officer brought Jax's left arm to the front and extended his fingers. Jax had on his wedding ring. It had a unique design, one that Annie had never seen before, which was why she had fallen in love with it the moment she'd laid eyes on it. It was a wide titanium band, dark silver in color, with a three-tenths section of the band cut out of the middle. A square diamond a fourth of a caret in size filled in the space, joining the two sides together. Annie knew the exposed corners of the open space, where the diamond didn't touch, could be sharp. More than once those edges had nipped at her skin when Jax had brushed his hand over hers.

Blood covered the ring, and a small piece of skin, snagged in the open space where the diamond sat, dangled in the air. Annie gasped for a second time that night.

Jax glanced into her eyes. What he saw brought his heart up to the back of his throat. Pain. Confusion. Fear. He'd let Annie down. He wanted to wrap his arms around her, to hold her close, but the officers held him tight. He tried to move, to step closer to her, but she drew away, a look of disgust on her face. That look of distrust burned a hole in his heart like a hot branding iron.

He spoke for the first time since Mr. and Mrs. Delfino had appeared. "It's not what you think," he whispered. "I didn't do anything."

Annie slapped him hard on the face, the sound echoing through the small apartment. Her voice cracked. "Don't lie to me."

A loud snicker came from the front door. Everyone turned. Mrs. Delfino stood in the open doorway, a conniving and evil glint in her eyes and a grin that spread from ear to ear. The sinister expression disappeared instantly as everyone turned to her, but Jax had seen it and so had Mr. Delfino. He turned to Jax; their eyes met.

Mr. Delfino's eyes were heavy and tired and filled with sadness. He stared at Jax for a moment longer, an unspoken understanding passing between them.

Mr. Delfino finally broke eye contact and turned to his wife. He said something in Spanish. It came out sharp and nasty. She snapped back with an elevated voice. Instantly, both their voices raised an octave as their words shot out of their mouths like machine gun fire.

Mr. Delfino, now yelling at the top of his lungs, raised his arms and gestured toward the door several times. Finally, Mrs. Delfino shut her mouth, her face flushed red, and she stormed out of the apartment, slamming the door behind her.

Mr. Delfino took two deep breaths, straightened out his suit coat, and slowly turned around.

"Officer Rodriguez," Mr. Delfino said, addressing the officer that had been giving orders. "You may leave. I will not be pressing charges."

"Mr. Delfino?"

"Please, let Mr. Tagget go. I've changed my mind. Your services are no longer needed."

Officer Rodriquez barked an order in Spanish and the three officers holding Jax let him go. Mr. Delfino opened the door and all four officers, with confusion on their faces, left the apartment. Mr. Delfino shut the door again and turned to face Annie and Jax.

"I'm very sorry about that," Mr. Delfino said. "There seems to have been a misunderstanding. Please forgive me."

"A misunderstanding?" Annie asked. "You came charging in with the police because of a misunderstanding? What about the cut on her face, the blood, and the skin on the ring?" Annie asked.

"An accident. Right, Mr. Tagget?" Mr. Delfino turned to Jax for confirmation.

"Right, an accident. That's all it was." Jax said.

"An accident?" Annie asked, staring at Jax.

"Yes, an accident."

Mr. Delfino pulled out a white handkerchief from the inside pocket of his coat. He reached out his hand toward Jax, palm up. "May I?"

Jax took off his wedding ring, placing it in Mr. Delfino's outstretched hand. He picked off the dangling fragment of skin, then polished the metal with his handkerchief. After running the cloth over it several times, he held up the ring for inspection. It shined under the lights. The blood having been removed, it sparkled like new again.

Mr. Delfino handed it back. Jax slipped it on his finger. Mr. Delfino turned silently to the door.

"Sir," Jax said. "What about tomorrow?"

Mr. Delfino hesitated with his hand on the door knob. "Tomorrow?" He turned slowly around. He paused, the gears spinning slowly in his head. "Tomorrow?" He said again. "Under the circumstances, I don't see how there can be a tomorrow. I'm sorry, but I'm going to have to let you go. I don't want to, but there's no other way. Please, see it from where I'm standing."

Jax did. He understood. He didn't want to see Mrs. Delfino again, not after what had happened tonight. It was better this way. He didn't want to go back.

Chapter 14

Jaxon

Welcome Home

Jax raised the axe high above his head aiming for the piece of wood standing on end. Working the mines had given him strong arms, back, and shoulders. It was late September, and the temperature was hot, even for Dillon, Montana. He had his shirt off, the veins in his neck and biceps pulsed with every beat of his heart. Sweat drizzled down his brow, into his eyes. His upper body glistened with perspiration.

Never taking his eye off the mark, he swung the axe, splitting the stump with one stroke. He bent over, picked up the pieces, and tossed them into the growing pile of wood.

Jax heard a car coming down the ranch lane before he saw it. He straightened up just as the vehicle rounded the corner off in the distance, coming into view.

A brand new black Cadillac Escalade thundered down the dirt lane, kicking up the dust behind it. It had no license plate, just the dealer's advertisement tags. It came with all the trimmings: chrome grill, lighted running boards, sun roof, spinning wheels, and several antennas sticking out the top.

Jax set up another stump; then, with his brute strength, he split this one.

The Escalade pulled up and parked. A young woman slid out. Dressed like she'd just stepped out of a fashion magazine, her poofy, shoulder-length, blond hair didn't move as she walked.

Took a whole bottle of hairspray to contain that hairdo, Jax *suspected*. A smirk crossed his face. The more he studied it, the more her hair reminded him of a lion's mane. Her makeup was just as flamboyant. Vibrant colors of red, yellow, and blue were strategically placed throughout her face, reminding him of a painter's palette.

Dressed in tight jeans and pointy high heels, she had a hard time walking over the gravel driveway. A wide belt, shiny and black to match her heels, loosely hung around her hips. She wore the belt as an accessory; her skin-tight pants weren't going anywhere.

Noticing the woman's form-fitting shirt that gaped open at the top revealing more skin than he was comfortable with, Jax quickly turned his head. High fashion stood out of place on the ranch—and in Dillon, with its country standards.

Before she was within fifteen feet, her perfume hit him in the face like a Mack truck. Jax swallowed hard, coughing twice. It had a nice fragrance and was probably very expensive, but it was strong.

Jax didn't know her. But he knew she didn't belong here in this part of the country. She was clearly the big-city type. *She must be here to see Annie.* He bent over, setting up another stump.

"I see the mines have been good to you," the woman said as she drew near. Jax could feel her gaze running up and down his body as he bent to steady the stump. Without so much as a nod to acknowledge her comment, he quickly grabbed his shirt, slipping it over his head and pulling it down over his body.

"Welcome home, Jax," the woman said in a friendly way. Shocked by her initial comment, Jax hadn't recognized her voice. Now that she spoke his name without using his full name, he recognized her. He glanced up.

"Beth? Beth Allen?" Jax asked.

"Beth Downs now, silly," Beth giggled, holding out her left hand for Jax to see the rock on her finger. The diamond was huge, twice the size as the Rock of Gibraltar.

"You and Easy?"

"Charles. He prefers Charles now. And yes, me and Charles." She giggled again.

Jax turned so she wouldn't notice the shock on his face. Fortunately for him, Beth had been inspecting her heels for dirt, so she hadn't witnessed his surprised reaction.

Jax and Annie were still at the university when they'd received the announcement of Easy's marriage to Samantha, a girl he'd met in college. Jax and Easy were close during high school, and Easy had requested that Jax be his best man. That was seven years ago. And now, Easy and Beth Allen? What had happened to Samantha?

"When?" Jax asked.

"Just last year."

"I'm sorry, but we hadn't heard."

"We sent your invitation to Venezuela. I distinctly remember sending you one because it was the only invitation we sent internationally." Beth giggled again.

"Must've gotten lost in the mail," Jax said.

He held up his hand after wiping it on his shirt. "May I see your diamond?"

She placed her hand on his. It was a large princess-cut diamond, and Jax could immediately tell that it was a high-grade stone; the color was brilliant.

"Wow, this is a beautiful stone," Jax said.

"That's Charles's doing; nothing but the biggest and the best for him. He treats me like a queen." Beth motioned over her shoulder with her head toward the Escalade. "He just bought me that new car yesterday."

"What's its weight?" Jax asked. Her brow furrowed.

"The diamond," Jax said, chuckling. "How many carats is the diamond?"

"It's three carats. Charles had wanted a four-carat diamond, but he didn't want to wait the three months it was going to take the jeweler to get it in, so he just bought the largest one in the store."

Jax wasn't a gemologist, but he had seen his share of diamonds in his field of study and through his work experience. This was a high-quality piece.

"I heard you and Annie had returned to the ranch," Beth said. "How long have you been home?"

"Just over a week." Jax adjusted the stone, angling it to catch more of the sunlight. "It's magnificent."

"Thank you." She drew her hand back.

"And, congratulations to you and . . . Charles." Jax drew out his friend's name, making it sound more formal.

"Thanks again." Beth turned toward the house. "Is Annie home?"

Jax was right: Beth had come to see Annie. "Yeah, she's inside."

Chapter 15

Annie

Visitor

Annie heard a car door shut. She grabbed a hand towel as she stepped from the kitchen into the living room, where a big window looked out to the front yard. From the corner, she had a commanding view of the front without being seen from outside. A black SUV had pulled into the driveway, and a woman stood talking to Jax as he bent down to adjust a piece of wood at his feet.

Annie didn't recognize her, but she knew the type. She had big puffy hair that didn't move when she walked. Her makeup, generously applied with a cement trowel and as thick as putty, was bright and flamboyant. What little clothes she had on were vacuum-sealed to her body, accentuating her voluptuous curves. The woman's shirt covered the right amount of skin to keep her legal, but enough skin showed to distract men's eyes. She looked and acted like many women Annie had seen before—women the corporate mining executives always had hanging on their arms.

Suddenly, Jax stood and put on his shirt. Annie hadn't seen the woman's face clearly yet, and now Jax's body was in the way.

Annie watched for a minute trying to get a good look at the woman. Body language was all she saw. The woman's hips bounced this way and that way as she talked, almost like she used them to give emphasis to what she said. Some people used their hands in the same way, not able to talk without gesturing. This woman used her hips. Her hands stayed busy too, flipping and twisting the ends of her hair and adjusting her collar, flirtatiously.

Annie's left hand immediately and involuntarily come up to the temple on the left side of her head, where her middle finger found the familiar scar mostly hidden by her hair. She gently rubbed the soft skin back and forth as she watched the woman.

Oh, the audacity. The woman stood on her ranch and flirted with her husband. Did he flirt back? Should she even question him? *Maybe.* The face of Mariana Delfino popped into her head. The dangling skin, the torn face, Jax almost getting arrested. It had only happened two weeks ago. It was still fresh.

That night in Venezuela after the police had left, Jax told Annie how the skin from Mrs. Delfino's face had ended up in his ring. On his way out of the office, Mrs. Delfino stopped Jax and asked for his help setting a plant on a high bookcase. She grabbed his legs while he was still on the ladder, causing him to fall. He landed on a couch, with Mrs. Delfino falling on top of him. When he pushed her off, his ring caught her face, snagging the cheek and tearing the skin. Mrs. Delfino screamed and Jax ran.

That was his story. It had sounded plausible, but it was full of holes. He hadn't explained much more than that, and Annie hadn't asked any questions, though she had plenty. But, she was exhausted, so she let it go.

Annie turned her attention to Jax, hesitating, afraid of what she might see. The nightmare in their apartment two weeks ago still flashed through her head.

Jax stood straight as a rail, leaning on his axe. No body language. He directed his full attention at the woman's face and eyes. Annie relaxed and her left hand stopped caressing the scar. Jax moved and Annie saw the woman's face clearly for the first time.

Beth Allen.

Annie and Beth had been friends in high school; at times they had been best friends. Varsity cheerleaders together all four years. They group dated to all the school dances. In their junior year they were on the homecoming committee together; they had worked hand-in-hand on the school float and the parade.

But two things happened at the start of their senior year that changed everything.

First, just before Annie met Jax, she was chosen to be the captain of the cheerleading squad. From that point on, a silent rivalry existed, each trying to outdo the other, from boys, to cars, to school, to friends, to hairdos. Practically everything became a contest.

Because Annie had been chosen as the captain of the team, Beth ran for student body president. Annie, true to her competitive nature, had also run—and had beaten Beth. At the end of their senior year they were friends, but not best friends.

Annie hadn't seen Beth in over six years, since Annie's wedding. Nothing had changed then; everything was still a contest for Beth. From the looks of things now, it still felt like they were in high school. Beth glowed with arrogance, probably showing up at the ranch to gloat. But Annie decided to leave the past in the past and greet Beth with open arms.

Jax stuck out his hand, and Annie watched as Beth placed her hand in his. Jax was looking at something, but Annie couldn't quite see what it was. Whatever it was, it sure had Jax's attention. Jax adjusted his position and Annie saw it, more like the sun reflected off it and Annie knew exactly what Jax couldn't keep his eyes off of. Jax was drooling over Beth's wedding ring.

Annie subconsciously spun the gold band on her ring finger, a habit she'd picked up over the years since Jax had given it to her. He had mined the gold himself from the old, abandoned Western Pleasure Mine on the ranch, and then he'd formed the band in metal shop. It was a beautiful piece, not perfect, but made with love. The ring's half-carat solitaire diamond had its flaws, which stood out to the naked eye, and the color was just a bit off. But Annie loved it, even with all its imperfections, because Jax had given it from his heart. He had given her everything he had. Annie spun the band again feeling the diamond pass between her fingers, surfacing to the top.

It was enough.

Annie quickly stepped out of the front room, heading back to the kitchen. Beth and her swinging hips were walking up the sidewalk toward the front door.

Just two knocks.

"Beth, is that you?" Annie said, acting surprised when she opened the door. She reached out and gave Beth a hug and invited her in. Annie had watched Jax admire Beth's ring, so she figured Beth's name had changed or would likely change in the near future. Annie hadn't said Beth's last name, hoping to avoid the inevitable conversation of her marital status.

"It's Beth Downs," she informed Annie, holding out her hand and displaying the large diamond on her finger. Beth couldn't wait to share her news and show off her ring. Annie didn't know much about diamonds, but the size alone of this one took her breath away.

"Beth *Downs*?" Annie managed to say. "You and Easy? I had no idea you two—"

"That's just what Jax had said, and he likes to be called Charles now. He's changed."

"Congratulations."

"Thank you. And welcome home to you. Are you glad to be back?"

"Thank you," Annie said sincerely. "Hmmm, are we glad to be back?" Annie restated the question as she thought about it. She let it hang in the air for just a moment before answering.

"Yeah, it's nice to be back, but I miss living abroad," Annie said. "Jax hasn't quite adjusted yet. He didn't want to leave. It had been a wonderful experience, and he wasn't quite finished when we needed to come home."

"I heard. Mr. Tagget, right? Cancer? I'm so sorry."

The day they arrived back in Dillon, they'd found out Jax's father lay in the hospital dying of cancer. It was just as good as any excuse to explain why they'd returned to the states. No need to tell everyone that Jax had lost his job because of a scuffle he'd had with the owner's wife. Even if Jax hadn't done anything, it wouldn't have looked good. Annie didn't share that with Beth, though.

They moved from the front door to the couch in the living room. Beth strategically placed her left hand on Annie's leg to comfort her; the diamond stood out again for Annie and the entire world to see.

A nauseating feeling swept over her. Annie swallowed hard several times to keep the bile from rising up. She stood, pacing back and forth several times to calm the queasiness. She passed it off as emotions.

"You poor thing," Beth said. "This must be so hard for you and Jax."

"The hardest part of living abroad is that you are out of touch with life back here in the states. We didn't hear that Jax's father had been sick until just a little while ago."

"No one told you?"

"Nope, no one told us. Since we've been home, we've learned that Jax's father has been sick for about two years, but he never let on. He just kind of kept it to himself."

"People in town started noticing things," Beth said. "Mr. Tagget missed the spring and summer cattle sale the last two years. People started wondering if he had given up the cattle business. Mr. Smith out at the WYOT cattle ranch came out to see him, but Mr. Tagget never let on about anything. I think Mr. Talon from over at the JH Ranch came by also. But Mr. Tagget didn't say anything about his cancer."

Annie turned to look out the window. A red Mercedes-Benz had pulled up right next to Beth's SUV; a man with a shock of silver hair and a dark three-piece suit stood talking to Jax. Annie didn't recognize him. Dillon, Montana, had changed since they'd left. A lot of new faces in town.

"Anyway," Annie said. She returned to the couch and sat next to Beth. "We arrived home in time to help Jax's parents with the ranch. And it turns out, of course, of all Jax's siblings, he was the only one willing and able to come. Plus, Jax knows the ranch and is probably the most capable of taking care of it."

"So you just packed up and came rushing back," Beth said. Annie sensed a note of sarcasm or maybe jealousy. She decided to let it go, passing it off as her own imagination.

"Yeah, it was the least we could do," Annie said.

Annie realized she'd been doing most of the talking. And although she didn't feel like it, she felt obligated to ask about Beth. "So, it's Beth Downs now. How long have you and Charles been married?"

"It's only been a year, but it feels like we've been married our whole lives. We're so in love." Beth clasped her hands together and looked out the window, her eyes glazed over, caught away in a daydream.

"Charles had been married to Samantha, right?" Annie asked. Annie knew Beth well enough to feel comfortable asking the hard questions that Jax might not have asked.

"Yes." Beth rolled her eyes and her shoulders visibly slumped. "Charles told me all about her. He said she was evil to the core."

Easy had brought Samantha to Annie's wedding, and she seemed nice then. When they all returned at MSU, they double dated occasionally and Samantha was always pleasant to be around. In fact, Annie remembered commenting to Jax that she and Samantha would probably be good friends if they ended up living by each other.

"Charles told me she always yelled at him. It seemed to him that he could never please her. Most of the time he'd come home from work and find a note stuck to the fridge saying she'd be out late and to not wait up for her. He said he lived off T.V. dinners those two years he was married to *that woman*." Beth said the last two words with disdain spewing from her lips.

"The poor man," Beth continued. "One night he came home from a hard day at work and found the same note on the fridge. He'd had enough." Beth's hands balled up into fists and her knuckles turned white from the pressure. She tensed, poised to strike at any moment. "He got in his car and went out searching for her."

"He did? And, did he find her?" Annie asked. She slid forward to the edge of the couch, her interest in the story piqued.

"Oh yeah, he found her alright." Beth paused to let the tension build. She waited for Annie to ask the next obvious question. Annie didn't disappoint.

"Where?"

"He found her in the arms of another man."

"No. Really?"

"Yes. She was cheating on him. So he filed for a divorce. What else could he do?"

"Did Charles tell you all this?"

"Charles told me everything. The poor thing. He is the kindest, most thoughtful man on the earth. I just don't see how anyone could be so cruel to him."

"Who was she with?" Annie asked.

"Charles didn't say. He said it wasn't important."

Annie had been listening intently. When she realized Charles had been the source of all the information, she questioned the validity of the story. It surprised her that Beth hadn't wondered about the truth of it herself. Annie knew Charles pretty well. Beth knew Charles just as well as she did. They had all grown up in the same small town, and they had all been friends forever. Maybe he had changed since high school, but he probably hadn't.

Charles had been the guy that never seemed to grow up. Life seemed to always be a party for him. The moment school got out for the weekend, he was looking to get drunk—if he weren't drunk already. And to make matters worse, he would wind up getting into a fight, and usually because of a girl. Half the time it was some other guy's girl that Charles had tried to put the moves on.

Charles wasn't called Easy for nothing. Actually, no one could remember how or why he got that name or when it started, but two theories had been floating around throughout the years. The first was that Charlie had the looks and was easy on the eyes. Of course only the girls thought that. Charlie was a drop-dead, knock-out—no question about that. But that theory didn't hold much water, especially with the guys. The other theory boiled down to one thought, that Charlie was an easy score, which, in all honesty, was the truth. So, word got around amongst the ladies that Charlie could be had easily on any day of the week. The name stuck, and he liked it because it helped him get what he wanted— the ladies. Ever since then, he'd been known as Easy.

With a name like *Easy*, Charles had a different girlfriend every weekend of his four years of high school.

Beth must have been reading her mind. "I know what you're thinking," she said. "How could Easy change? I've wondered the same thing the whole time we went out. But, it didn't take me long to see what kind of man Charles really is; he is a kind and sweet, loving man. He even told me he worships the ground I walk on. He treats me with respect, and he is always showering me with gifts. He has changed. You'll have to see it to believe it."

Annie *would* have to see it for herself.

Beth, never having left Dillon after graduating from high school, knew all of the town gossip, and she was more than willing to share everything she knew. Although Annie got sick every time Beth waved her ring around to show it off, it was nice visiting with her and catching up about the lives of all their old friends.

Once the stories started flowing, time seemed to fly, and an hour had disappeared before they knew it.

Beth stood. She announced she needed to run and finish some errands she'd promised to do for Charles. Annie walked her to the door and stepped out on the front porch to say good-bye. They hugged and promised to have lunch in a few days. Jax and the silver-haired man still stood by the wood pile talking. Annie's brow furrowed. What could be so important to keep them talking for so long?

Chapter 16

Zeren

Hide

For the hundredth time that day, Zeren Carr read the text message from Tish, his girlfriend. "Someone's at the house looking for you." It contained only seven words, relatively short. He had it memorized, but he read it anyway, trying to decipher any hidden message in the tone, length, or construction of the words. None existed and he knew it.

"Cops?" Zeren had asked.

"No. Three black suits."

That was all he'd needed to know. The time had come to leave Las Vegas. The text had arrived from Tish at about ten that morning, an hour after he'd arrived at work. He worked at Office Supplies in the customer merchandise loading department. It was a mindless job. When a customer purchased a large item on the showroom floor, they would drive to the back of the store and Zeren would load it into the customer's vehicle.

With a bottle of water he'd grabbed from the employees' lounge, he'd told his boss he wanted to take his scheduled ten o'clock break out in his car.

He never returned.

He'd first gone to his bank to close his account. The teller didn't ask any questions. When an account that size closed, no one cared. Zeren showed his driver's license, signed a few forms, and the teller counted out with painful deliberation, by twenties at his request, the three hundred dollars and change that made up his entire life savings. With that completed, he'd grabbed I-15 heading north, leaving Las Vegas, probably never to return.

He'd come to Vegas right out of high school. With only five bucks to his name, he needed money. He quickly had gotten in with the right group, hustling tables and working the slots. There was a trick to it, and he picked it up, and the money started flowing.

He was lucky, he kept telling himself. Most kids his age had to work for their money. For him, it was a game. It all came so easily.

For the first couple of years, he couldn't lose. He paid cash for his candy-apple red Nissan Nismo 370Z. It was the first thing he'd purchased after his first big win. Zeren Carr was his given name, but ever since he could remember, he went by Z-Carr. So, when he came into the money, the 370Z occupied the top spot of his wish list.

After the car, he'd purchased a diamond-studded gold watch. He wore Italian leather shoes and imported clothes from Europe. He lived in an expensive apartment down on the strip. And the women—he had several girlfriends all at the same time—all lined up outside his door.

Life was grand—until he started to lose. His rise to fame and fortune ended just as quickly as it had started. The harder he tried, the bigger he lost. He'd run out of money, but he knew he could get it all back again, so he borrowed.

He lost what he borrowed.

So he borrowed more. He lost that also. He moved apartments several times to save money and to avoid the "collection agencies" (the dark suits) that seemed to always be one step behind him.

The women, the parties, and the clothes had all disappeared overnight. No money, no friends, no treasure. Just as well, he didn't need those leeches. He got a job to keep him going until his luck changed. But his luck never reappeared.

When he received Tish's text that morning, the time had come for him to leave.

That was twelve hours ago.

A yellow light on his dashboard came on, the gas needle resting on empty; he planned on making it home tonight, so he needed to fill up. Plus, he hadn't had anything to eat since his last gas stop. His stomach had been screaming at him for the past several hours. If he didn't eat soon, he would faint.

According to the last road sign he passed, he would hit the small town of Dubois, Idaho, in sixteen miles; he could survive just a little bit longer, and he knew his car had just enough gas.

Dubois, Idaho, population 677, or so the sign read as he drove into town, looked like a ghost town at eleven at night.

He took the first and only exit in Dubois, dropping down onto Main Street. Ike's 66, the first gas station he came to, with its single, naked light bulb swaying in the night breeze, looked deserted as he pulled up to the pump.

The door to the station opened when he tested the handle, so he stepped in.

"Hello," he yelled into what he thought had been an abandoned store.

"Hello," a man's voice out of the shadows answered back. "How can I help you?" The voice had a country drawl to it. Definitely not in Las Vegas anymore.

"Are you open? I need gas."

"Sure." A tall, slender man in his mid to upper twenties, about the same age as Zeren, stepped out of the shadows. He wore blue jeans pulled over a pair of cowboy boots worn down in the heels. He wore a Mack truck baseball cap, tilted up, on his head. His button-down shirt was clean and tucked in, but old and faded. He stuck out his hand.

"Name's William, but everyone around here just calls me Ike."

From William to Ike? Was that even possible?

Zeren, his brow furrowing, took Ike's hand and gave it a few pumps. Ike was friendly, but Zeren had been on the road all day. His back hurt, his legs throbbed, and his stomach hadn't had anything in it for hours. Zeren didn't feel like making a new friend just at the moment.

"About the gas?" Zeren asked, hoping to get what he needed so he could get back on the road.

"Just go pump then come and pay."

Zeren turned back toward the door, and as he did so, he saw in the darkened area toward the back of the store a few tables covered with red and white checkered tablecloths. Instantly, as if right on cue, his stomach growled. "Any place to eat around here?" he asked Ike.

"Most places in town are closed at this hour, but my restaurant," he motioned toward the tables in the back, "is always open." Ike quickly handed him a piece of paper. Across the top, in bold print, the word menu had been printed. It looked like Ike had probably created it on his own personal computer and then printed it with an HP inkjet.

"Why don't you pick what you want," Ike said, "and by the time you're done pumping, I'll have your meal ready."

"Wow, that's fast." Zeren scanned the menu. There weren't very many items: hamburgers, hot dogs, and chicken platters seemed to be the most prominent. He settled on the hamburger, fries, and drink combo meal.

"It'll be ready by the time I'm done pumping?"

"It'll be on your table waiting," Ike said with a toothy grin.

"Do you want to put some money on it?" Zeren loved to bet—it added spice to his life. He took out a twenty and laid it on the counter. He didn't have much money left. He'd spent most of it on food and gas just traveling this far, but he couldn't pass up the chance to earn a quick buck. Zeren quickly glanced at Ike, sizing him up. This guy didn't look too quick on his feet. Anyway, he had an idea on how he could guarantee that he would win. "Twenty says I'm in here before the burger gets off the griddle. It's a fresh burger?"

"Oh it's fresh, alright. I'm going to go make it right now." Ike looked at the twenty on the counter. "You want to bet, like a little wager?"

"Yeah, you up for that kind of thing?"

Zeren watched his face, looking for creases in his forehead or maybe a twitch at the corner of his eye, anything that might show signs of doubt or fear, but he saw nothing. Ike had a poker face, a stone cold poker face. Suddenly that toothy grin crossed his face. "You're on," he said as a twenty materialized from his pocket. He laid it on the counter next to Zeren's.

Zeren sprinted out the door. *Sucker*, he thought as he raced to his car and pumped the gas.

A moment later he flung open the front door to the gas station. He rushed in, sure he'd finished first. To his surprise, a hamburger, a plate of fries, and a tall drink stood on a table in the restaurant.

He'd lost.

"You didn't pick out a drink, so I just poured you a Coke. I hope that's what you like," Ike said. He sat at the next table looking like a rooster with its feathers all puffed up, as if he were strutting through the barnyard for all the hens to see.

"Coke is fine," Zeren groaned as he slumped down into a chair. He could smell the freshly grilled hamburger and the hot greasy fries. If he hadn't been so hungry, he probably would have paid for the food and his gas, and then just left.

Ike stood and took both twenties off the counter and disappeared into the back.

Zeren sat eating his food, still in shock. How had he been beaten, even after he cheated? To guarantee he would win, Zeren only pumped a few gallons of gas, just enough to make it to the next town. And yet, he'd still lost. He ate in silence stewing over his predicament. With the lost money, the cost of the gas and the food, he only had sixty-three dollars and a pocket full of change. Since he'd only pumped a few gallons of gas, he would need to stop again soon. He had enough to make it home to Dillon tonight, but not much more.

※

At twelve thirty in the morning, the house was dark as Zeren parked his 370Z on the street in front. He sat there for a moment looking at the house. He knew every nook and cranny of it. His parents had purchased it thirty-five years ago, and it still looked brand new as it did on the day they'd bought it. That's because his father, a fanatic for preventive maintenance, painted the house every summer, no questions asked. By the time Zeren turned five and could hold a paintbrush straight up, he'd been enlisted for the job.

During those summer months when the house received a fresh coat of paint, his father would study every shingle, every siding board, and every window for problems. Any signs of weakness or deterioration in the house, the painting would stop and the repairs, whether needed or not, would commence. Every summer and all summer long, Mr. Carr had the house under repair. Zeren could see his old man's bright yellow scaffolding tower on the left side of the house.

As Zeren stared at the house and the scaffolding, painful memories flooded over him, memories of him and his old man arguing. "Paint faster!" his old man would yell.

"Don't miss a spot." "Go to college, and get an education." "Get a job." "Do something with your life."

And yet there he sat, staring at the nightmare. He had been gone seven years, but sitting at the curb looking at the house, it felt as if he'd never left. Just seeing the freshly painted house made his stomach turn.

He started the car, put his hand on the stick shift, and pressed the clutch down with his foot. He shifted into first and pressed down on the gas pedal. The engine revved. Without lifting his foot off the clutch, he shifted down to second, and then back to first.

The muscles in his jaw tightened. He hit the steering wheel with his left hand, then revved the engine again. He closed his eyes, his right hand leaving the stick shift and finding the key in the ignition, he turned the car off.

Silence.

Eyes still closed, his head dropped. He had nowhere else to go.

***

He walked up the front steps of the porch. He swung the number three to the side, the last number of their address, revealing a small hole drilled into the siding. He removed the hidden key. Why his father still kept a key there amazed him. Everyone in town knew about his father's "secret" hiding spot, and yet he'd still kept one there. Zeren had told his father years ago to change his hiding place, but obviously he hadn't listened. And right now, with the key in his hand, at such an early hour, he praised his father for not listening.

Zeren opened the front door and stepped inside. Instantly a light flashed on and his father stood, shotgun in hand, staring at him. "Zeren?"

Chapter 17

Valentino

An Empty House

Valentino Fattore had dark hair, which matched the bushy eyebrows and heavy sideburns that he wore down to the bottom of his ears, much like most of his colleagues. Born of Italian immigrants, he looked and dressed the part, although he'd never been to Italy.

He was born in New York.

When his parents were newly married, they emigrated from Savona, Italy, to the United States to find work. Shortly after their arrival, Valentino came into the world. His father, a skilled laborer, worked in a machine shop, which he later purchased. Valentino's three older brothers and his little sister, Evelina, all worked in the family-owned business.

Valentino wanted a different life, though. He didn't want to be stuck in the family business, punching the clock from nine to five, same routine day after day.

His brothers and sister had a good life, he knew. They all had homes in New York, their kids went to private schools, and occasionally they frequented the shows on

Broadway. They told him it was a good life. But it was their life, and it wasn't for him.

Valentino wanted adventure. He wanted thrills and excitement. He lived his life on the edge, one foot planted on solid ground while the other foot flirted with danger.

After working a year in the family business, he said his good-byes, boarded a plane, and left New York, heading straight for Las Vegas, Nevada. His money running low, he looked for work. The first couple of casinos he inquired didn't have any openings. He would do anything, he told them, but still they said no.

The third casino he came to was the Grand Palace. He went to the management office and inquired about job openings. They gave him the same response. Nothing available for the moment; try back in a couple of weeks.

Tired and dejected, he turned to leave the offices of the Grand Palace and ran into a short man, knocking the man to the floor.

"I am so sorry, sir," Valentino said. He extended his hand to help the man off the floor. Instantly, four big men wearing dark suits surrounded Valentino; they lifted him off the ground.

"Easy boys," said the man on the floor. The personnel manager, the woman that had just turned Valentino away, quickly stepped forward and helped the short man from the floor. "It was an accident? Wasn't it?" The short man looked right at Valentino and asked.

"Yes, sir," Valentino quickly added. "I just turned to leave when I ran into you."

The man appeared to be in his mid-fifties. He had salt and pepper hair. When he was up and had straightened his rumpled clothes, he came and stood by Valentino. He was markedly shorter than Valentino by over a foot.

"You knocked me flat on my back when we collided. You didn't even budge when we connected. You're like a brick wall." The man reached up and squeezed Valentino's bicep. "Strong as an ox. How tall are you?" The shorter man asked.

"Six-five."

"Weight?"

"Normally around 240, but I think I'm down a bit because I've been walking so much lately," Valentino said as his brow furrowed. "Why do you ask?"

"I could use someone like you. My name is Adrian Sebasti. I own this place." He swept his raised arm across the room, taking in the entire place with one gesture. "How would you like to work for me?"

"Actually, that's why I'm here; I'm looking for work."

"Then it's settled," Mr. Sebasti said, putting his arm around Valentino's waist. "You work for me now." Mr. Sebasti motioned to the personnel manager.

"Get this young man's personal information, buy him some new clothes, and get him on my payroll."

"Yes, Mr. Sebasti."

"When that's all taken care of, send him up to my office."

※

That was five years ago.

He had worked his way up in Mr. Sebasti's organization. He now ran Mr. Sebasti's collection agency. Valentino was in charge of *collecting* any money owed to Mr. Sebasti or the Grand Palace Casino.

In the past five years Valentino hadn't made a mistake. He collected on every debt owned. He had a perfect record, and Mr. Sebasti was generous in his praise—and with his annual bonuses.

However, today was different. He'd made a mistake and he knew what the consequences would be, having been the enforcer of Mr. Sebasti's orders for other employees who had made mistakes.

A drop of sweat escaped from his left side burn and rolled down the side of his face until it reached his jaw. It then fell to the floor. The little droplet had tickled his skin as it made its way through the two-day growth on his face. Valentino wanted to wipe it away, but he dared not move.

Valentino stood in front of Mr. Sebasti's desk on the thirty-seventh floor of the casino. Although he didn't enjoy standing before his boss, he did love the view. The entire back wall of the office was glass and had a commanding view of the city lights of Las Vegas.

This was the first time that Valentino had ever questioned his choice of employment. He ever so gently shifted his feet as he wondered if there might still be a position available for him in the family business in New York.

"I've heard you lost the trail," Mr. Sebasti calmly said, staring at him with cold eyes. "Tell me your pitiful story."

"We've been on Zeren Carr's trail for about six months. We've almost caught him three times, but each time he seems to know when we are coming and then he disappears. He's always just one step ahead of us. We had a good tip this time, and we showed up at his apartment, but he'd already left for work.

"We waited around for an hour hoping he might return when his live-in girlfriend showed up. She wasn't any help; said she didn't know anything. We did catch her texting Carr while we were there, though." Valentino pulled a cell phone out of his pocket and handed it to Mr. Sebasti. "None of his texts revealed where he was. The last text she received from Carr came in at about ten this morning. Since then, there have been no additional communication between the two. His girlfriend warned him, and now he's disappeared; we've lost his trail."

"Again . . ." The way he shouted it, Valentino could tell that Mr. Sebasti was losing control. Mr. Sebasti must have noticed it as well. He took a deep breath before he continued.

"Where's the girl now?"

"We brought her in for further questioning. We are going to use some of the standard techniques to help jog her memory. Paolo has her down the hall in room six."

"Don't leave her alone too long with Paolo; we want her alive."

"I'm headed there right after I leave here, sir," Valentino said.

Mr. Sebasti walked behind his desk and opened his top draw. He pulled out a large hunting knife and raised it in the air, the light in the room reflecting off its large stainless steel blade. "Bring the girl to me; I have a few of my own questions to ask her."

Valentino pushed the girl into the office. Mr. Sebasti sat on the corner of his desk, the knife, standing on the tip of the blade on a book, spun around and around ever so gently in his hand. Mr. Sebasti stared at the girl for a long moment without saying anything; he just kept spinning the knife around and around. Valentino had never seen that look in Mr. Sebasti's eye before. Filled with pure evil, it scared him, not so much for his life, but for the girl's life.

In his line of work he had threatened many, and he had even hurt a few that wouldn't cooperate. But, never had he killed an innocent person, someone strictly associated with the wrong guy.

"You're a pretty little thing," Mr. Sebasti said, finally breaking the silence. "What's your name?"

"Tish," the girl said, barely above a whisper.

"Well, Tish, this is how it's going to go. I'm going to ask a few questions. If I don't get the answers I'm looking for, I'm going to carve my initials into that pretty little back of yours. Then I'm going to ask more questions, and if I don't get the right answers I'm going to remove the fingers of your left hand one at a time—one finger for every wrong answer." Mr. Sebasti jumped off the desk, landing on the ground in front of Tish, the knife outstretched in front of him.

This quick unexpected motion startled Valentino and Tish at the same time. Valentino recovered from his initial shock, just in time to grab Tish by the shoulders as she started to run for the door.

"No you don't," Valentino said. "Not until we get a few answers." Valentino swung Tish around, slamming her hard against the desk, forcing her to bend down until her face smashed against the top of it.

Tish screamed.

"Scream all you want. No one will hear you," Mr. Sebasti said. "This office is sound-proof, made especially for these types of occasions."

Tish wore a shirt with the entire back missing, the front held together by a single spaghetti strap that ran from side to side. Another spaghetti strap looped around the neck to keep the shirt up. Mr. Sebasti didn't have a hard time finding an exposed area of skin on her back where he could start carving. He placed the tip of the blade at the small of her back. "First question. How long have you been with Zeren Carr?"

"About three months."

"How well do you know him?" Mr. Sebasti pressed the tip into her back and drew a drop of blood. Tish screamed.

"I barely know him," Tish gasped. "We party at night, we share the same bed, and then he goes off to work. That's about it. It's not like we're married. We just hang out."

Mr. Sebasti turned the blade, drilling the tip in a little deeper. Blood began to flow more freely, a small drop making its way down her side. The muscles in Tish's back shuddered under the pressure. Valentino turned his face to hide the pain he felt as he watched her muscles twitch.

"Where does he work?" Mr. Sebasti asked.

"He works at Office Supplies down on twenty-fifth."

"Is he there now?"

"No. He's off at four." Mr. Sebasti looked at his watch. Valentino did the same: twenty minutes past five.

"Where is he now?"

"I don't know."

"When did you last hear from him?"

"I got a text from him this morning—that was it."

"Do you know where he's from?"

"I . . . don't remember."

Mr. Sebasti lifted the point from off her back and the girl's muscles relaxed. Valentino relaxed as well, drawing most of his weight off the girl.

To Valentino's horror, Mr. Sebasti pressed the point of the blade in a new spot on the girl's back, causing her to scream. Valentino adjusted his weight pinning her down again.

"Maybe this will help you remember," Mr. Sebasti said. He turned the knife in his hand, drawing blood. The girl's muscles spasmed out of control.

"Montana," she screamed. "Somewhere in Montana. I can't remember the name of the city. I think it's a boy's name; something like David, Daniel, or Donny. I can't remember."

"Dillon?" Valentino asked.

"Yeah, that's it. He's from Dillon, Montana," Tish said.

Mr. Sebasti stepped back from Tish, holding his knife in the air, showing off the blood on the blade as if it were a sign of honor.

Valentino's stomach turned sour. At first, working for Mr. Sebasti had been exciting. The clothes, the women, the food, the parties, and the occasional roughing up the "bad guys," as Mr. Sebasti called it. Valentino had killed before, but only when needed. He'd beat up his fair share of punks too, but this, the knife in the back of . . . an *innocent* girlfriend. This was torture.

Maybe the time had come to find a new line of work.

"Get your boys and go and see if Carr returned home to Montana," Mr. Sebasti said. "And if you find him, bring him back so I can talk to him, face to face." He stabbed the knife down into the book on his desk, a foot from Tish's face.

She screamed.

"What about her?" Valentino still had Tish pinned down. "Take her shopping for a new pair of shoes."

Concrete shoes. *Kill her*, is what he meant, and dispose of the body at the bottom of the lake so that no one would find her. Horrible time to have a conscience.

Chapter 18

Annie

Double Trouble

"Who came by this afternoon?" Annie asked Jax after dinner. He gave her a funny look, squinching his nose until wrinkles covered his forehead.

"Beth Downs came by," he said.

"Not her, the silver-haired man you were talking to out front. He came by the same time as Beth."

Understanding crossed his face. "Oh yeah, Mr. Windsor, president of the bank."

Annie waited for Jax to go into the details. He didn't elaborate. The silence grew heavy. Annie didn't say anything; she stood and went into the kitchen. She busied herself cleaning up the dinner. She covered the leftover meatloaf and put it in the refrigerator. She put the empty vegetable dish in the sink; she would wash it in a minute.

She watched Jax stare off into space. The gears in his head worked overtime, processing some seriously deep thoughts.

Jax's chair slid back from the table. From the corner of her eye she noticed him leave the room. After a minute or two he returned carrying his rifle case and a gun cleaning kit. He set the case on the floor and placed a blanket on the table. Soon he had his gun on the table and the cleaning kit out.

Annie gathered the remaining dishes from the table. There weren't very many left since it was just the two of them. The only other person who would normally be at the home was Jax's mom, but she usually stayed at the hospital with Mr. Tagget, which left Annie and Jax alone most of the time.

Whenever Jax was this quiet, something was wrong. Annie could read him like an open book. In the past two weeks since they'd been back in Dillon, this wasn't the first time she'd notice how quiet he was. At first, she'd passed it off as stress caused by her own silent treatment she'd been giving him.

Ever since that night in Venezuela, when Mariana Delfino arrived with the police accusing Jax of attacking her, Annie hadn't spoken to him. He'd tried to explain what had happened, giving her all the details. But Annie couldn't get that scratch on Delfino's face out of her mind. Had he tried something on her? Had she fought back? *Jax wouldn't do something like that*, she kept telling herself. But she couldn't deny the scratch and the skin stuck in his ring.

Annie had slapped him hard. Since then, they hadn't really spoken much, other than Jax trying to explain what had happened.

Jax kept his distance, giving her the space she needed so she could sort through everything. Maybe he was cracking under the pressure? Maybe the distance between them was too much? She'd felt it herself. She wanted him, needed him, longed to reach out and touch him again; but, as of yet, she hadn't allowed herself to trust him again. So, she kept her distance as well.

Of course, Jax's quietness could also be related to Mr. Tagget. It was a shock to come home and find his father in the hospital dying of cancer. No one had even tried to let them know. Mr. and Mrs. Tagget, with their old-school mentality, had kept everything to themselves. It would be hard for anyone to handle.

His quiet mood might also be due to the rigors of managing the Double T. She quickly dismissed that idea, knowing that her husband, director of VMI mining operations, could handle the ranch, even though it was a large responsibility.

Jax seemed extra quiet tonight, and she wondered if something Mr. Windsor had said had added to his problems. She would just have to wait a little longer and then, at the right moment, give an encouraging nudge, and Jax would open up.

Annie finished cleaning the kitchen and sat next to him. "What did Mr. Windsor want?"

"Not much." Jax didn't even look up.

This was going to be harder than she'd thought. Something must really be bothering him. Usually a simple question would cause the flood gates to open and Jax would spill every little detail.

Not tonight.

Annie decided on a different approach. "Can you believe the size of Beth's diamond? I mean, that thing was huge. And she kept waving it around, like we were back in high school."

Jax raised his eyebrows slightly, and as he turned back to his rifle said, "That was a big stone."

Time for a frontal attack. Annie put her hand on Jax's shoulder. "What's wrong Jax?"

"Nothing, I'm fine."

"Come on, you can tell me. Is it something Mr. Windsor said? Is it something about the ranch?"

Lucky guess. Annie had hit a cord. Jax put down his cleaning rod. "Mr. Windsor came by to tell me that Dad hasn't paid the mortgage on the ranch for the past year."

"I thought your dad owned the ranch free and clear."

"So did I. It turns out my parents didn't have health insurance."

"Really? No insurance?"

"Yeah, no insurance. When my dad got sick, he refinanced the ranch. He took some cash out to help pay his bills."

"Can we help? With our savings, maybe we can help pay the mortgage and his hospital bills."

Jax's shoulders slumped. He took Annie by the hand. "That's sweet of you. That was my first thought, too."

"How bad is it?"

"After Mr. Windsor left, I contacted the hospital. With Dad's extensive chemotherapy and radiation treatments, his current bills are bordering a million dollars."

"What?" Annie couldn't keep herself from exclaiming. "What about the money from the bank?"

"It's all gone, used up a year ago, some for bills and some for living expenses."

"Oh Jax, I'm so sorry."

"We're in pretty deep." Jax said.

"What are we going to do?"

"I don't know yet. I'm still thinking about it. I haven't come up with any feasible options."

"What about last year's selloff?" At the end of every summer the Taggets always had extra money from the spring and summer cattle sales. "Surely there must be money left over from the cattle sales, it's only September."

"My parents didn't have any money to pay the hands last year, so they all left."

"No one stuck around to help a sick old man?"

"No one knew he was sick, remember? We didn't find out until we got home. Everyone left. No one stayed to help get his cattle to market.

Annie dropped her head into her hands. "What about the cattle?" she asked.

"They're still out on the range. It would take some time to round them up, and by the time we did there wouldn't be any buyers. Any potential buyers have already filled their quotas during the earlier sales. We're too late for this year. Even if we did sell the cattle now, we'd only get half the price."

"What about next year?"

"Yeah, we could be ready, but we need money now. Mr. Windsor has been trying to hold off the creditors. The Double T is prime real estate, and there are a few groups itching to get their hands on it; if we don't pay the mortgage, the Double T goes up on the auction block soon."

"Isn't he the president of the bank?"

"He can only stall for so long," Jax said. "He's already prevented foreclosure proceedings for a year."

"What about your dad's plane? Maybe you could sell it."

The Double T, a 15,667 acre ranch, was difficult to cover by horseback even in a week. Jax's father had purchased a new Cessna 206 in 1984 as a way to more efficiently scout the ranch, spot cattle, and search for any potential problems on the range. The plane turned out to be useful in working the ranch, but it was more of a toy for Mr. Tagget.

"That would help. But, it would literally kill my dad if he knew I'd sold his baby."

At the encouragement of his father, Jax had earned his private pilot's license the month before he'd turned sixteen and obtained his driver's license. He and Annie had gone on several flying dates in the plane; but since they'd left for the university and Jax had started working, there had been little time for that. Annie knew that Jax loved the plane just as much as his father did. It would kill Jax to have to sell the plane as well.

"It's an option," Annie said. "I mean, if we want to help. But there has to be something else we can do first."

"Mr. Windsor feels bad about the situation, but against his wishes, the board has given the ultimatum."

"Really? What, we have to move out by the end of the week?"

Jax shook his head. "Not by the end of the week. The bank was kind enough to give us a month. We have until the end of October to get current on the mortgage or move out."

"Seriously? One month."

"I spoke with the hospital today as well. They figured now that we've been home for a couple of weeks, we would have things arranged to start paying Dad's bills."

After a moment of silence, Jax picked up his rifle and resumed his cleaning.

Annie watched for a moment, then asked, "What are you going to do with that? Planning on taking out the banker and the head of the hospital?"

"The way I figure it," Jax picked up the rifle and sighted down the barrel, pretending to shoot an imaginary target, "if they aren't around, they can't come collecting." Annie laughed, knowing Jax wasn't serious.

"You've heard the saying, 'When it rains it pours,'" Jax said.

"Yeah, and with the hospital and bank bills screaming, I'd say it's raining pretty hard. Don't tell me there are more problems?"

"The foreman I hired when we first got here reported that we've been losing cattle. In the past week he's found five dead out on the range."

"Any idea what's killing them?" Annie asked.

"Only large and healthy cattle have been killed, and the way the cattle are being dragged off and eaten, the foreman thinks it might be a bear. It could really be anything, but bears have been known to kill cattle. And right now we can't be losing cows, so I'm planning on going out on the ranch tomorrow to watch the herd and scout the area. I'll be gone for a couple of days. It'll give me some time to think about the ranch. Maybe by the time I get back, I'll have an answer."

"Today is Tuesday. Do you think you'll be back by the weekend?"

"I hope I'll be back by Friday for date night. If not then, for sure by Saturday morning."

Annie smiled. It had been a couple of weeks since they'd been on their regular date night, and she needed some time alone with Jax.

Chapter 19

Jaxon
The Mine

With the bills piling up, it looked as if the longest-held privately owned ranch in the Beaverhead Valley was about to come to a fiery end.

Jax didn't like the ranch life anyway. He had never wanted to be a rancher. Ranching required hard work. He knew how to work hard, but ranching wasn't his kind of work, though he loved the Double T. To be a rancher you had to be patient, always keeping your eye on the end of the season when the cattle were sold and the big payoff occurred. He had lived his whole life like that, and all he could think about as he grew up was leaving as soon as he could find a chance. And that chance had come when he'd secured a job in Venezuela.

Living overseas, he thought he couldn't be touched—too far away to come running home.

He was wrong.

He couldn't believe his misfortune; of all the places in the world, the ranch was the last place he wanted to be.

Jax started his 700cc Yamaha ATV, backed it off the trailer, and parked it. In the early morning hours, amber streaks of sunlight slowly began to light up the sky, the sun peeking over the horizon. His breath came out in puffy white clouds, the summer temperatures had faded fast. The brisk fall temperatures Dillon was known for had arrived.

Jax was now deep on the ranch, the farthest distance from the house, the location where the foreman had said they had been losing cattle. Although he should have kept the ATV on to warm up the motor, he'd turned it off. It was quiet, except for the gurgling of the Beaverhead River. Peacefully quiet.

He stood for a moment, looking down the Trapper's Valley that opened before him. He saw gentle, rolling tree-shrouded hills that surrounded the lush valley carpeted with fire red, amber yellow, and violet purple wildflowers. Light from the rising sun reflected off the river as it meandered northeast through the valley. It had been a while since Jax had been out on the ranch; he'd forgotten how serene it could be.

Jax took a mental photograph in his mind, promising himself he would share it with Annie when he got home.

He took a deep breath of fresh air and let it out slowly.

Not one to dillydally on sentimental things, he quickly turned back to the task at hand. He packed his gear on the ATV, fired it up, and started out.

He planned to scout the area, find a spot to set up camp, and then watch and wait. Jax had instructed the foreman to push the cattle back into Trapper's Valley for the next couple of weeks to lure whatever had been attacking them to strike again. Jax hoped not to lose any more cattle, but he didn't want to have to continue coming out on the ranch for extended periods of time. If it meant losing one or two more cows to quicken the process, so be it. He would make that sacrifice so that he could be home with his wife sooner than later.

The cattle grazed through the valley and along the river—they were in position. The majority of the kills on the cattle had occurred along the edge of this valley. Jax decided to circle the area to look for any recent signs of predators, and to also look for the best place to set up for the next couple of days, a sort of base camp that he could operate from.

By noon he had only covered a third of the east side of the valley. It was a tedious process, partly because he didn't actually know what he was searching for and also, because every time he came upon a set of tracks, he had to get off the ATV and study them. He didn't want to miss anything, so he stopped for every little thing.

Ever since Jax was twelve and could legally carry a gun, he had been hunting with his father on the ranch. He was familiar with the signs of most animals in the area. His father would wake him up when it was still dark out. Jax would quickly dress, grab a bite to eat, and take his gun. He had learned quickly that to his father, hunting meant studying tracks. On these so-called hunting trips, Jax spent most of the time on his hands and knees studying dirt.

However, every year without fail Jax and his father would always fill their tags with a deer and an elk.

Although Jax hated studying dirt, it didn't take long to realize the connection between good tracking skills and meat in the fridge. While his friends from school seemed to only sporadically kill an elk or a deer year after year, Jax never missed. His mom had attributed his success to Jax's skill at shooting. He could shoot, he knew that. Rarely did he miss. But Jax's father had always told him that successful hunters, meaning good trackers, spent 90 percent of their time tracking and 10 percent shooting.

He came across deer, elk, and antelope signs. He examined the prints, looking at the ridges in the dirt created by the hoof. With the ridges of the tracks falling in, the tracks had been made hours before, even days before. He did find some fresh tracks, with ridges of the dirt still straight and tall, made within the last thirty minutes or so. Jax also tested the scat of the animals. With a stick he pushed and smashed the animal droppings, checking for dryness.

But it was an uneventful morning; lots of signs, but nothing that might be killing cattle. After lunch Jax came across the track of a mountain lion. The print was large in size, probably a three- or four-year-old cat. Mountain lions were known to take down a cow, but usually only the small calves or the sick ones. On the Double T, only large, healthy cattle had been killed.

Although the prints appeared to be more than a couple of days old, Jax decided to follow them anyway to see where they might go. So far, the mountain lion was the only promising lead.

He followed them for a couple of hours, growing tired as the afternoon wore on. He had to cross streams and skirt large rock outcroppings that the cat seemed to effortlessly scale. Several times Jax lost the trail, but found it again after widening his search pattern.

Two Hearts

The sun began to set. Jax hadn't found the cat yet, but the tracks had been slowly heading out of the area. Jax started looking for a place to set up his base camp.

The ideal spot would provide the best view of the valley without having to move around much. He figured if he stayed in hiding, whatever had been killing the cattle might show itself again. And, if it did, Jax would be ready.

Douglas fir, Lodgepole, and Ponderosa Pine trees covered the hillside that rose in front of him, making it difficult to see ahead. With Trapper's Valley to his back, he didn't see anything that looked promising as a base camp. Up ahead, as he passed through the trees, the terrain rose to what appeared to be a small clearing on the hillside—just what he'd been looking for, an unobstructed view of the valley floor.

When he came out of the trees, what he saw surprised him. He had been to this spot before many years ago, but had forgotten about it. Before him, framed with railroad ties, stood the entrance to the Western Pleasure Mine, the same place he'd found the gold to make Annie's wedding ring and two hearts pendant.

Jax pulled up to the entrance and turned around toward the valley floor stretched out below. From the entrance, slightly elevated off the valley floor, he could see almost the entire valley and the river with the cattle grazing in the lush green grass.

He turned on the lights and backed his ATV deep into the mine. There was plenty of space to park his machine out of the elements and to set up camp.

In no time he had a small fire burning, which warmed the area inside the mine. He used his backpacking stove to prepare his dinner. When he had eaten and cleaned up, he got out his binoculars and his rifle and went to the front of the mine entrance.

The sun had completely set.

He sat down, leaning against the framed entrance, listening to the noises, and trying to figure out where they were coming from and what might be making them. He could hear the cattle gently mooing. He could hear the river gurgling as it made its way through the valley. He could hear a gentle buzz of insects. Everything appeared to be normal.

Jax woke with a start in the same position from the night before, sitting against the framed entrance, his gun lying across his lap. He knew he had been tired, but he hadn't realized how much. It was pitch black, and a shiver ran down his spine. His small fire had died several hours earlier. Jax slipped his cell phone out of his pocket. He'd brought it for its clock, knowing he wouldn't have any signal bars of reception. He glanced down at the time: three in the morning. He'd slept for several hours.

But something had startled his sleep. It could have been the cold that woke him, but he didn't think that was it. His body temperature normally ran hot, and he could sleep through almost any weather condition, covered or uncovered. He listened intently, not moving a muscle, trying to discover the source of any potential disturbance.

Suddenly he heard it, a low growling noise. It faded and then disappeared. Then he heard grunting, and the low growling noise came again.

A bear, Jax thought. A big bear, judging from the deep sound of the growling and grunting. Jax turned toward the noise, which was coming from a clump of bushes about twenty-five yards away. Too dark to make out any shapes or see anything clearly, he could only see the bushes moving. He looked down, his gun clutched in his hands with the barrel pointing in the direction of the bush.

He sat ready to shoot, but unless he knew exactly what and where to shoot, he would wait. Shooting blindly into a bush could be stupid and dangerous. What if the noise hadn't come from a bear? What if the noise had been a dog from a nearby ranch? What if it was one of his own cows stuck in the heavy brush?

But, if a bear had made those noises, and he shot it now—he raised the barrel slightly—he could be home in a couple of hours, done with this ordeal quickly. But, if it was a bear and he shot blindly into the bush and only wounded it, he would have an angry bear to deal with. He lowered the barrel. He didn't like the idea of wounding a bear.

Jax waited and watched, hoping for an opportunity to shoot. It never came. The growling and grunting slowly faded into the distance and then disappeared. Whatever it was had wandered off.

He leaned back against the railroad ties. He tried to stay awake, but he was still tired. He quickly fell asleep again. By five thirty in the morning, light began chasing the darkness away, the amber rays of the sun appearing in the east.

Jax woke at the first shades of light. He ate a quick breakfast: a double bag of peaches and cream instant oatmeal, a cup of hot chocolate, and a cold dinner roll. After he'd cleaned up, he grabbed his rifle and went out to investigate the bushes.

He wasn't prepared for what he found.

Jax had resolved that the morning's disturbance had been caused by a bear. Black bears were not an uncommon sight in the area. With the Beaverhead River full of trout, black bears often hunted along its banks. Wild blackberries and raspberries that grew along the banks also attracted the bears.

Jax knew the animal had left the area early that morning, but he still approached the bushes cautiously. He gently parted the branches and stepped through. He found the tracks easily, scattered all over the ground. And, as he had guessed, it had been a bear. But the size of the prints didn't look like an ordinary black bear. They looked as large as dinner plates, about ten to twelve inches across, Jax guessed. All of the five claws of the paw were visible in the dirt. Very unique and distinctive. He knew enough about bear signs to know that a black bear hadn't made those prints. Jax took a deep breath and let it out slowly. A grizzly bear, a very large grizzly, had made those tracks.

With a grizzly killing his cattle, he would lose more before the end of the week. When a bear finds a good source of food, they usually stay nearby until the food supply is gone. Jax looked down the valley and watched as the cattle grazed undisturbed. With over a thousand head of cattle spread throughout the valley, chances were good that the bear would strike again.

After discovering the tracks of the grizzly, Jax widened his search circle to take in more ground. Three hours of painstakingly slow nose-to-the-ground searching revealed nothing, which he half expected. Jax bent to examine an indentation in the dirt at the edge of the game trail he'd been following. As he did so, a loud rumble, like the crackling of thunder, came from his stomach. A quick peek at his cell phone showed 12:42. Jax figured he better stop for food before his stomach mutinied.

Back at camp, inside the mine shaft, Jax placed his rifle in its case attached to the ATV. He dug out a couple of sandwiches from the ice chest strapped to the rack on the back of the ATV. Annie, knowing of Jax's voracious appetite, had packed as if a small army had come with him, just the way Jax liked it. She sent a large ice chest packed with drinks and a variety of cold cuts, peanut butter and jelly, and fish sandwiches. There were fruit cups and homemade chocolate chip cookies in a Ziploc bag. One thing was for certain, Jax would not starve.

He had already been out on the ranch for over a day, and the food in the ice chest had stayed cool. The temperature inside the mine stayed ten to fifteen degrees cooler than outside. Jax's stomach growled again, reminding him of the grizzly he'd heard last night.

He sat down in the dirt at the back of the ATV and stretched out his legs, resting them on the old iron rails that ran down the center of the shaft. He leaned back against the wall and took a bite of his sandwich. Turning his head to his right, he glanced down the darkened mine shaft. On the ground about twenty feet away and in the middle of the shaft between the two iron rails, he noticed a right angle in the dirt. He grabbed his flashlight from his pack and went to investigate.

He placed the beam of light on the object, quickly realizing it was his old wooden-handled rock pick which he'd left behind after finding the gold nugget all those years ago. He bent over and picked it up, feeling the weight of the steel head at the end of the handle. He swung it through the air several times. It felt good. He struck the wall with it. There was a loud clang as the tip bounced off the rock. The pick was still solid.

He peered down the darkened shaft. Western Pleasure Mine was a gold mine. It had been abandoned for nearly a century, but he'd found gold in it. Not much, but enough to make Annie's ring and pendant. Incredibly, it had taken him nearly three months to find just that small amount, which was little in comparison to what he would need to find now if he were to fix his family's problems.

He took another bite of his sandwich. As he chewed, he thought about the mines in Venezuela he'd worked in. Gold was never the primary target of those mines, but they'd always found it as they tore up the earth digging for other minerals. Unfortunately, he didn't have the luxury of time or the resources to rip open Western Pleasure to look for gold.

But he was a miner—a real one, now. This was where he belonged. He breathed in deeply. The dusty smell brought back fond memories.

He flashed his light down the shaft. It reflected off the rough surface of the ceiling and walls, illuminating the single internal infrastructure of wood framing fifty feet in front of him. The cross beam in the ceiling had broken in the middle and it sagged dangerously, as if the ceiling would collapse at any second. Part of the ceiling had already fallen, partially filling the floor of the shaft.

He took his last bite of sandwich and stuffed the now empty Ziploc bag into his back pocket. With the beam of light showing the way, he stepped down the darkened shaft.

Maybe just a quick look.

He approached the broken cross beam with caution. It wasn't completely broken in half, only part way. It sagged heavily in the middle, where the weight of the ceiling had put most of the pressure. It hadn't been this way before when he was last there. He scanned his light over the ceiling. Only a small portion, maybe the size of two basketballs, had caved in. But, it had been enough to break the thick wood beam.

He reached up and placed the head of the rock pick against the bowing cross beam. He pushed. Nothing happened. The beam appeared to be still in place, practically broken in half but not moving anymore. Jax stepped back and placed the head of the rock pick against the wood beam against the wall that supported the broken cross beam. He pushed. It moved, and then a loud groan echoed down the shaft. The cross beam shrieked, as if it were in pain. It shifted and then moved with the motion of the support beam.

Jax jumped back just in time as the ceiling beam came crashing to the ground followed by a large section of the ceiling.

Rocks, dirt, and dust filled the shaft, making it hard for him to breath. Jax moved back, just out of reach of the billowing dust cloud. He waited five minutes to let the dust settle before stepping forward to investigate.

He flashed his light over the mound of rocks in the center of the shaft. It was a large pile, filling up half of the mine from wall to wall. The broken ceiling beam was now in two pieces, partially buried, with an end of each piece sticking up in the air on either side of the pile.

He cautiously approached the mound of rocks. He'd been in a few cave-ins before, three to be exact. In all of them he'd come out unscathed. Wiser but uninjured. Right now he didn't feel like going through another one. He stopped at the edge of the pile and flashed his light over the ceiling, scanning it for any loose rocks that might be waiting to tumble down.

To his surprise, the ceiling was gone. In its place was a hole about five feet wide by fifteen feet long. The hole was five feet deep, extending the original ten-foot ceiling to fifteen feet off the shaft floor.

Along the edge of the wall, a foot above where the original ceiling had been, a paper-thin line reflected his light. He flashed his light over the reflecting area for a better look. The ceiling had crumbled to the ground, exposing a small seam of . . . gold. Standing on the pile of rock, he reached up and very gently traced his finger over the seam.

Gold! Pure Gold!

He took a deep breath and let it out slowly. He had accidentally found gold in this old mine. He tried digging at the wall, wanting more of the rock to crumble to the ground, but it didn't move. He wondered how deep and wide the seam went.

Jax stepped back and flashed his light on the pile of rocks at his feet. Tiny bits of gold reflected in various spots. He flashed the light on the wall again, and from this vantage point, having moved slightly away from the wall, he could see two other smaller gold veins just like the first one he'd found.

This could be it! This could be what he needed to save the ranch. He grinned with the thought that he had just stumbled, purely by accident, upon a small gold mine. Jax sat down and leaned against the opposite wall. His eyes stayed focused on the seams of gold. His mind raced. All thoughts of the grizzly bear and the cattle had quickly disappeared. Gold was on his mind.

He needed a sample of ore. He needed to have it tested.

He looked at the pile of rocks on the floor of the mine shaft. He could take that to be tested. But the gold seams on the wall appeared more promising. To remove that he would need tools, and right now, he didn't have any. Nor did he have any back at the ranch.

He stood and ran his hand over the freshly exposed wall, brushing over the three veins of gold. He needed a pick, a hammer, a shovel, and several buckets.

Chapter 20

Annie

A Sighting

By Thursday evening, Jax had been gone almost two days. He'd said he might be home by Friday night or Saturday morning. Knowing Jax, he would do all in his power to be home Friday night. If there was one thing Jax didn't like, it was missing Friday date night with Annie.

Annie pulled up and parked in front of Vans grocery store. She'd come to town to buy a few things, knowing Jax would be hungry when he returned from his hunt.

She entered the store and grabbed a cart. She wound her way through the aisles picking out the essentials: Rocky Road ice cream, Oreo cookies, milk, eggs, and a couple boxes of Cap'n Crunch Berries, Peanut Butter Crunch, and Lucky Charms. After filling her cart, she stood in line at the checkout stand.

"Annie Tagget?" a female voice asked from behind. Annie turned. "How are you?" Linda Emmett asked.

"Mrs. Emmett, how nice to see you," Annie said, forcing a smile.

Linda Emmett was a lovely person. Always the first to lend a hand to someone in need, or the first to bring dinner to someone sick. She was the first to volunteer to help build the annual float during the high school homecoming parade. Mrs. Emmett had a huge grin that never left her face, even when it seemed like things weren't going her way.

But Mrs. Emmett had one flaw. Mrs. Emmett liked to gossip. She knew anything and everything about everyone's business. She seemed to think she had the answer for everyone's problems. And, no matter the situation, she would tell you her opinion.

To make matters worse, Mrs. Emmett worked at the post office—probably not the best place for the town gossip. Nothing went untouched. She handled everyone's mail, and she either new all the dirt or she guessed at it based upon the mail they received.

She knew which homes had been foreclosed on, sometimes before the homeowners did. She knew when employees got their walking papers from their bosses. She knew who received smutty magazines, and she made sure the pastor at church knew also. And, Mrs. Emmett didn't mind spreading the news.

Annie had to be careful.

"I heard you and Jax had returned to the ranch. How is Tru doing?" Mrs. Emmett asked. Everyone knew Mr. Tagget had cancer. In a small town, news traveled quickly and nothing stayed hidden. Annie saw the expression on Mrs. Emmett's face; genuine concern showed.

"Not good," Annie said. "Mr. Tagget didn't tell anyone, not even his own family, and now the cancer has spread. The doctors don't think there is much they can do for him."

"I had no idea it was so bad," Mrs. Emmett gasped.

"The doctors are trying to make him as comfortable as possible."

"Have they given him a time frame?"

Annie shrugged. "Yes, but the doctors are still uncertain."

"How long?" Mrs. Emmett asked, her dropped voice betraying her fear.

"They've given him several options, and of course he's chosen the longest promised time frame. The doctors said it could be a couple of weeks to half a year."

"A couple of weeks? That isn't very long."

"Honestly, the doctors are surprised he's lasted this long. Under his current condition, they said he should have died a long time ago. That's why they can't give him an exact time frame. One doctor said Mr. Tagget could live a whole entire year."

"A year? Wow, that would be wonderful," Mrs. Emmett said. She raised her index finger to add emphasis to her next thought and Annie knew what was coming, Mrs. Emmett's dreaded sage advice. "I am so sorry he's sick, but I tried—"

"Annie?" the clerk at the register asked. "Do you want paper or plastic?"

Saved by the clerk.

"Excuse me for one moment," Annie said, cutting off Mrs. Emmett in the middle of her thought. The clerk, starting to run Annie's grocery items over the scanner, had created the perfect opportunity to excuse herself from

Mrs. Emmett. Annie turned and started placing more of her grocery items on the conveyer belt. As she did so, she said over her shoulder, "I'll tell Jax I ran into you and that you said hello."

"No need to. I just saw him thirty minutes ago in Twin and I said hello to him myself," Mrs. Emmett smiled.

Twin Bridges, Montana, or Twin, as the locals called it, was a small town approximately twenty-nine miles northeast of Dillon, with I-41 running right through the middle of it.

Annie turned from her cart and faced Mrs. Emmett. "You couldn't have seen him. Jax is out on the ranch hunting."

"But I did. I just saw him in Twin."

"What was he doing?" Annie asked, doubt still registering in her voice.

"I was in Twin picking up a few things at Mission Mercantile, and I stopped at the grocery store to see if I could find some crystallized ginger. As I was walking in, Jax came bursting out and about ran me over."

"He was buying food?"

"He did have a couple of bags in his hands. I don't know exactly what it was, but it looked like food."

"That can't be. Jax is supposed to be out deep on the ranch, hunting," Annie shot back.

"Did I say something wrong?" Mrs. Emmett asked.

"No." Annie took a deep breath. "I'm sorry, but I'm just surprised you saw him. He left Wednesday to go hunting and I wasn't expecting him until late Friday or Saturday. You sure it was him?"

"Oh, I'm sure." Mrs. Emmett gave Annie a great big smile. "I stopped and chatted with him for a moment. Maybe he's going to surprise you and come back early?"

"Maybe," Annie mumbled. *Or maybe he's up to something*, she thought.

"What?"

"Did you see if he was with anyone?" Annie asked, trying to distract her.

"Nobody came out of the store with him, but there was a girl already in his truck when he got in."

"A girl?"

"Well, *she* had long blond hair, and it was pulled back into a ponytail. From where I stood, it looked like a girl." Mrs. Emmett shrugged. "I guess it could have been a man."

The look on Mrs. Emmett's face told Annie everything. It wasn't a man. It was girl in Jax's truck. *So that's it*, Annie thought. Jax hadn't gone hunting; he'd gone to Twin to meet a girl.

Instantly her hand shot up to the left side of her head where her middle finger found the scar.

Despite the sixty-five-degree air-conditioned temperature in the grocery store, heat steamed up the back of her neck. She adjusted her collar, tugging at it to let the heat escape. She wiped her hand across her brow and pulled it away, wet with perspiration.

Her head started spinning in circles. She leaned back against the checkout stand to steady herself. She felt a heavy weight pressing against her chest. Something had a hold of her heart, squeezing it like a vise. The crushing sensation caused Annie to instinctively look down for the source of the pain. With her head still spinning out of control, she lost her balance.

Her vision blurred as the blue and red speckled design in the vinyl floor rushed to meet her. Her arms, like five-hundred-pound lead weights, were too heavy to move. Her right arm stayed at her side. The left arm, frozen in place, held its position at the side of her head. Annie hit the ground with a thud. The lights went out.

Annie opened her eyes. Three industrial light fixtures, the kind that hold four tubular fluorescent light bulbs, hung from the ceiling. One of the bulbs needed to be replaced. It flickered. She lay on her back on a couch, her arms crossed and resting on her chest like she was dead. The orange fabric of the couch, probably made in the early 70s, felt matted and brittle. A spring, out of place, poked her in the right shoulder blade, causing her pain. She adjusted and the pain faded. A man sat next to her. When she stirred, he turned, took her by the hand, and began stroking it gently.

"Easy . . . is that you?" Annie stammered. She pulled her hand away, hiding it at her side. The store clerk, the young girl that had helped Annie ring up her items, stood back a few steps. "He goes by Charles now," she said.

Charles turned to the girl, and raising his hand as if to ward off any further attack said with a calm voice, "It's okay, Joanie." Charles turned back to Annie.

"That's my little sister, Joanie. You remember her." Annie gave her a little smile. "She was scared when you fainted and didn't know what to do. My office is just down the street, so she called me for help. I came as quickly as I could."

Annie's mind finally cleared. Charles wore khaki pants, a blue button-down shirt, and a yellow paisley tie. He leaned over her with his left arm stretched over her body, resting against the back of the couch. Annie could see the face of his gold Rolex watch that hung loosely from his wrist. He looked sharp, as always.

"Where am I?" Annie said as she tried to sit up.

Charles put both his hands on Annie's shoulders and gently but firmly pushed her back down. "You need to rest. The doctor is on his way."

"The doctor? But, I'm fine." Annie tried to sit up again. This time Charles didn't try to stop her. Annie sat up and leaned back on the couch, scanning her surroundings. "Where am I?"

"Vans' employees' lounge," Charles said. "I sent Mrs. Emmett to get the doctor while Joanie and I carried you back here."

Suddenly, the double swinging doors leading into the lounge burst open.

"Annie? My dear Annie?" Beth Downs announced for the whole world to hear as she came charging in. "Mrs. Emmett told me all about it, how Jax is off cheating on you behind your back. You poor thing, you poor little thing." Beth dropped on the couch and picked up Annie's hand. "Tell me all about it."

Charles followed suit, and they both began stroking Annie's hands as if that would take all the pain away.

Everything came rushing back: Mrs. Emmett, Jaxon being seen in Twin, the girl with the ponytail, and the pain. Reliving the pain just about crushed her heart again. Annie stood. Shaking off Beth and Charles, she started pacing in front of the couch. The pain started to fade, anger filling in the empty space with a rolling boil.

"First off," She punctuated her statement by pumping her fist in the air a couple of times.

Beth slid to the edge of the couch, her eyes bulging with excitement. "Anger, that's a good sign. What're you planning?"

Annie turned on Beth. "As I was saying, first off, Jax isn't cheating on me. I'm sure he has a logical reason for being in Twin and not out on the ranch hunting."

"What about the girl?" Joanie asked. "Mrs. Emmett said she saw a girl in Jax's truck."

"Mrs. Emmett said she *thought* it was girl. She said it could have been a man." The way she said it didn't convince anyone in the room that she believed those words for a second. Before anyone could say anything in response, the double doors swung open again and Dr. Goodman came in, followed by Mrs. Emmett. Both were breathing heavily.

"Sorry it took us so long; we came as quickly as we could," Dr. Goodman said between breaths. The doctor's office was located two blocks away, and from the looks of it, he'd probably run the entire way. The doctor was at least seventy years old. Annie figured that his body, with its all-encompassing triple X figure, hadn't seen this much exercise in the past twenty years.

"I'm fine," Annie said, placing her hand on his elbow as she directed him to one of the empty chairs in the lounge room. The doctor sat down and placed his black doctor's bag at his feet. His breathing had slowed a little, but he still gasped for more than his fair share of the oxygen in the room.

"Let me catch my breath for a moment and then run a few tests," Dr. Goodman said.

"I'm fine, really."

"Just to be safe," the doctor added.

"Fine, just to be safe."

After a short pause in the conversation, Annie cleared her throat. "Right now, everyone in this room believes that Jax is cheating on me. This is based upon Mrs. Emmett having seen Jax with a 'person,'" Annie added her own quotation marks in the air around the word *person*, "that she believes was a girl."

"Sweetheart, don't make it harder than it is," Beth said. "You will heal faster if you just accept the facts as true and move on."

Annie gestured with her hands in a wide circle encompassing everyone in the room. "Guilty until proven innocent? Is that how it is now in America? I know I've been out of the country for a little while, but I thought the saying went 'innocent until proven guilty.'" Annie looked everyone in the eyes willing them to contradict her. No one said anything.

"Here's what we're going to do," Annie looked directly at Mrs. Emmett, "Nothing. Nobody says anything until I've had a chance to confront Jax when he gets back."

Mrs. Emmett nodded several times as Annie stared hard at her, but she couldn't take the pressure from Annie's glare, so she turned away. Annie looked around the room. Beth and Charles were still looking at her. Everyone else had their heads down.

"Are we all in agreement?" Annie asked.

Five heads nodded in unison.

Chapter 21

Annie

Jaxon's Return

The unexpected gathering at the employees' lounge ended as quickly as it had started. After everyone had agreed to say nothing until Annie could confront Jax, Annie went with Dr. Goodman to his office. She told the doctor she was fine. But he insisted.

His office was only two blocks away, so Annie walked with him. He took her blood pressure. Checked her heart with his stethoscope. She flinched when he pressed the little silver pad against her skin. It was cold. He placed it on her back and checked her lungs. She had to breathe in deeply several times. Dr. Goodman took a blood test, pricking Annie's finger with a razorblade lance. It hurt.

When he finished his tests, Annie returned to the ranch. She quickly put her groceries away, started a load of laundry, and folded the pile of clothes in front of her bed. She wanted everything cleaned when Jax came home. He would have his own mountain of clothes that would need to be washed.

Every time she passed the windows in the front room, Annie looked out toward the front yard and glance down the dirt road that led to the ranch. Each time, she saw nothing but the dry, dusty road.

Needing to keep busy, she next went to the garage to tackle the storage closet. Annie opened the garage door to let the fading afternoon sunlight brighten her way. She also wanted to keep an eye on the road. It had been years since Mr. or Mrs. Tagget had done anything to the closet except throw things in and shut the door.

Every noise or passing shadow drew Annie's attention to the front of the opened garage and toward the dirt road. It was late Thursday, and Jax had said he wouldn't be home until Friday or Saturday. But she couldn't help thinking or hoping that he might return early. So she watched and waited in anticipation. Once she saw dust clouds rising from the road. She stopped and set down the two old, empty picture frames she'd just removed from the closet. Annie looked at her watch, six thirty in the evening. Still too early for Jax to return. But she couldn't help feel her heart race a little faster as she watched in anticipation for him to drive up.

Since she returned from Dr. Goodman's office, she'd been rehearsing the first thing she was going to say to Jax, though it continually changed as the time passed and as her mood swung back and forth like a pendulum, from frustration and anger to heartache and tears.

The dust cloud was drawing closer. Jax had finally returned. Her blood started to boil. Instead of taking the soft approach, Annie decided to confront him and get it out in the open, over with as quickly as possible.

The dust clouds came closer, but then turned and faded away. No one. It wasn't Jax. Although she hadn't actually seen the car, she knew it had left the interstate and driven on the dirt road that led to the ranch house. However, since the vehicle didn't come all the way to the ranch, Annie assumed that it must have turned onto the road that led to Lover's Flat. Probably parkers getting the first dibs on Lover's Flat's prime spots, although six thirty in the evening on a Thursday night was a bit early to start parking.

After putting the groceries away, folding the laundry, and cleaning out the storage closet in the garage, Annie dropped on the couch in the front room exhausted. She had kept herself busy to keep her mind off Jax, but it hadn't helped. No matter what she did, all she could think about was him.

Mrs. Emmett was wrong, Annie had kept telling herself throughout the evening. Jax loved her, and she loved him. He wouldn't cheat on her. The bloody red scratch on Mariana Delfino's face kept flashing through her mind. She saw the dangling piece of skin. Jax had explained it. According to him, nothing had happened, so there must be a logical explanation for Jax today, too. She fought to stay in control.

It could have been a man, but as hard as Annie could think, she couldn't remember anyone in Dillon, boy or girl, that had a long blond ponytail. And what was Jax doing in Twin anyway? He was supposed to be out on the ranch hunting. *A secret rendezvous?*

Annie considered herself a homemaker; she kept a clean house, she kept Jax's shirts pressed, and she always tried to have a home-cooked meal ready on the table when he came home from work. But that evening, as Annie pulled her precooked chicken pot pie from the oven, she wondered if maybe she'd been slipping just a little.

Annie stepped from the kitchen with her dinner in hand when she heard a car pull up to the front of the house. With the passing of the hours and her anticipated excitement waning, her vigilance toward the dirt road had lessened minute by minute. Two hours had passed since she'd last looked toward to road, and now someone had pulled up out front. *Could it be Jax?*

Annie set her plate down on the table and pulled off her apron. She stepped into the half bath just off the kitchen to examine herself. What she saw in the mirror frightened her. She was a wreck; her hair was disheveled, and the old T-shirt she wore had dirt smeared on the front from working in the garage, but that wasn't the worst of it.

Her face was a mess. Her mascara was smeared from the sweat that dripped from her brow. She'd wiped at it with the sleeve of her shirt. Dirt had gathered on her forehead, accentuating the furrow lines on her brow. She looked scary.

And emotionally she wasn't ready to see him.

She'd fought all day with her emotions, telling herself that nothing was wrong, that there was an easy explanation for why Jax was in Twin with a girl. And that really, it probably wasn't Jax, and if it had been, he wasn't with a girl.

Annie had told herself these things a hundred times throughout the day; but, no matter how hard she'd tried to convince herself that they were true, there was always that shred of doubt that lingered in the back of her mind, whispering in her ear.

She looked at her red, swollen eyes, which were irritated and puffy from the dust in the garage. It looked like she'd been crying nonstop, all day long. But she hadn't. She'd fought all day with her emotions, not allowing herself to cry. She wouldn't do it.

A knock at the front door brought her back. She scratched her head. Jax wouldn't knock at his own home. Annie wiped at the dirt on her brow with a hand towel, fluffed her hair once, and hurried to front door.

"Beth?" Beth Downs stood on the porch with a plate of homemade cookies, a plant with bright yellow flowers in her hand, and a sorry look on her face.

Chapter 22

Jaxon

A Grizzly

"This is the last bucket, I swear." Jax raised three fingers in the air, mouthing the words *I promise, scout's honor.* "How many buckets does this make, anyway?"

"This will be the fifth bucket of ore hauled out of this old mine," Zeren said as he dumped a shovel full of dirt into an empty bucket. "Don't you think you have enough?"

"I probably do, but every time I try to stop, I see the pile of dirt sitting there, knowing it is laced with gold, and I can't stop. I keep telling myself, just one more shovelful." Jax added a shovel full of dirt to the partially filled bucket.

"I don't really care if we load ten buckets of ore." Zeren stopped shoveling and leaned against the wall of the mine. "I'm just exhausted." He pulled out his cell phone and hit the power button. "It's already two in the morning. Maybe we should stop until tomorrow."

Jax stopped working, leaning against his shovel. He wiped his brow with his sleeve. "No more. I promised this would be the last bucket."

"What do you plan to do with this stuff, anyway?" Zeren asked.

"Well, first I'm taking it home to show Annie. Then, I'm taking a sample over to Mr. Collin to have it tested."

"The local assayer? I hate that guy."

"He's not so bad," Jax said. "Once you get to know him, he's a pretty nice guy."

"He gives me the creeps, with his tiny buggy eyes." Zeren made small circles with his index fingers and thumbs and placed them up to his eyes, as if he had round glasses on. In the dark mine, illuminated by a small flashlight laying across the back seat of the ATV, Jax could barely see what Zeren was doing; but, having known him practically his entire life, he knew Zeren was trying to imitate Mr. Collin. Jax laughed. It was actually pretty funny, the way Zeren walked around pretending to be half blind, stumbling around and bumping into things.

"I know it's rich with minerals and gold, but I want to have it certified so I can market the mine to potential investors. With a certificate in my hand, investors will be knocking at my door for a chance to reopen the mine. Let's load this last bucket on the back of the ATV and then hit the sack. First thing in the morning, we'll head back to the ranch."

"Don't forget my car back in Twin."

"Oh, yeah. It was lucky for me I found you wandering the streets," Jax said. "I probably could have loaded all this by myself, but with you, it cut the time in half."

"I wasn't wandering the streets," Zeren said. "Like I told you, I was looking for work."

"You should've come out to the ranch; you know you'll always have a job at the Double T."

"Serious?" Zeren asked.

"No question about it. Today is Thursday." Jax glanced at his cell phone, even though he knew it was past midnight. "I mean Friday. On Monday you start working at the Double T."

By two thirty in the morning Jax and Zeren had finished loading the last bucket of ore onto the ATV. They didn't take time to clean up their tools and supplies. They could do it in the morning when there was light and after they had rested from the backbreaking labor.

"Thanks for the sleeping bag and the food," Zeren said as he slid into the bag and pulled it up to his chest.

Jax, nervous about a possible change in weather and getting stranded out on the ranch without supplies, had brought double of everything. He let Zeren sleep in the extra sleeping bag.

"I'm glad I brought an extra one." Jax slipped into his bag and rolled to his side. "Goodnight, buddy." He sighed from exhaustion.

It had been a long day, but a good day. A smile crossed his face. The ore would test positive for high traces of gold. His mind raced with all of the possibilities. He could pay his father's medical expenses. He could pay off the mortgage on the ranch. He could buy a truck. He could take Annie on a trip. Sleep began to overcome him, his mind going fuzzy.

Suddenly, a scream shattered the silence, tearing Jax from his sleep. Zeren and Jax bolted out of their beds. Jax grabbed the flashlight and snapped it on.

"What was that?" they asked in unison. Within seconds another scream tore through the mine, bouncing off the walls. Now that they were fully awake, it sounded more like a moan than a scream.

"The cattle," Jax said. He stared down the mine shaft, toward the entrance. It was dark, but moonlight illuminated the framed entrance.

"Something's been killing the cattle, and I came out here to scout the herd," Jax said, as he pulled on his last boot and tied the laces. "I traced its steps, and I think it's a grizzly. He's out there right now having one for breakfast." Jax stood, picking up the flashlight. He fumbled through his gear until he found his rifle.

Zeren pulled on his boots. "Wait for me. I'm coming with you."

Once Jax found his rifle and checked its load, he turned off the light to allow his eyes to adjust to the darkness again.

He could still hear the dying moans of the cow. "Come on. We've got to get out there before it kills again." Jax said.

He and Zeren silently crept up to the framed entrance, each standing partially inside, concealed by the railroad ties that made up the doorway.

The moon sat high in the sky, creating good visibility. He could see clearly for about three or four hundred yards. However, as he scanned the meadow, it was empty.

There were no cattle. Jax assumed that the cattle had scattered at the first scream of the dying cow. He scanned along the edges of the meandering river. Nothing. Jax stared out into the meadow, to the farthest point of his visibility, scanning back and forth. Nothing.

Jax started to panic. The moaning cow had stopped. The seconds and minutes ticked by; if he didn't spot the victim or the perpetrator soon, he might miss the opportunity altogether. In his anxiety he began scanning the meadow faster, going back and forth, left to right.

Movement.

Something caught his eye on the right side of the meadow, along the edge of the tree line. There, two hundred yards out, Jax saw a dark spot, a shadow that had moved.

Wind, maybe, brushing the trees?

Jax focused his eye on the spot for several seconds. Movement again.

Jax raised his right arm and pointed to the dark spot in the meadow. "Do you see that thing right there, just out there at the edge of the trees?" he whispered, getting Zeren's attention.

Zeren came and stood behind Jax, following the end of his finger. "I see it. Something is moving, almost as if it's backing up into the trees."

"What do you see?" Jax asked

"Too far, I can't tell for sure."

"Does it look like a bear?"

"Yeah, I guess it could be a bear." Zeren stepped slightly forward and put both of his hands on his forehead, shielding his eyes from the moonlight. "The moonlight is helping, but with the distance I can't quite make it out."

Jax motioned Zeren out of the way and raised his rifle to his shoulder. He positioned his eye up to his Leupold

VX-6 hunting scope, scanning the general area where he'd seen the movement. His scope wasn't actually a night scope, but its thirty-millimeter wide-angled lens practically sucked in all remaining available light in the sky, making it appear as if it were high noon on a sunny day. He watched for any movement. The dark spot materialized through the scope. He saw a huge bear dragging the carcass of a cow toward the trees.

Two hundred yards. An easy shot, under normal conditions.

But with the distance, the downhill slope, the trees, and the darkness, he didn't want to risk missing.

Jax lowered his rifle.

"Aren't you going to shoot?" Zeren asked.

"Not under the current conditions. I might miss."

"Jaxon Tagget, miss what he's shooting at? Impossible. Unheard of."

"It's happened before," Jax said.

"You never miss, and you know it."

"I've missed before."

"When?"

Jax didn't respond.

He took a step forward.

"You going down there?" Zeren asked.

"Just a little closer to find a better shot."

Jax and Zeren slipped down the hill, heading for the safety and cover of the trees. They were on the hunt. Jax's blood pumped through his veins with the thrill of the hunt. He imagined that Zeren's did the same. The previous night's work and consequential exhaustion was completely forgotten.

It was darker under the trees, the moonlight struggling to penetrate the canopy of the tree tops. They lost sight of their target, but they worked their way quietly but quickly, always in the general direction of the last know location of the bear.

Jax had never hunted at night. It wasn't illegal in Montana, but it was definitely more difficult. The darkness and the shadows played tricks on the eyes and mind. Distances were difficult to accurately estimate, and the game seemed to disappear a lot easier. Shadows cast eerie images, exaggerated by the imagination.

He planned to spot the bear at about a hundred yards while still in the trees and then, without alerting the animal, take aim and shoot. In the morning, they would return and haul the bear out.

They walked in silence for a while. Jax stopped and whispered, "I don't know exactly where the bear is and I don't want to accidentally walk in on it. We should step out of the trees and get our bearing and see how close we are."

"Sounds good," Zeren responded with a nod.

Jax stepped out of the trees ahead of Zeren and instantly froze. Zeren slammed into the back of him.

"What's up?" Zeren asked, stepping to the side of Jax. Zeren's mouth opened, but nothing came out. Not more than fifty yards in front them, the grizzly bear stood, hunched over the dead cow.

At the sound of Zeren's voice, the bear glanced up at them. For an instant, time seemed to stand still. No one moved, not even the bear; but the hypnotic trance didn't last long.

The bear roared, renting the stillness of the early morning darkness, and charged. With the speed of a racing horse in full gallop, the grizzly, on all fours, charged up the hill.

Zeren screamed, high-pitched. He turned and ran.

Jax stepped forward, holding his Winchester Model 70 Alaskan rifle at his side. Shooting a .338 Winchester Magnum, it could stop any large game animal in North America. He didn't have time to raise it and aim, so he gripped the rifle tightly with both hands, then pulled the trigger. The rifle jumped in his hands, an explosion of fire shattered the dark night. Zeren screamed again, falling to the ground. Jax had worked the bolt action of his rifle, sending a spent shell in the air, hitting the prone and petrified figure of Zeren. A second explosion echoed through the meadow.

The grizzly kept charging, unfazed by the two direct hits, rapidly narrowing the gap, its loud thunderous roar chilling Jax's blood.

The grizzly was close—twenty yards. Jax had to stop him with the next shot, or he and Zeren were goners. No time to properly aim, he pointed the barrel of his rifle at the head of the grizzly. Within half a second a third explosion flashed. The bullet slammed into the bear's mouth, jerking its head to one side. The bear stumbled and crashed to the ground three yards in front of Jax.

The bear lay on the ground, a gigantic mountain of black fur. Jax chambered another shell and discharged the rifle one more time through the bear's head.

No one moved. Jax stood over the bear, legs spread wide, his heart rate elevated, but his breathing slow and steady. He drew back the bolt, metal sliding against metal, the sound amplified in the silence. He chambered another round, clicking the bolt back into position.

After what seemed like an eternity, Zeren finally got off the ground and stood next to Jax. Zeren let out a soft whistle.

"I thought we were dead."

Chapter 23

Annie

Confrontation

Annie rolled over in bed, peering at the clock: 7:52 a.m. Exhausted because of all the late-night planning and scheming, last night's raging bonfire inside of her had died down to only a few smoldering embers. She'd slept in. She was usually up by six, but last night she'd tossed and turned, her mind actively roleplaying different scenarios for when Jax returned. She hadn't quite made up her mind whether to confront him the moment he stepped through the door, or whether to play the wait-and-see game—let things play out after he got home. She didn't know what would be the best.

One way or another, Annie would be ready for his return.

Although she could see light through the blinds, it still appeared a little dark outside. She stretched, her arm gliding over Jax's side of the bed. It was empty and . . . cold.

Since returning to Dillon just over two weeks ago, Annie had not allowed Jax to share the same bed with her.

She'd been sleeping in the bedroom Jax had used growing up in the house. Jax had been sleeping in a spare bedroom down the hall. Still reeling from the incident in Venezuela with Mariana Delfino, she had struggled to allow her guard down. She hadn't been ready to trust him yet. He'd patiently kept his distance.

But Tuesday, the night before he'd left to go hunting, they had a talk. They talked about the ranch. They talked about the hospital bills. They talked about Beth and Charles. It was so hard not to call him Easy. It would take some time, they both agreed, but they were willing to make the transition. They talked about being back in Dillon. They were both happy and sad about being back. Mariana Delfino came up. Jax had explained it again. He said he was sorry. He promised nothing had happened. Delfino had jumped on him, and when he'd pushed her off, he'd cut her face with his ring.

It had been a good talk. Long overdue. By the end, they were friends again. Annie had even invited Jax to share her bed with her.

She got up, stepping over to the window. She parted the blinds. Overcast. Dark clouds blanketed the sky, threatening rain. She glanced back to the bed, the covers on Jax's side were still made. A lump caught in her throat. She fought back the tears, feeling just as the sky looked—dark and gloomy, threatening rain.

"Not today," she quietly said to herself as she swallowed the lump in her throat. "I've got to be strong when Jax gets home." At that, she turned to the bathroom to take a shower.

Annie dressed, put some makeup on, and headed to the kitchen. She cooked scrambled eggs, two slices of bacon, and wheat toast with raspberry jam. She walked by the front room, glancing out the big window to the front yard. She didn't see Jax. If she sat around waiting for him to show, she would drive herself crazy.

She could go shopping. She really needed a new pair of jeans, so she found her keys and headed to town.

She'd been in town for two hours when her phone rang. With her hands full, she couldn't answer it. By the time she dropped everything, it was on the third ring, only one more before it went to voicemail. She didn't have time to check the caller ID. She grabbed the phone, sliding her finger across the screen, and answered.

"Hi, this is Annie."

"Hey baby." Hearing his voice caught her off guard.

"You're home?" Annie asked, the tone in her voice not hiding her surprise. She grimaced. So much for all the planning she thought.

"Yeah, is that okay? You sound surprised."

No it wasn't okay. *Why would it be okay that you're home? You've been off seeing someone else?* But after all the scheming she'd done the night before, she didn't say it. Under pressure, she'd folded, taking the soft approach.

"Of course it's okay," she finally said. "Why wouldn't it be okay?"

"Where are you?" Jax asked. The words came out so quickly, all slurred together as one word, Annie could barely understand him.

"I'm in town, shopping."

"When will you be back?"

"Is everything okay?" Annie asked. She knew Jax. When his words came out at the speed of sound, all slurred together, he was either really excited or really nervous.

"Everything is fine. When will you be back?" Jax asked again. His words came out a bit slower this time.

"I'm just wrapping things up. I should be home in half an hour or so. Why?"

"I have a big surprise for you," Jax said.

I bet you do. Annie sat at a picnic table display in the store she was shopping in. She wanted to be seated when Jax shared his news. "What is it?" Annie asked, hoping he would tell her now instead of making her wait until she got home.

"I'll tell you when you get home," came his quick reply. "This is too big to tell you over the phone. I can barely wait. Hurry home."

He clicked off.

"Jerk," Annie said out loud.

※

Annie didn't rush home. She tried on a few more jeans, found a pair she liked, and went through the checkout. She went to Vans to pick up a few things she'd forgotten to get yesterday. She stopped at the salon to set up a hair appointment for the following week. She could have called, but the salon was just down the street.

She glanced at her cell phone—almost one. Before she left town, she stopped at Subway to grab a sandwich, taking her time to eat it in the restaurant. Annie stretched out the half hour to two hours.

The two-mile section of I-41 leading up to the entrance to the Double T was long and straight. As Annie drew near the entrance to the ranch, she saw a red sports car leave the gravel road, enter the interstate, and head in her direction. By the time the car had passed her, it had reached maximum speed. Annie couldn't see the driver.

It was Friday, but probably too early for anyone to be leaving Lover's Flat. Could it have been Jax's visitor leaving the ranch?

Annie took a deep breath, slowly letting it out as she turned her car onto the dirt road. It wouldn't be long now until she heard the big news.

Annie pulled up to the house. As she got out of the car, she glanced over to the large barn two hundred feet to the left of the house. Both sixteen-foot-tall bay doors were down, shut tight. The main entrance door on the side stood open. If Jax was in the barn, he would have heard Annie pull up, yet he hadn't exited to come see her.

It had been three days since she had seen him, and under normal conditions, Annie would have left her bags in the car, rushed over to the barn, and thrown herself into his arms.

But these were not normal conditions.

Hearing his voice on the phone earlier had brought back all the hurt she'd felt the last few days, and with all of the pain building inside again, the fire started raging out of control.

She got out of her car and went around to the back to grab her things from the trunk. She loaded the bags high in her arms, carrying them on her left side as a shield. She had a hunch Jax was outside in the barn, and she didn't want to be able to see the door in case he came out. As she walked up the steps of the front porch she heard Jax call her name. Just as she'd expected, he'd come out of the side door of the barn and called to her. It took everything she had not to stop and turn around. But, she pretended not to hear. She stepped into the house. It killed her not to respond, but anger and hurt boiled inside her, and she was afraid of what she might say if she spoke to him right now. It was better that she hold her tongue.

Within seconds after entering the house, Annie heard the door behind her.

"Hey, baby," Jax said. He followed her into the kitchen, where she laid her things down.

"Hey, Jaxon," Annie answered back, her voice soft, barely over a whisper. She didn't speak louder, nervous her voice might crack with emotion and betray her. Annie didn't turn, not ready to face him yet.

He came up behind her, placing his hands on her hips. He leaned down, gently brushing his lips across the skin of her exposed neck. He kissed her lightly, several times. "I missed you," he whispered. His warm breath on her skin sent a chill down her back. A warm burning started to grow in the bottom of her stomach.

"I . . . missed you too," she said. She closed her eyes. Mixed emotions ran through her. She longed to be with him, to reach out and put her arms around his waist and kiss him. But the hurt was too much to bear. Had he been with someone else? Should she ask him? Could she trust him to tell her the truth?

Jax turned Annie around slowly. She decided halfway through the turn to ask him straight out.

"Jax," she said, "were you . . ." She stopped.

His eyes were lit up as big as a five-year-old standing in front of a Christmas tree on Christmas day. The giant grin on his face confused her.

"Annie, you've got to come out to the barn and see my big surprise." Excitement oozed out of every pore in his body. He didn't wait for a response. He grabbed her hand, practically dragging her outside.

Her slow, hesitant steps didn't damper his spirits. He kept pulling until they reached the barn door, where Jax quickly put his hands over her eyes. He helped her over the threshold of the door, leading her ever so carefully inside. Annie followed along, definitely not in the mood for games, but Jax's excitement was contagious.

"Surprise." He pulled his hands away. What she saw did surprise her, but also confused her. In the middle of the barn, clustered in a circle, were five white, five-gallon buckets full of dirt. Twenty feet behind the buckets toward the back of barn, Jax had parked the trailer. The ATV, secure on the right side of the trailer with nylon tie-downs, seemed small in comparison to the mountain of black fur in the space next to it.

Annie turned away from the buckets, taking two steps toward the trailer. As she drew closer, she could see the bear's face slumped over the side of the rail. One of the paws of the bear hung off the side of the trailer. Annie's eyes grew wide at the sight of the claws dangling over the edge. The paw was enormous, and its razor sharp claws were caked with dried blood. An involuntary shudder went through her. She stepped back.

"That's a bear," Annie said.

"A grizzly, actually. It's been feasting on our cattle."

"When did you kill it?"

"Earlier this morning, at about three, while it munched on one of our cows."

"It's huge."

"Totally huge, but that's not the surprise."

"It's not? What's the surprise?"

"Over here," Jax said. He'd moved back over to the five buckets. Jax bent down, shoving his hand into the dirt of the bucket closest to him.

"What is it?" she asked, her curiosity piqued. She stepped forward to get a closer look.

"This is the answer to all our financial problems."

"Dirt?"

"Gold."

"Gold?"

"Yes indeed, gold." There was a twinkle in his eye as he reverently spoke the word. Jax raised his hand, letting the dirt sift through his fingers. "I hid out in the old Western Pleasure Mine the whole time while I watched the cattle, and I found my old rock pick. After lunch on Thursday, I went to investigate a small cave-in that had happened since I'd last been there. When I leaned on the support beam, it moved and set off a chain reaction, which ended up knocking down a huge section of the ceiling. After the dust had settled, I saw in plain sight three veins of gold where the ceiling used to be."

Annie heard Jax talking about the gold as his hand sifted through the dirt. He explained how he'd found it, but none of it really registered in her mind. She'd locked onto three words Jax had said at the beginning of his explanation. *The whole time.* She felt the smile on her face as the corners of her lips curled up. For the first time in days she had something to smile about.

"Jax," Annie interrupted her husband.

"Yes?" Jax stopped digging, turning his attention to his wife.

"You said you were in the mine *the whole time*?"

"Yeah, practically the entire time."

"The whole time in the mine?" She mumbled half in a daze.

"I did some initial scouting around the meadow, where the previous attacks had occurred, but the cave-in incident happened Thursday afternoon, right after lunch. Once I saw those veins of gold, I forgot all about the cattle. Ever since then I've been focused on removing this ore to have it tested." He patted the top of the pile of dirt he had his hand on. "This is a gold mine, literally. We need to have it tested to see how much gold is in it."

She stared at Jax as if she were gazing off into space, his face not coming into focus.

"Baby, are you okay?" Jax asked. He stood, wrapping his arms around her.

Annie visibly came back to the present at his touch. "You were in the mine the whole time?" she asked again.

"Yeah, most of the time. I did leave the ranch once, though, to get some mining supplies in Twin. Oh yeah, you'll never guess who I ran into in Twin."

She stepped back. Her brow furrowed. "Was it a . . . girl, with a blond ponytail?" Annie asked, holding her breath.

His face squinched up.

Annie grimaced, all her fears came rushing back. Her smile instantly disappeared.

"A girl? No, it was Z-Carr from school. You know, Zeren. And, you're right, he does happen to have a blond ponytail. Some sort of act of rebellion against his father."

A logical explanation. A complete misunderstanding, just like the Delfino thing. Exactly what she'd hoped to hear.

She didn't hesitate. Annie threw her arms around his neck, planting a big wet kiss on his lips. She kissed him long and hard. She didn't want to let go.

When they pulled back, Annie whispered in his ear. "I love you, Jaxon Tagget."

She laid her head against his chest, closing her eyes. She let out her breath softly, the exhaustion of the past three days suddenly catching up to her. She sagged in his arms. As the heavy burden dropped off her shoulders, she was happy and tired, all at the same time. He wrapped her up, pulling her in close, rocking her gently back and forth. "I missed you," he whispered in her ear.

She peered into his eyes, kissing him gently on the lips. "I missed you too." This time she meant it.

Chapter 24

Annie

What If

Jax stepped back from Annie and examined the cluster of buckets—something seemed out of place. He picked up a bucket and placed it toward the back of the group. He picked up another from the back, moving it to the front of the group. He stepped back.

He nodded a couple of times, content with his placement.

"How many times do you think you'll do that before Monday comes around?" Annie asked.

"I don't know, maybe at least a hundred more. I can't stop thinking about it. I just want to stay here all night long running my hands through the dirt. When I pick up a bucket and feel the weight of it in my hands, I know it's real and not just a dream." He smiled. "It probably sounds a bit weird," Jax added, as he shrugged, "but I can't help it."

"You're crazy, Jax."

"Just a bit, I know, but it's that little bit that keeps me sane."

"Is this stuff really going to fix everything?"

"Yes. On Monday we'll know for sure after Mr. Collin tests it."

Mr. Collin's office wouldn't be open until Monday morning at nine—two more days. To Jax that seemed like an eternity.

"What's your plan B?" Annie asked.

"Plan B?"

"What if this is just dirt? What if there is no gold? What's plan B to save the ranch?"

"I don't know yet. I haven't thought about anything else this week, except for this dirt. It has to work."

"We're running out of time, Jax. Don't you think you should figure something else out, just in case?"

"It's going to work. Trust me."

"Okay . . . I'll trust you." She placed her arms around his waist. "You planning on staying out here until Monday?" She leaned her body against him, teasing a strand of his long black hair. He could feel the curves of her body, as she pressed against him.

"There are still a few things I need to do before I come in. I won't be out here much longer."

She stepped back, a hurt look crossing her face. "Don't tell me I'm competing against a couple of buckets of dirt for time with my husband," Annie said, her lower lip sticking out. She looked cute when she pretended to pout. He scanned the barn noticing the ice chest and rifle that needed to be cleaned, the bear that still needed some attention, and his camping gear that was still out. A hundred things still needed to be done.

But they could wait until tomorrow.

Chapter 25

Jaxon
Mr. Collin

Monday finally arrived, sunny and bright. Friday's storm had disappeared by Saturday evening, bringing with it only a few scattered showers. Anxious for Mr. Collin to test the dirt, Jax left for town a half hour earlier than he needed to.

Located in old town on South Montana Street, the building where he found Collin Assayers and Laboratories was built of red brick and had two large front windows, flanking a rustic log door. A *CLOSED* sign hung in the window at the right of the door. A large metallic sign hung over the door advertising the name of the establishment. Jax sat in his truck parked along the curb. He held a chocolate-covered doughnut in his left hand. A bottle of milk sat in the cup holder next to him. He'd already been waiting fifteen minutes, but there didn't seem to be any life in the office yet. He pulled out his cell phone: 8:55 a.m. Almost nine. The lab would open soon.

He glanced down the street. Two cars drove past him. It was pretty quiet—typical for a small town, even on a Monday. He could see the neon sign down the street were he'd picked up the doughnut and milk. A few cars were still parked in the lot, the drivers enjoying a late breakfast.

Movement to his right caught his eye.

The clerk at Collin's stood at the right window. The *CLOSED* sign Jax had been studying for the past fifteen minutes was now flipped over. *Finally open.*

The front reception room was sterile. No pictures hung on the walls. No trees stood in the corners. A waist-high Formica laminate-covered countertop positioned to the left of the door greeted him. To the right of the door, a small waiting room, complete with a vinyl-covered couch and chairs that lined the walls, sat empty.

The young man behind the desk wore a royal blue polo shirt. The company's logo, embroidered in gold lettering over the left breast, read:

Collin Assayer & Labs

Did You?

Jax gave the clerk a weird look. He didn't understand the question on the shirt. Jax knew the clerk from school, but he couldn't remember his name—he was three years younger than Jax, but his older brother Scott was Jax's age. Jax and Scott had been in the same grade.

"How's Scott?" Jax asked.

"He's fine. Got a job in Denver after graduating from MSU."

"What's he doing?"

"He's an accountant with some big firm. Crunching numbers all day long, as he puts it."

"Did you what?" Jax asked, curiosity about to kill him. "Why does your shirt have a question on it?"

"Did you strike it rich? That's the question. I'm assuming you brought your dirt in to be tested?"

Next to Jax stood two white, five-gallon buckets filled to the top with dirt, one on the right and the other on the left.

"Yeah."

"Well, you've come to the right place. Here at Collin Assayers & Laboratories, that's what we do. We help you answer the question, did you or didn't you strike it rich?"

Jax was sure the clerk had given that little speech a thousand times. He'd delivered it with a monotone voice.

"Let me go get Mr. Collin. He's just in the back." The clerk disappeared behind a swinging metal door.

Within a short time, Mr. Collin, with his round glasses, slipped through the swinging metal door. No more than five feet tall, one hundred and twenty pounds, he was a small man. What hair he had left on the sides of his head was salt-and-pepper in color. The top of his head shined, reflecting the fluorescent light bulbs.

"Jax, welcome home." Mr. Collin took Jax's right hand in both of his, vigorously pumping it up and down. Jax felt like a giant compared to Mr. Collin.

"Thank you, Mr. Collin. It's good to be home."

"How's your father? I heard from Mrs. Emmett that the doctors have only given him a short time."

"As well as can be expected, under the circumstances," Jax said.

The clerk returned through the door. He stood behind the counter waiting for instructions from Mr. Collin.

Mr. Collin leaned his head forward slightly, lowering his voice as if what he was going to say was highly confidential. "I've heard he only has two weeks left."

Not embarrassed to talk openly about his father's condition, Jax spoke loud enough for the clerk to hear.

"Well, we've also been told that he has an entire year, which is what we are counting on."

"That's wonderful. If there was ever a person that could beat the odds, it's Tru Tagget—he's a man of *true* grit."

"Thank you, Mr. Collin."

"Well, I'm sure you didn't come here to talk about your father," Mr. Collin said, as he bent down and ran his hand through the dirt of the bucket closest to him. "Looks like you found gold, Jax."

"Do you really think so?" A chill ran down his spine when he heard Mr. Collin's declaration.

"I've been testing ore for the past twenty-five years. This sample looks as promising as anything I've seen in a while. You have to realize, though, that what I've just said is my initial assessment. Unofficial, of course."

"Oh, sure. Of course."

Mr. Collin picked up a sizeable clod, holding it up to the light. "Real promising," he mumbled as he studied the dirt more closely.

Mr. Collin put the clod back into the bucket. He turned to the clerk. "Tyler, will you take these two buckets to the back?" Turning back to Jax, he said, "We should have an answer for you real soon."

Two Hearts

Tyler came around to the front of the counter, picked up the buckets one in each hand to balance the weight, and disappeared through the swinging door.

Mr. Collin stepped around to the backside of the counter and disappeared from view for a second. When he reappeared, it was as though he had swallowed instant growth pills. He now stood practically eye to eye with Jax. He laid a pad of paper between the two of them and pulled out a pen from a drawer. The pad had a blank form on it with the company logo at the top and a bunch of empty boxes ready to be filled in.

"I just need to get a bit of information before you leave," Mr. Collin said.

"Sure."

"Should I just put the Double T for your address?"

"Yeah, that's where we are right now."

Mr. Collin scribbled *Double T* on the address line.

"Give me your phone number again—I'm sure I have it somewhere, but it would just be easier for you to give it to me now."

Jax gave him his cell number.

"As soon as I have something, I'll be sure to call you," Mr. Collin said. He extended his hand to Jax. They shook. Jax thanked him and left the office.

It was a waiting game now, but he left the office in high hopes. Mr. Collin's first impression had lifted his spirits. As the butterflies settled in his stomach, Jax couldn't believe his luck. He immediately called Annie to give her the good news.

Chapter 26

Jaxon

Negative

Tuesday morning the sun peeked over the horizon in the east. Jax had been up for an hour already, and from his vantage point on the back patio of the house, he had a view of the beautiful sunrise. Yet, he barely noticed it, his mind preoccupied with the day's responsibilities. The ranch took a lot of work every day. Sure, he could take a few days off here and there, but if he relaxed his daily work schedule, the chores, as his dad called them, would pile up on him and he'd pay the price by having to work double-time.

The thing that preoccupied his mind the most this morning, the thing that caused him to barely notice the colorful sunrise, was Mr. Collin.

After receiving the initial assessment, Mr. Collin's unofficial declaration, Jax had floated five inches off the ground the rest of the day. Jax waited for Mr. Collin to call, but he never did.

Two Hearts

Even though Mr. Collin had said the results would be available real soon, he never indicated how soon was *real soon*. Jax just assumed it would be the same day. Monday had come and gone without any word.

Maybe there had been a problem and Mr. Collin didn't know how to tell him. Jax picked up the phone and dialed the lab. Before it had time to ring, Jax hit the end button after he saw what time it was: 6:32 a.m. He hung up quickly.

Maybe there wasn't a problem and Jax was just overreacting. But why hadn't Mr. Collin called yesterday? He took a deep breath, letting it out slowly. His mind was working overtime, and making him crazy. He stood, stretched, and went back to the barn to start on his chores.

No word from Mr. Collin the entire week. By Friday morning Jax was so jittery he could hardly sit still. Every time he talked to Annie, his words came out so fast that she had a hard time understanding him.

Finally, by three in the afternoon Jax couldn't take it anymore, and he decided to run a couple of errands to get his mind off things. While in town, he received a call from Mr. Collin: the tests were done. He could pick up the report at the office any time.

"This can't be!" Jax yelled. He slammed the yellow folder onto the dining table.

"What does it say?" Annie asked. She picked up the report.

"It's not good news."

"Obviously," Annie said, with a hint of sarcasm.

Jax snatched the report from her.

"Fine, I'll tell you." The tension was high as he tore open the folder and pointed. "Right there. 'Traces.' Only traces of gold."

Jax shoved the report at her. "Here, look for yourself."

"Jax, don't."

He knew what she was saying. He shouldn't be so upset with her. She wasn't the one that had prepared the report, and yet he was taking it out on her, as if she were the cause of the bad news.

His head slumped down out of frustration with himself. With her sarcastic comment, he had turned on her and she became the target of his destructive mood.

Jax sighed. "Sorry," he whispered.

"I'm so sorry too, Jax," Annie said, placing her hand on his arm. "There must be something else we can do to save the ranch."

Jax slammed the table with his fist again, trying to release his anger. He hit the table again, this time hard enough to jostle the flowerpot sitting in the middle. Annie instinctively grabbed for the wobbling pot before it toppled over.

"Just traces, but nothing of significance. What are we going to do, Annie?"

"Maybe we could sell off a piece of the ranch."

"No. I won't be the weak link. I won't be the Tagget that lost the ranch. I have to keep it intact. I was hoping the mine was going to be the answer." Jax picked up the report again and began fanning the pages as he thought.

"We might not have any other choice. Time is running out," Annie said. She stood and picked up Jax's dinner plate. "We only have a couple more weeks before the bank forecloses."

"Maybe I should get a second opinion on the ore."

"I hate to be pragmatic, but how long is that going to take? We're about out of time."

"There aren't any other options at the moment. I'm not selling any of the ranch." Jax placed both hands on the table and stood up with an air of confidence. "I know good ore when I see it. I'm going to have it tested again."

Chapter 27

Jaxon
Kris Dirkfield

Jax sat at the little desk in the living room of his parents' home, an HP laptop open in front of him. The computer whirled and a Google-populated list of the latest search filled the screen. The light in the living room was dim. His profile reflected off the backlit screen, where he could see the blank expression on his face. It was late Sunday night, and his mind was numb. He'd been staring at this same screen for the past three days.

The yellow notepad lying next to the computer was practically empty. There were five lab names written on it, but three of them were crossed off.

After receiving the bad news from Mr. Collin, Jax had spent the rest of Friday, Saturday, and now Sunday searching the internet for a second lab that could test his dirt.

Friday night, he and Annie had had their second real fight in only three weeks. Annie figured that the mine had been abandoned for a reason and that he shouldn't waste any more time trying to find a second opinion. He wasn't wasting time, he'd told her. He was trying to save the ranch. She couldn't see that, so Jax had screamed at her to get his point across, which only caused Annie to disappear to their room for the last three days.

He scanned the notepad.

Company two on the list wanted three weeks to test the dirt—but by then, no matter if the tests were positive or not, it would be too late. He'd crossed out their name.

Company four wanted a nonrefundable $2,500 retainer before they would test the dirt. At first they seemed promising because they guaranteed test results within a week, which was what Jax needed—a quick turnaround. But he crossed their name off the list because once they tested the samples, they requested the option to invest in the mine, with the owner of the mine fronting 65 percent of the operation cost to extract the dirt. He couldn't afford that.

Jax googled company five's name, just like he had all the others, and an FBI report immediately popped up. Company five was under investigation for fraud and money laundering. He immediately crossed it off the list.

Companies one and three on his list were still options, but Jax was not completely sold on either one of them. He kept searching.

Jax decided to expand his search internationally. Immediately after hitting the return on the computer, a list revealing the top international labs populated.

Jax clicked the first one—Kris Dirkfield International. When the website popped up, he thought he'd accidentally clicked on a different link, so he hit the back button. The same Google list of international labs popped up again.

Jax read the brief description under the first link—"Kris Dirkfield International, a leading gold assayer's office headquartered in Germany, a world leader in mine reclamation and gold assaying." He'd read that before, which was what had prompted him to click on the link in the first place.

He clicked on the link again.

Sure enough, the same website popped up. What had confused him, causing him to hit the back button the first time, was what he saw on the home page. A beautiful woman stared back at him. She wore a full-length black satin evening gown, with a long slit up the side, showing off her tan legs. She stood against an all-red background. The woman's long blond hair cascaded over her exposed back. The tailor of the dress must have run out of material before finishing it. The entire back side of the woman, the part not covered by her golden locks, was exposed, revealing the sensuous curves of her spine and hips.

A dazzling diamond necklace swooped down the front of the women's chest, where the evening gown was gently open. At an angle to the camera, with her arm raised slightly in front of her, delicately outstretched from her body, the woman wore a brilliant gold bracelet. He leaned in for a closer peek. From what he could see of the details on the bracelet, the craftsmanship was a work of art.

This didn't seem like the website for an international assayer's office. It appeared more like the home page for a jewelry store.

Amazing. It hit him. A gorgeous woman decked out in gold and diamonds was bait—or more appropriately, advertisement. To confirm his suspicion he glanced at the web address in the address line. He was in the right spot. *Effective*, Jax thought, but still confusing. If this was the home page of the company, where was the information on how to get ahold of them?

He rolled the mouse pointer around from corner to corner, hoping that something would pop up or stand out as the pointer scrolled over it. There was nothing except the beautiful woman.

Jax scanned the page one more time, running the mouse pointer over and over the red backdrop, following a systematic pattern so as not to miss any hidden key or drop-down link.

He finished his complete scan of the page. In disgust, he slid the mouse pointer to the complete right edge of the page, about the middle of the screen, and let go of the mouse. He leaned back in his chair.

What was he missing?

Then he saw it. Where the pointer had come to rest, the word *ENTER*, in small, three-dimensional lettering, almost the exact color as the red backdrop, had popped up. Jax grabbed the mouse. He clicked on the word.

The beautiful woman disappeared and the Kris Dirkfield International company profile page appeared. Jax read the rest of the night.

Chapter 28

Jaxon

The Receptionist

On Monday morning at eight o'clock, and not a minute after, Jax dialed the 1-800 number he had obtained from the website the night before.

"Kris Dirkfield International, Dallas office," a female voice answered the phone in perfect English.

"Dallas, Texas?" Jax asked without even saying hello, his heart leaping for joy. He'd half expected the phone to be answered by an operator from a call center in Germany.

"Yes, this is the Dallas, Texas, office."

"Dirkfield International has its headquarters in Essen, Germany, right?"

"Yes, but we also have several laboratories throughout the United States, one of which is in Dallas, Texas. How may I help you, sir?" The receptionist spoke politely, but professionally.

Jax couldn't believe his luck. Dallas wasn't within five hundred miles of Dillon, but it wasn't on the other side of the world either. Maybe, just maybe, he could have the samples tested in a week.

"I have some ore samples I need tested, and I was wondering what your turnaround time might be." Jax held his breath, praying she would say a week.

"Our company policy is four weeks."

Jax let out his breath all at once. "Four weeks," he gasped.

"I'm sorry, is that a problem?"

"Yeah, I was hoping you were going to say a week."

"Only under extreme circumstances, sir, can we have the results back within a week—four weeks is our normal time."

"This is an extreme circumstance," Jax said. "I need this ore tested within the week or else I'm going to lose my ranch."

Jax didn't want to divulge all of his personal problems, especially to this woman he didn't know. But under the circumstances, he was willing to do or say anything that might help him get the answers he needed.

"That sounds serious," the woman said, still maintaining her level of professionalism. Jax however, noted a hint of genuine sincerity in her voice. She continued, "But . . . unfortunately the only person that can authorize any expedited test results is gone for the next two weeks."

"Can you contact the person and get authorization over the phone?"

"Normally yes, but right now the owner is out of cell range for a few days."

He slammed his fist on the table.

"Thank you for your help," Jax said. He hung up the phone without waiting for the woman's response. He stared out the front window, looking out over the front yard. His luck had turned in his favor. An international lab located in Texas—close enough to home—that could test the ore within a week, if he got the right authorization. But then his luck had run out—the owner was gone, gone for two weeks.

The owner?

Jax picked up the phone.

"Kris Dirkfield International, Dallas office," the same female voice answered the phone.

"Hi again," Jax said. "I just called about having my ore tested within a week."

"Yes, I recognize your voice," the receptionist said. "How may I help you?"

"I really need to have this ore tested within the week."

"Yes sir, but there is nothing I can do."

"You're my last hope. Please, there must be someone there besides the owner that can authorize the tests this week, a manager or a crew boss, or superintendent, somebody, anybody." Jax was begging and he knew it.

"There is no one here. I'm sorry. Company policy—any expedited testing must first be authorized by the owner."

"You can't make an exception?" Jax pleaded.

"I'm sorry sir, but I don't make the rules, and I don't grant exceptions. I'm really sorry." The receptionist's voice changed, no longer did she sound like an operator answering the phone. "What's your name, sir?"

"Jaxon Tagget."

"Where do you live?"

"Dillon, Montana."

"Mr. Tagget, I'm sure there is a lab where you live that can test the ore."

"Collin Assayers & Laboratories. They tested it last week, but the results came back negative."

"And now you want a second opinion," the woman said.

"Yes. I've been in the mining business for the past three years and I know this is good ore."

"Where have you worked?"

"I worked for Venezuela Mining Industries."

"I'm familiar with that company."

Jax didn't know where these questions might lead him, but he felt a genuine concern in her voice, so he decided to share a little more about his current situation with her.

"Upon returning to the states from Venezuela about three weeks ago, we discovered that my father was dying of cancer."

There was a slight gasp from the woman. "Oh, I am so sorry."

"And, to make a long story short, my father is about to lose his ranch in a couple of weeks if I don't do something immediately."

"These ore samples are your only answer?" she asked.

"Yes. I really don't have any other option at the moment."

"I really feel sorry for you, Mr. Tagget." She paused. "I wish there was something more I could do . . . to help."

"Thank you for listening," Jax said.

"Mr. Tagget," the woman said in a hushed voice, "the owner is in Las Vegas at a mining convention. He will be stopping in Pagosa Springs, Colorado, on Wednesday for the weekend, before heading back to Germany."

"Really?"

"You didn't hear that from me."

"Where?"

"Pagosa Springs, Colorado. Wednesday to Sunday, at the Springs Resort and Spa."

"Thank you," Jax said.

Returning to her professional voice, the receptionist said, "Thank you for calling Dirkfield International." She clicked off.

Instantly, a plan began to formulate in Jax's head.

Chapter 29

Jaxon
The Trip

The yellow notepad sat on the desk in front of him. The name *Kris Dirkfield International*, written in the center of the pad, had several blue circles around it.

Pagosa Springs, Colorado, was approximately 540 miles from Dillon. Closer than Dallas or Germany.

Jax couldn't allow this opportunity to pass him by. A crazy idea had popped into his head. What if he were to fly down to Pagosa Springs and *accidentally* run into the owner? Jax could explain his dire circumstances, and he was sure that once he met the owner, he would be able to get the needed authorization.

Pagosa had a small airport. He could fly there in his dad's 1984 Cessna 206 Stationair. He calculated the distance and the speed of the plane. It would take him just over three hours. If he left on Wednesday, he figured it would take him just one day to meet the owner and get the authorization. By Thursday he could be home. Over the weekend he could make the necessary arrangements and by Monday he could sell the mine. The entire trip would take about two days on the short end or three days on the long end.

Once the ranch was secure, he and Annie would be free to see the world again. The possibilities were endless.

The biggest question that faced him now was Annie—would she be up to the idea of his running off to Colorado? The idea of bumping into the owner at a hot springs resort was a long shot. He knew it. To complicate matters, not only did Jax have to find the owner, but he needed to convince the owner that his cause was worthy of an expedited test. It was a crazy idea, but under the circumstances, Jax was willing to do it.

Jax was still reeling from their recent argument. They'd been married for just over five years, and Friday's argument, when Jax had lost control and yelled at her, had been a real blowout.

Three days had passed since the incident, and he had apologized to Annie every day since that night, telling her over and over again how sorry he was for blowing up. But no matter how much he tried, it didn't seem to help. Annie was still giving him the silent treatment, and rightly so.

Sounds were coming from the kitchen. He could hear Annie moving about as she prepared lunch. Breakfast this morning, like the past two mornings, was a quiet affair. Annie ate in the kitchen, and Jax ate in the dining room.

She was initially upset at him for wasting time chasing after the mine. Now she was upset because he'd lost control, and that hurt even more. He'd messed up, and he knew it.

The trip.

Annie wasn't going to approve, not in her present state of mind, anyway. Should he still go? Would he disappoint her again? Would it cause another argument?

But the mine *was* valuable, and he knew it. It was the answer. Dirkfield International was it. He would pursue this one last shot, and if it didn't turn out, he would focus his efforts on something else.

Annie stepped through the doorway into the dining room with two plates in her hands. Each plate had a hoagie sandwich, a pile of potato chips, a dollop of ranch dip, and three Oreo cookies, double stuffed—just the way Jax liked them.

"I found a company that can test the ore within a couple of days," Jax said.

Annie didn't glance up when she responded. "That's great." Her voice carried no emotion. She set the two plates down, one in Jax's spot, at the head of the table, and the other in Annie's place, next to Jax. He noticed the placement of the plates. Today she was sitting at the table close to him.

Things were improving. And yet, he still sensed a strain in her voice, her delivery dry and lifeless. He glanced furtively in her direction as he reached down for his sandwich. Was she watching him, waiting for an additional comment? Was she going to add more to her two-word response? From the corner of his eye, he watched her pick up her sandwich and take a bite. Her eyes stayed focused on her plate.

That was it? Two words? Well, it was better than it had been for the past couple of days, so Jax took courage and pressed forward.

"It's not a local company, but the owner is going to be in Colorado on Wednesday." Jax stopped right there. He let that sink in for a moment as he got ready to unload some more. He couldn't provide all the details of his planned trip, or she would reject the idea without question. The delivery had to be slow and deliberate. One piece at a time.

She glanced up from her sandwich, which was approximately four inches away from her opened mouth. "Where's the company located?"

"It's in Germany."

Annie's eyes flicked up and stared at Jax. He quickly added, "But it has several laboratories in the United States, one in Dallas, Texas, and another somewhere in California."

She didn't respond. She took another bite of her sandwich and then started on the chips and dip. Jax waited. Annie's brow wrinkled as she ate chip after chip. He knew better than to interrupt her as she processed the information; she was thinking over the last thing he'd said, wrapping her mind around the whole idea.

After the chips were all but gone, she finally responded. "How long will it take to get the results back?"

"A few days."

"And then what?"

"We sell the mine."

"But what if . . ."

Jax knew where she was going, and before Annie could finish her thought, Jax added, "If the results come back negative, I promise I will drop the mine issue and pursue another avenue."

Annie finally turned to him. Jax knew this was what she'd been waiting to hear for the past three days.

"You promise?"

Jax held out his hand to her, and as she took it, the warmth of it sent a jolt of electricity shooting up his arm and straight to his brain. He hadn't touched Annie in almost three days, and just the contact of skin to skin was exhilarating—every sensory neuron in the palm of his hand and in his fingertips were screaming out of control, sending electrified impulses to his brain. He looked her in the eyes and they shook hands. "I promise," he said.

The corners of Annie's mouth turned up ever so slightly—a smile started to grow. Jax hadn't seen one of those in a while, and it brought a smile to his own face. She looked down at their hands, still clasped together, neither one of them wanting to let go.

"How long will you be gone?" she asked.

"It's a very quick trip. The owner won't be in Colorado until Wednesday. I figure I can do my chores in the morning and then leave on Wednesday afternoon. If all goes as planned, I will meet with the owner on Thursday morning and be back late that evening."

"That fast?" Annie asked, the surprise registering in her wide open eyes. "How can you get to Colorado, do your business, and get back so quickly?"

"I was planning on . . . flying my dad's plane."

Just as he'd expected, Annie suddenly didn't like the idea. She drew her hand back, breaking their intertwined fingers. She turned away from him, facing the table.

Before he had approached Annie with the idea of having Dirkfield International test the ore, he had gone over and over in his mind what would be the hardest thing for her to accept, him running off to Colorado to "accidentally" run into the owner, or that his plan involved his flying his father's plane to Colorado.

Jax had his private pilot's license, and he had taken Annie flying several times in high school. But once they had moved to the university, the flying had practically died off. He'd flown occasionally, when they'd come home to Dillon on long holiday weekends—Jax needing to keep his hours up to maintain his license. But since high school, Annie hadn't flown with him. When they'd gone overseas, Jax thought his flying days were over, at least until he returned to Montana.

Since he and Annie had been home, close to a month now, he'd taken the plane out twice, each time by himself. Both times he'd asked her to come, but she'd had an excuse.

"Is it the plane?" Jax asked.

"No," Annie said, practically firing the word out of her mouth like a cannon ball. With that rapid, explosive response, Jax sensed there was more to the plane idea then she was letting on, but Jax wasn't quite ready to push the issue—not yet, anyway.

"What, then?"

"You can't find someone closer to test your dirt?"

"I've looked."

"There's got to be someone here in Montana that can test it."

"Sure there are," Jax said trying not to raise his voice. They'd already discussed this earlier at length. He took a controlled breath, nothing too exaggerated. "All of the labs here in Montana want at least four weeks to process the results, and by that—"

"—by that time we'll be on the street," Annie said, completing his thought for him.

"Exactly."

"There still has to be someone else that can test it without you having to fly to Colorado."

There it was, the *flying* issue.

"Are you sure the plane has nothing to do with my going to Colorado?" Jax said.

"Nothing." She was looking at her hands as they tied and retied the drawstrings of her apron.

"Nothing?"

Annie sat there for a moment undoing the knots and then twisting the string around her fingers. Jax waited patiently.

"On the news last week, there was a plane crash, a small plane," Annie said, looking up into Jax's eyes. "All four passengers died."

"How?"

"There was a fog bank that unexpectedly rolled in. The plane flew right into a mountainside obscured by the fog."

"I've already checked the weather report for Montana and Colorado: clear skies on both ends for the next ten days."

"Something else could happen," she pleaded. "I don't think it's a good idea. I have a bad feeling about this, Jax." Her hands trembled as she twisted and knotted up the drawstrings again.

She'd used his nickname—that was a good sign. Things were looking up. His courage rising, he leaned toward her, kissing her on the neck. He took her fidgeting hands in his.

"It'll be alright," he assured her. "It's not that far of a flight. I'll leave on Wednesday and I'll be back on Thursday. Friday morning at the latest."

"And then you promise you'll stop with this mine thing and figure something else out?" she asked with a slightly raised voice. Jax sensed that even though she didn't want him to travel to Colorado in his father's plane, she was willing to let him do it, knowing that the quicker he got the ore tested, the quicker he could return and pursue a different solution to their financial problems.

"You promise?" Annie asked again, catching his eyes with hers.

Inwardly, he was grinning. He was going to Colorado on a trip to see Kris Dirkfield.

"I promise," he said.

Chapter 30

Annie

Friends Again

After lunch with Jax, Annie spent most of the afternoon on the couch, too tired to move. She was definitely coming down with something. She felt guilty lying around for hours while Jax worked, so she tried to read but ended up dozing off, never quite being able to finish even one page.

Maybe she'd caught the flu. Dr. Goodman had told her two weeks ago that there were two hundred different strains of the flu bug going around. She remembered him saying the sickness was running rampant throughout Dillon right now, which kept him more than busy.

The rest definitely had helped. She got off the couch, heading for the front door.

The sun dipped in the west, a ball of fire stuck on the horizon, the last rays of light illuminating the sky with multiple shades of oranges, reds, and yellows.

Just outside the door hung the ranch's wrought-iron dinner chime. It wasn't a regular garden-variety triangular chime. This one was in the shape of a rustic cowboy boot. The striker, matching the rustic beauty of the boot chime, was a black metal rod with a horseshoe welded to the end.

Annie picked up the striker, but before she shattered the stillness of the evening with the clanging of the chime, she stopped one more time to admire the sunset. This view from the front porch of her in-laws' home was one of the many things she liked about being back in Dillon. She leaned against the door jam and closed her eyes. She took a deep breath, holding it for just a second. The air was fresh and crisp. With September almost in the history books and summer officially over, the season and the air were changing. Fall was coming and so were the beautiful colors that it brought. The leaves on the trees had already started to change.

She loved Dillon and she loved the ranch. It hurt deep down inside to think that they might lose it. She reassured herself that Jax would fix it. That's what he did. He fixed things, and he would fix their financial problems. She just needed to trust him more.

She raised the striker, sounding the dinner bell.

All throughout dinner Jax kept rambling on about wanting to take Annie on a trip or maybe buying her a new car. She'd liked Beth's Escalade, but she told Jax she didn't need that expensive of a car. A new car would be nice, though, she agreed. After they discussed exotic vacation spots they'd always dreamed about, the conversation changed to the mine. Jax's eyes lit up again as he spoke about how lucky they'd been that the ceiling of the mine had fallen in, exposing the three veins of gold. Jax's excitement was contagious, she couldn't help dream a little herself—maybe a new car or a trip to Hawaii, liked they'd always talked about.

In his excited state of mind, Jax talked a mile a minute. Annie, knowing she wouldn't be able to get a word in at the pace he was speaking, sat back and listened with a smile on her face.

Since finding the company that could test the dirt in such a short time, Jax's mood had changed dramatically. He was himself again—happy and full of life. It made Annie happy to see him this way—she didn't like it when he was grumpy.

Dinner ended, and Jax helped clean up. As he passed into the kitchen with the last things from the table, Annie met him in the doorway. She took the plate of food and pitcher of water he carried and placed them in the refrigerator. She turned back to him. He stood at the kitchen sink rinsing their two plates. Reaching around him she turned off the water. She gently spun him around.

"Those can wait," she said. She reached up, placing her arms around his neck. She laid her head against his chest. "You smell nice," she whispered. While she'd prepared their dinner, Jax had cleaned up after having worked in the barn all afternoon. After his shower he had put on Annie's favorite cologne.

His arms found their way around the small of her back. He squeezed, drawing her in close.

"I'm sorry for blowing up at you," he said. He gave her another squeeze. "I've missed you," he added, as he kissed the top of her head.

"Thank you." She squeezed him back. "I was wondering...," she paused just for a moment for dramatic effect, "if you could carry me to *our* bed tonight?" She intentionally added emphasis to the word *our*, drawing out its pronunciation, to give it more attention.

"Our bed?"

"Yes, our bed. We're married, aren't we?"

"Yes, but what about the dishes?"

"They can wait until tomorrow."

Jax bent down and picked her up. As they passed through each room of the house, heading toward the bedroom, she turned off the lights. As they entered their room, she didn't turn on the light—she knew Jax could find the bed, even in the dark.

The window in Jax's old bedroom, the room that Annie and Jax had been staying in since they'd returned from Venezuela, faced east. Every morning, light from the rising sun would pierce through the blinds, and inevitably, no matter how many times she had asked Jax to adjust them, a speck of light always found its way to Annie's eyes. She rolled over to find a spot out of the sunlight, and at the same time she reached for Jax. The bed was empty. She grabbed his pillow, pulling it over her face. Jax had always been an early riser.

After a minute, she rolled out of bed and slipped into a pair of comfy sweats and one of Jax's worn-out T-shirts. After she'd dressed, she went to look for him.

Not finding him in the living room or the dining room, she entered the kitchen, but he wasn't there either. Last night's dishes had been washed, dried, and put away. The kitchen was spotless.

Turning to the refrigerator, she noticed Jax's handwritten note for the first time.

"Gone to town to run a few errands. I will be back by ten. Love, Jax. P.S. Thanks for the fun time last night." She blushed, heat turning her cheeks red. Making up was the best part of an argument.

She glanced at the clock on the wall: eight fifteen. She ate breakfast and curled up on the living room couch to wait for him.

Chapter 31

Annie

Hunting Trip

Jax returned promptly at ten, but he wasn't alone. Thomas and Zeren, riding in Zeren's candy-apple-red Nissan 370Z sports car, followed behind Jax's truck down the lane to the ranch. Not expecting visitors so early in the morning, Annie quickly ran to her room to change. She still had on the same hole-ridden T-shirt and sweat bottoms she'd grabbed when she'd slid out of bed.

She slipped on a pair of jeans and grabbed a cream-colored blouse out of the closet. She pulled it on. As she passed by the open door of the bathroom, she stepped in to take a peek at her hair. It was a tangled mess. She ran a brush through it, straightening out the knots. Her hair now somewhat presentable, she quickly glanced at her face in the mirror. No makeup yet, and not enough time to worry about it, even if she'd wanted to. She didn't wear much makeup anyway. She pinched her cheeks to bring up the color. That helped.

Two Hearts

Annie made it to the front room just in time to see Thomas and Zeren climbing out of the red sports car parked in front of the house. Annie didn't recognize Zeren as he approached the porch. She knew it was him, but it didn't look like him, at least not the old him. He wore an expensive black leather jacket. Under the jacket he wore a fancy blue silk shirt. He wore designer jeans, not his usual faded and torn wranglers, and he had on what appeared to be pointed Italian leather shoes. His customary down-in-the-heel cowboy boots where gone. To top it all off, he had long, very long, blond hair, which was pulled back into a ponytail that dropped to his shoulders.

If she had only seen him from the back, with his long hair and designer clothes, she would easily have mistaken him for a girl.

Thomas, same old Thomas, hadn't changed a bit. He was tall and lanky, and he still appeared to be as shy as ever—standing back, keeping his distance.

Annie saw them approach the house, but Jax wasn't with them. It would be only a matter of seconds before they were at the front door. She didn't wait. Going straight to the door, she swung it open and stepped out on the porch.

"Look what the cat dragged in," Annie said.

"Well, well, what do we have here?" Zeren responded. He stepped forward, scooping Annie up in a massive bear hug. He picked her up off her feet, swinging her around several times. Zeren set her down, then stepped back, sizing her up and down. He nodded several times. "Dang girl, you look good. You were always the prettiest girl in school, and now if you aren't the prettiest girl in the county."

Annie blushed slightly. "And you're the biggest liar too—you slick-lip," she laughed. "How much did Jax have to pay you for that one? Where is he, anyway?"

"He went to park around back by the barn," Thomas said.

Annie held out her arms, and Thomas hesitantly stepped forward. He gently put his arms around her, making sure not to step in to close. They hugged. Mild compared to the mauling she'd gotten from Zeren.

"I haven't seen either one of you in ages. How are you both?" Annie asked.

"We're good," Zeren answered for both of them.

"Thomas, are you still working at your father's hardware store?" Annie asked.

"Yes."

"How's that going?"

"Fine."

"You planning on taking over some day when your dad decides it's time to quit?"

"Yes."

"You serious with a girl?"

"No."

That was all he said. She turned to Zeren.

"And what about you, Mr. Long-haired Hippie?" Annie asked. "What've you been up to?"

"Well, not much, except that I . . . went straight to Vegas after high school and struck it rich playing the tables." He grabbed the front lapels of his leather jacket, as if he were some kind of big shot.

"If you struck it rich, what're you doing back here in Dillon?" Annie asked.

"I've learned by watching the pros that no matter how lucky someone is, they are always bound to hit a streak of bad luck. It's usually during that time when everything blows up in your face. So, I left Vegas before it happened to me. I returned to Dillon to give the tables a break."

"That was kind of you. I'm sure the tables were grateful for your mercy." She peeked at Thomas to see if he were buying all this bull from Zeren. Thomas's eyes were as big as full moons at the first of the month. He was practically drooling on Zeren's shoulder, so caught up in his lies. "The way you make it sound, you must have been giving it to them pretty hard."

"Every night when I left the casinos with buckets full of money, the tables would be begging for mercy. It really was the only humane thing to do."

"Buckets of money?" Thomas whispered behind Zeren, his eyes growing even bigger at the thought of carrying buckets full of money through the casino doors.

"How long do you think you'll be here before you go back? You will be going back, won't you?" Annie asked.

"Oh yeah, I'll be going back." He glanced over his shoulder at his little red sports car. "The money's too good not to. I'll probably be here for a couple of months, or until my old man throws me out, whichever comes first."

"What're you going to be doing while you're here?"

"Get a job. I know that sounds weird; it's not like I really need the money, but I just need to get out of the house, away from my old man. We aren't actually seeing eye to eye right now."

"Jax told me he gave you a job on the Double T. Why haven't we seen you?" Annie asked.

He raised his hands out in front of him in a defensive gesture. "I'm thankful for Jax's kindness. I don't want to sound ungrateful, nor do I want to offend you or Jax, but I am weighing all my options before I make a commitment."

Annie smiled. Weighing all his options? What options? She knew Zeren had never worked a day in his life if he could avoid it. He was lazy, always had been and always would be. She took no offense at his comment, or by the fact that he hadn't showed up on the ranch to work. In fact, when Jax had told her that he'd offered Zeren a job, she knew Jax had wasted his breath.

Before she could come back with a clever response, Jax stepped onto the porch at the end of the house, carrying his rifle case.

"Why's everyone standing outside?" Jax asked as he passed through the open front door.

Everyone followed him through the door into the dining room, where he placed his gun case on the table.

"Can I get you something to eat or drink?" Annie asked Thomas and Zeren as they sat down at the table. "Jax, anything for you?"

"Just a glass of ice water, thanks," Jax said. Thomas declined, but Zeren asked for a root beer, which Annie went in the kitchen to retrieve.

When she returned, Annie set the drinks in front of Zeren and Jax and sat down on the couch in the living room. Jax had his rifle out on the table with a towel covering the surface to protect the table and the gun from scratches. Even with her back to the group, Annie could hear their conversation.

She picked up her book, the one she'd tried to read yesterday, and, opening to her marked spot, began scanning the page, pretending to read. She listened to their conversation, catching everything Zeren said. He spoke loudly. But from Thomas, ever the shy one, with his low voice, she could hardly hear anything. She only got part of the conversation. Jax's voice was right in the middle. She could hear him.

From what she heard, they were talking about hunting, and the way Jax ranted and raved, he was telling them his story about killing the bear a couple weeks ago. It was a good story, but she'd already heard it several times before, so she decided to tune it out, focusing on her book. Then she heard Zeren say something that caught her attention.

"You've got to bring your rifle tomorrow, in case you decide to go hunting with us."

Annie glanced over the couch at the three men. Jax stared at her, smiling. It was one of those I-didn't-intend-for-you-to-hear-that smiles. There was pleading in his eyes, the kind of look that sent a message: *Please, can they come?* and *Please don't make a scene.*

"Going hunting tomorrow?" Annie asked gently, catching Jax's messages loud and clear.

"Well, it's kind of a funny story," Jax said.

"You know me," Annie said. "I love stories, especially funny ones." Annie got up from the couch and took a seat at the opposite end of the table facing the three men.

"Well, when I went into town this morning, I stopped by Edison Hardware to pick up some things for the ranch, and I found Zeren talking with Thomas."

"Yeah?" Annie tried to act interested while at the same time hiding her frustration.

"I told them I planned to head off to Colorado tomorrow for business and that I was taking the plane."

"Totally lucky for us," Zeren said. "I have a buddy who guides big game hunts out of Pagosa, exactly where Jax is going."

"Really, that is lucky," Annie said. She started to see the big picture now, but she didn't like where it was going. "So you just thought . . ."

"Yeah, I figured that since he was going down there, Thomas and I could catch a ride with him. Kill two birds with one stone, you know. We go hunting while he does his business. When he's done, he can come hunting with us."

"I had planned on telling you when we got back, Annie," Jax quickly added, "but it happened so quickly."

"Do you want to hear what else is so crazy?" Zeren asked.

"Sure," Annie said.

"As soon as I heard Jax was going down there, I immediately called my buddy. He said he's guiding a trip that leaves tomorrow. Here's the crazy part: three members of tomorrow's group cancelled at the last moment." Zeren held up three fingers. "So, there are three extra tags that haven't been filled." Zeren had a big grin on his face as he waited for her to say something. When she didn't respond, Zeren asked, "Do you know what that means?"

"No, fill me in," Annie said with a calm voice.

"We all have tags to go hunting for the weekend."

Slowly and with total control, Annie turned to face Jax.

Chapter 32

Annie

Weekend Getaway

Thomas and Zeren stayed for a couple of hours planning their trip. The three were leaving early in the morning to catch the last driver of the guided group. Most of the hunting party would leave first thing in the morning, but one driver would stay back until noon to pick up Thomas and Zeren. Obviously, Jax's plan to work on the ranch in the morning and leave in the afternoon had changed.

His initial plan of coming back the following day would also no longer work with the two joining the hunting party. Annie had heard Zeren say that if they hadn't gotten anything by Saturday, they would have one of the drivers bring them out, which meant that Jax wouldn't return home until at least Saturday. What had happened to the quick down-and-back trip Jax had described earlier?

By the time they'd finished their planning, it was one fifteen. Annie prepared lunch for all of them, and as soon as they'd finished, they left.

The rest of the afternoon Annie and Jax hadn't talked much. By dinnertime she had calmed down some, gaining more control of her emotions. Yet, the conversation at dinner remained light.

"It's not what you think," Jax finally said, breaking the silence as Annie cleaned up the evening dishes.

"Are you sure?" Annie asked.

"They're going hunting while I meet with the owner of the testing lab. That's it. I will be doing my business while they're off playing."

"You said it would be a quick trip. 'Down and back' were your exact words."

"Okay, so it's a few more days."

"Two days you could be home working on another solution to our problem. Do I need to remind you that we're running out of time?" Her words came out in quick, short bursts. As she reached for the last dish on the table she noticed her hand trembling. Annie placed her hands on her hips to steady them. She looked him straight in the eyes.

"Tell me why you need to take your gun," she said.

"Zeren thinks I'll get my business done quickly and—"

"You didn't tell him why you're going down there, did you?" Annie interrupted. Her frustration had turned to anger. She sat down at the table to steady herself. Zeren was the last person she wanted to know that Jax was trying to find someone to invest in their gold mine. He was one of Jax's best friends, but she didn't trust him.

"Zeren knows I'm having the ore tested from the mine, but he doesn't know that's why I'm going to Colorado.

"I don't trust him." There, she said it out loud.

"I've known him since grade school."

"So, I still don't trust him."

Jax rolled his eyes. "Okay, I won't tell him, I promise."

"So, what about the gun?" Annie asked.

"Zeren wants me to join the group when I get done doing business."

Annie stood up, her face flushing red. Her voice betrayed her as she spoke, even though she tried to calm it down by taking two deep breaths. Even so, her words came out in a pitch higher than she had expected—or wanted.

"It's exactly as I thought: a weekend getaway for the men."

"No. Totally wrong."

"The dirt's the angle, but the hot springs and the hunting with the gang are the real reason why you're going," she barked. Annie immediately sat down again as her legs started to tremble under her. She laid her right arm, visibly shaking, on the table to steady it. Her shaking left hand involuntarily rose to her left temple, her middle finger instinctively finding the half-buried scar. She started gently rubbing it back and forth, back and forth.

"I'm surprised that Easy isn't going with you, then all the gang would be back together," Annie snapped. "Just like in high school." She kept her eyes focused on the table in front of her, not giving him the satisfaction of looking at her in the face.

Jax came and sat down by her, placing his arm around her shoulders. She shuttered, drawing away slightly.

"It's not like that at all, Annie," he said in a calm, reassuring voice. "This hunting trip just sprang up this morning, I swear."

Annie turned to him and said, "Jax, if you need time to yourself, all you have to do is ask. I really don't mind."

"Really, it's not like that. I'm headed to Pagosa Springs to meet with the owner of Dirkfield International to get my dirt tested. That's why I'm going."

"Honesty, Jax. Just call it what it is, a guys' trip."

He pulled her in close. She tried to draw away, but he kept her firmly within his embrace.

"I won't go," he whispered in her ear.

She stopped moving. "Really?"

"Really. I won't go."

"Just like that?" She turned to him, sensing the sincerity in his voice.

"Just like that." He stared back at her, looking deep into her eyes. He gently kissed her on the lips. "If my going to Colorado is causing you that much pain, than I won't go. You're more important."

"What about . . . the dirt?"

He stared down, taking a deep breath before he responded. As he glanced up, Annie saw it in his eyes before he even spoke.

"It's . . . over. I'll . . . have to figure something else out." He sounded dejected. It was in his delivery, in the hesitation, in the intonation, and in his eyes, like all the life had been drained out of him. Annie felt it, the pang of guilt knotting up inside her stomach.

All Jax had ever wanted to do was take care of her. When they were in high school he was always kind and respectful, always opening doors for her. The same thing happened at the university. He would help her with her homework. He was a gentleman, always trying to get her home early when they went on dates—not wanting to keep her out too late. He proposed on graduation night, wanting to get married right after high school, but she wasn't quite ready. Having skipped a grade, she was seventeen when she graduated from high school. She felt she was still too young to get married, so she asked if he would wait. He gladly waited two years.

The knot in her stomach started tightening more, making her feel even worse. How could she ask him to not go to Colorado? It was the same thing; it was his way—Jax was still trying to take care of her.

"No, it's not over," she said. "I still want you to go. Go get your dirt tested. And if you get the chance, I want you to go hunting with the guys."

He turned to her, surprise registering in his face. "Really?"

"Yes, really. You leave tomorrow. When you get back on Saturday you will still have a couple of weeks to figure out another solution to our problems."

"You still want me to go?"

"Yes, it's final. You're going."

Jax leaned forward, kissing her on the cheek. "Thank you. You won't be disappointed."

Jax helped with the last of the dishes. Although it wasn't late, Annie was exhausted from the long day and went off to bed. When he finished cleaning up, Jax went outside to the barn and pulled out his cell phone. He dialed a phone number and hit the send button.

"And?" A female voice answered without saying hello.

"It's all set, I'm still coming," Jax said with a sigh of relief.

"Was it hard?" the female voice asked.

"Harder than I thought, but she finally gave me her blessing."

"Won't she be surprised?"

"Totally," he said. "I'll see you tomorrow." He clicked off his phone.

Chapter 33

Valentino

The Last Job

Valentino had an apartment on the fiftieth floor of the Grand Palace Casino and Hotel, where he worked—one of the many perks of being employed by Mr. Sebasti. There was a separate living room, complete with a couch and a love seat. There was a coffee table and a fifty-inch plasma T.V. on the wall. There was a full kitchen with stainless steel appliances. The apartment had two separate bedrooms, one on each side of the living room. The master had an in-suite bathroom with a sunken Jacuzzi tub. His room had a view of the city, but nothing like Mr. Sebasti's entire back wall of windows in his office.

Mr. Sebasti had told him to take the boys to Montana and bring Carr back to Las Vegas. Valentino should be able to find Carr in one day, but, to be on the safe side, he'd planned for three. How big could Dillon, Montana, be, anyway?

His duffle bag sat open at the end of his bed. He stuffed an extra pair of socks into the top. He'd already counted out enough pairs to last the entire trip, but he didn't like being without clean socks, so he'd stuffed one extra pair in for good measure.

Before packing his bag, he'd laid everything out on his bed. That's just the way he liked it, being organized. Planning his packing helped him not to forget anything. With his clothes packed, he stuffed in a couple of *Car & Driver* magazines in the top just in case he had some down time. He glanced across his bed. It was empty, except for his Beretta 92FS 9mm handgun, two extra clips, and a box of fifty rounds of 9mm Parabellum shells. The term Parabellum came from the German weapons manufacturing firm Deutsche Waffen-und Munitionsfabriken. Their motto was Latin, si vis pacem, para bellum: "If you want peace, prepare for war."

Valentino always carried a weapon on his assignments for Mr. Sebasti. Initially, he'd told himself it was necessary to defend himself against an irate client. But on more recent collection assignments, it had been necessary to put one of Mr. Sebasti's clients "down," as he'd been told. He hadn't had a problem with that before.

Paolo and Lucero, "the boys", as Mr. Sebasti liked to refer to them, were coming with Valentino to Montana.

Paolo would kill Carr if given the chance; he wouldn't even hesitate. Carr had never done anything to Paolo, but that didn't matter. It didn't have anything to do with Carr. Paolo had no conscience—killing came second nature to him.

He stared at the gun. Would Valentino need it? Maybe for self-defense. He picked up the gun, weighing it in his hand. *He would use it if he needed to*, Valentino thought.

Two Hearts

"Where're you going with her?" Paolo had asked as Valentino pushed Tish out of Mr. Sebasti's office the day before. Paolo sat in the lobby outside Mr. Sebasti's office. Paolo held an ivory-handled knife with an eight-inch blade perfectly balanced in his opened hand.

"Mr. Sebasti told me to get rid of her."

"Perfect, I was hoping I might find someone to play with before lunch." Paolo quickly stood, flicking his knife in the air. It did a full flip with a twist before Paolo grabbed it by the handle, the business end pointing straight out, ready for action.

Paolo stepped in front of Valentino, stopping him from advancing toward the elevator. Paolo was a little guy, five-five in height and not weighing much more than a buck forty with his clothes wet. Valentino knew he could crush him with one hand if he needed to, but there was an underlying fear of Paolo that ran through the Grand Palace family. It wasn't his size, it wasn't his weight, nor was it even a special skill or talent that he possessed that scared others. It was his mind. He could snap at any moment. Valentino had seen it on several occasions. Paolo was crazy.

"Hand her over, I'll take her from here," Paolo said.

Valentino peered into Paolo's eyes; something he saw in there told Valentino that when Paolo was done playing with Tish, there wouldn't be much left of her.

It was simple. Give the girl to Paolo. The two would disappear for a few hours, then Paolo would return to the casino offices alone. All done. Clean, with no mess. It had happened before. It could happen again.

Something in the way Mr. Sebasti had treated Tish had rubbed him the wrong way. Tish was Carr's girlfriend for maybe a couple of months. She hadn't done anything to Mr. Sebasti, except maybe getting hooked up with the wrong guy. Mr. Sebasti had put his knife to Tish's back, torturing her.

Valentino wasn't a saint. He'd employed similar techniques making collections for Mr. Sebasti. But Tish, she was nothing to Mr. Sebasti. Valentino couldn't get it out of his mind, the muscles on Tish's back quivering under the point of Mr. Sebasti's knife blade. Before he'd left Mr. Sebasti's office, he'd decided that this was going to be his last job, he was going to find Zeren Carr, bring him back to Las Vegas, and disappear.

Valentino took a deep breath. He pushed his way through Paolo, dragging Tish toward the elevator. Valentino pulled out his nine, jamming it to Tish's side as they stood waiting for the elevator doors to open. Tish tensed in Valentino's grasp. Valentino spoke over his shoulder, "Mr. Sebasti told me to get rid of her myself, and that's exactly what I plan to do."

"You get all the fun," Paolo said. He slumped back down into the lobby chair, dejection sounding in his voice.

Once inside the elevator Tish asked, "Where're you taking me?"

"Shut up." Valentino barked. "You'll find out soon enough, sweet thing." He jabbed the gun harder into her side. Tish jerked in pain, trying to pull away. Valentino held her tight as the doors closed. He saw Paolo grinning.

As soon as the elevator doors opened at the garage level, Valentino shoved Tish out the door. She stumbled, falling to her hands and knees. Valentino grabbed her by the shoulders, and then jerked her off the ground. She couldn't weigh more than ninety-five pounds, Valentino thought.

Valentino dragged Tish to a dark blue four-door sedan. He opened the driver's door, shoved her into the front seat, and then slid in next to her. Valentino pressed the gun to her side. "Move over, or I'll do it right here and I won't even bat an eye."

Tish slid over, not saying a word.

Valentino put the car in drive. He made his way through the parking garage. He found the exit, then pulled onto the strip. As soon as they were two blocks from the Grand Palace, Valentino pulled the gun from Tish's side. He held it in the air, then, with one hand, he operated the mechanism that released the clip in the gun. The clip dropped with a loud clank to the seat in the space between them.

Tish glared at him, eyes opened wide.

While holding the steering wheel steady with his left leg, his left hand and right hand discharged the bullet in the chamber. The shiny brass round clattered to the floor. The gun was now empty. Valentino dropped his leg as his left hand took control of the steering wheel. He threw the empty gun into the back, followed by a thud as it bounced on the back seat.

"We don't need that anymore," Valentino said.

"What are you doing?" Tish asked in surprise.

"Bus, train, or plane?"

"What?"

"How do you want to leave? Bus, train, or plane?"

"I don't understand?" Tish turned in her seat toward Valentino.

"You're leaving Las Vegas right now. Is it by bus, train, or plane? I personally would take the bus or the train—less watched by the wrong people. But then again, the plane is so much faster," Valentino said. "It's up to you, but you need to decide quickly so I know where to take you. I don't have much time before I need to be back. My boss will be expecting a full report."

"And what do you plan on telling your boss?"

"That I got rid of you." Valentino glanced at her. His brow furrowed. "What'd you expect?"

"That you were going to kill me!" Tish screamed.

"Really, you thought I was going to kill you?"

"Yeah. What else was I supposed to think, that we were headed out to dinner and a show?"

"You thought all that was for real?"

"Yes."

"There are surveillance cameras everywhere. Everyone, including my boss, was watching. I had to make it seem real or they would have known something was up."

There was a moment when Tish just stared at him, her mouth slight agape.

"You're not going to kill me?"

"No. Do you want me to?"

"No."

Tish faced forward. She placed her head into her hands. She stared down at the floor of the car as she let out her breath. Her shoulders visibly slumped.

After a moment Tish asked, "Why are you doing this?"

"Let's just say in the last few hours I've grown a conscience."

"Thank you," Tish whispered.

Two Hearts

A moment of silence passed again. Still slumped forward with her head in her hands, Valentino didn't want to interrupt her thoughts, but she needed to answer his question.

He couldn't wait any longer. "Bus, train, or plane?"

"Train," she responded.

Valentino was glad to bring Paolo along. If Carr needed to be killed, he would rather have Paolo do it then have to do it himself. He glanced at the box of 9mm Parabellums at the end of his bed. If you want peace, prepare for war. He packed his nine, the extra clips, and the box of Parabellums into his bag, just in case. He would shoot Carr if he needed to.

Chapter 34

Zeren

Leaving

Zeren was in his room packing when his old man arrived home from work. A knock sounded on his bedroom door. Before Zeren could ask who it was, his dad let himself in.

"Going on a trip," his dad said. It wasn't a question. Zeren sensed an edge in his old man's voice.

"Yeah, Jax is going on a business trip down to Colorado, so Thomas and I set up a weekend hunting trip with a guide I know down there."

"You've been home for about two weeks, you haven't found a job yet, and now you're already leaving?"

"Just for the weekend—it won't be long."

"Don't you think you should stay home and search for a job?"

"It's just for the weekend. Seriously, Dad. I'll have plenty of time to look for a job when I get back."

"Where's your sense of responsibility?" his dad asked. "Life isn't always about just having fun."

"Life isn't always about working, either."

Responsibility, or the lack thereof, had always been at the center of their arguments for the past twelve years. The day Zeren turned sixteen and was legal to work, his dad had been pushing him to get a job.

"Stop being a free loader," his dad had always told him. "Get a job." "Be a responsible citizen in the community." "Leave your mark on the world." Zeren didn't quite understand what that meant anyway, "leave your mark on the world". For all he knew, he was leaving his mark on the world just by being a wild and crazy guy.

His leaving on the trip was exactly the kind of thing that always made his dad mad, but Zeren didn't care. He was going, and he wouldn't think about his dad the entire time he was gone.

The temperature in his room started to rise as their voices raised in volume. Within a very short time they were both yelling at each other. Zeren could tell that he was in a no-win situation, so he decided to pack his things in his car and sleep in the parking lot at the airport. They were leaving in the morning anyway, so he figured he would just be there a little early.

When Chet arrived at six to open the service center, he let Zeren crash on the lobby couch. Jax showed up at seven, exactly when he'd said he would.

By the time they'd loaded everything in the plane, which was not much since they were only going to be gone for four days, Thomas arrived. He loaded his small bag and rifle in the back of the plane.

The plane, a Cessna U206 Stationaire, built in 1984 as a six-seat hauler of people, stuff, or both, depending on the mission, would be their transportation. At the assurance of Zeren, Jax removed two of the six seats to make room for Zeren's elk he promised he was going to bag. Zeren wanted Jax to remove a third seat to give them more space, but Jax insisted he might need the extra seat. With only four seats remaining in the plane, the cargo area was quite large, especially since their gear was light.

Zeren's guide friend had assured him that everything would be provided for on the trip, except for the warm body, the gun, and the ammo. They didn't need sleeping bags, tents, food, or anything else.

Zeren ran to his car to check one last time to make sure he hadn't left anything behind.

Coming from the parking lot, he passed through the lobby of the service center before heading out onto the flight deck. As he entered the lobby, he saw through the windows, a beautiful jet taxiing on the flight deck behind Jax's Cessna. A ground crew with red beacon lights flashing in each of his outstretched hands, directed the jet to the space right next to the Cessna.

The jet had an artistic paint scheme that caused Zeren to stop in mid-stride. As soon as his foot landed on solid ground, he froze. The base color of the jet was white. From the nose of the plane, stripes of blue and red ran parallel along the belly to the back edge of the wings. Then they swirled up from the bottom of the plane, completely covering the tail. Zeren knew this paint scheme well, and without having to look, he knew what was on the tail. But out of curiosity, he peeked anyway.

Two Hearts

The initials GP were stenciled in black on the tail, larger than life, staring at him.

The jet had stopped and the door was opening.

Zeren ducked around the corner, clear of the big windows that looked out onto the flight deck. How had they found him? He'd hid his tracks so well. Tish, it had to have been her. She must've squealed, Zeren thought, and knowing Mr. Sebasti, Tish was probably wearing a new pair of concrete slippers at the bottom of Lake Mead.

"She deserved everything she got coming to her," Zeren said. "The little snitch."

Zeren peered around the corner. A pretty flight attendant stood on the ground at the bottom of the steps. One man, already having descended the stairs, stood at the bottom next to the flight attendant. Two more men could be seen negotiating the stairs. They all wore dark suits.

The three suits had found him.

Zeren quickly glanced towards the Cessna. Jax stood with his back to the little plane, glancing toward the service center lobby.

The Cessna, a model U206, the U standing for utility, had a pilot-side door and a large clamshell rear door that provided easy access to the backseats and easy loading of oversized cargo. Right now, that clamshell door stood wide open, waiting for Zeren to climb aboard.

Zeren watched as Jax glanced at his watch and scanned the flight deck and areas of the front parking lot looking for him. Thomas was sitting in the copilot's seat of the Cessna, already onboard quietly waiting. Thomas had won the toss not fifteen minutes earlier to ride in the front on the way down, which meant Zeren would start out riding in the back.

All he needed to do was get out of the service center and into that plane without being seen.

Peering around the corner into the lobby area, Zeren searched for something that might give him an idea. To his right, visible through the floor-to-ceiling glass windows, he could see the three suits—they were crossing the flight deck, heading to the lobby entrance.

He recognized the suit in front, it was Mr. Sebasti's henchman—the debt collector Valentino. Every time Zeren had obtained a loan from Mr. Sebasti, Valentino had been introduced to him as part of the guarantee of repayment. "Meet Mr. Valentino," Mr. Sebasti said. "He makes sure you repay the loan on time." Zeren knew it was more of a scare technique that probably worked on 90 percent of Mr. Sebasti's customers, but it hadn't worked on him. Sure he'd been scared out of his wits at the size of the guy. Valentino was physically intimidating. But the moment Zeren had walked out of the office with his pockets full of money and the promise of his luck returning, he'd forgotten all about Valentino. That was until right now, as Zeren watched his monstrous frame approach the lobby entrance.

Chapter 35

Valentino

The Service Man

Valentino pulled open the door to the lobby of the service center, and a gust of warm air escaped from the heat inside, greeting him as he entered. It was late September and the morning temperatures in Dillon were brisk, unlike Las Vegas, where the temperatures, even for the mornings were pushing into the nineties by eight.

After getting off the G-V jet, the cold morning air had hit him hard, chilling him to the bone. Now, as he entered the warm lobby, he breathed deeply, the smell of freshly brewed coffee filled his nose. The warmth of the room was inviting, which seemed to help immediately. He scanned the room, but was unable to locate the source of the aroma.

The place seemed to be empty.

"Welcome to Montana, boys," he said over his shoulder to Paolo and Lucero as they entered the lobby behind him. "Eight in the morning and dead as a doorknob. Hello?" he yelled out, but no one answered.

A service man appeared around the corner carrying a large cardboard box on his left shoulder.

The service man was short, consistent with his seemingly short blond hair that was barely visible under the cover of a blue Dillon Airport baseball cap. Under the visor he wore dark aviator glasses. Matching his blue cap, he had on a blue Dillon Airport service jacket. Positioned over the left breast, a white patch, outlined in red stitching, bore the name of Chet, embroidered with the same red thread. Chet was heading for the door leading out to the flight deck.

"Hey," Valentino said, holding out his hand to stop the service man. Valentino flicked the patch with his finger bearing Chet's name and said, "Chet, we are wondering if we can get some service around here."

"Sure," a baritone voice sounded out, which seemed out of place for the man's stature, but Valentino made nothing of it. "How can I help you?" With the box on his left shoulder, the head of the service man was hidden from view. Valentino stepped to the side of the box to face the man. The service man didn't turn away, but instead kept his gaze focused down.

"We are looking for . . ."

"Breakfast," Lucero said behind Valentino. "Let's get some breakfast first."

"Where can we get some breakfast?" Valentino smiled.

"Ring the bell on the counter. Someone should be right with you." With that, Chet pushed passed the three men, walked through the door, and entered the flight deck.

Valentino stepped up to the front desk and rang the silver bell sitting on the counter. The sound bounced off the walls in the empty lobby.

Two Hearts

The three waited a moment, but growing impatient from an empty stomach, Valentino rang the bell again, this time with a little bit more force. They all turned their heads toward a noise coming from the hallway on their right that ran the length of the building. They all stepped over and glanced down the hall—someone was coming through a door that appeared to lead to the shop area of the service center.

"Hey," Valentino said to get the man's attention. "Can we get some service here?"

"Hey, buddy," the man said. He raised his hand and waved. A big grin crossed his face. "Sure can."

The man stepped behind the counter, picking up a clip board. "You guys here with that G-V? Man, that is a beautiful plane. Where are you all coming from?" The man talked while scanning the paperwork on the clipboard. The man was still grinning from ear to ear. *One of those happy types*, Valentino thought—always smiling.

"Vegas," Valentino responded.

"No kidding. Vegas, huh? What're you doing up here in Montana—hunting? Hunting season seems to bring everyone around, though. I mean, we get people from all over; we've had people fly in from New York and Florida. I remember one time we even had a group from Hawaii fly in to go hunting."

Not only was he one of those happy types, but he was also a chatterbox.

"Can you believe that, all the way from Hawaii to come here? If it were me, I'd have stayed in Hawaii. But that's me, you know what I mean? Vegas, huh? Hunting?" The man glanced up from his paper work to see if Valentino was still part of the conversation.

"Yeah," Valentino said. "You could say that. We're here to hunt."

"Well, if there is anything I can do to help, you let me know." A grin crossed his face again as he slid the clipboard across the counter to Valentino. "I'll need you to fill this out first."

Valentino grabbed the pen and started filling out the form.

All heads in the lobby, even the smiling man behind the counter, turned his head as the Cessna, the little plane parked next to their G-V, started up its engine. It could easily be heard, even through the heavy-platted glass windows.

The guy behind the counter seemed friendly and willing to help, so Valentino decided there was no better time than the present to start looking for Carr.

Valentino asked, "How long have you lived in Dillon?"

"My whole life. I've never left, except for the time I spent two long and grueling semesters at the university."

"You must know everyone in town, then."

"Sure do, most everyone. Although, Dillon is growing, and there are a lot of new faces around. But I know almost everyone." Valentino slid the clipboard back.

"We're here to meet a buddy of ours—he used to live in Vegas."

The motor on the Cessna rose in volume, and they all turned to watch as the little plane taxied away from the service center heading toward the runway.

A big grin, one of those that reveal all the person's teeth, popped out on the man's face.

"I knew it. I knew it. The moment you said Vegas, I figured you were Z-Carr's friends."

"You know Carr?" Paolo asked, hope flashing in his eyes.

"Know Z-Carr?" the man asked, a puzzled look wrinkled his brow. "I sure do. I've known him since preschool. He lives just down the street from me."

"Do you know where we can find him?" Valentino smiled. This was too easy. They'd only just arrived ten minutes ago. If things kept falling into place like they had, they would have Carr within minutes and head back to Vegas. Mission accomplished. They would be home sooner than they all thought, even sooner than what Mr. Sebasti had expected. He'd given them until Sunday to be back with Carr. If they showed up before lunch today, there might be bonuses for all of them on the next payday.

"You just missed him," the man said as he leaned over the countertop, pointing out the big glass windows. "That's him right there. He's taking off in the little plane."

Chapter 36

Valentino
The Boss

Valentino ran outside and watched as the plane flew away. It slowly disappeared into the horizon until it was only a tiny black speck in the sky. He cursed as it disappeared.

He turned back to the service center, noticing for the first time a cardboard box on the ground at the side of the door up against the brick wall. He cursed again. It was the box Carr had carried out on his shoulder as Chet the service man. The muscles in his jaw tightened, his fist clenched. The box only reminded him of how close he'd been to grabbing Carr. His blood boiled even more.

Valentino returned to the warm lobby, but just before he entered, he kicked the box, sending it skidding across the asphalt.

"Thanks for all your help," he said to the man behind the counter as he entered. "I didn't get your name."

"The name's Chet." He grinned when he said it, which only made the muscles in Valentino's jaw grow even tighter.

With a controlled voice Valentino asked, "Chet, can you tell me where we can get some breakfast?"

"Shouldn't we call Mr. Sebasti first?" Lucero whined.

"It won't matter if we call him before or after," Valentino said. "Carr is already gone. Frankly, I'd rather face Mr. Sebasti on a full stomach." Paolo and Lucero both nodded.

No matter how many angles he tried to present the story in his mind, anyway he looked at it, he knew Mr. Sebasti was going to be upset. All the stories ended the same; Carr had escaped again, and that was the bottom line. Yeah, they were closer. They'd actually seen him—Valentino had reached out and thumped his chest, which made him even more frustrated. But in the end, they didn't have him, and that was what Valentino was afraid to tell his boss.

He turned his attention back to Chet.

"Is there somewhere nearby we can walk to to get something to eat?"

"No. The airport is just outside of town. It's too far to walk. I'll have to call you a cab."

"Fine." Just as he turned to walk over to the couch to take a seat, Valentino nonchalantly asked with a half grin, "Oh, by the way, you don't happen to know where Mr. Carr went, do you?"

"Oh, sure." Chet picked up a different clipboard from the one Valentino had used earlier. Pointing to the second sheet of paper, Chet said, "I helped Jax register his flight plan last night, and according to this, they are headed to Pagosa Springs, Colorado. Z-Carr told me they were going hunting with a guide buddy down there while Jax ran off to do some sort of business deal."

"When do you expect Z-Carr to return?" Valentino had picked up on Chet's use of Carr's nickname and he decided to use it as if he and Carr had been the best of friends.

"Saturday at the latest, is what I heard."

Before he and the boys had left Las Vegas, Mr. Sebasti had given Valentino his private cell number to keep him updated on their status. He wanted to be updated every hour, or sooner, if the situation required it. And this situation with Carr required it. According to Mr. Sebasti, Carr owed him close to two million dollars.

"Mr. Sebasti," Valentino said when the lines connected after the third ring.

"Valentino, tell me you have the rat." He didn't waste any time, which Valentino had anticipated all morning.

"No sir . . . we don't. But we do know where he is," he quickly added.

"And? Don't waste my time; just tell me."

"He left this morning in a private plane heading to Pagosa Springs, Colorado. He is expected to return on Saturday." Besides having to come up with some clever, non-blood-boiling excuse of why they didn't have Carr, he knew that his boss would want him to come up with a plan B now that plan A had failed. So, without letting Mr. Sebasti ask the question that was inevitably coming, Valentino volunteered his plan B.

"Sir, we plan to stay here and wait for Carr to return, then we'll grab him."

"Pagosa Springs?" Mr. Sebasti said. With that rhetorical question hanging in the air, Valentino practically could hear the wheels turning in his boss's head as he thought through the situation. "I've been there before; it's a nice little resort town centered around the hot springs."

"Yes, sir, that's where they went."

"Pagosa, that's pretty close to Vegas." Valentino just listened. Mr. Sebasti was thinking out loud, and he knew not to interrupt him or it might cost him a month's wages. It had happened before.

"Valentino?"

"Yes, sir."

"Get to Pagosa Springs, Colorado, immediately, I have a new plan. Call me when you get there."

"Yes, sir."

Chapter 37

Jaxon

The Springs

Jax stood on the sidewalk watching the San Juan River wind its way west. Highway 160 was elevated above the river at its north edge, running parallel and bending with every curve of the river. The sidewalk adjacent to the highway gave him a bird's-eye view of everything on the other side, including the Springs Resort and Spa, one of Pagosa Springs' hottest tourist destinations.

The resort, set high above the river on the opposite bank, had twenty-three naturally heated outdoor pools, strategically placed throughout its terraced backyard, which backed right up to the banks of the San Juan. The guests to the resort not only had excellent views of the sparkling water as it rushed by, but also had the freedom of going from hot to cold water within seconds.

Jax watched as several brave patrons, their bodies glowing red from the hot pools, scurried down the pathway that lead to the cold water of the San Juan River. Most approached the water laughing and giggling, eager to take

Two Hearts

a quick swim, but after dipping their feet in, many quickly turned and hurried back to the comfort of the hot water. The fearless ones waded in partway, only to succumb quickly to the cold. Like their smarter friends, they too hurried back to warmer water. Jax smiled as he watched the little show start and end quickly.

He glanced at his cell phone: 12:36—lunch time. The afternoon was turning out perfectly. For early October, the weather hovered around a mild forty-five degrees with the sun shining high overhead. It was cool enough that he could see steam coming from off the hot pools at the resort.

The air was heavy with a pungent sulfuric smell, which Jax knew was typical of mineral hot springs. But what he didn't know, until he'd read the brochure he'd picked up at the airport, was that of all the minerals in the water, sulfate was the highest by far, with 1400 milligrams per liter, compared to sodium, with the second most at 790 milligram per liter. This heavily lopsided sulfate mineral count was the sole cause of the "rotten egg" smell in the air, as stated by the brochure.

He stretched. His body ached. The flight was uneventful, and the weather had cooperated beautifully, but he'd risen early, and sitting in the pilot's seat for four hours had drained him. Tired and hungry, he turned and scanned the storefronts behind him for a place to eat.

The driver for the outfitters had been waiting at the airport when they'd arrived just a little before noon. It hadn't taken long to transport their gear from the plane to the back of the truck. Zeren and Thomas were off. Jax caught a ride with them to town, and the sidewalk where he stood was where he'd been let off.

In front of him was the Shady Nook, the old Victorian home that had been converted to a bed and breakfast where he'd reserved a room. He wasn't staying at the resort. It was too pricey for him, especially under his current financial circumstances.

The Spring Café, adjacent to the bed and breakfast, looked promising. He headed in that direction first.

After lunch Jax checked in. He found his room toward the front of the house on the second floor. There was a double bed to the right of the door. An arm chair, positioned directly across from the door, was against the far wall. A desk stood to the left of the arm chair with a lamp that had an old-fashioned shade on it. There was a large armoire to the left of the door against the interior wall. Opposite the bed, at the front of the house, was a window. Jax entered the room, dropped his bag on the bed, laid his rifle next to his bag, and placed a small package in the corner of the room. He stepped up to the window, parted the curtains, and peered out. He could clearly see the resort and its numerous pools.

The pools were teeming with guests. Jax silently tried counting the number of bathers, but there were too many. They kept moving about from pool to pool, which made it almost impossible to count them as they moved about. Glancing at all the resort guests, he stopped counting, the reality of his task quickly settling over him. How was he going to find the owner of Kris Dirkfield International among all those people?

He slumped down on the corner of his bed and let out his breath. He glanced out the window from where he sat, realizing for the first time that maybe his plan wasn't the brightest idea he'd come up with in the past ten years.

He heard Annie's voice in his head. *You're wasting time going down there when you could be doing something else.* For the first time, doubt started to invade his thoughts. Maybe she was right. Maybe he was just wasting time. Maybe he was just fooling himself into believing this little adventure was the answer to all their problems. He glanced out the window again. So many people.

Jax quickly pushed out all the negative thoughts from his mind. He wasn't the type to just give up without a fight. He first had to try, or he would never know if he would have been successful.

Set in the corner of his room where he'd put it when he arrived was a five-pound tightly sealed container of dirt from his mine. To prove it was valuable he needed to have it tested again, and the only way he figured to do that was to find Kris Dirkfield.

He changed into a pair of swim trunks, a T-shirt, and a pair of flip-flops and headed off to the resort.

Chapter 38

Jaxon
The Needle

He entered through the bathhouse, paid the admission fee, and walked through the doors to the pool area. The sulfuric smell, stronger here then it had been at his bed and breakfast, wasn't so overpowering to make one sick, but the rotten egg smell was everywhere.

Jax stepped through the doors, surveying the area. He now faced the proverbial, needle-in-the-haystack task. With so many people, he knew this was going to be a long day. Doubt, still a shadow lurking in the back of his mind, tried again to creep its way forward and overtake him. He rolled his shoulders a couple of times and shook his arms to get the jitters out. It worked; the doubt receded back to its hiding place.

He scanned the pools, assessing a strategy. He first noticed the number of children. Some were laughing and playing in the shallower pools of water. There were some children with families sitting at metal picnic tables having lunch. He didn't think he would find the owner with children. He checked those groups of people off his list. No families with children.

He noticed several groups of teenagers, some splashing in the water, while others were cuddled up close together, each enjoying the hot pools in their own way. Not with the teenage crowd either. He made quick work, checking off each group where he knew the owner wouldn't be.

There were a few older couples that seemed to be scattered throughout the pools, the age group that interested him the most.

He decided to visit each pool, just to be thorough.

As he began walking through the resort, he noticed that each hot pool had a different name, like The Burg or Treasure. There was one named Boulder and one named Lobster Pot, which didn't surprise him at all. Jax went from pool to pool, discreetly scanning the faces of the occupants, but nothing jumped out at him.

He spent just under an hour gazing at each person, studying their faces, but he found nothing.

Walking past the Venetian pool, Jax heard a noise to his left, which drew his attention from the path in front of him.

He turned and watched as a little girl around six years old held her father's hand and crossed a submerged bridge through the mineral hot pool, the Golden Pond. The girl squealed as her foot slipped on algae growing on the wooden slats of the bridge. He watched until the child and her father had made it safely across.

Jax turned back to the walkway leading to the next pool, and accidentally ran into a man.

"Excuse me, sir," Jax said. The man mumbled something inaudible. The man continued on his way without stopping. He wore a thick and fluffy white terry cloth bathrobe. Jax watched the man walk up the path. Jax glanced ahead in the direction the man walked. Twenty feet in front of the man, a small rectangular wooden sign positioned at the side of the path read *Adults Only*.

Most of the guests in this area of the resort, the ones not in the pools yet, had robes on. Jax saw a few draped over chairs positioned next to the pools. A couple coming from the hotel to the left of him passed him on the walkway. They were both wearing the same white fluffy robes. Nonchalantly he turned in their direction, scanning their faces, but didn't notice anything telling about them. Just normal people, doing normal things.

But the robes?

Those coming from the bathhouse had towels; but, those coming from the hotel wore robes.

He followed the path. A family, a father, his wife, and two children, a boy and girl, all wearing robes, were walking in front of him, headed toward the hotel. The family stopped at a gate. The boy, maybe ten years old, held out his hand. His mother, right on cue, placed a plastic hotel room card in the boy's hand. He quickly swiped it through the security system. There was a click. The gate unlocked. The family passed through and entered the hotel lobby.

Jax peered up at the two-story structure. The receptionist at Dirkfield International had told him the owner would be staying at the resort. He glanced back over the numerous pools. So far, he hadn't seen anyone that might possibly look like the owner. *Probably still in the hotel*, he thought.

Jax looked around, scanning the tables and chairs for a robe that seemed unattended. He wasn't a thief. He was sure he could follow a hotel guest through the gate, pretending he'd left his key card in the room, but he wanted one of those robes. When he was done using it, he would simply leave it in the hotel somewhere. No harm done.

He spotted one draped over a chair sitting next to an empty table. It appeared to be abandoned. As he walked by, he picked it up. With the same motion and without breaking his stride, he slipped his arms through the sleeves and tied the belt around his waist.

As he finished tying the knot in the belt, an older woman approached the gate. Her arms were full with three heavy bags. Toys and towels and clothes were spilling out of the tops of the bags. She had pure silver hair pulled back into a tight bun. Perfect for staying neat and tidy while getting wet at the same time. She appeared to be in her late sixties and wore a white fluffy resort robe. She fumbled with her key, trying to swipe it through the security system.

"May I help?" Jax asked, holding out his hand as he slowly approached from behind.

The woman was startled just a bit, but seemed to recover quickly when she noticed the smile on Jax's face.

"Yes, please," she said. "Thank you."

Jax took the key card from the woman's hand and swiped it through the security system. The green light flashed, and there was a click as the gate unlocked. Jax stepped through, holding the gate open. As the woman walked through, he handed the card back to her.

"Thank you so much," the woman said. Motioning toward the bags in her hands, she said, "All my grandkids' toys and things. I'm ferrying everything to the room before it gets too late, but I think I might have grabbed too much this trip."

"May I help you with some of those?" Jax asked, flashing his friendly smile again. This time the woman hesitated.

"Thank you, but I think I can manage." Just as the last word passed her lips, a bag slipped from her grasp.

Jax reached out, grabbing it before it fell to the ground.

"At least let me help you to the elevator," Jax said, hoisting the bag up. It was heavy. No wonder the woman was having a hard time carrying it all.

"To the elevator then," the woman said.

Jax led the way, holding the door to the hotel lobby as the kindly grandmother entered before him. At the elevator, he pushed the up button.

The doors opened. Jax set the bag he'd been carrying on the floor of the elevator. "Thank you ever so much for your help," she said as she stepped on.

"You're welcome."

In reality, he should have been thanking her for getting him through the gate, but he didn't saying anything about that.

When the doors closed he turned, facing the lobby. He quickly scanned the room. Instantly he saw her. There she was, a tall, blond woman standing in the center of a circle of couches in the lounge area of the lobby. Her golden locks, salon perfect, draped over her shoulders. It was the same woman from the home page of the Kris Dirkfield International website. The long legs. Elegant. Tan. Firm.

The shoulders. Poised. Proud. Confident. The eyes. Crystal blue. Intense.

This was who he'd come to see.

She was more beautiful than he'd remembered, and her outfit wasn't helping either. She was wearing a white, silky, shear swimsuit cover-up, teasingly transparent enough to just barely show the cut and color of the two-piece swimsuit underneath, allowing the imagination to dangerously wander a bit. Like every other guy in the lobby, he followed her with his eyes.

Breathtaking.

Jax approached, taking slow, deliberate steps. As he drew near he said, "Kris Dirkfield?"

She turned her beautiful eyes on him and smiled.

Chapter 39

Annie

Lunch Date

Annie spent most of the morning cleaning the house after Jax's early departure. By eleven she felt completely exhausted and sick to her stomach. Throwing up had rarely been part of the flu when she'd gotten it before, just headaches, body aches, and an overall yucky feeling, which was exactly how she felt now. Except this time, she felt like she was about to lose her breakfast.

She lay down, glancing at the clock on the wall. Ten minutes, then she would start a load of laundry. Exhaustion overcame her. As soon as her head hit the armrest she fell asleep.

※

She heard the ringing, but it barely registered, her mind heavily in a fog. The ringing stopped. Instantly she started to fade, the thick dark fog engulfing her mind, when she heard the ringing again. This time, partially awake, she recognized the ring tone—it was her cell phone sitting on the end table next to the couch.

She sat up and grabbed the phone on the last ring. She noticed Beth Downs's name on the glass as she swiped to answer the call.

"Hello?" her voice croaked, her throat dry from her nap. She swallowed two times.

"Annie?" Beth asked. "Is that you?"

"Yes," she said, her voice sounding a little more normal.

"Did I wake you?"

"Yes, but it's okay, I needed to get up." She peered at the clock, expecting ten minutes to have passed since she'd laid down—twenty at the most. 12:39. She blinked a few times to clear her vision. She looked again—still the same time. She'd slept over an hour and a half. It wasn't like her to sleep so much, but, by the way she'd been feeling this morning, she knew she needed it. She shook her head slightly. *An hour and a half.*

"I called to see if you'd like to have lunch." Beth asked. "Charles is sending me on a surprise shopping trip to Denver for a few days, and I thought we might get together before I leave. Plus, I figured with Jax gone you could use some girl time. Am I right?"

"Girl time?" Since she'd been married to Jax, she'd given up all that so-called *girl time*. She and Jax had always hung out, doing things together. There really never had been any guy friends or girlfriends that got between them. They were each other's best friends. That was all they seemed to need.

Before Annie responded, she stood up. She normally would've made up an excuse to get herself out of spending time with Beth, but with Jax gone, she liked the idea of having company, even if it was Beth. Maybe she did need some *girl time*.

She walked around a bit, testing her legs. The body aches had subsided; the yucky feeling had all but disappeared. She felt better.

"Sure, how about a late lunch in an hour, say one thirty," Annie said. "Let's meet at—"

"Hey, it's my treat. I want to take you to the Den."

"That's kind of pricy for lunch. Are you sure? You really don't need to."

The Lion's Den, one of the local favorites, served a variety of dishes, including steak, prime rib, and chicken. But, it also had a variety of pizzas, salads, and soups. It was well known for its sauerkraut-topped pizza, which usually scared off customers. The kraut provided a unique sour pizza experience that the locals loved and that was always recommended to brave first-timers.

Annie loved the Den just as much as anyone in Dillon, but she didn't want Beth to pay for her meal. She didn't want to owe anyone anything, especially Beth.

"Please? It will be fun." Beth whined. "It's settled. I'm taking you to the Den. I'll see you there in an hour." Beth terminated the call, not waiting to hear Annie's excuse, which was just on the tip of her tongue when the line disconnected.

Annie arrived five minutes early. Beth hadn't arrived yet, so Annie sat on a hardwood bench in the lobby. Beth showed up fashionably late, as always. Sheila, the hostess of no more than eighteen showed them to a booth. The Den, laid out like most restaurants, had a row of booths against the outside walls and a row of tables in the inside area. In the center, there was a large horseshoe-shaped bar.

Like Annie had anticipated and dreaded, the conversation immediately gravitated to Beth's shopping trip to Denver. Beth gloated, bragging about how Charles doted over her, giving her gifts, taking her on trips, and sending her shopping all the way to Denver, which caused Annie's stomach to turn, reminding her of how she'd felt earlier. This was why Annie had hesitated at first to accept Beth's invitation, knowing that any chance Beth had to brag about herself and her *fantastic* life, she would take it.

Although it made her sick, Annie couldn't help feeling a little jealous.

Yes, right now she and Jax were in a situation. The image of Mariana Delfino with the red scratch on her face flashed through Annie's mind. Maybe it wasn't Jax's fault they were back in Dillon. But, knowing Jax would come out on top, as he always did, even if it meant starting over, allowed her to absorb Beth's look-at-me attitude.

Annie's life wasn't perfect, but she was happy. She had Jax. He was good man. He worked hard. He loved her. He provided for her, met her needs. She'd lived abroad and had seen amazing things. She had her one true love. It was enough.

Annie glanced down the row of booths for their server. They'd already been seated for ten minutes, and all they had to show for their time were two glasses of water. She glanced the other way. No server. Lunch was going to take forever.

Finally, after five more minutes, the server showed up, providing something else to occupy Beth's mind instead of herself. But Beth simply changed directions with her conversation, almost as if in mid-sentence, and started asking questions about Jax.

"Now, where did Jax go?" Beth asked. But before Annie could answer, Beth asked another one. "I heard it was somewhere in Colorado—some resort place?"

"Pagosa Springs." Annie said, trying to keep her answers short and simple.

Annie didn't want to talk about Jax's trip, but she figured Mrs. Emmett had already spread the news about it. If Beth had missed any details, Annie didn't want to be the one filling in the gaps that Beth might be fishing for.

Annie waited, watching patiently for any chance to change the subject.

"A business trip?"

"Yeah."

"I heard—"

Here it comes, Annie thought. She held her breath as Beth continued.

"—Jax went down to see the owner of a mining company, *Dirkfield* or something, located in Germany."

Well, she got part of it right. But, typical of gossip, only part.

"You've been back in Dillon for just under a month, and now you're already planning on leaving again? This time to Germany?"

Annie smiled, her shoulders relaxed. She silently let out her breath. Beth was way off track.

"Something like that," Annie responded.

Beth pulled out a stylish maroon leather case that held her iPad. She flipped it open, tilted it on its stand, and hit the power button. After waiting for it to warm up, Beth started tapping the screen with her silver stylus.

"What was the name of the company? Dirkfield what?" Beth asked as she typed.

Annie hesitated. Jax's being in Colorado wasn't any of Beth's business. The gears in Annie's mind spun at breakneck speed, trying to think of a firm but polite way of redirecting the conversation without being too obvious.

Beth must've sensed Annie's hesitation, because she glanced up and said, "I just want to see where you will be living in Germany."

Annie didn't believe her for one second, but looking at the iPad, with its Google search page up, her interest was piqued. Ever since Jax had mentioned the mining laboratory, she'd wanted to go online to research the company as well. But, between trying to help get Jax off, cleaning the house, and feeling sick almost every day, she'd never taken the time to do it.

"Dirkfield International," Annie said. "That's what Jax told me." Beth typed in the name and hit the return button.

"Kris Dirkfield International is the first name on the list that popped up," Beth said leaning forward to tap on the link. "Do you think that's it?"

"That might be it, but Jax only said Dirkfield International. He didn't mention the name of Kris." Annie stared at the screen in anticipation, not knowing what she would see. But, what she did see was the last thing she'd expected.

"That's Kris Dirkfield International?" Beth shrieked. "That's who Jax went to see?" A couple of heads turned at Beth's raised voice.

Shocked by what she saw, Annie wasn't prepared to answer Beth's outburst. Annie's eyes glazed over as she stared across the restaurant, her left hand rising to the side of her head. The middle finger, out of pure instinct rather than from a controlled brain function, found the partially exposed scar. She started rubbing it back and forth.

"Annie? Annie?" Beth said.

Annie could hear Beth's pleading, it registered in her mind, but she couldn't answer. She turned her focus back to the iPad, locking her gaze on the screen. She kept rubbing the scar back and forth, back and forth.

"Annie, are you alright?"

There it was again, the pleading, but it didn't faze her. The only thing that penetrated her mind was the image on the screen—a tall, scantily clad, beautiful blond bombshell. What had her mind frozen in place was the amount of exposed skin. The woman was slightly turned, revealing her backside, which was completely exposed, the evening gown swooping down her back just above her buttocks.

The woman's right leg, raised slightly on the tippy toes of her matching black high heels, parted the slit in the side of her dress that ran almost all the way up her leg. Her tan skin was visible up past mid-thigh.

Annie's mouth opened, parting slightly.

Mesmerized by the woman, Annie failed to see the jewelry the woman wore. If she hadn't been so distracted, Annie would have seen gold bracelets, diamond necklaces, diamond earrings, and gold chains sparkling on the woman's ankles.

She missed all that.

Annie saw Kris Dirkfield, the owner of the mining laboratory, the same owner that Jax went to see, the one he'd failed to mention was a woman, no, a beautiful, striking, elegant woman.

The rubbing of the scar became more pronounced as she processed this information.

"Annie?" Beth grabbed Annie's left arm, forcing her to stop moving. Beth got in Annie's face. "Annie, are you okay?"

"Daddy?" Annie whispered.

Chapter 40

Annie
The Scar

Annie Bradley laid her head down on her desk. She placed her right arm under the desk, resting her hand against her tummy. She pressed gently. It felt squishy, like a balloon partially filled with air. It gurgled. Pain shot to her left side. She twisted and groaned. Mrs. Chatsworth, Annie's fourth grade teacher, stood at the front of the class, teaching about the beautiful state of Montana, where they lived.

"From your homework over the weekend, can anyone tell me why Montana is called the Treasure State?" Mrs. Chatsworth asked.

Smart aleck Bobby Law's hand shot up at the same time he yelled out, "Because Blackbeard the pirate buried a chest of gold in the Pioneer Mountains."

The class burst out laughing. Annie laughed too, causing her tummy to rumble even more. Pain bounced around the walls of her tummy, like a silver ball bouncing off the bumpers in a pinball machine. She felt dizzy. She grimaced with her face down on her desk so no one would see.

Kind Mrs. Chatsworth, not wanting to hurt Bobby's feelings, couldn't tell him he'd been totally wrong. "That is partially correct, Bobby. Would anyone else like to answer the question?"

Annie raised her hand. "Yes, Annie?" Mrs. Chatsworth called.

Barely raising her head, Annie said, "I don't feel good."

"Oh dear." Mrs. Chatsworth hustled down the aisle to Annie's desk.

The school nurse called Annie's mother. "Mrs. Bradley?" she asked.

"Yes?"

"This is Jessica, the school nurse at Parkview Elementary."

"Is Annie okay?"

Annie was lying on the bed in the nurse's office as the nurse spoke to her mom. The nurse's desk was right next to the bed. Annie could hear the entire conversation, even the agitation in her mother's voice through the phone.

"That's what I'm calling about."

"Is she hurt?" Mrs. Bradley asked with sharpness in her voice.

"She's not hurt, but she's not feeling well."

"The flu or something?"

"Yes. She has a temperature of 103 degrees—she's pretty hot. She's also complaining of stomach cramps. She hasn't thrown up though, which I would've expected with her symptoms. Nine out of ten students that have been in my office in the past two weeks have vomited. There's a pretty bad flu bug going around."

"Annie doesn't throw up when she gets sick. In the entire eight years of her life she's never thrown up once."

"Amazing," the nurse said.

"May I speak with her?"

"Sure." The nurse passed the phone to Annie, who weakly sat up. She took the receiver, and cradling it in both hands, she raised it to her head.

"Hi, Mommy."

"Hi baby. Not feeling good?"

"No. I hurt all over. My tummy doesn't feel good."

"I'll tell Mr. Miller I need to take my morning break, and I'll come and get you—he'll understand. He has a family too."

"Thanks, Mommy."

"Let me talk to the nurse again."

"Mrs. Bradley?" The nurse asked when Annie gave the phone back to her.

"I'm coming to get Annie."

"That'll be best."

"The poor thing sounds exhausted," Mrs. Bradley said.

"She definitely needs rest."

"Thank you for calling."

"You're welcome. I'll have her checked out of school by the time you get here."

"Thank you again," Mrs. Bradley said.

※

Annie stayed curled up in a little ball in the backseat of the car. Normally a little chatterbox, the ride home was quiet. She stayed that way, except for the occasional moan or groan when the car jostled from a pothole or from the uneven road.

As the car turned the corner heading down their street, Annie's mom said, "Your father's home? Why would he be home?" The way she asked the questions, it seemed her mother wasn't looking for a response from Annie.

As the foreman of the local lumber yard, her father's work schedule never allowed him to come home during the day. Annie wrinkled her nose. Her eyebrows furrowed with the thought that her dad might be home early from work. With her mother's puzzled statements, even in her weakened condition, Annie perked up, interested to see what her mom was seeing.

She sat up and leaned over the front seat for a better view. They were still several houses away from theirs when Annie, pointing straight at her house, said, "Who is that?"

Mrs. Bradley focused down the street. A woman had exited her own home followed by her husband. He was oblivious to anything and everything else around him, except for the woman walking a step ahead of him. With his left arm raised, his hand rested on her shoulder. With the woman's left arm raised and bent at the elbow, her hand was resting on his.

Mrs. Bradley quickly pulled to the curb and stopped. She and Annie watched as their husband and father walked the woman to a car parked in front of their home. He opened the driver's door for her. Before she got in, he turned the woman around to face him. He affectionately wrapped his arms around her waist. Then, lifting her off the ground ever so slightly, he pulled her body into his. He kissed her hard on the lips.

Mrs. Bradley gasped.

"What is Daddy doing?" Annie asked.

"Daddy's . . . kissing that woman," Mrs. Bradley said, her voice cracking with emotion.

Annie turned to her mother, sensing the strain in her voice. Tears welled up in her mother's eyes. Her body trembled. Seeing her body shake and tears roll down her cheeks, Annie asked, "Mommy, are you okay?"

Her mother wiped at the tears with the sleeve of her right arm. Annie noticed her mother's left hand, gripped tight on the steering wheel, her knuckles as white as the chalk from her fourth grade classroom.

"I'm fine," Annie's mother said through gritted teeth.

She didn't seem fine, but Annie didn't have the strength to pursue the issue much further.

Annie turned back to watching her house. The woman had gotten into her car and had driven away already. Her father walked up the steps to their house. He opened the door and went in.

Annie moved back to the back seat, exhausted from her curiosity-spurred exertion. She laid down and curled up into a ball.

Her mother pulled away from the curb, drove to their home, and parked the car in the driveway next to her husband's car.

Mrs. Bradley glanced over the front seat and said, emotion still registering in her voice, "Baby, I know you're not feeling well, but I want you to stay in the car for just a moment while I go talk to Daddy, okay?"

"Okay, Mommy," Annie said, nodding her head slightly.

"I'll be back to get you real quick," Mrs. Bradley said with a tight smile on her face. She got out of the car and went inside the house.

It wasn't long after her mother entered the house that Annie heard her parents screaming at each other at the top of their lungs. Annie sat up expecting her parents to be standing on the front porch. They weren't.

She'd never heard anything like it. Her parents had never fought before, at least not in front of her. They seemed to be so in love, always holding hands, always sitting next to each other at the dinner table, and always cuddling in front of the T.V. on the weekends.

Annie rested her arms across the front seat to keep them from twitching. She turned her head, glancing down the street both ways. The street and sidewalks were empty. No one was there that might have heard her parents yelling. Her body began to tremble with fear. She didn't know what to do.

She placed her hand on the door handle. She knew she'd told her mother that she would stay in the car. But their elevated voices set her insides tumbling over and over and around and around.

She'd told her mother she would wait, so she withdrew her hand. She bit her lip as she let go, wondering if it was the right thing to do. Instantly, a crash like breaking glass came from inside the house, followed by more screaming and yelling.

Body trembling with fear, Annie opened the car door. She climbed the front porch steps, taking deliberate steps with unsteady feet. Still very weak, with a trembling hand, she turned the door handle on the front door. She stepped inside.

"Daddy? Mom—?"

Something heavy slammed into the left side of her head. She crumpled to the floor, blood spilling from a severe gash at the hair line on her left temple. Blood stained the carpet of the living room floor.

Chapter 41

Annie Attack

Annie, hesitant to speak, didn't know how Beth was going to react to the story she'd just told her. Annie sat back in the booth, not making a sound, staring down at her hands. Sitting across the table, Beth had her own eyes down, watching her fingers twist her napkin into a knot.

No one spoke for a minute.

Annie finally spoke, breaking the silence. "A clock hit me in the head. My father, trying . . . to hit my mother, threw it right when I stepped through the door." Annie pulled back her hair revealing the scar at the side of her temple. Her middle finger found the edge, the skin still warm to the touch, having just been agitated. "I had twenty-five stitches and a mild concussion, which put me in the hospital for a couple of days."

"I'm so sorry. I didn't know."

"Nobody knew. I've never told anyone."

"What about the hospital?"

"My mother told everyone I was there because of the flu."

"And the stitches?"

"Caused by a fall from being weak with the flu," Annie said. She grinned and shrugged. "Anyway, that was the story we told. After that incident, my father and mother quickly but quietly divorced. I think he felt bad about what he'd done to me—so he just agreed to everything my mother asked for and left. My mom and I, we've been on our own ever since."

"What happened to your father?" Beth asked.

"He moved in with his girlfriend, but that didn't last long. Later he moved to Bozeman." Annie shrugged. "We pretty much didn't see him after that—he didn't want to be part of our lives at all."

"Wow, just like that. One minute you have a dad, and the next minute he's gone. That must have been hard."

"It was, at first. But it was also uncomfortable being around him. Every time I was with him, I could tell he wanted to be somewhere else. That hurt, and I think he could tell, but that didn't change how he felt about us. So he started distancing himself, drawing away from us. That hurt too. But, once he moved to Bozeman, we hardly ever saw him again."

"I'm so sorry, Annie," Beth said, as she reached across the table. She placed both of her hands on Annie's.

Silence again, even in a noisy restaurant with televisions and people clamoring to be heard.

Their lunch, Beth's steak salad with tomato basil soup and Annie's grilled chicken salad with creamy broccoli soup, arrived just in time to help fill the awkward void.

The steam rising from the soup carried the spice-laden fragrance to her nose. It smelled good, but she wasn't hungry. She knew she should eat, not having had breakfast that morning, so she took a couple of bites—it was divine. The flavor, creamy and smooth, was exactly as Annie had imagined it would be. But a few bites was all she could eat. She pushed her food away.

The iPad was standing there, powered down after a lack of use. A reflection of Beth's soup was showing on its darkened screen. Despite the image of the soup, she could still see the shapely figure of that woman. Annie wanted to smash it, to get rid of the very thing that had showed her whom Jax was with.

Beth noticed Annie staring at the iPad and must have sensed what Annie was thinking. "Jax wouldn't, would he? I mean, he couldn't, could he?" Beth asked.

That was the question. Annie didn't answer, not sure what to say. Her mind told her what she didn't want to believe, that Jax could, but in her heart she felt that Jax loved her and that he wouldn't. Not trusting her heart, she said what was in her head.

"I don't know, he might," Annie said. "I don't think he would, but that is exactly how my mother felt about my father, and he did."

"But, this is Jax."

"I know, I keep telling myself the same thing."

"Charles was the same way. He was just as surprised when he found out his first wife was cheating on him."

"I just can't believe this is happening to me," Annie said. She buried her face into her hands. Her arms trembled. "I thought . . . I thought we were so in love." Her voiced betrayed her, shaking as much as her arms.

Annie folded her arms in front of her, squeezing tight, trying to hide the shakes. She swallowed twice and took a deep breath, which seemed to calm her down.

"Sure we've had our problems, but who hasn't?" Annie said. "You work through them, right? That's what normal people do. You don't just go off and throw everything away."

Beth just sat there not saying a word. After a moment, Beth asked, "Now what?"

Now what? Annie didn't hesitate.

"Attack."

Chapter 42

Jaxon

The Real Kris Dirkfield

Crystal blue sapphires with a sprinkle of light, the color of the eyes of the beautiful woman before him. Jax stopped. He shuffled his feet, trying not to stare.

"Kris Dirkfield?" Jax reached out a hand.

"Yes?" a man's voice boomed from behind the woman. The lovely lady stepped to the side, revealing a large muscular man sitting on the couch. He had short, well-groomed, blond hair with a sprinkle of gray. Early to mid-fifties, Jax guessed. He stood, taking Jax by the hand. He was tall, six five, and probably weighed close to 250 pounds. And, by the looks of it, he was all muscle. He was a presence. With a crushing grip that matched his broad shoulders, he said with a deep German accent, "I'm Kris Dirkfield."

"Mr. Kris Dirkfield?"

"Yes?"

Jax, his brow furrowing, turned back to the woman.

"This is my lovely wife, Sophia," Mr. Dirkfield said. Gentleness was what first came to mind. Respect came next. That's how Mr. Dirkfield presented his wife.

"Jaxon Tagget," he said. She extended her hand. The skin was soft, warm, but she had a firm grip.

"Mr. Kris Dirkfield," Jax said, turning back to the man.

"Yes? You've said that before. You seem surprised. Were you expecting something else?"

"Your name, Kris, K-R-I-S, and the picture of your wife on the home page of your website . . ."

"You were expecting Kris to be a woman?"

Jax hesitated. "Yes?"

"Kristoffer is my given name, but I go by Kris," he said. "As for the website . . . effective advertising; you can't even begin to imagine the number of phone calls we receive and orders we take because of how we display our jewelry on our front page."

"But, you're a . . ."

"Mining laboratory. I know. And we don't sell jewelry." Mr. Dirkfield stood next to his wife. He brushed back her hair from off her shoulders, revealing a gold chain that hung loosely around her neck. "The gold of this necklace came from one of the mines we tested and which we later invested in. All of the jewelry displayed on the front page of our website came from mines we've invested in."

"Tricky."

"Powerful," Mr. Dirkfield said. "Nothing sells better than a beautiful woman, no matter the product." Mr. Dirkfield motioned for Jax to take a seat on the couch where he had been sitting. Mrs. Dirkfield sat next to her husband.

Two Hearts

Once seated, Mr. Dirkfield said, "You probably didn't come here to talk about advertising, so how may I help you?"

Jax started at the beginning, when he came home from Venezuela and found the problems with his parents and the ranch. He told them about his father's cancer and about the situation with the mortgage.

Mr. Dirkfield listened intently, never interrupting. He nodded several times to indicate he was paying attention.

Jax continued. He told them about the hospital bills and about the cattle being killed. He mentioned the old abandoned mine and the three veins of gold he'd found, which seemed to perk Mr. Dirkfield's interest.

Jax finished off his story with the bank's ultimatum for Jax to come current on the mortgage by the end of the month or lose the ranch. When he finished, he sat back, waiting.

"Have you contacted my lab in Dallas?"

"Yes, but they can't have the results back for at least four weeks. I'm running out of time."

"What do you want me to do?"

Jax shifted in his seat before answering. "Authorize an emergency test on the ore from the mine on my ranch."

"I'm sorry to have to tell you this, but you came a long way for nothing—I don't grant emergency authorization so easily."

"But, if you—"

Mr. Dirkfield raised his hand, cutting Jax off. "Didn't you say it had already been tested once, the report coming back negative?"

"Yes." Jax didn't elaborate—he already knew where this conversation was going and how it was going to end. His eye contact with Mr. Dirkfield faltered ever so slightly. Discouragement settled over him.

"I'm sorry about your parents and the ranch, but I would be taking a huge risk, and who knows if the ore is even viable. Plus, I'm on vacation."

"Mr. Dirkfield, I've been mining for the past three years, which isn't long, I realize, but in my experience I know good ore when I see it. I know I've received a negative report already, but all I'm asking is for a second opinion."

"Send it to my lab and we will have it tested . . . in four weeks."

Jax dropped his head. He sighed and glanced up. "Sir, I don't have that kind of time. I need it tested immediately—I need the results by Monday at the latest."

Mr. Dirkfield stood. His wife followed.

"What did you expect? That you could just accidentally bump into me while I'm on vacation and tell me your sob story and that I would have compassion on you? First off, I don't appreciate being approached while I'm away from the office. Second, I'm truly sorry about your father's cancer, but I can't take the risk of authorizing an emergency test based upon a sad story. Third, the ore has already been tested and proved not viable. I'm sorry, but I won't be able to help you." Mr. and Mrs. Dirkfield turned and walked away.

Chapter 43

Jaxon

The Drop-Off

Jax stood in the lobby of the Springs Resort with his arms limp at his side, his mouth slightly agape, his eyes fixed straight ahead. He stared at the backs of Mr. and Mrs. Dirkfield as they walked to the elevator. A few guests of the hotel passed through his line of vision which didn't faze him. His eyes stayed riveted on the Dirkfields.

He raised a foot, taking one small step forward. With eyes wide open, he forced himself to stop. He couldn't believe it. He was about to throw away all inhibition, run over to the Dirkfields, and, falling on his knees, beg them for help.

He couldn't do it. Begging was beneath him, and yet . . . he still stood there glaring at them, willing them to turn around and see the pitiful look he knew was on his face, hoping it might change their minds.

The elevator doors opened. The Dirkfields entered the elevator. The moment the doors closed and they had disappeared from sight, his heart thudded in his chest. His subliminal message hadn't been received.

The first thing he thought of was Annie. His chin dropped to his chest in disgust. He'd let her down. More importantly, he should have simply listened to her in the first place. Like she'd said, he was wasting time chasing after a pipe dream when he should have been pursuing a more viable solution to their problems.

Jaxon shrugged off the white hotel robe from his shoulders, letting it slip to the ground where he stood. Eyes down, he dragged himself out of the hotel.

With his business done, he was ready to leave—time to go back to Dillon and face the fallout from his stupid choices. He made his way back to the bed and breakfast. He trudged up the stairs. He unlocked the door to his room. He dropped into the small armchair, the only furniture that fit in his small room. He grabbed his cell phone still charging on the end table next to him.

He selected Annie's number at the top of his contact list and pushed the call button. Her voicemail picked up after the fourth ring. His shoulders slumped, his head sagged. He knew if he could just hear her voice, his spirits would lift. She'd always had that calming effect on him.

"Hey Annie . . . this is Jax," dejection evident in his voice. "I just called to say hi. Call me back when you can."

He hung up. He leaned back in the armchair, slumping down to recline his head against the back.

The weight of the world, heavy with all the responsibilities of his family, the ranch, and his parents' situation suddenly seemed to press down on his shoulders all at once. He took a deep breath, letting it out slowly through pursed lips.

He dialed Zeren. No rings, straight to voicemail. Either no service where they were or Zeren had his phone off, not expecting any calls. Jax left a message for Zeren to call as soon as he could.

It was late afternoon. He was hungry. On his way to the restaurant he dialed Annie again. Voicemail. He didn't leave a message this time. He had an early, quiet dinner. Not having anywhere to go, he stayed in the restaurant for a couple of hours.

His server, Sven, a young guy with an Old Nordic name, filled him in on all the local gossip. Maybe a senior in high school, he knew a lot about what was going on in town.

By eight o'clock, Jax returned to his room after getting every little detail he could out of Sven. He called Annie one more time. No answer. It was unlike her to not answer her phone. Could she be out with Beth or some other girlfriend? He'd never had a problem getting ahold of her before. He didn't leave a message. The same with Zeren. When his phone went directly to voicemail, he didn't leave a message.

He would try tomorrow.

Thursday morning. He rose early, as usual, and with his mind fresh from the previous night's rest, an idea popped into his head. It was a long shot, but there were no other alternatives. In fact, he didn't expect anything to come of it, especially after the Dirkfields' cold reaction to his request yesterday.

He first dialed Annie, four rings, and then voicemail. He dressed in less than five minutes and went to the restaurant for breakfast. When he'd finished, he dialed Annie again. Still no answer. He crossed the street to the resort with his specially prepared package.

Jax entered through the front door. A girl probably in her early twenties greeted Jax as he approached the front desk. Her nametag read *Piper*. She was a perky brunette with a big smile. Jax placed the small package on the front counter.

"I'd like to leave this package for Mr. and Mrs. Dirkfield," Jax said. "Can you see that they get it?"

Piper smiled, revealing a large dimple in her rosy right cheek.

She leaned over the counter slowly, scanning the area left and right. She whispered, "It's not, like, a bomb, is it?"

"No, it's five pounds of dirt."

"Dirt? No way." She flashed that perky smile again. "Like, why would you give someone dirt?"

She had a valley-girl way about her. Jax instantly liked her; she was fun.

"Mr. Dirkfield owns a mining laboratory. I want him to test this dirt."

"Cool, right? Like, what's your name so I can tell them who it's from?"

Jax pointed to his business card sealed to the top of the package with the clear packing tape he'd gotten from the owner of the bed and breakfast that morning.

"My name, address, and phone number are right here."

Piper withdrew a piece of paper from under the counter top, placing it in front of him.

"You'll need to, like, fill out this form with your personal info: address, phone number, and email. And I will also need to make a photocopy of your driver's license—it's not, like, for me, though, in case you were wondering." She gave him a playful wink and flashed him her perky smile as she picked up the license from off the countertop.

It was done. He'd delivered the dirt, not the way he'd originally planned it, but it was out of his hands.

By the time he reached his room, it was nine in the morning. He dialed Annie again. It had been over an hour since he'd last called her. Voicemail.

Where could she be? Something had to be wrong.

He called his mother at the hospital. She hadn't heard from Annie. He didn't mention to his mother that he hadn't been able to reach Annie all last night nor this morning. He didn't want to give his mother anything more to worry about. They chatted for a moment before Jax said he needed to go.

He walked down the street window-shopping, trying to pass the time. He didn't know how long he was going to have to wait until he heard from Zeren or Annie, but he wasn't going to spend the day cramped up in his room.

At 10:43 a.m., his phone rang. He about dropped it trying to get it out of his pocket—it could be Annie and he didn't want to miss her call.

It was Zeren.

"Hey, dude," Zeren said. "We're about an hour outside of town."

"You coming in already?" Jax asked.

"Yeah, dude. I shot an Elk early this morning, but Thomas hasn't, and . . ."

"Does he want to stay so he can fill his tag?" Jax crossed his fingers.

"No, he doesn't really care. Says he came just to hang out with me. The tag was free, so it's not like he's losing anything."

Perfect.

"We'll have the driver drop us off at the airport at twelve," Zeren said.

"I'll be there." They both clicked off at the same time.

Chapter 44

Jaxon
The Text

By the time Zeren and Thomas arrived, Jax had been waiting for over an hour. He checked his watch as they jumped out of the truck and grabbed their stuff. 12:37. He was hungry, which didn't help, and he could barely breathe. The air circulation in the airport office, a corrugated metal warehouse, was poor.

Under the circumstances, he would've been in a better mood, except for the fact that he still couldn't reach Annie. He'd been dialing her all morning, and there still was no answer.

His mind had been racing, conjuring up different scenarios of the worst types of accidents she could have had, an accident being the only thing he could think of that would prevent her from answering the phone. Maybe she'd been in a car crash as she entered I-41 from the ranch road. Maybe a horse had kicked her while she was in the barn. There could have been a gas explosion on the ranch, but probably not. Maybe she'd been bitten by a rattlesnake.

Most of the things he'd thought of involved being out on the ranch alone, which meant no one would find her until he got home tonight.

He was sure she was hurt, so he needed to get home quickly to help her. By the time Zeren and Thomas showed up, he was anxious to leave.

They loaded what little gear they had. And, just like Zeren had promised, they loaded the meat from his elk into the extra cargo space of the plane. Jax, wanting to get in the air, quickly ran through his preflight check. All looked good.

They were finally off.

Zeren filled Jax in on all the details of their hunting trip. They'd been flying for about an hour, and so far the trip was uneventful. Exhausted from their hunt, both Zeren and Thomas drifted off to sleep.

Suddenly, Jax's phone buzzed in his pocket. He pulled it out and pressed the button on the side to wake it up. He slid his finger across the screen to unlock the phone. He'd received a text.

It was from Annie.

Finally.

He opened the message.

"Why'd you do it?" His brow furrowed. That was it, that's all the message said.

"What?" He texted back.

"Don't play dumb."

"What do you mean? What's going on?"

"I'm not stupid."

"No, really, what's going on?" Jax texted.

"Your business trip, was it really just a business trip?"

Two Hearts

"Yes."

"Liar, you were with a woman," Annie texted.

Jax touched the icon for contacts. At the top of the list was Annie's name, which he tapped once with his finger. Then he tapped the call button that immediately popped up—the phone dialed her number.

It rang, once, twice, three times, and then one more before her voicemail picked up. He hung up. Just as he did so he received a text from Annie.

"Don't want to talk."

He dialed again. He got her voicemail. He didn't leave a message.

Another text from Annie. "I can't talk to you right now."

Jax dialed a third time—voicemail again.

"Stop calling me, I said I don't want to talk right now," Annie texted.

"What's going on? What's happened? Are you okay?" Jax texted back.

"I'm too emotional. I can't talk right now."

"Has something happened?" Jax texted.

Jax didn't receive a text for several minutes. He started drafting another text to Annie when he received a response from her.

"Kris Dirkfield, you cheater, that's what's going on."

Jax, holding the phone in his right hand, dropped his hand into his lap as he stared out over the horizon. He shook his head from side to side.

Cheater? *Me?* No, never.

He ran his hand through his hair, feeling the dampness along the edge. He was sweating, even though it was cool in the cabin of the plane. He took a giant gulp of air. He let it out slowly like a steam engine releasing its pent-up gas.

He quickly deleted the text he'd been preparing and started another one.

"A complete misunderstanding. Kris Dirkfield is a man," he texted.

"You're with a man?"

His brow furrowed again. He read his last text, the message coming into focusing on the last part—*Kris Dirkfield is a man.*

He laughed, realizing his mistake and Annie's misunderstanding.

"Business trip to meet Kris Dirkfield of Kris Dirkfield International. Kris is really Kristoffer—he is a man."

"Liar."

"Annie, come on, it's me."

"I saw the website; I saw the woman. I saw Kris Dirkfield."

It would be so much easier if he could just speak to Annie and try to explain. He knew he could clear this all up in seconds if he could just talk to her.

He dialed her number again. She didn't answer. He immediately got another text from her.

"Stop calling. I told you I can't talk to you right now."

"We're on our way home. We've been flying for over an hour, and we'll be home soon. I'll explain everything when I get home."

Sitting on the couch and staring at the black screen of the TV, Annie read the text over again. Jax was coming home. She would have to face him. Her middle finger involuntarily found the scar on the side of her head. She started to lose focus.

No, she screamed inside her head. Not now. Rage burned inside her as her surroundings came back into focus. She forced her left hand down, grasping her cell phone with both hands. She drafted another text. "Don't come home to this house. You're not welcome here."

Annie's trembling finger hovered over the green send button. She'd never before been so bold. She'd never before spoken this way to Jax, and she didn't know if she could do so now, even through an emotionally disconnected text message. She started to waiver. Her finger moved across the screen until it hovered over the red end button.

Suddenly the image of Kris Dirkfield, in her black satin dress, her back completely exposed and her tan leg being thrust through the slit in the side, flashed across her mind. Then another image, this one of Mariana Delfino and the red scratch on her face, instantly replaced the image of Kris Dirkfield. The muscles in Annie's jaw tightened, the knuckles of her left hand, gripping the cell phone, turned white. The muscles in her back went rigid. She sat up, gritting her teeth. Annie's finger, moving with purpose, straightened out and pushed the send button. She'd done it.

Chapter 45

Jaxon

Crash

"Can you believe it?" Jax asked. He handed the phone to Zeren sitting in the copilot seat, pointing to the text visible on the screen. The plane, hitting a warm pocket of air, had lurched and both Thomas and Zeren had woken up. "Annie thinks I flew to Pagosa to meet a girl."

Zeren, not taking the time to read the text, immediately raised his hand toward Jax. "Give me a high five dude. You're my hero—double dipping."

"Shut up, I'm not double dipping."

"Didn't know you had it in you," Zeren said.

"Shut up," Jax yelled. "I'd never do that to Annie."

"Okay, so just call her and tell her."

Jax rolled his eyes, and his shoulders slumped. "I've been trying, but she won't answer the phone. She'll only text."

"Sounds like she's too emotional to talk," Thomas said, leaning over the front seats.

"That's what she said," Jax responded.

"Dude, where'd that come from?" Zeren asked. "When did our shy little Thomas become an expert on women?" Zeren ruffled Thomas's hair, messing up his perfect part.

"I'm not, but from what you guys were saying, it sounded—"

"Dude, when was the last time you went on a date?" Zeren asked.

"Well, just so you know, Tayla Olsen and I've been dating for the past couple—"

"You and freckle-faced Tadpole?" Zeren teased. "You can't be serious. What, you two going to have little tadpoles for babies?"

Jax glanced over his shoulder at Thomas, noticing the corners of his mouth turned down slightly at the mention of Tayla Olsen's high school nickname. In school she wore thick, coke-bottle glasses that seemed to make her eyes pop out, which reminded someone of the tadpoles they'd been studying in biology class. Ever since then, she'd been known as Tayla the Tadpole.

"You and Tayla?" Jax asked.

"Yeah, for a couple of years now."

"So, you and Tadpo—" Jax shot Zeren a look that could kill, cutting him off before he could finish the nickname. "So, you and Tayla for a couple of years? That makes you an expert?"

"No, but Jax said Annie wouldn't answer his calls—she would only text. Under the circumstances, if she believes Jax is on a trip to see a woman, she's probably hurting inside, so much so that she probably can't talk to Jax without crying."

"But, you big idiot," Zeren said sarcastically, "you forgot one major part: Jax isn't seeing a woman in Pagosa, is he?"

Thomas either didn't notice Zeren's condescending tone or chose to ignore it when he answered. "No he's not, but Annie doesn't know that. She thinks he is and that's enough to get her all worked up inside."

"Okay, Dr. Phil, whatever you say," Zeren shot back.

But, before Thomas could respond, Jax's phone buzzed in Zeren's hand; he held it up so Jax could see. "You got another text from Annie."

Suddenly there was a loud explosion. The plane lurched violently, dropping out of the sky like a speeding elevator dropping twenty floors in an instant.

Zeren shot out of his seat, having taken off his seat belt five minutes after takeoff because the belt was uncomfortable. His head, followed by his body, crashed into the ceiling, causing the plane to jolt at the force of the impact. Zeren's hand, still grasping Jax's cell phone, slammed into the ceiling, sending the phone hurtling through the air into the front windshield.

The phone smashed into the glass, shattering all over the cockpit. The main body of the phone went in one direction while the back casing and the battery shot off into another.

Jax and Thomas, still in their restraints, remained in their seats.

Short bursts of flame flashed out of the nose of the plane, immediately followed by black smoke pouring in from the engine compartment.

"We've lost the engine," Jax yelled.

The altimeter, spinning backwards, showed their rapid descent. Jax pulled back hard on the yoke, causing the altimeter to slow, but not stop.

"Mayday, Mayday, this is Cessna-seven-seven-one-mike-lima. Mayday, Mayday."

"I don't want to die," Zeren squealed, a wild, high-pitched shrill escaping from his opened mouth.

"Cessna-seven-seven-one-mike-lima, this is Grand Junction Airport, go ahead."

"Mayday, Mayday, we've lost our engine, we're going down," Jax said.

"Seven-seven-one-lima, can you restart the engine?"

"Negative, the engine's on fire," Jax yelled.

"Seven-seven-one-lima, what's your altitude?"

"2,500, and falling fast."

Jax rapped his knuckle on the altimeter hoping that he might slow it down. The needle bounced several times, but it kept spinning backwards. It now read two thousand.

"Seven-seven-one-lima, do you have an emergency transponder?" Grand Junction asked.

Jax tapped the little beige box under the VHF radio. "Affirmative."

"Seven-one-lima, squawk 7700."

Jax spun the knobs on the transponder until the numbers read 7700.

Jax knew once he'd set the transponder to 7700, Grand Junction would be able to pick them up on radar, that way when they went down, any rescue party would be able to find their location quickly.

"Seven-one-lima, we're not picking you up on radar. What's your location?

"We're flying over a valley covered with trees. There are mountains and peaks all around us.

"Seven-one-lima, the mountains maybe interfering with the signal—we don't have you on radar. Can you find a place to land, a road, field, or a meadow?"

"I'll look," Jax said.

An hour and a half from Pagosa Springs put them right in the middle of nowhere, and below them was nothing but a vast carpet of trees—a dense forest with nowhere to land.

Thomas, with his eyes shut tight and his hands clasped in front of him, could be heard praying in the back, repeating over and over the same prayer. "Please don't let us die. Please don't let us die. Please don't let us die."

"I see an opening in the trees," Jax yelled pointing toward the front.

"Trees?" Zeren squealed. "Trees?"

"Grand Junction, this is seven-one-lima, I see an opening in the trees, an open meadow in the valley. It's about three to four miles ahead.

"That's too far, that's way too far," Zeren screamed. "We'll never make it."

"Seven-one-lima, lower your nose just enough to keep it from stalling and aim for that meadow. At your altitude you'll only have one shot at it."

"Affirmative," Jax said.

Jax's natural inclination was to pull back hard on the yoke to keep the nose up, but he forced himself to ease off the pressure to allow the nose of the plane to lower. The effect was immediate. The backwards spinning altimeter sped up, the ground appearing to rush at them, drawing closer than ever.

"We're going to crash!" Zeren screamed. "We're going to crash."

Zeren was losing it. Thomas had quieted down. With his eyes closed tight, his lips were still moving, repeating the same prayer.

"Seven-one-lima, what's your speed and altitude?" Grand Junction asked.

"One thousand feet; sixty-five knots."

"Seven-one-lima, try to maintain your speed and call in after you've landed."

"Affirmative," Jax said. The strain of the moment could be heard in his voice and in his shaky delivery.

Jax ran through his normal landing procedure, even though there was nothing normal about this landing. He checked the throttle. He adjusted the trim on his flaps. He checked the speed—still sixty-five knots. Perfect for landing. The altimeter read five hundred feet. At their current rate of decent they would be on the ground within the next minute or less.

The meadow lay stretched out in front of him, long and skinny. Maybe a hundred yards wide and a half a mile in length, there was plenty of room to land. They were going to make it, he kept telling himself. They had to . . .

He had to for Annie.

An image of Annie's face shot through his mind, just before the wheels hit the meadow floor. They bounced once, then one more time, before making contact with the thick green grass.

"Whoa," Jax yelled, adrenaline pumping through his body. It wasn't a perfect landing, but they were on the ground.

Suddenly, a dark line in the grass appeared out in front of them, cutting across their path.

A stream.

The high grass had concealed the banks of the stream and now there was no time to react.

The front nose wheel dropped into the stream, hit the opposite bank, and then ripped off, flipping the plane over. They nosedived, smashing into a large, flat granite slab, instantly stopping the plane. A hailstorm of loose objects erupted inside of the cabin.

The world was in entire chaos, slamming, smashing, and crashing. Then in one second, there was nothing but silence. No one moved.

Chapter 46

Annie

Home

A bird chirped, its sound crisp and sharp and mingled with a chime. Five chirps. The chirping stopped, replaced by a beautiful chorus of music. Annie felt the smile on her face.

She rolled over on the couch and opened her eyes. She stared at the cuckoo clock, suspended three-fourths of the way up the living room wall. She'd counted correctly. It hadn't been a dream, it was five o'clock—dinnertime. She glanced over to the front window. The sun, visible from the front room, hung above the horizon as it began its western descent. Still early October, the sun wouldn't completely set for another two hours.

She sat up. Dazed and exhausted even though she'd slept for the past three hours, she leaned back against the couch, her head spinning. She glanced around. She couldn't see Jax, nor could she hear him.

Where could he be?

Five o'clock. Of course he wouldn't be in the house at this hour. He'd probably still be out on the ranch. He still had two solid hours of light left to work. He'd be tired and hungry after a hard day of work. She would need to make him dinner. She scooted to the edge of the couch attempting to rise. Her head felt heavy. Her stomach felt queasy. Her body ached. She still had the flu. When she first felt sick, she'd hoped it was the twenty-four-hour flu, but that was a few days ago. She didn't like being sick, not that anyone did. She'd read somewhere that the flu could last up to two weeks. She hoped she wouldn't be sick for that long. Her movements were slow and deliberate. She placed both hands on her knees to steady herself, but something was in her left hand. She glanced down.

Her cell phone.

Like a flash of lightening, it all came back to her—her confrontation, Jax's repeated calls, and . . . her text.

She sagged back into the couch, her hands dropping to her sides. She'd actually done it. She'd told Jax not to come home.

Her mouth noticeably dropped open. Oh, the audacity, the courage behind those last words she'd texted. She'd actually hit the send button. She sat there a moment remembering it all. The reality of what she'd done slowly settled over her. She thought she would have been elated with the fact that she'd been strong, that she'd stood up for herself. But she wasn't.

She scanned the house. Empty. Quiet. Too quiet.

She took a deep breath. It didn't help. She still felt lousy. What had she done?

Before she'd sent her final text, Jax had said he would be home in a couple of hours. Glancing at the clock, he was already two or more hours late.

Annie peered out the front window, but his truck wasn't there, which she already knew.

He would come home. She knew he would. He'd have flowers, a note, and some chocolate. That's what he did. He'd apologize. He'd say he was sorry over and over again. She'd told him to not come home, and she would remind him again, even though she would be glad that he was home safely.

But where was he? He should have been home by now.

She got up and made her way to the kitchen even though she wasn't hungry. She had a queasy stomach and didn't feel like eating much. But she hadn't eaten since late that morning, and she didn't want to have a migraine when Jax showed up to perform his little show. She would just find something small to nibble on.

By 6:45 p.m., the sun had set, but there was still no sign of Jax. Annie considered driving by the airport to see if his plane was in its usual spot, but after putting on her jacket and grabbing the car keys, she'd talked herself out of it.

Don't chase after him. Let him come to you. She returned the keys to the key rack and hung her jacket in the closet. She found a comfortable spot on the couch and turned on the T.V. She surfed the channels for a while, scanning the front window at every creak of the house. Nothing.

She turned off the T.V. just before the ten o'clock news came on, which she hated watching. It was always bad news, and bad news she could do without right now.

She changed into her pajamas. She stepped into the bathroom to brush her teeth. Noticing the Dixie cup dispenser was low, she crossed the front room, peering out the window on her way to the storage room at the back of the house. Nothing. On the way back to the bedroom, she glanced out the front window again—still nothing.

She brushed her teeth and went back to the front room to turn off all the lights, which was something Jax had always done their entire married lives. She peeked out the window again, but the front yard was the same as before—empty.

The click of the light switch and the sudden darkness caused her to jump. She turned the light back on.

Don't be silly.

She turned off the light and made her way down the dark hallway to the bedroom. She turned off the bedroom light and climbed into bed. Jax hadn't come home, just like she'd told him. Maybe he'd listened to her this time, and maybe . . . he wasn't coming home. The house was empty and dark.

She was alone.

Chapter 47

Jaxon

Alive

It was silent except for the gurgling stream underneath them. The sound of moving water is usually peaceful, which helps some people go to sleep.

Except Jax wasn't trying to go to sleep. His plane had flipped over, and now Jax hung upside down, suspended in the air, being held in place by his seat belt. The weight of his body added a great deal of pressure to the belt across his lap, which cut into his left hip. With delicate fingers, he managed to operate the latch on the buckle, dropping him from the seat. He crashed into the ceiling, which was now the floor, with his head. He groaned at the impact.

His right leg hadn't come all the way with him. When his body dropped from the seat, his right leg twisted, still pinned tightly against the hood of the plane. Bolts of electricity shot through him. He quickly got his arms under him and pushed off the ceiling, raising his body, which relieved the pressure on his leg. He was in a precarious position. His strength would soon run out, and he would drop again. He had to free his leg.

Jax scanned his surroundings.

Sunlight streamed in through all sides of the now damaged plane. All the windows had been smashed out, and he could feel a light breeze filtering through the open crevices. He smelled pine trees, wildflowers, and water.

He turned his head to the right toward the copilot's seat.

"Zeren, Thomas," he said, whispering their names.

He could hear noises coming from where Zeren had been sitting. He heard nothing from the back seat.

"Zeren?" Jax asked again. "Are you okay?"

After a moment's pause and some moving around, Zeren responded. "Yeah, I'm okay, just a bit shaken up."

"Thomas?" Jax asked again.

Nothing.

"Thomas, are you okay?" Jax asked again, but there was still no response.

Jax could barely move with his leg pinned down, but he twisted his body slightly to the right, trying to look into the back seat. Pain shot up his right leg, but he held his position, using his arms to stabilize himself. He closed his eyes, as the muscles tightened over his entire body, fighting off the pain. After a moment, he opened his eyes. He tried to locate Thomas, but he was still out of position. He gritted his teeth to find a better angle, twisting a little more despite the pain.

He found it. Jax could see the top of Thomas's head as he hung suspended in his seat belt. His arms, hanging straight down as if he were a referee signaling a touchdown, were motionless.

Jax reached back with his hand and gave Thomas a gentle nudge. His body moved with the force, but then it swung back into position. Lifeless.

"I think Thomas is dead," Jax said.

"What?"

"He's not moving. I can't tell if he's breathing."

"Really?" Zeren said.

Jax stretched. "I can't quite reach him. My leg is stuck. Can you reach him?" Jax asked.

"No, I'm not in a good position."

Jax could see Zeren out of the corner of his eye. He was sitting cross-legged on the ceiling of the plane. He didn't seem to be in any kind of distress. *You can't reach him or you don't want to reach him? Jerk.* Either way, Jax had to get closer to feel for a pulse.

Jax planted his left foot on the side of the plane and pushed, trying to gain a couple more inches. He gasped from the pain, but he didn't stop pushing, as even more pain shot through his leg. He closed his eyes, stretched out, and reached.

He first tried for the neck, wanting to place his fingers against Thomas's throat. It was just out of reach.

He next tried for the wrist. Both of Thomas's wrists were further from Jax than the throat, hanging straight down from his body. He couldn't reach them directly, so he pulled on Thomas's sleeve, bringing the left wrist closer to him.

He took Thomas's wrist between his thumb and first two fingers and pressed lightly while holding his own breath.

"I feel a pulse," Jax said, exhaling. "He's still alive."

"Oh good," Zeren said. Jax craned his neck to glance at Zeren, even though it brought immense pain from the effort. Zeren's delivery was all wrong. It was cold and flat, without any emotion.

"That's all you have to say?" Jax said through clenched teeth.

"What?" Zeren snarled. "Okay, so he's alive, that's great, but have you noticed?" He tried the handle on the door that was right next to him, "we're stuck in the plane." He shrugged, as if the door being jammed was the end of the world.

"Seriously, Zeren?" Jax's head dropped down in disgust. "Thomas could've been dead."

"Yeah, so. If we don't get out of here, we'll be dead too."

Jax glared at Zeren. He didn't mean it. He couldn't have. Thomas was their friend. After a moment, each staring at the other, Jax shifted his gaze to the door. "Why don't you put both feet against the door and try kicking it out."

"Good idea," Zeren said.

Zeren spun around, positioning his feet against the door.

"Wait," Jax said. "Let me brace myself before you start rattling the cage."

Jax lowered himself back to his side of the plane, easing the pressure on his pinned leg. He planted his free foot in the space next to the brake pedals. He fumbled around with his hands blindly at his sides, grabbing anything attached to the plane.

"Okay, I'm ready," Jax said.

Zeren kicked once, violently shaking the plane—Jax let out a squeal of pain.

Zeren didn't even look up. He kicked again and again. Each time he kicked, the enormous object that was pinning Jax's leg vibrated, sending sharp stabbing pains up his leg and into his body.

After the fifth kick, Jax couldn't take it anymore. "Stop," he yelled, but he was too late. Zeren was already in motion, kicking the door a sixth time. Jax clenched his teeth against the pain.

"Just a couple more and I think it will come open," Zeren said.

"Give me a second," Jax breathed heavily. He shifted his weight, trying to find a slightly more comfortable spot. He braced himself again. "Okay, I'm ready," he said.

Zeren kicked the door three more times, each time harder than the last, violently shaking the plane, causing Jax's leg to ignite with pain. The door finally burst open on the last kick.

"I'm free," Zeren yelled. He quickly rolled through the open door, disappearing from sight.

"Hey!" Jax yelled. "Come help us out!"

After a moment, Zeren's head appeared in the doorway. "Relax, dude. I was coming back." He drew up close to Jax, observing the situation.

"Inspecting the plane from outside, you can see where the engine jammed into the cockpit when it hit the ground. That's probably what pinned your leg."

"Can you do anything to help me get out?"

"Yeah, let me see if I can push the engine enough to free your leg."

Zeren sat down and spun his legs around, this time facing into the plane. He placed both feet against the hood of the plane, inches from Jax's pinned leg.

"Don't kick. That will hurt too much," Jax said.

"Relax, Jax. I'm just going to push it with both of my feet first." Zeren situated himself at an angle in the cockpit, his feet crossing over the middle of the plane into Jax's seat compartment, resting on the hood, while his back found a spot against his now upside down chair. "But, if I have to kick it, I'll do whatever I have to do to get you out."

Zeren closed his eyes, took a deep breath, and, straining every muscle in his body, pushed with everything he had. His face turned bright red, the veins in his neck popping out as he surged.

Jax felt nothing at first. Then suddenly the pressure on his leg lessened.

"It's working," Jax said. "Do it again."

Zeren relaxed, took another breath, and pushed again.

This time there was a cracking sound as the hood of the plane shifted. The noise seemed to inspire Zeren. He didn't relax this time to take a breath, but instead he grunted as he strained harder. His face turned dark red as the blood raced through him.

The hood shifted again. Jax's leg fell from its hanging position, dropping him onto the ceiling. *Freed at last.*

"You did it," Jax said. "Thank y—"

But Zeren had already climbed out of the plane and disappeared.

"Hey, help me get Thomas out!" Jax said.

After a minute, Zeren came back and squatted in the doorway. His shoulders slumped as he glanced back at Thomas. Jax knew what he was thinking.

Self-centered smuck, only thinks of himself.

Jax, with his hurt leg, and Zeren, with his all-too-important attitude, got Thomas out of the plane. They'd crashed directly in the middle of the meadow, about fifty yards from the forest in either direction. They carried Thomas to a large ponderosa pine set back thirty feet from the edge of the meadow, moving him out of the sun. Jax propped his head up with his jacket and put a blanket over him to keep him warm.

Jax returned to the plane and grabbed his flight pack, which had flown from the back storage compartment to Thomas's seat during the crash, now lying on the ceiling of the plane. Whenever he flew, Jax always carried a small survival backpack with him in case of an emergency. He'd never had to use it until now. When he got back to Thomas and Zeren, he suggested they retrieve the rest of their gear from the plane.

Zeren stood as if he were getting ready to follow Jax. "I'm going to scout the area," Zeren said. "You know, search for any signs of people, like roads, cars, or cabins, that sort of thing."

Jax stared at him hard. "You're going to scout for signs?" He and Zeren had grown up together. Jax knew Zeren couldn't tell the difference between the mark of a ten-speed bicycle tire and that of an ATV tire.

Scout for signs? Jax wasn't stupid. Zeren just didn't want to help. *Typical, lazy Zeren.* Jax was too tired and too much in pain to worry about it.

With a great deal of effort, Jax stood up from where he'd been sitting next to Thomas and hobbled over to a wall of rocks. He leaned against them to catch his breath before continuing on.

Jax forced a smile. "Don't be gone long. It'll be dark soon."

"I won't be long."

Right, just long enough for me to get everything out of the plane by myself.

Zeren turned, took one step toward the forest, and stopped. Suddenly he turned back, excitement in his eyes. Zeren stared out toward the meadow. "Do you hear that?" he asked. Jax turned to the meadow. He heard it now. Jax's heart rate increased a beat as he recognized the sound of a distant rotor blade pounding the air. They'd been found.

Jax could see a helicopter heading in their direction a hundred feet off the ground at the south end of the valley. It had no under-carriage rails to land on, nor did it have any wheels protruding from its body. Retractable wheels, for sure. This was a sleek, elongated helicopter, corporate executive in style, that looked built for speed and comfort. It had a distinctive paint scheme. The body was primarily white, with red and blue stripes running parallel down the middle. There was some type of detailing in black, but it was indecipherable at that distance. Jax had seen those colors before, but he couldn't remember where. Zeren stepped up beside him, peering down the valley.

The helicopter was coming fast.

Jax started screaming. He waved his arms, frantically jerking them up and down as if the very act would launch him into the air to his would-be rescuers. It was unnecessary though. The helicopter was already flying directly to them.

Chapter 48

Valentino

In Plain Sight

Valentino pointed straight ahead through the front windshield of the helicopter. "There they are, coming out from under those trees." He climbed from the cockpit into the back compartment where Paolo waited with his AK47. Valentino picked up his own weapon, a Heckler & Koch UMP9 semi-automatic machine gun, lying on the back seat. Exclusively used by law enforcement, you had to have special connections to get a weapon like this one. Fortunately for Valentino, Mr. Sebasti could get him practically anything he wanted.

With a flick of a switch, the H&K UMP9 could be set to a single shot, a two-round burst, or a full automatic trigger configuration. For this evening's target practice, Valentino chose the two-round burst setting, which would allow for better control and accuracy. Since his targets were standing in plain sight, they would be easy pickings.

Two Hearts

He turned back to the pilot. "Bring us in low and make a sweeping pass. We'll finish what our little plane accident didn't."

Missing Carr by seconds in Montana, Valentino and the boys were sent to Pagosa Springs to rendezvous with a mechanic, another one of Sebasti's henchmen. While Valentino, Paolo, and Lucero chatted with the single airport attendant in Pagosa Springs, the mechanic went to work on the Cessna. Five minutes later, the mechanic had finished. He'd fixed it so the engine of the plane would explode an hour or so after takeoff. The plane would crash, killing all occupants, including Carr. Kill Carr and be done with it, that's what Mr. Sebasti had wanted.

Valentino cocked the weapon cradled in his hands. The pilot dropped the helicopter down to fifty feet off the ground as they drew closer.

A gust of wind filled the back compartment as Valentino slid open the back door of the helicopter. He spread out his feet and leaned against the back of the opened doorway while Paolo stood at the front of it. Lucero wasn't with them. He'd flown back to Las Vegas with the mechanic.

Paolo had a nasty grin on his face, and Valentino knew what was going through Paolo's mind. They were about to kill Carr, and Paolo was in his element. He lived for this kind of action. Nothing pleased him more. Real live target practice. Bracing himself against the door frame, Valentino pointed the muzzle of the H&K outside, waiting for the targets to come into view.

"They've seen us," Jax said. He stopped flailing his arms. "We're saved—that didn't take Grand Junction that long to send help."

From where he stood, Jax could see the side door of the helicopter slide open. It was still too far to make out any details, but he could see two men wearing black clothes standing at each side of the open doorway.

Suddenly, gunfire burst from the helicopter. Rock fragments, exploding from the rock wall in front of him, sprayed him and Zeren in the face. They both dove to the ground just as a second round of fire came from the helicopter.

"What the . . ." Jax screamed.

The helicopter passed by, but not before a third burst of gunfire peppered the rock wall. Jax and Zeren clawed the ground, trying to keep as low a profile as possible while bullets whizzed over their heads.

"Who are those guys?" Jax yelled. "Why are they trying to kill us?"

Zeren didn't respond.

The sound of the helicopter faded as it made a wide sweeping arc, positioning itself for a second pass.

This gave Jax the opportunity he needed.

Commando style, Jax used his arms and elbows to pull himself over the ground to his flight pack leaning against the tree next to Thomas. Ripping it open, he rifled through the contents, pulling out a compressed rain poncho and a Ziploc bag containing four Clif bars, four small square boxes of purified drinking water, and a first aid kit. He got to his wool sweater stuffed in the bottom. He'd packed this backpack the night before they left, and he knew what was under the sweater before he lifted it out.

There, sitting in the bottom of the pack, was his father's Model 1911 semiautomatic Colt .45. Blue in color, it had a dark walnut hand grip. Next to the pistol lay a box of fifty extra rounds. It was loaded, carrying a full magazine of seven rounds.

Jax always envisioned crashing in a remote part of Montana where he'd have to survive several days, facing extreme weather conditions, lack of food, and wild animals like grizzly bears, wolves, and mountain lions. He never thought he would have to use it to defend himself against someone trying to kill him.

He grabbed the .45 and the extra rounds from the pack and dragged himself back to the rock wall. Zeren's eyes went wide when he saw the gun. "What's that for?"

"Survival."

"What, you planning on killing someone?"

"Whatever it takes." Jax rolled to his back and grabbed the gun with both hands. He cocked it, putting a round in the chamber. "Whatever it takes," he said again.

Partially hidden by the rock wall, he pointed the pistol in the air, taking aim at the approximate position the helicopter would pass on its next flyby. Jax closed his left eye, sighting down the barrel with his right. He then opened his left eye and, with his peripheral vision, watched the helicopter as it completed its arcing turn.

The helicopter was coming from the opposite direction this time. The two men in black were standing on the opposite side of the helicopter at the opened back door.

They pointed the muzzles of their automatic weapons in Zeren and Jax's direction.

They were coming in slow and low, not planning on making a fast pass this time.

Jax lowered his weapon, concealing it for the moment. He didn't want to give them any forewarning that he was prepared to fight back. Although he had plenty of bullets, he knew he would only get one chance. They had automatic rifles. He had a pistol. The odds were not in his favor.

Zeren was to his left, the side the supposed rescuers were coming from. "Do you have a good view of the helicopter?" Jax asked.

"No better than you do," Zeren responded with a slight edge in his voice. Jax brushed it off, attributing the edge in his voice to the stress of the situation.

"I want you to lie down at the edge of the pile of rocks. When you see the helicopter directly in front of us, let me know."

"What you planning on doing?"

Jax sighed. He didn't have time to explain all the details, so he just said, "Spray and pray." He'd heard that term before and figured it applied to what he planned on doing.

He wouldn't have time to aim and select his targets—he'd be dead before he got off his first shot. If he pointed the .45 in the general direction of where he wanted to hit, firing as quickly as possible, he could empty the magazine, all seven rounds, and he might hit something. That's what he was praying for.

Zeren, kissing the dirt with his chest, slid down to the end of the rock wall. He peered around to the open meadow. Jax lay against the rock pile, his head at least a foot below the top. He waited and listened. He could hear the thump of the rotor blades getting louder. The limbs of the trees rattled violently as the blades of the helicopter created chaos with the air. *Anytime now, Zeren.*

"Now?" Jax yelled.

"Not yet."

A dust cloud swirled in the air, and the leaves on the trees ripped from the branches. The helicopter must be about to land on them, they seemed so close. Jax held to his hiding spot, waiting for the signal.

"Now!" Zeren yelled.

Jax didn't hesitate. Clenching the .45 in both hands, he leapt to his feet. The helicopter hovered twenty feet off the ground one hundred feet in front of them.

He pulled the trigger as fast as he could, aiming his shots at the engine. The second he started firing, rock fragments and dust kicked up around him, but he didn't move, intent on emptying his weapon.

One, two, three, and four, he counted in his head as he pulled the trigger, the pistol leaping in his hands.

A bullet burned his side, just under his left arm. He felt the searing pain, but he didn't stop. He pulled the trigger, five and six, he counted. A bullet slammed into him, hitting him like a sledge hammer, violently throwing him to the ground. He hit the dirt hard. His arms jerked up. He lost his grip on the Colt, sending it flying over his head.

Chapter 49

Jaxon

Hit

It was quiet. With his eyes closed, Jax rolled his head to the left and then gently to the right. There was no sound. No rifle fire and . . . no helicopter noise.

Was he dead?

He opened his eyes. Through the canopy of tree branches overhead, he could see the last rays of sun turning the sky on fire before it disappeared. He tried to move, but as he did so, burning pain shot through his left side.

So much pain. He definitely wasn't dead.

Reaching over with his right hand, he touched his left side. His shirt was wet. He raised his right hand over his eyes. Just as he feared, it was red with blood. He rolled to his right side.

He gently probed around with his fingers where he'd been shot. Drenched with blood, his shirt clung to his skin. Through his shirt he could feel two holes in his side. He'd been hit twice, both times in the fleshy part of his body, just below his rib cage, and just above his hip bone. But, the position of the holes bothered him. One was on the front side and the other one more toward his back side, almost as if. . .

The bullet had gone completely through him. He'd only been hit once.

He let out his breath, which he'd been holding as he examined the wound, fearing the worst. Getting shot wasn't good news, but at least he didn't have any broken bones, and it appeared that the bullet was out of him.

He'd been lucky.

He rolled to his back. He tried to sit up, but mind-numbing pain shot through him. He just lay there.

He craned his neck back and forth, searching behind him the best he could for his .45. Nothing. He'd fired his Colt six times, and more than likely, missed every time. But the gun still had one more round in it, and he would feel better with the weight of it in his hand. But he couldn't see it anywhere.

"Zeren?" Jax groaned.

"What?"

Rolling his head to the side from his prone position, Jax could see Zeren still curled up in a little ball behind the rock pile, his arms wrapped tight around his head, protecting it from flying debris. He hadn't moved during the entire shooting spree.

"Are you hit?" Jax asked.

"No."

Jax tried raising his left arm, but burning pain shot through his side. He gritted his teeth, closing his eyes tight until the pain had faded.

Raising his good arm over his head, Jax pointed in the direction of the bushes behind him. "My gun, I've lost it back there. Can you help me get it?"

"You don't need it right now."

"What?"

"You hit the helicopter or the pilot. Maybe both."

"What do you mean?"

"It's gone," Zeren said. He sat up, leaning his back against the rock pile.

"What do you mean, it's gone?"

"It's gone, okay? The helicopter, it flew away after you shot it."

"It's gone?"

"Get up here and see for yourself if you don't believe me."

"I'm hit, you idiot. I can't move. Just tell me what you saw." Jax bit his lip, trying to hold back his frustration.

Zeren sighed, letting out his breath. He rolled his shoulders and dropped his head before he spoke. "From what I saw, you must have hit the helicopter. After you shot the last bullet and just before you fell down, the helicopter started spinning out of control. It rose slightly off the ground, tilted its nose downward, and flew off down the valley, smoke pouring from its engine."

Jax needed to get up just to see for himself. He reached over with his right hand, securing his left arm tight against his body. With great effort he rolled to his right side with his right arm pressed against his chest, keeping his left arm and shoulder as still as possible. He positioned himself in the right spot so he could get up.

So far so good.

He took a deep breath and let it out slowly. This next part was going to require a great deal of core body strength, strength that would put pressure on his injured side. He clenched the muscles in his jaw and grunted, partly from exertion and partly to shield against the pain he knew was coming.

He moved again.

Using his bent right arm as a wedge, he pushed himself off the ground.

Pain. A lot of pain. As his stomach muscles tightened with the exertion of sitting up, electricity shot through his side. Gritting his teeth again and grunting harder, he didn't stop until he was completely upright. He was still sitting on the ground, but he was up.

His chest heaved from the effort, sucking in gallons of air with each intake.

When his breathing had slowed, he inched his way over to the rock pile. With his good arm, he pulled himself to his feet and leaned his body against the pile of rocks for support.

"And just for the record," Jax said, "I didn't just lie down to take a nap. I got shot and knocked off my feet trying to save your neck."

"Whatever."

Ungrateful pig. Jax stared at Zeren in total disgust.

Jax turned his attention back to the meadow, scanning it from left to right.

The helicopter might have left the scene, but it wasn't gone. Jax could see smoke rising in the distance at the southernmost point of the meadow. He could barely make out the top of the rotor blades of the helicopter. Now he understood the source of the acrid smell he'd detected in the air. The wind, blowing slightly in their direction, had carried the smoke from the helicopter to their makeshift campsite.

"The helicopter, it's down there." Jax pointed south. "I must've hit it, forcing it down. But it doesn't look like it crashed—it's just sitting on its wheels."

"At least they're gone," Zeren said, coming off the ground and standing next to Jax.

"For the moment," Jax said.

"You don't think they'll come back, do you?" Zeren asked.

"I do. They mean business, and I think they intend to come back and finish what they started."

Zeren turned away from the meadow and took his frustrations out on a little sapling. He kicked and stomped on the helpless tree, pulverizing it in the dirt. He screamed as loud as he could.

"Why won't they just leave me alone and go away?"

Jax turned to Zeren. "Why won't who leave you alone?"

Zeren's eyes flared, fear dilating his pupils. "Those guys—why won't they just go away?"

"Zeren," Jax stared at his friend. "What aren't you telling me?"

"Nothing."

Zeren turned away from Jax, brushing dirt off his pants. He bent down and fiddled with his shoelaces.

"Zeren, do you know those guys in the helicopter?"

"No . . . not personally."

"Zeren!" Jax yelled, not able to control his frustration any longer. "Who are they, and why are they trying to kill us?"

"They're not trying to kill you. They are trying to kill me."

"Excuse me," Jax said, pointing to his bloody side. "I'm the one shot here." Jax hobbled the best he could on his one good leg. He managed to draw himself within two feet of Zeren as he knelt down adjusting his shoelaces.

Jax bent down, fighting through the pain, and with both hands grabbed Zeren by the collar, jerking him off the ground. Jax was at least a foot taller than Zeren and weighed at least sixty pounds more. Jax's upper body was like granite from years of working in the mines. Jax pulled Zeren up, drawing his face within inches of his. "Why are they trying to kill us?"

Zeren, unable to keep eye contact, turned and stared off into the distance. He mumbled, "I owe them money."

"Figures," Jax said, not at all surprised. "How much?"

"It's none of your business," Zeren shot back, regaining some of his composure. Zeren struggled under Jax's vise-grip hold, but was unable to break free. As he twisted around, Jax winced in pain but didn't let go. He drew Zeren closer, narrowing the gap.

"How much?" Jax snarled, spit shooting from his open mouth.

Zeren hesitated, but finally said, "Two million."

That surprised Jax. That was a lot of money.

Jax tightened his grip. Maybe he should just keep Zeren pinned here against these rocks and turn him over to his friends when they showed up. Maybe they would let him and Thomas go once they had Zeren. But Jax wasn't stupid. Even if those guys from the helicopter had Zeren, they wouldn't let Jax and Thomas live.

Jax shoved Zeren hard, causing him to stumble backward and fall to the ground.

Jax turned away, not able to look at his friend. An awkward silence filled the air. But it didn't last long.

"If they're coming back, we better get out of here," Zeren said.

"We aren't going anywhere. This is as good a place as any to make a stand."

"We going to fight?"

"We're going to survive."

Jax glanced out to the open meadow at his upside down plane. He would need his rifle if they were going to survive the night. They would also need food and water. Zeren, sitting on the ground with his back to the pile of rocks, was useless, so Jax didn't even bother asking for his help.

Jax started making his way toward the plane. With his eyes going from the crashed plane to the southern portion of the meadow, he kept an eye out for any movement from the downed helicopter.

Once Jax got out in the open meadow, he moved as fast as he could despite the injuries to his leg and side.

"Hey, where're you headed?" Zeren called to him.

Jax shook his head. He stopped walking. Maybe it was the tension. Maybe it was the heat of the day. Or maybe it was Zeren's attempt to be funny. He wanted to let it go, but the stupidity of the question wouldn't let him. With great effort, he turned and glared at Zeren. "You honestly don't know where I'm going?" he asked.

Zeren shrugged, which just about drove Jax crazy. Jax sighed and said, "It will be getting dark in an hour or so, and I'd like to have my rifle before your friends show up again." Not waiting for a response, Jax turned and hobbled to the plane.

Chapter 50

Annie

Empty

Friday morning, Annie slipped out of bed and went into the bathroom. Jax's toothbrush holder was empty, he hadn't returned last night. Annie found one of Jax's big T-shirts and pulled it over her head. The T-shirt smelled like Jax, which drew a smile to her lips.

She picked up her cell phone. No missed calls. No waiting text messages.

With just the T-shirt on, she wandered through the house, hoping she might find him curled up on the couch in the living room. Maybe he'd come in late and hadn't wanted to wake her.

The couch was empty.

Standing in the empty living room, she held up the phone. She wanted to call him, but she couldn't. She had to wait to hear from him. He had to be the one that called. How would it look if, after telling him not to come home, she called to see where he was? Stupid.

Annie ate a light breakfast, wanting to save her appetite for when Jax returned. She knew he'd be hungry.

She showered and dressed. On her way into town to pick up a few groceries, Annie drove by the airport parking lot. Jax's truck was still in the same stall. It hadn't moved since Wednesday.

After completing her grocery shopping, Annie returned home. She made some lemonade. She filled her cup with ice and poured herself a tall glass. She carried the cup and the pitcher with the remaining juice outside to the front porch swing to wait.

He would be home any minute.

It was the first weekend of October, and the weather was pleasant. The temperature for early October normally hovered around seventy degrees for a high. Glancing at the outside thermometer nailed to the support beam of the covered front porch, the temperature had already hit seventy-five degrees. At ten o'clock, the sun hadn't reached its zenith yet, but the day was turning out to be a warm one.

Annie drank her lemonade and waited. After finishing her first glass of juice, she poured herself another one.

She heard a honk, and her heart leapt, skipping a beat. The sound surprised her at first, not knowing where it had come from. She glanced down the lane until it curved and disappeared. Nothing.

She heard a honk again and then another and another. The honking intensified—it was all around her. It wasn't coming from the lane. She stepped off the porch and stared up. Geese, hundreds of them, flying south for the winter in a V formation, passed overhead. She watched for a minute as they flew over, then, lowering her head, dejected, she returned to the porch.

It wasn't Jax.

She picked up her glass and emptied it. She poured herself another and dropped into the swing.

Geese honking? It didn't even sound like a car horn. Who was she kidding? But she knew the sound had quickened the flow of blood through her veins—it had made her look down the lane toward the state highway.

The sun now straight over head, the temperature had risen by four degrees. Seventy-nine. Dillon, Montana, was experiencing a heat wave.

The pitcher of lemonade was half gone. At this rate, the heat spurring her on, she was going to have to make more.

She was hungry. Annie went to the kitchen and made a turkey sandwich, hurrying as quickly as she could. She wanted to be on the front porch when Jax drove up. She grabbed a lunch-size bag of Nacho Cheese Doritos, Jax's favorite, loaded a plate of Double Stuf Oreos, also Jax's favorite, and returned to the porch. She placed her food on the small wicker table next to the swing and sat down.

Picking up her plate, she scanned Jax's regular parking space out in front of the barn. It was empty. She let her eyes wander down the lane, not missing an inch, until she came to the curve. Nothing. She swallowed hard, a lump rising in her throat. Still no Jax.

She picked up her sandwich, scanning the lane one more time before taking a bite. The road stayed empty. She peered at the sandwich in her hand. Suddenly, she wasn't hungry anymore.

She pulled her phone out of her pocket. No missed calls. No text messages. She hit the contact button. Jax's name was at the top with two capital A's placed at the beginning of his name so it would show up first on the list. She tapped his name, but before it started to dial, she hit the cancel button. No, he had to call first.

He isn't coming back, a little voice inside her head whispered, *just like you told him*. He'd said he was coming home. She knew Jax. He would try to apologize. But he still hadn't returned. No box of chocolates. No flowers. No card. He never tried to call. He wasn't here. He'd done what he was told, and now he was with another woman.

Annie set the sandwich back on the little white paper plate sitting in her lap, and with a trembling hand, she set the plate on the table next to the swing.

With her elbows on her knees, she dropped her head into her hands, covering her face. She could feel a slight vibration in her face from her trembling arms.

What surprised her were the feelings that raced through her. She half expected the lump to return to her throat and the tears to start pouring out, but that wasn't how she felt. She felt the opposite, like her blood was about to boil right out of her skin.

With nostrils flared, she planted her feet firmly on the porch and stood. She placed her hands on her hips with her elbows out wide. She thrust out her chest.

He wasn't coming home because he was with *her*. The words Annie had heard her mother say so many times when she was growing up flooded her mind. *You can't trust men. They only think of one thing, and one thing only: themselves.*

Whether she said it out loud or the words only sounded in her head, she didn't know, but she distinctly heard, "Two can play this game."

Chapter 51

Jaxon

Survival

What should have taken less than five minutes took just over twenty, but when he was back under the cover of the trees, Jax had three rifles and Thomas's backpack, which was the easiest to get at in the upside down plane. With Thomas's backpack stuffed with food, water, and several boxes of rifle shells for all three weapons, they were now prepared to make a stand.

Jax cleaned and dressed the wound at his side, wrapping his body three times with gauze to slow the bleeding. He examined his leg, cutting open his pant leg to reveal the damage. It felt just as it looked. Miserable. All of the skin around the knee was a ghastly yellow and black. The skin on the inside of his leg was torn and mangled just below his knee, where it had been pinned against the plane.

He could deal with the discoloration from the bruise and the torn skin. His knee caused him the most concern. It was swollen to the size of a small melon. With the discoloration, it looked more like a rotten melon. To make things worse, his leg, slightly bent at the knee as a result of the swelling, was locked in place at a bad angle, making it difficult for him to stand on his good leg.

He blew out his breath, glancing over his handy work. With supplies from his first aid kit, he'd cleaned and wrapped his leg with gauze. It was going to slow him down. He would just have to make do—like he always did.

Jax glanced out in the meadow toward the helicopter.

He figured the first attack would come from the side. Zeren's friends knew that he and Zeren had at least one weapon, but that was about it. He didn't think they would charge from the front again, fearing they might take more casualties.

Thomas still hadn't regained consciousness. He was lying at the back of the base of the large tree that had provided them shelter during the initial attack. Purely out of luck, Jax figured, Thomas hadn't been hit by flying debris or a stray bullet. During the next attack he may not be so lucky, though, and Jax wanted to make sure he was well protected.

"Zeren, we need to move Thomas back, further into the trees behind a rock shelter or a fallen log to keep him safe."

"He's fine," Zeren said. "Let's just leave him where he is."

"We aren't leaving him there—he has to be moved, and you're getting off your lazy butt to help me." Jax had moved while he was speaking and now stood towering over Zeren.

"Get up," Jax said, "before I make you."

Zeren rolled his eyes before speaking. "Whatever." He took his time, but finally got to his feet and stood next to Jax. "We going or not?" Zeren swung his arm, turning at the same time, gesturing in Thomas's direction.

A shower of dirt spat up from the ground five feet behind Zeren and directly where he'd been standing. The report of a rifle immediately followed.

Pure luck. He'd turned and saved his own life.

Zeren and Jax dove for the ground. There were several follow-up shots, just in case the first round had missed its target, which it had.

Jax rolled to his side, picking up his rifle in the process. He crouched below the top of the rock pile and laid his gun across the top. Gradually poking his head over the top of the rocks, he raised his rifle. He peered over the scope to the other side of the meadow where he thought the shot had come from. The shadows were long in the meadow, the sun suspended above the western horizon, just about to disappear. Maybe another half hour of light.

He positioned his eye up to his scope, scanning the general area. He panned, slowing, watching for any movement on the other side of the meadow.

Suddenly, to his right a flash of fire caught his attention. A bullet shot across the meadow, tearing through the branches of the trees overhead. It was high and to his left. Then another one, still to the left, but by the sound it made through the trees, it seemed a little lower. Fifteen seconds later another bullet slammed into the trunk of a tree behind him and to his left.

Zeren's friends were fishing, probing the area with bullets, hoping to get lucky. They had no visible targets—Jax and Zeren lay behind the rocks—so they were shooting random shots hoping to score a hit.

Jax glanced over his shoulder. Thomas, on the other hand, was still partially in the open. The shots coming into their protected oasis were high and to the left. But, if and when the shots straightened out, Thomas would be exposed. He'd be in danger. He had to be moved to safer ground.

Jax peered through his scope across the meadow and to his right, where the flames from the muzzle had given away the shooter's position. He could easily see three distinct men standing relatively close together. Jax estimated their range at one hundred and fifty yards.

The three stood in the trees, not out in the open meadow. No other cover. They weren't standing behind any trees, nor did they take shelter behind any rocks, and from Jax's vantage point, there were plenty rocks to choose from. They were out in the open, as if they didn't expect any return fire.

They knew he and Zeren had a weapon, but they must have figured it was empty and that he and Zeren had no more rounds. Or maybe they thought they were out of range. They probably felt safe where they were standing.

He scanned the three men. One was short and carried a rifle, and the other two were tall. Only one of the tall guys carried a rifle. The other tall one must be the pilot.

Jax decided to give the three visitors something to think about. At one hundred and fifty yards, a shot he could probably make with his eyes closed, he could pick a fly off any one of their foreheads.

A head shot? Easy. The Bible said not to kill, but . . . under the circumstances . . . he would make an exception.

Killing one of the three, though, would make it too easy for them. If they had an injured person to take care of, that would slow them down. Even the playing field.

A shoulder shot then. Plus, injuring a shoulder might make it difficult to shoot a weapon. What shoulder? Depends on if the shooter's a righty or a lefty.

Suddenly, a rifle cracked and a bullet whipped overhead, thudding into a tree behind him. This one was closer to the center. The shots were slowly moving inward.

Jax pulled up his rifle, positioning the scope to his right eye. He closed his left eye. The short one, kneeling down in a shooting position, had his rifle pulled up to his right shoulder. Crack. Jax saw the flame break from the muzzle. Dirt kicked up from the ground just behind him. Getting closer. Jax kept his eye glued to the scope, waiting for the right moment.

The short one dropped the rifle from off his shoulder to cock the weapon. Just what Jax had been waiting for.

He placed the crosshairs on the short one's right shoulder, took a small breath and held it. He pulled the trigger.

There was a deafening boom as the rifle leapt in his hands. A .338 Winchester Magnum bullet at 200 grains of powder has a muzzle velocity of 2,950 feet per second, more than twice the speed of sound. With only 450 feet to travel, it took the bullet a fifteenth of a second to reach its target. When the bullet hit, with its 3,866 foot-pound of muzzle energy, it was as if its target had been hit by a Mack truck traveling at turbo speed. He lifted into the air and slammed into the ground ten feet back from where he'd been kneeling. Immediately he let out a blood-curdling scream.

Nailed him.

Jax surveyed the scene. The two tall ones had disappeared, hidden behind either a tree or a rock. The short one, lying on his back, his left hand holding what was left of his shoulder, squirmed in pain. Perfect shot—injured but not dead. The short one wouldn't be using his weapon anytime soon.

One down, two to go.

Chapter 52

Valentino

A Promise

"I'm hit, I'm hit," Paolo cried. "Help me, Val, help me."

Valentino poked his head out from behind the tree where he'd been hiding and watched as Paolo squirmed on the ground fifteen feet in front of him.

What he saw instantly made him sick to his stomach. Valentino turned away. He doubled over, dropped to the ground and breathed heavily, trying to turn back what he knew was coming.

Paolo had no right shoulder. There wasn't just a hole where the bullet had entered. Practically the entire shoulder had been blown off. Paolo's heart raced, and with every beat, his blood pumped out of what was left of his shoulder. Like the Old Faithful geyser in Yellowstone National Park, blood spewed out steadily.

In his line of work, Valentino had seen blood before, but not like this. This was more than he could handle.

Doubled over on all fours, Valentino retched once, hard, and then again.

"Val?" Paolo moaned.

Not looking Paolo's way, Valentino stood up, and with his back against the tree he'd been hiding behind, he stared into the blackness created by the dense forest. He took three steps toward the forest before he heard Paolo's voice again.

"Val?" Paolo's voice sounded weak.

Valentino stopped, but he didn't turn around. He didn't want to go back. Like a comfortable blanket, the darkness of the forest called to him. He wanted to ease into the forest and disappear into its many folds. He could leave Paolo. Valentino didn't owe him anything. In fact, Valentino knew if the roles had been switched, Paolo wouldn't hesitate—he would just leave.

But he and Paolo weren't cut from the same cloth—it would bother Valentino the rest of his life if he just left Paolo to die.

Valentino turned back.

He knelt down at Paolo's side, fighting back the nausea that quickly returned upon seeing the blood. Even in the shadows of the trees, Valentino could tell that Paolo's face was white—he looked like a ghost. They were miles, if not hundreds of miles, from the nearest hospital, and that was exactly what Paolo needed to survive.

"Val?" Paolo asked.

"Yes, I'm here." Valentino reached out and touched Paolo's left arm that was lying across his chest.

"How bad is it?" Paolo asked, his voice weak from the loss of blood.

"It's bad," Valentino said, not wanting to sugarcoat the reality of the situation. "You've lost a lot of blood, and I don't have anything to stop it."

Paolo closed his eyes. "What about the other guy?"

Valentino's brow creased—the other guy? Steve, the pilot?

Valentino scanned the area quickly, but didn't see any sign of the pilot. When Paolo had been shot, Steve and Valentino had both gone for cover. From behind the tree where he'd been hiding, Valentino had seen Steve crouching behind a large granite boulder the size of a house. Now, Steve couldn't be seen anywhere. From where he knelt by Paolo's side, Valentino couldn't see behind the boulder.

"Steve," Valentino whispered. No response.

"Steve," Valentino said a little louder. Nothing.

"Steve," he said one more time, practically yelling his name, but there was still no response. Steve had disappeared, just as Valentino had wanted to do.

"Steve's gone," Valentino told Paolo.

"What about the other guy," Paolo asked?

"What other guy?"

"The one I shot at. Did I get him?"

It didn't register in Paolo's mind how bad off he was, that he was about to die. He just wanted to make sure the other guy had gotten the worst of it.

Unfortunately, Valentino didn't know what had happened to the other guy. But he was fairly certain their probing shoots were useless. He hesitated for a split second, not sure what to say. He didn't want to lie to a dying man. But he was also uncertain what the truth might do to him.

Paolo must have sensed his hesitation. "That bad, huh?"

"Well, I didn't quite know how to tell you, but . . ."

"I missed?"

"Yeah, you missed."

"Well . . . I guess, I can't get them all," Paolo said with a smile curling the corners of his lips. "I'll just have to get him the next time."

But for Paolo, there wasn't going to be a next time.

"Sounds good," Valentino said.

Paolo opened his eyes and raised his left arm off his chest, holding it up with his hand open, an invitation for Valentino to take it.

"Promise you'll get him for me," Paolo said.

Valentino glanced at the forest, the darkness waiting patiently with open arms. He wanted all of this to be over, and the curtain of darkness through the forest was the answer. He wanted to disappear like Steve had.

Here was Paolo, asking him to finish the job he wasn't able to do. Mr. Sebasti also wanted Valentino to get Carr.

Then there was the darkness.

Valentino took Paolo's opened hand, giving it a squeeze. "I promise."

Paolo closed his eyes and took his last breath.

Valentino held Paolo's hand for a moment before laying it across his chest.

He scanned the area—he was alone. He had no food, no shelter, and no water. He wasn't prepared for the night. Their plan, to follow behind the plane until it crashed, after the mechanic had fixed the fuel line, was hastily thrown together. After the plane had crashed, Valentino and Paolo had planned on finishing off any survivors. It was a simple plan, one that hadn't taken in all of the variables, like the occupants of the plane fighting back or the unlikelihood of their helicopter being forced down by a lucky shot to the engine. Their plan hadn't included surviving in the wilderness, nor had it included Paolo being killed.

Had Valentino or Paolo truly thought about all the possibilities, they probably would have shot Carr before he boarded the plane in Pagosa Springs. It definitely would have been much easier.

Now he was in the wilderness alone, up against an armed opponent. The odds were not in his favor.

Valentino glanced out across the meadow into the fading light. For all he knew, they might be watching him right now. It didn't matter, though. He had a job to complete and a promise to fulfill, and he meant to do it, no matter the outcome.

He stood and walked over to the tree where he'd been hiding. He picked up his H&K. He pulled back the lever, ejecting the spent cartridge. He let the lever go, the spring-loaded system performing flawlessly, a live round loaded into the barrel.

He peered at his watch: 6:23 p.m. No better time than the present.

Chapter 53

Jaxon

It's Over

Jax watched the short one on the ground for just a moment, the man not able to get up. One of the tall ones poked his head out behind a tree, then, after disappearing behind the tree for a moment, he rushed to the short one's side. The tall one knelt at the injured man's side, his profile to Jax.

He couldn't have asked for a better shot. Number two down.

Jax sighted through the scope, positioning the crosshairs on the shoulder of the tall one kneeling down. He took a breath in anticipation of pulling the trigger, but before he could let it out, movement at the edge of his peripheral vision drew his attention. He swung his rifle to the left of the injured one on the ground, scanning the area for movement.

Nothing. He had seen something. He moved the rifle, peering through the scope, focusing on a rock. Nothing. He moved to a tree, scanning it for life. Nothing. He was just about to return his attention back to the tall one kneeling down, when he saw movement again.

The second tall man darted from behind a tree, running away from the other men. He stopped and hid behind a large rock. Jax kept his scope focused on the rock. The man ran again, farther away from the other two. He hid behind another rock.

Jax watched as the tall man fled from his hiding space, widening the distance between him and the other two. The tall man moved one more time, hiding behind a tree, until he finally stopped taking any more precautions about hiding from his companions. He ran at a full speed through the trees, leaving his two friends behind. It seemed he'd had enough of this dirty work.

Only one more left. The odds were now in Jax's favor.

Jax turned his rifle back to his target, but it was gone, and so was the injured one.

He's coming.

"Zeren," Jax whispered. When Zeren didn't answer, Jax turned around. Zeren had disappeared. "Zeren," Jax whispered again. Still no answer.

He heard some noises coming from behind the tree where Thomas lay. Jax, with great effort, got up and made his way over to Thomas.

Stepping around the tree, he wasn't surprised at what he saw. He found Zeren kneeling next to Thomas's backpack, clasping the last buckle on the back of the pack.

"Going somewhere?" Jax asked.

Zeren jumped. "Don't do that!" Zeren barked. "You scared me half to death."

"Why so jumpy?"

"Well . . ." Zeren stammered. "I thought . . . that, if, well. Since they're after me, I figured that if I left, they would leave . . . you know . . . you and Thomas alone."

"On your way out, were you planning on telling your friends that you were leaving, or were you going to just let them come over here and find us on their own?"

"Yeah, exactly."

"And you figured that once they got here and found that you'd left, they would just leave me and Thomas alone?"

"Yes, I'm sure of it. I mean, all they want is me, right?"

Zeren stood. He picked up the pack, slipping his arms through the shoulder straps.

Jax nonchalantly directed the muzzle of his rifle at Zeren.

"So you figured you were saving our lives by directing your friends' attention away from us and onto you," Jax said. He shifted his one good leg, which automatically shifted the point of his rifle directly at Zeren's stomach.

"You've . . . got it," Zeren quivered, watching Jax's hand as it shifted to the trigger guard on his rifle. Jax placed his finger on the trigger.

"Take the pack off Zeren. You may leave, but you won't be taking the only food and water we have."

"Or what? You threatening me?" Zeren challenged. Jax didn't back down.

"Yes."

Immediately Zeren changed tactics. His voice went soft. He started to beg. "Come with me. Let's run. You can still move." He dropped the backpack to the ground at his feet, placing both hands on top of it. "There's enough food and water for the both of us. We can last a couple of days. We can make it out of here."

"What about Thomas?" Jax said. "We can't just leave him."

"He's unconscious. Heck, he may be dead by now. When was the last time you checked his pulse?"

"He's unconscious, not dead. If we leave him here, he will surely die without us." The rifle muzzle lowered slightly.

"Look," Zeren said. "If we leave, we can find help. Then we can come back for him. I promise."

The word *promise* changed everything. Jax didn't trust Zeren, especially not now that he wanted to leave Thomas to die. The muzzle came back up, pointing directly at Zeren's chest. "Go if you want to, but I'm staying here with Thomas," Jax said. "Leave the pack."

Zeren's body jerked violently, the silence of the night shattered by the loud explosion of a two-round burst that tore Zeren's chest apart. Zeren's eyes flashed wide in shock as he fell backward, dead before he hit the ground.

Jax spun on his one good leg, dropping to the ground. It saved his life, but it wasn't enough to avoid the two bullets aimed in his direction. The first bullet missed, coming within an inch of his head, but the second one caught him in the back, just below the right shoulder, slamming him into the ground. He landed hard on top of his rifle.

He was hurt, this time badly. He tried to roll over using his left arm, which seemed to function without much pain. No matter how hard he pushed, though, everything seemed to move in slow motion. He grunted, pushing harder. Finally he rolled to his back, his shirt wet with blood.

Suddenly, the last tall man was standing next to him. Jax slowly reached out his arm, grabbing for his rifle lying next to him. But the tall man was faster. Getting to it first, he kicked it away.

"You won't be needing that now," Valentino said.

"You got Zeren," Jax said with slurred speech, his words coming out with great effort. "So . . . leave me alone."

"I can't do that. See, I made a promise to my friend." Valentino gestured over his shoulder with his head. "I promised I'd get the person that shot him. And, seeing that it was probably you, the one with the rifle, I'm now going to kill you."

There was a loud metallic scraping sound as Valentino chambered a round in his rifle.

Valentino stood over Jax, pointing the barrel of the rifle six inches away from his head. Jax closed his eyes. This was the end—he was never going to see Annie again.

Annie, I love you, forever.

There was a loud explosion.

Chapter 54

Annie

Night-Out

The parking lot of Sparky's Garage was full when Annie pulled in, which she'd expected on a Friday night. *Everyone in Dillon must be out on the town*, Annie thought. She found an open space in the back lot of the restaurant and turned the wheel to pull in.

Annie hesitated.

Don't be stupid. You're Annie Tagget, married to Jaxon Tagget.

She slammed her hand on the steering wheel. "Stupid, stupid me." She turned the wheel, nosing the front of the car away from the open space.

She was going home.

She took her foot off the brake pedal and started to pull away. Suddenly, a young couple holding hands walked between parked cars and stepped in front of her. Annie stomped on the brakes. The car jerked to a stop. She watched the couple pass, laughing and giggling, already enjoying the evening.

When the couple had passed, Annie didn't take her foot off the brake. Instead, her nostrils flared. She watched as the couple stopped between two parked cars. They embraced and kissed. Annie's lips tightened and flattened.

Her heart pounded. That should be her and Jax. Jax would have returned, and they would have gone out to eat since he'd been gone for the last couple of days. She should have been the one laughing and giggling with Jax as they walked to the restaurant holding hands.

Instead, Jax was with another woman, and Annie was by herself, about to go home to an empty house.

She gripped the steering wheel with both hands, her knuckles turning white. Heat flushed through her body. She didn't want to go home alone.

Not tonight.

Annie turned the wheel, pointing the front of the car back to the empty stall. She pulled in and parked. She knew if she hesitated again, her resolve would break, so she quickly grabbed her jacket and her purse and climbed out.

She walked through the parked cars quickly, feeling a little conspicuous walking by herself. She kept a sharp eye out, scanning over the tops of the cars in case she spotted someone she knew.

She'd already worked up a story in her mind. She planned to tell people that Jax was out of town on business, that there was no food in the house, and that she'd come to Sparky's to eat. That sounded reasonable.

Dillon was a small town, but she'd been gone for just over seven years. When she went shopping or to the grocery store, she hardly recognized any of the people. Just as well. She hoped tonight would be the same—she didn't want to use the made-up excuse if she didn't have to.

When she got to the door, she grabbed the handle, pulled on it, and stepped in. Katy Perry's song "Roar" blasted loudly over the sound system, greeting her as she entered. The lobby was packed with people standing shoulder to shoulder. She made her way through the crowd to the hostess station.

"How long's the wait?" Annie asked, practically yelling to be heard over the music.

"How many in your party?" the hostess girl yelled back. She had a short blond bob. Fortunately Annie didn't know the girl.

"Just one tonight," Annie said with a tight smile.

"It will be about thirty minutes."

"Thirty minutes," Annie mumbled as she stepped back. She definitely didn't want to wait in the lobby. She was certain she would be recognized by someone. She wasn't quite ready for the small talk she knew would ensue.

Just as Annie had made up her mind to leave, the hostess said, "If you want, you can sit up at the bar—there's no wait there." The hostess pointed out a few empty seats at the bar.

"If I sit at the bar, can I still order off the regular menu?"

"Yeah, it's just the same as if you were sitting at a regular table."

"Okay, that would be fine."

Annie followed the hostess, which seemed unnecessary because there were several seats available, and the hostess had said she could pick whatever seat she wanted. Annie was sure it was protocol for the hostess to seat all the guests, so she didn't make a fuss.

Sparky's was a sports bar, and, as is common with sports bars, there were numerous T.V. screens strategically placed throughout the restaurant showing various live national sporting events. Directly to the left of her, a sixty-five-inch flat screen T.V. hung on the wall. A football game was on.

The bartender came by and placed a black and red coaster with *Sparky's* on it in front of her. "What can I get you?" he asked.

Her stomach felt fine now, but she remembered how queasy it felt yesterday morning. She didn't want to upset it again, so she ordered a sparkling water, which she hoped would be soothing. If she'd been out with Jax, she might have ordered something with a little more kick to it, like a beer or maybe a white wine. She was alone, for now, which meant she might have to drive home tonight, and she didn't want to sit behind the wheel after a few drinks.

The bartender placed a wine glass in front of her with the word *Sparky's* stenciled across the glass. Pulling a white speckled hose with a nozzle on it from the soda fountain on the inside of the bar, he filed the glass with water. Most of the bubbles from the carbonation rose to the surface, but some clung to the sides of the glass, like barnacles hanging on for dear life to the side of a boat. Annie picked up the glass and took a small sip.

"Annie?" a male voice sounded behind her.

Two Hearts

Just as she feared, someone had already recognized her, and it had only been five minutes. Annie turned to see Charles Downs standing next to her.

"Easy . . . I mean Charles," Annie said.

"You can call me Easy. Beth prefers people to call me by my given name, but, to be honest, I like the name Easy."

"Okay, Easy it is. What are you doing here?"

"Beth's gone to Denver to shop, and there's no food in the house, so I decided to see what Sparky's had cooking tonight. What about you, Jax not home yet?"

Easy had used the same excuse that Annie had cooked up. She didn't know what to say without sounding lame, so she scanned the restaurant, hoping to see something or someone that she could point out or bring up to distract him. She saw a couple of familiar faces, but no one that she could mention that would start a conversation.

"Yeah, Jax is still gone," she finally said. She didn't elaborate. Her brief reply didn't seem to bother Easy.

"May I?" he asked, gesturing to the empty seat next to her.

"Sure."

Annie turned back to the bar and placed the glass down. Without Easy seeing, she dropped her hand to her side and snapped her fingers as the muscles in her jaws clenched tight. *Dang it*, she wanted to say, but kept it to herself. She had come to Sparky's to pick up a man, but now she had to somehow get rid of Easy and that might take all night.

They ordered. Annie got grilled chicken over angel hair pasta. She noticed what Easy ordered, the walnut-crusted balsamic salmon and vegetables, the same thing Jax would have ordered. Jax loved fish—he ordered it every time they went out.

Conversation was lighthearted. She had known Easy just as long as she'd known Jax, since high school, and there were many things they could talk about. They talked about old friends from high school and growing up in Dillon. Conversation naturally touched on their days at the university and about Annie and Jax going overseas. Annie tried to stay away from mentioning Easy's first wife, Samantha. Annie didn't want to open a can of worms that might stink up the whole place, so she left that alone. She preferred the light talk they were having over any heated, drama-filled conversation.

Easy was easy to talk to, and several times she found herself laughing at things he would say or the stories he would tell or just the way he put things. He was just plain funny, which made her laugh even more. She was actually having a good time. She let it go, rationalizing that Easy wasn't a threat and lowered her guard a little.

The food arrived. They both reached for the salt at the same time, but Annie got there first, her fingers clasping around the shaker. Easy's large hand closed around Annie's and the shaker, drawing it and her hand toward him.

"Excuse me, but I got there first," Annie said.

Easy didn't let go, pulling Annie's hand closer to him. His skin felt warm against hers, soft. It felt good. She tried pulling away, but not too hard.

"Yup, you did get there first, but I'm bigger, so now it's mine. Let go."

"I can't, Easy. You're holding my hand."

With that, he let go, slowly dragging his fingers across hers as he did so.

"Easy." Annie gave him a stern look, as if to say "back off." But the way she'd said it, alarmed her, almost as if she were flirting with him. *Was she?*

What was he doing anyway, trying to hold her hand? And, what was she doing? This was Easy, one of Jax's best friends. Easy was married to Beth, Annie's friend and . . . high school rival.

Then it hit her, practically ran her over like a prized thoroughbred racing at the Kentucky Derby. *Easy?* It was perfect. Jax's best friend and Beth's husband.

If she was going to get back at Jax, and really make it hurt, she couldn't have asked for a better situation.

She glanced his way, catching his eye. She gave him a soft smile, which he readily returned. Target sighted.

Conversation continued without any direction or agenda. She laughed at the appropriate times. She made comments where she needed to. Easy followed along nicely, going along with the whole game, or that's what it seemed like to her, a game.

He would reach over and touch her arm during their conversations to give emphasis to what he said. He would glance her way when she wasn't looking and turn his head only after Annie had noticed him staring.

This little back-and-forth action amused her. It also frightened her, because, like catching a fish, if she landed it, she wouldn't know what to do with it. She had Easy on the line, with the hook set deep in his mouth. She tried to fight down the feeling in the back of her throat that was rising up from her churning stomach, realizing that the only way to get this one off the hook was to bring him all the way in.

Dinner ended, but the evening was still young. Easy stared at Annie. He didn't turn when she glanced back. He leaned forward and said, "Would you like to go somewhere quiet?"

She had been anticipating something like this, but when it came, she wasn't prepared for her reaction. Heat flashed up the back of her neck, turning her cheeks hot. There it was. It was on the table. It was simple now. She would leave with Easy, the starring role in her own small-town scandal. The skin on the back of her neck began to tingle as beads of perspiration came to the surface.

"Yes," she said, her mouth as dry as a cotton ball.

Chapter 55

Annie

No Survivors

Annie winked at Easy. "I'll meet you outside," she said. "But, first I need to use the ladies' room."

"Great, I'm parked on the south side. Let's go in my car." Easy smiled. He had a mischievous glint in his eye that frightened her, causing her right leg to twitch under the bar. She returned the smile, trying to hide her fear, but it came out flat. Easy didn't seem to notice. He winked back. "See you soon," he said.

He left the bar, making his way through the crowd of people to the front door. He paused, turned, and glanced back at her. She'd half expected him to look back, so she was ready for him. She smiled and gave him a small nod with her head. He disappeared through the door.

Annie turned back to the bar. She covered her face with her hands. *Oh crap.* Her stomach turned. *I've actually got a live one.*

She hurried to the bathroom, bursting through the door. She grabbed the sink with both hands, her knuckles turning white. She shook uncontrollably for a minute, waiting for the hysteria to pass. She couldn't believe what had just happened. She'd actually picked up a guy, and not just any guy, Easy.

She glanced under the stalls for legs, needing privacy. Empty, just as she hoped.

Her hand jerked with spasms as she frantically pulled paper towels from the dispenser. She moistened them under the faucet, spilling water everywhere. She first swiped the base of her neck. The wet towels felt cool, providing instant relief, but she had so much internal heat that the coolness disappeared within seconds.

She quickly moistened the towels again, reapplying them, repeating the process every few seconds, as the coolness in the compress disappeared. Gradually, after about the sixth application, she could feel her body temperature dropping.

She sighed, taking a deep breath.

She refreshed her towel supply with new ones, and then, after moistening them, she applied the cold compress to her forehead this time, wiping off the sheet of sweat on her brow. It was like cold water being poured onto a hot frying pan. She did it again and again, until finally she gained control.

Annie threw the paper towels away and glanced at herself in the mirror. She straightened her shirt, smoothing out some of the wrinkles. She pulled out a small brush from her purse and ran it through her hair a couple of times.

She stared at herself. She squared her shoulders. "You've got this," she said to herself, trying to imbue confidence. "It's perfect." Jax and Beth were both gone. Easy waited for her outside in his car, ready to take her to his place. The moment couldn't be more perfect. Won't Jax and Beth both be surprised when they find out? Annie wouldn't keep it a secret. She didn't want to. She wanted them to know. In fact, she might even be the one to start the juicy gossip rolling through town. She would spread the word to Mrs. Emmett. After that, the news would spread like a blazing hot forest fire.

She smiled at the thought, hoping it would make her feel good. But it didn't. She felt lousy, all wrong inside. She thought married life would have turned out differently. Hers was a true love—a forever love—one that was supposed to last through all of life's bumps in the road. That's what Jax had promised her all those years ago—that he would love her forever and ever. Nothing could ever come between them, he'd said.

The smile immediately disappeared. *Nothing except . . . another woman.*

She swung her purse, smashing her reflection in the mirror. "I hate you, Jax," she yelled. "I hate you, I hate you, I hate you."

She let her purse fall to the ground as she grabbed the edges of the sink again, glaring at herself in the mirror.

The bathroom door opened, a waitress stepped in. "Ma'am, are you . . ."

"I'm fine," Annie snapped, her eyes cold and hard, sending daggers at her unsuspecting victim.

The waitress's hand came up in defense, to shield against another attack.

Annie grabbed her purse and stormed out of the bathroom, pushing past the waitress, who stood there with her mouth slightly agape, the hurt showing in her eyes. Annie didn't care. She just wanted to get out. She headed toward the front door, knowing Easy still waited for her outside.

She grabbed her jacket and fed her arm through one sleeve. She pushed her other arm through the second sleeve. She stopped and stood still, her arms falling to her side.

She glanced up. The song blasting through the sound system caught her attention. A lump lodged in her throat as the chorus played loud and clear. Her head dropped, her chin resting on her chest.

Their song, "Two Hearts," played loud throughout the restaurant. Jax had requested this song on the night he'd proposed.

Her chin brushed the chain hanging around her neck. She placed her hand on her chest, feeling the pendant through her shirt. Since the night he'd given her the necklace, she'd never taken it off. It symbolized who they were—husband and wife forever. She pulled out the pendant and held it in her hand. Two hearts overlapping to create a figure eight—eternity. That's what Jax had promised her—eternal love.

Annie looked at the front door. She'd promised it to him as well, and now here she was, about to break that promise. The front door opened, and Annie bit her lip in anticipation. Had she waited too long? Had Easy decided to come back in? If Easy came back through the door searching for her, she was done.

A woman with long, dark hair stepped through the door followed by a man with a handlebar mustache and a felt cowboy hat. It wasn't Easy.

Annie peered down at the necklace in her hand. The gold appeared to be turning bright red-hot, as if it were on fire. She dropped it, letting it bounce on her shirt before it had a chance to burn her. Guilt washed over her. She still loved Jax, even though he obviously didn't love her. She'd made a promise and she wasn't going to break it, no matter what.

She turned, stumbled to an empty seat, and dropped down into it. She placed her elbows on the bar, burying her head into her hands. She made no eye contact. She spoke to no one, lost in her own world. Once, a man came by and asked if he could sit in the empty seat next to her. She didn't respond—she didn't even move. The bartender never came by to see if she wanted a drink. With her head buried in her hands, she noticed through her fingers the waitress she'd yelled at in the bathroom. The waitress stood talking to the bartender, pointing in Annie's direction.

Just as well, she hadn't wanted to be bothered anyway.

Annie didn't move for fifteen minutes. Easy never came back for her, which didn't surprise her. He'd probably figured out by now that she'd decided to stay inside instead of leaving with him. She'd had enough of Easy for one lifetime. If she never saw him again, that would be fine with her. It takes two to be unfaithful, and she wasn't going to be one of them.

Annie lowered her arms and stared across the restaurant, not focusing on anything.

She waited another five minutes and then stood, thinking it would be safe to leave Sparky's. Easy would have left by now. She wanted to go home, empty house and all. Jax would return at some point in time, and when he did, they would talk.

Could she live with him, knowing that he was unfaithful? Would he want to stay with her? Maybe. But, she wouldn't be able to live with herself and stay with him at the same time. Maybe he would promise to never do it again. Could she ever trust him again? Probably, but would she? Absolutely not. It's not easy to trust when someone has lied to you.

There would be a lot to talk about when he got home, but for right now her mind was numb from the emotional rollercoaster she'd just been through.

Go home, that's what she wanted to do. Get in her pajamas, curl up into a ball on her bed, and disappear from life for a couple of hours, maybe days, if that's what it took.

As she turned to leave, she saw a group of people standing below the flat screen T.V. hanging from the wall. They were pointing and talking about the program on the T.V. Football season having started over a month ago, every screen in the place had some college game on it, except for the one in front of her.

Across the bottom of the screen were the words *NEWS FLASH*. A special report had interrupted the game. In the upper-right-hand corner of the screen, a reporter gave an update. With the sound turned down, captions appeared at the bottom of the screen.

Annie walked over and stood to the side of the small group.

What initially caught Annie's eye and caused her to stop was the image on the screen. Coming from what appeared to be a camera on a helicopter was a picture of a green, grassy meadow in the mountains. But she'd seen plenty of green meadows before. What stood out to her was the image of a wrecked plane lying upside down in the grassy meadow, its wheels sticking straight up in the air.

The captions reported that the Grand Junction Airport, after receiving a mayday call from the pilot on Thursday afternoon, lost radio contact with the plane just before it went down. A rescue team had been sent out immediately to the plane's last known location, which turned out to be many miles and several mountain ridges away from the actual crash site. After searching through the night on Thursday and all through the next day, the plane wasn't found until late Friday afternoon.

The helicopter flew overhead, scanning the scene of the wreck. The door on the passenger's side and the cargo door on the pilot side were open and the personal belongings of the occupants were strewn everywhere.

The camera man zoomed in on the wreck. Annie's hand shot to her mouth. Inadvertently, she took a small step back. Her eyes started blinking rapidly.

She knew the plane—she recognized the paint scheme. It was Jax's plane.

Jax had crashed.

Annie's head spun. She felt dizzy. She tried to read the captions, but the words faded in and out of focus. She saw the words "blood everywhere," appear at the bottom of the screen, which made her head spin even faster. She started to lose touch with her surroundings.

A new caption flashed across the bottom of the screen: "Three bodies recovered." Instantly Annie thought of Jax, Zeren, and Thomas. A nightmare image flashed through her mind, three bodies lying next to each other, each covered with a blanket.

Dizzy, she reached for the chair next to her. She touched someone, a woman.

"Sorry," Annie mumbled. She grasped the back of the chair.

Annie, stabilized with the help of the chair, glanced back to the T.V. Her eyes came into focus. She saw the captions, but all her mind registered were the last two words. *No survivors.*

"No survivors?" Annie stammered.

Jax . . . dead?

Chapter 56

Annie

Where It All Began

Annie stepped back, bumping into a chair behind her. She sagged against the chair as her body went limp, losing all control of her motor functions. Just as she felt her body crumbling to the ground, a man jumped up and grabbed her by the shoulders. He was strong, just like Jax. He practically lifted her off the ground. He raised his voice to be heard over the music, but it sounded louder than needed. Those sitting two tables away could easily hear the frustration in his voice. "Excuse me, ma'am, but we're trying to have a peaceful dinner here."

Annie focused on the man's face, strength coming back to her limbs. "I'm sorry," she said. "Really, I'm sorry." She wiggled her body, struggling to break free from the man's hold. He let her go. She landed on her feet and quickly stepped over to the bar, leaning up against it. She was ten feet from the T.V. She stared directly at it. The news flash had ended, replaced by the previously aired football game, but Annie knew what she'd seen—it hadn't been a dream.

Jax's plane had crashed . . . yesterday, that's why he'd never made it home last night. He'd died yesterday. Annie had warned him before he'd left. She hadn't felt right about him flying to Colorado.

Annie dropped her head into her hands, grabbing fistfuls of hair. She pulled, practically ripping her hair out. Her face turned red as the pressure built up inside her head. Tremors racked her body. She gasped for air over and over again. Her heart pounded in her chest, the beats reverberated loudly in her ears. She started to hyperventilate. Trying to gain control, she closed her mouth, forcing her to breathe through her nose.

The muscles in her jaw clenched tight. She squeezed her eyes shut. *Jax*, she screamed inside her head. *Jax*, she screamed again.

She grabbed her cell phone, pressed the side button to wake it up, and touched the message icon at the bottom. Jax's text threads, as the last person she'd texted, were at the top of the list. She touched the screen. The messages opened.

She slid her finger down the screen to his last message. The date was yesterday and it showed a time of 1:15 in the afternoon. Jax had crashed sometime after that, but when?

She stared at the text, willing it to tell her more, hoping the harder she looked the more information she would get, but nothing happened. Jax's text was in yellow, and just below his text, outlined in blue, was the edge of her response, the last message in the thread. She slid the screen down a little further to see the full text message.

Two Hearts

Her chin quivered. She read the last words she'd sent him. Her gaze lowered, staring blankly into the glossy bar top. Instantly she felt cold even though she had her jacket on. Her arms closed around her chest, drawing herself up tight, and her shoulders slumped forward.

The last thing she'd told her husband was "Don't come home to this house, you're not welcome here." Now, he was dead.

With her arms held tightly across her chest, she started slowly rocking back and forth. *I'd yelled at Jax just before he died. Now he's gone and I can't say I'm sorry..*

She knew now that if he had come home she would have apologized. She would have told him she was sorry for overreacting. She knew he would have apologized, and she would have listened to him and believed every word he said.

They would have hugged and kissed, and then they would have made love.

She knew that now, but it was too late. In anger, she'd told him not to return; now he was dead, never to come home again.

"Ma'am?" The bartender touched Annie on the shoulder. Annie jumped, startled at his touch. She lashed out with her left arm, her closed fist smashing a half-filled glass on the bar top next to her. The glass shattered against the bar top, a piece of glass cutting her little finger just below the knuckle. Annie didn't even feel the impact or the glass cutting her hand.

"Ma'am, your hand, you're bleeding," the bartender said, as Annie stood to leave. "Let me help you."

"I'll be fine," Annie said. She grinned, a genuine smile crossing her lips for the first time that night. A peaceful calm settled over her. "I'm going to see my husband; he'll take care of me."

She winked at the bartender, and without saying another word, she turned, shouldered her purse, and glided out of Sparky's.

Chapter 57

Annie

The Edge

It was dark when Annie left Sparky's—she'd been there a good part of the evening. She calmly walked through the parking lot until she found where she'd parked. She eased into the car, buckled her seat belt, and started the engine. She took her time backing out, maneuvering the car through all of the vehicles packed into the back lot.

She wasn't in a hurry. She knew where she was going, and she knew Jax would be there when she arrived.

She made her way out of the parking lot, passing a late model Ford pickup truck that had been raised. She chuckled to herself when she saw the Texas Long Horns fastened to the hood of the truck. Jax would've laughed too. Only here in Dillon, he would have said. Only here would you see something like that. She would have to remember to tell Jax about it.

Annie headed out of town, catching I-41 to Twin Bridges. Eighteen minutes, that's how long it took to reach the ranch—not long at all.

She smiled. It wouldn't be long now, she would see him soon.

She turned off the interstate onto the dirt road that led to the ranch house. It was dark and hard to see, but she knew that a hundred yards after leaving the interstate, the road would tee, another road coming in from the right-hand side. She slowed at about the right spot, her headlights illuminating the entrance to the dirt road coming in from the side. She turned right. This road wouldn't take her to the ranch house. It would take her to Lover's Flat.

This was where it had all begun for her, and she knew it was the same for Jax. It felt like the right place to meet Jax again, for the last time.

The road switched back and forth several times before she made it to the top. The surface of Lover's Flat wasn't very big. Jax had said it was a little smaller than the size of a football field.

Annie turned off her lights and left just the fog lights on, as Jax had done many times before. He'd always say that the lights from other cars were too bright for those already parked. It just made sense to dim the lights out of common courtesy for the others.

She smiled. Jax would be happy that she'd dimmed her lights. She'd have to remember to tell him that too.

Lover's Flat had a commanding view of the Beaverhead River as it made its way through the valley below. The east side, sloped slightly, allowing the road to make its way to the top. The west side, the side that faced toward the city of Dillon, was a sheer cliff, two hundred feet straight down to the valley floor.

Jax had warned her many times to stay away from the edge. A fall from the top would kill you instantly on impact, he'd told her.

She pulled her car up to the edge, the front wheels within a foot from the lip, the bumper hanging over the edge slightly. She kept her foot on the brake and the motor running—and the car in drive.

The lights of the city were beautiful from where she sat. She could see the dark spot where the high school gymnasium stood. She could see the lights of the cars snaking their way through town. It was Friday night, and the high school kids were cruising Main Street—she knew because she and Jax had done it many times before.

It wouldn't be long now—she would see Jax soon.

A bead of sweat rolled down her spine. She would see him soon. She very gently eased the pressure off the brake pedal and the car began to inch forward.

Annie's cell phone, sitting in the passenger's seat, rang. She slammed down hard on the brake, startled. The car jerked to a stop.

A bit angry from the interruption, she grabbed the phone, intent on hitting the off button.

The caller ID showed Beth Downs's name on the screen. Beth wasn't supposed to be home until late Saturday night. She was probably calling to tell Annie how much fun she was having in Denver—exactly what Annie didn't need right now.

On the second ring, Annie almost answered it. Maybe it would be good to talk to someone, even if it was Beth.

Maybe Beth could . . . nah, Annie didn't need any help; she was busy at the moment. She hit the ignore button, sending Beth directly to voicemail.

Annie set the phone on the passenger's seat and eased her foot off the pedal. The car inched forward. The cell phone rang again, causing Annie to jump. She slammed on the brake, this time out of frustration more than fright.

"Beth," Annie grunted through clenched teeth. She grabbed the phone. She would answer it and get rid of Beth quickly so Annie could finish what she'd started. The sooner she did, the sooner she would be with Jax.

Without noticing the caller ID, Annie slid her finger across the screen and held it up to her ear.

"Beth, how are you?" Annie said in the happiest voice she could muster under the circumstances.

"Baby, this is Jax." The voice was weak and sounded distant, but Annie recognized it immediately.

"Jax?"

Chapter 58

Jaxon

Head Shot

Point blank shot to the head—instant death. No pain. Cord unplugged. Lights out, instantly. But there was pain, lots of it, but not in his head. Jax's shoulder throbbed, his side hurt, and his leg felt numb.

A heavy thud shook the ground next to him. Jax opened his eyes. He rolled his head to the right where he'd felt the earth shake. The tall man lay on the ground three feet away. He still grasped the assault rifle in his right hand, but his left arm was lying under him, bent out of place. The man's eyes, wide open, stared back at Jax. The man looked alive, but he wasn't.

A shadow loomed over Jax, blocking out the last bit of remaining light from the setting sun.

"Hey, buddy. It's good to see you," Thomas said casually, as if they were meeting at a café for lunch. He held Jax's Colt .45 in his hand, the chamber open, the last cartridge spent.

"Where've you been?" Jax asked.

"Well, I woke up when you and Zeren were arguing, but my head was really heavy, and I was pretty dizzy. I just lay there with nothing really registering in my mind. I couldn't quite figure out where I was. I could see trees and mountains in the fading light, but I didn't know why. I figured we were still hunting, but couldn't understand why you were with us. Then there was gun fire. I watched as Zeren fell to the ground and then you got hit. By this time the dizziness had faded, and I was starting to think clearly. Then that guy showed up with the rifle. When he pointed the barrel at your head, I put my arm out to get up. That's when I felt your pistol lying next to me. As they say, the rest is history."

"It's good to see you too," Jax mumbled with great effort. He raised his head and at the same time he tried to position his right arm under him in an attempt to sit up. Electrifying pain shot through his shoulder. He dropped his head back, letting his arm fall to his side. He shut his eyes, took a deep breath, and then let it out slowly.

"Going somewhere?" Thomas asked.

"Yeah, I thought I'd catch a flick. Anything good showing?"

"No, just a couple of sci-fi movies, one war show, and this comedy love story—all a bunch of run-of-the-mill stuff," Thomas said. Jax could tell he was trying to lighten up the situation. Talking this much was out of character for Thomas. As if it was a last-minute thought, Thomas added, "Do you need any help? You look pretty bad off."

"No, I got this."

"Of course you do. By-the-way, I'm free for the next, say, ten minutes or so, if you need anything." Thomas gestured to a large rock. "I'll just be over there reading the help wanted section if you need me."

"Punk," Jax said without glancing up.

Thomas set the .45 on the large rock he'd gestured to earlier and knelt down next to Jax. "I heard that," he whispered.

Jax opened his eyes and stared at Thomas.

Thomas said, "You need to pick better friends. This guy," Thomas gestured to the tall guy lying next to Jax, "doesn't seem to like you very much."

"Thanks, Thomas," Jax said, the playfulness gone from his voice. Thomas just nodded.

Silence ensued as Thomas leaned over Jax, gently unbuttoning Jax's shirt. Blood saturated the shirt, causing it stick to Jax's skin. As Thomas peeled back the shirt, Jax winced, gritting his teeth.

"Sorry, buddy," Thomas said, but he didn't stop peeling until he'd completely uncovered the right shoulder.

"How bad is it?" Jax rasped, his breathing low and shallow.

Thomas didn't say anything for a moment. He just stared at Jax's shoulder. Jax licked his lips. The fingers of his left hand found a button on his shirt. He started twisting it around and around.

"Thomas?"

"Blueberry cheesecake, it looks as good as blueberry cheesecake, and you know how good that is."

"That bad, huh?" Jax closed his eyes again, the pain excruciating.

"Well, if you want to know the truth, I've seen worse."

Even though Jax was certain Thomas was lying, what he said made Jax feel a little better.

"Thanks for trying to cheer me up."

Thomas stood up and disappeared for a minute. Jax could hear Thomas rummaging through the backpack. When he'd found what he'd been searching for, Thomas returned to Jax's side.

"First thing we've got to do is stop the bleeding," Thomas said. He opened the first aid kit he'd retrieved from the backpack and set in on the ground next to Jax.

"I'm going to rinse out the wound before I bandage it," Thomas said as he held up a bottle of water.

Jax raised his good arm and placed it on Thomas's forearm positioned above Jax's chest. "Don't, Thomas, don't waste your time," Jax said.

"What are you talking about?"

"It's no use. I'm not going to make it."

Thomas took Jax's arm and laid it at his side. "Don't go talking crazy like that. You're going to make it; we both are."

Thomas raised the bottle over the wound. Before he poured, he said, "This is going to sting a bit."

Before Jax could respond, Thomas poured the water over Jax's exposed shoulder, causing him to wince. Holding his breath against the pain, Jax gritted his teeth and squinched up his face, the skin gathering at the corners of his eyes.

"Hey, I wasn't ready," Jax stammered.

"I know."

Jax let out his breath as the pain subsided.

"I just wish I could have seen Annie one more time—I wanted to tell her I love her," Jax whispered, pain still registering in his voice. "Will you tell her for me, please? Promise me, Thomas. Promise you'll tell Annie I love her."

"I won't promise anything, and I won't tell her anything either, because you're going to make it, Jax."

"Thomas, promise me?" Jax coughed a deep throaty cough. His whole body shook.

"Okay, I promise you're going to make it. How's that?"

"Don't lie to me."

"Seriously, Jax, you can tell her yourself."

"Thomas!" Jax spoke sharply, with what little strength he had left.

Thomas sat back on his haunches, holding a roll of white translucent gauze that he was about to apply to Jax's shoulder.

"Jax, I heard what you said to Zeren just before he got shot, how you wanted stay with me, that you wouldn't leave me. Did you . . . mean that?"

"Yes," Jax said.

"Well, I'm telling you right now, you're my friend, and you've always been there for me. Do you remember that night, our high school graduation night, when you set me up with Tayla?"

"Yeah, I think so," Jax said, a vague recollection of their graduation night flashing through his mind. "What about it?"

"Well, I knew before I got to the party that night that you and Annie had arranged for me to take Tayla home after the party."

"You did? Why didn't you say something? How come you didn't run and hide?"

"Because I thought it was cool. It really showed me what kind of friends you and Annie were. You went to so much effort just to help me. Me, Thomas Edison, a big nobody in school. It meant a lot to me."

"You're not a nobody."

"Exactly. That's how you always made me feel, that I was somebody. You and Annie were the most popular kids in school, and that night you made me feel like an equal."

"You are somebody," Jax said. "You're Thomas, my friend."

"Thank you, Jax." Thomas wiped a tear from his eye. "And, you're my friend. That's why you're going to tell those three special little words to Annie yourself." Thomas placed his hand over his heart. "I promise I'm going to get you out of here alive, if it's the last thing I do.

No one spoke for the next ten minutes while Thomas worked on Jax's shoulder. Thomas washed it again, pouring water over the wound, cleaning it one more time. After letting it air dry, Thomas wrapped Jax's shoulder, moving it as little as possible. But no matter how carefully he wrapped it, Thomas couldn't help but cause Jax more pain. Several times during the process Jax winced, his jaw clenching tight, the muscles on his neck squinching up as he fought through the pain.

Two Hearts

Thomas wrapped the shoulder, placing a stabilizing splint in the wrap to support the damaged area. The bleeding finally stopped.

Thomas sat admiring his handiwork. "Hey, Jax, would you mind telling me where we are, and why I had to shoot that guy to stop him from killing you?"

"You don't know where we are?"

"No. Well, I realize we're in the mountains, but I don't know why. Did we stop to hunt?"

"What's the last thing you remember?" Jax asked.

"The last thing I remember was Zeren and I arriving at the airport in Pagosa after our hunt."

"Do you remember the engine exploding?"

Thomas's eyes grew wide. "The engine blew up? You're kidding?"

"Nope. About an hour after we left Pagosa, the engine burst into flames and we went down." Jax raised his one good arm, and without looking, he pointed toward the meadow where he knew Thomas would be able to see the outline of the remains of his plane even in the early evening darkness.

Thomas let out a low whistle. "We crashed?"

"We landed, not crashed. I didn't see the little creek that ran through the middle of the meadow and once we were on the ground the wheels hit the creek, flipping us over." Jax paused, closed his eyes for a moment, and breathed in and out slowly.

Thomas didn't say anything.

"When we flipped over, you hit your head pretty hard, which knocked you unconscious. You've been out ever since we landed, which was around one."

"What happened to Zeren?" Thomas asked.

"A couple scrapes and bruises, that's it."

"And you?"

"The engine smashed into the cockpit, pinning my leg against the plane, twisting it up pretty badly. With Zeren's help, we got it out."

"So who's the guy I just killed?" Thomas asked.

"One of Zeren's gambling buddies, here to collect on some old debts. I killed one on the other side of the meadow. Then I watched the third one run off. I suspect they're the reason the engine blew up, why I'm shot, and why Zeren is lying over there dead."

"You've been busy," Thomas said. He sat back, leaning up against the rock. "Do you have any idea where we are?"

"Just over an hour as the crow flies from Dillon, somewhere in the Colorado Rockies."

"Anybody coming to get us?" Thomas asked, concern noticeable in the tone of his voice.

"We lost radio contact with Grand Junction airport just before we went down. With the mountain interference, they were unable to locate us on their radar. I'm sure someone is searching for us, but . . . they don't know exactly where we are."

At that news, Thomas's head noticeably dropped two inches as he stared at his feet stretched out in front of him.

"Before we crashed, I mean landed," Thomas corrected, "did you see any roads or structures?"

"No," Jax said, before he broke out in a coughing fit. "That hurt," Jax said when he'd finished. He lay there exhausted. Thomas raised the bottle of water to Jax's lips. Jax drank, taking careful sips.

"Better?" Thomas asked.

"A little, thanks." Jax's voice cracked. "Help me sit up, please."

Thomas carefully placed his arms under and around Jax's back and pulled Jax into a sitting position. He was up, but not for long. Instantly, electricity shot through his shoulder as the weight of his body shifted from a relaxed, prone position to an upright position. Gravity pulled at his upper body.

"Back down, put me back down," Jax yelled.

Thomas obeyed without hesitating, tilting Jax to his back. Jax's chest rose and fell, rose and fell, as searing pain shot through his body.

"That wasn't such a good idea," Jax finally said in between breaths.

"We're going to need some help to get you out of here," Thomas said.

"Just leave me, Thomas. Save yourself. I've lost too much blood. I'm too weak to go anywhere."

"We've already talked about this—you're not going to die."

Chapter 59

Jaxon

Three Special Words

Jax wanted to see Annie. Would he? The odds were against it. He was hurt, really hurt. Jax tried to look at his bandaged shoulder. From his horizontal position he could see very little of it, but what he did see was crimson red, covered with his own blood.

He'd lost a lot of blood. He was weak, barely able to lift his head off the dirt or use his good arm.

A promise, that's what Thomas had given him. Would he be able to keep it? Would Thomas be able to get Jax out—alive? An empty promise? Maybe. If he was going to see Annie again, he had nowhere else to turn but to Thomas.

Jax looked at Thomas kneeling next to him. "Now what?" Jax asked.

"First, I'm going to get us something to eat. Then I'm going to make you as comfortable as possible. After that, I'm going to scout the area to see if I can find some help."

And by the time you find help and get back, I'll be dead. He wouldn't see Annie again. Jax wasn't afraid to be by himself. Animals might smell the blood and come for him, but he would have his .45 for protection.

He wasn't afraid that the third guy might come back. Jax had watched him run off, and from the direction he'd run and the way he'd run, it seemed like he'd had enough. He'd cleared out, not to return.

A dull ache in his back started to manifest itself; he'd been on his back in the same position for a long time. Jax squirmed a little, trying to find a new, more comfortable spot. As he adjusted his hips slightly to reposition his back, his right shoulder moved, sending a bolt of electricity pinging through his body like a silver ball bouncing from side to side in a pinball machine. The pain shot to his toes, then side to side as it ricocheted through his body toward his head.

Jax grimaced, his contorted face telling the whole story.

"You okay?" Thomas asked. "Maybe I shouldn't leave."

Thomas had to leave, had to find help. He was their only hope. They could sit and wait for someone to stumble across them by chance, but that might take forever. Jax was almost certain rescuers were out searching for them, but how long would that take? Hours? Days? A week?

"I'm fine," Jax lied. "It's just a little pain. Don't worry." What he didn't tell Thomas was that his shirt was wet under him. When he'd shifted to find a more comfortable spot, he'd reopened the wound, and the blood had started to flow. He could feel it trickling down his side.

That was what he was afraid of. Thomas would be gone too long, and by the time he returned, Jax would be dead from the loss of blood.

But, there was no other way, Thomas had to leave.

Thomas made small talk as he put together a quick meal. He helped Jax eat it. Thomas finished quickly, after Jax had eaten. He then packed the backpack with supplies for his scouting trip.

Thomas put a bottle of water in Jax's left hand and the .45, with a full magazine, next to him.

"Don't be gone long," Jax said as Thomas swung the pack to his back.

"I'll be back faster than you can scramble two eggs." Thomas winked at Jax. "And don't forget, I promised to get you out of here alive so that you can say those three special words to Annie." Thomas mouthed the words—I love you. "Just in case you forgot what they were."

Thomas turned and disappeared.

Utterly exhausted from the intensity of the last six hours, Jax fell asleep the moment he shut his eyes.

Chapter 60

Jaxon
Cell Phone

Jax woke at the sound of an engine. He cracked his eyes but didn't see anything—it was too dark. He was uncertain of the time, not knowing how long he'd been out. Jax's mind, foggy from the sleep still lurking in the corners of his head, was unable to focus.

Jax closed his eyes again. He started to fade, letting sleep take him. The sound of the engine grew stronger, drawing him back from the depth of sleep that was pulling him deeper and deeper into the darkness.

He cracked his eyes again, which helped him focus. He heard voices over the sound of the engine. Two voices. Directions. One voice told the other which way to go.

A beam of light swept over him, then disappeared. The voices searched for him. Jax struggled to raise his good arm. He wanted to raise it up like a flag on the Fourth of July. He wanted the light to pass over him again with his arm raised high, waving in the air. He wanted the two voices to see him. But he couldn't. He was too weak.

The light passed over him several more times, until finally it settled on him. It stayed this time. The voices had found him. The noise of the engine grew louder.

Jax, fully awake now, could hear Thomas's raised voice. "Pull up alongside him so we can load him from the back."

"You bet," the other voice said.

The light swept over Jax and then disappeared, throwing him into complete darkness.

"Hey, buddy," Thomas said. He was now kneeling next to Jax.

"Thomas?" Jax asked.

"Yeah Jax, it's me."

"You made it back."

"Totally. Just like I said, I found someone that can get us out of here."

An ATV pulled up next to Jax, and the engine shut off. It was too dark to make out the type of machine, but there was enough moonlight for Jax to see the uncommonly large rack on the back of it.

Suddenly another face loomed over him, right next to Thomas's. Even though the new face was almost entirely covered with a bushy handlebar mustache, Jax could still see the man's toothy grin as he beamed down on him.

"This is Cody Steiner," Thomas said. Jax didn't move. He couldn't. "I found his outfitters camp an hour ago. We're going to haul you to his camp, where he has a bush plane. From there, he said it would only be a half-hour flight to the nearest hospital."

Half an hour to the *nearest* hospital? Jax didn't like the sound of that. He liked the idea of being rescued, but he didn't want to go to the nearest hospital—he wanted to go

Two Hearts

home. He wanted to see Annie. He hadn't spoken to her in two days, and he wanted to see her one last time before he...

Jax spoke, his voice barely a whisper. "Thomas, you can't take me to the hospital. I've got to see Annie."

"But Jax, you need to go to the hospital."

"Annie, Thomas, you promised me Annie."

"Annie?" Cody asked.

"He doesn't want to go to the hospital," Thomas said. "Jax wants to go to Dillon to see his wife, Annie. I promised him I'd get him home to see his wife."

"Dillon, Montana, is a two-hour flight from here," Cody said, scratching his head. "The hospital is so much closer."

"Can you take us to Dillon?" Thomas asked.

After a moment's hesitation, Cody nodded his head. "Sure, I'll take him to see his wife."

A smile crossed Jax's lips. He would see Annie one last time.

After making a suitable bed on the back of the rack, Thomas and Cody loaded Jax on top. Every inch of his body hurt, and no matter how gentle Thomas and Cody were, Jax grimaced in pain with every step they took.

They laid Jax on the makeshift bed and secured him the best they could. Jax felt like a prized bull elk riding on the back of the ATV, except that when an elk rode on the rack, it was dead. As for now, Jax was still very much alive, and he felt every stick or rock the ATV happened to drive over. Any slight vibration or twist of the machine sent a shock wave of pain through his body.

They crawled along at a snail's pace, with Cody driving, Jax riding on top, and Thomas walking on the side to keep Jax steady. Several times Jax asked to stop so he could catch his breath. The jostling ride, even though very slight to an uninjured person, was almost too much to bear.

The pace was slow, painstakingly slow. It took them two hours to cover the ground that Thomas had crossed in only one. But, after an excruciatingly slow pace, they crept into Cody's base camp in the dead of night, worn out and exhausted.

The camp had been set up at one end of a meadow from which Cody could easily land and take off in his plane. The camp was ready for guests with six white wall tents set up in a half moon, all facing a large fire pit ringed with basketball-sized rocks. Logs for sitting were evenly spaced around the fire pit. Off to one side was another wall tent, set back from the fire pit toward the edge of the meadow, which served as the kitchen.

The camp was set up for guests, but the place was empty.

"Where is everyone?" Thomas asked.

"Gone," Cody said. "We're in between parties. Monday my two partners bring in a pack train with the next hunting group; then it's back to work."

Luck, that's what ran through Jax's head. Luck was on his side.

Parked just outside the camping area, already facing an open meadow, a yellow plane was ready for takeoff. Jax had seen that kind of plane before, but only on the internet. He'd never actually seen one in person. It was an Aviat Husky taildragger. A stable high-wing plane with over-exaggerated tires that looked like they belonged in a circus act. The tires were out of place in a municipal airport with a concrete runway, but they were in their element in the back country, perfect for landing in rough terrain, where holes and rocks lay hidden under overgrown grass. The big fat tires could practically handle any type of runway, improved or unimproved.

Thomas came to Jax's side. "How you feeling?"

Jax coughed before he answered. The truth was the trip on the back of the ATV had opened the wound on his shoulder again. The bandage Thomas had previously applied was saturated. With the loss of more blood, he was even weaker. He didn't want to tell Thomas, though, afraid it might change his mind about taking him to see Annie.

"Fine," he rasped. Jax blinked his eyes a couple of times as he tried to smile. He was too weak. He couldn't even curl his lips to grin at Thomas.

Thomas wasn't fooled. "You don't look fine." With the aid of a flashlight, Thomas bent down and examined Jax's shoulder. At the slightest touch, Jax grimaced. Cody came up to Jax's side.

"I think he needs a better bandage on his shoulder," Thomas said. "He's still losing a lot of blood."

"Be right back," Cody said as he turned and ran off. He quickly returned with a large white suitcase with a red cross on the top. He flipped it open, revealing a well-stocked first aid kit. Cody pulled out a roll of gauze wrap.

"Should we remove the old bandage first?" Thomas asked.

"No, let's just apply more gauze and reinforce the old one," Cody said.

Cody and Thomas worked together quickly. Thomas lifted, while Cody wrapped, but no matter how careful they were, Jax felt every movement and every shift of his body. He fought to stay conscious. When they were done, there was so much gauze on his shoulder, it looked like he was wearing football shoulder pads.

Jax glanced over at the plane that was waiting to take him to see Annie. "Ready to go," Jax said.

Cody looked at Thomas. Thomas looked at Jax. Thomas's shoulders dropped. "Jax, Cody thinks you're too weak to fly."

"Look," Cody said. He came and stood next to Jax. "If we fly out of here right now, you'll be dead by the time we arrive in Dillon."

Jax was in no position to argue. He wanted to see Annie, but he didn't want to die before he had the chance. "What do you suggest?"

"Rest," Cody said. "Get some fluids into your body. Eat. Build your strength back. Then we'll see." Cody shrugged. "Maybe tonight or possibly tomorrow you'll be ready to fly out of here."

Tomorrow? That seemed like a long way off. Too long for him, but he had no other choice. "Okay," Jax finally whispered.

Cody and Thomas laid Jax on a cream-colored canvas cot in one of the white wall tents used for the guests to the camp. For most of the morning, he ate, slept, and drank bottle after bottle of Gatorade, desperately trying to regain as much strength as he possibly could. He wanted to leave as soon as he could. By noon of the same day he'd entered Cody's camp, he was improving. Cody and Thomas came to check on him.

"How you feeling?" Thomas asked.

"Better."

"You look better. Your face has color—it's not deathly white anymore."

"Can we leave now?" Jax asked.

"Have some lunch first, rest a little more, and then we'll see," Cody said. "We don't want to rush it."

Jax did. Jax wanted to see Annie. But Cody was the pilot, so Jax would have to wait.

After lunch he slept. He hadn't realized how tired he was. He didn't wake until five thirty, when the sun was already halfway through its descent in the west.

Thomas came to see Jax. "Cody's getting the plane ready. He thinks you're ready to fly."

By the time Thomas and Cody loaded Jax in the cargo space of the plane, the light of the day had disappeared. The cargo space was large enough to allow him to stretch out to his full length. Cody and Thomas both sat in front, with Thomas in the copilot seat. Once Cody climbed aboard, they were off.

An hour went by. "Cody," Jax called from the back of the plane.

"Yes?"

"May I use your cell phone?"

"Sure, but I can't promise good reception." Cody handed his phone to Thomas.

"Tell me Annie's number, and I'll dial it for you," Thomas said.

"You probably should wait another half hour," Cody said. "By that time we should be closer to Dillon, and you will have at least two bars."

"Sounds good," Jax whispered. He waited, but it was hard.

Thirty minutes later to the second, Thomas opened Cody's phone and dialed Annie's number. Thomas reached over the front seat and held the phone to Jax's ear.

It rang only a half a ring when Annie answered it. She sounded happy, but her words surprised him.

"Beth, how are you?" Annie said.

"Baby, this is Jax."

Chapter 61

Annie

Ambulance

Annie screamed.

"Annie," she heard Jax say. Annie screamed again.

She dropped the phone in her lap.

Had she heard right? Jax was dead. No survivors. Three bodies recovered. That's what the news had reported. But she'd heard his voice. That was his voice. It was Jax. She grabbed the phone, took a deep breath.

"Jax, is that you?"

"Yes."

"Really?"

"Yes, it's me."

"Where are you?"

Nothing. Suddenly she heard coughing. A lot of coughing. Annie could hear Jax hacking. That didn't sound like Jax. She'd never known him to cough so violently.

"Jax? Are you okay?"

"No." Annie could barely hear him, his voice was so soft.

Instinctively she raised her voice when she spoke. "Where are you?"

"I'm in a plane," Jax said.

"But, I saw the news—the plane crashed."

"Yeah," Jax said, his breathing hard and labored. Each word coming with great effort. ". . . a different plane."

"Jax, a different plane? Where?" Nothing made sense. Jax's plane had crashed.

"Baby, this . . . may be . . . the . . ." Jax's voice trailed off.

"Jax? Are you there?" Nothing. "Hello, Jax?"

Annie glanced at the screen of her phone. Still connected. She put the phone back to her ear. She could hear muffled noises in the background, but nothing distinguishable.

"Annie?" A male voice finally asked.

"Jax?"

"No, this is Thomas."

"Where's Jax? What's wrong with him?"

"He's been shot twice."

"Shot?" Annie's mouth dropped opened. "Jax has been shot?" Annie asked.

"Yeah. I can explain later, but right now we need you to call the ambulance to meet us at the Dillon airport."

"How bad is he?" Annie asked.

"Bad, really bad."

"Is he going to live?"

"He's going to live, but he needs the ambulance."

"How long?"

"We should be there in the next fifteen minutes."

"I'll meet you there with the ambulance."

Thomas and Annie both clicked off at the same time.

Two Hearts

Annie queued up the dialer pad on her phone, and with trembling fingers, she dialed 9-1-1. When the operator answered she relayed the emergency situation, requesting an ambulance be sent to the airport. Annie told the operator what she knew—multiple gunshot wounds and that the injured would be arriving in an airplane in fifteen minutes, if not sooner.

The operator dispatched the ambulance, and they disconnected.

Jax was alive. He'd survived the crash. But he was shot. Everything was so confusing.

Annie glanced out over the valley floor at the city lights. She was going to see Jax just like she'd thought. She put the car in reverse and gently backed away from the edge. She turned the car toward the road heading down from Lover's Flat. Jax was coming home.

Chapter 62

Jaxon

Reunited

Even though the Husky had extraordinarily large tires, which compensate for rough terrain and which could make any pilot look like an expert at landing, Cody was in a hurry to get Jax on the ground as quickly as possible. He came in hard and fast, slamming the plane down on the runway, botching the landing and causing Jax to flatten out against the floor of the plane.

Jax barely felt it, though. He was fading in and out. Unknown to Thomas or Cody, the long, bouncy flight had opened both of Jax's wounds, and he'd lost more blood. He was weak, and as a result, he'd lost consciousness while on the phone with Annie.

When they bounced on the runway, Jaxon stirred. "Annie," Jax yelled reaching out for her with his one good arm. Thomas, having abandoned the copilot seat after Jax dropped the phone, was now sitting in the cargo space next to Jax. Thomas reached out and took Jax by the hand.

"Right here, buddy," Thomas said.

"Annie," Jax yelled again.

The airplane taxied across the runway, heading for the service center. With red, blue, and yellow lights flashing, an ambulance, a fire truck, and a police car waited at the service center for Jax's arrival. As they drew near, a lone figure stepped out in front of the police car, arms crossed in front of her.

"Jax, I can see Annie. She's here." Thomas squeezed Jax's hand. "She's here, buddy, she's here."

Before the plane came to a complete stop, the cargo doors popped open. Emergency personnel immediately rushed the plane, going to work on Jax. In between the sounds of the winding down of the propeller and the noise from the emergency personnel, Jax could be heard yelling, "Annie! Annie, where are you?"

Thomas, having exited the plane from the passenger's door, made his way through the crowd, pulling Annie with him until they reached Jax.

There she was, standing by his side, her eyes filled with tears. He raised his left arm. She took his hand in hers, drawing it close to her chest. He had so much to tell her he didn't know where to begin.

"I've a story to tell you," Jax said, "but this one doesn't have a happy ending."

"Shhhh," Annie said, holding her index finger to Jax's lips. "Your story does have a happy ending, because you're alive and you're home. The mine, the ranch, those things don't matter. All that matters is that you're alive and home with me."

Chapter 63

Annie

Mr. Windsor

Jax spent two days in the intensive care unit, where he received a blood transfusion and reconstructive surgery to his shoulder. Annie never left the hospital, sleeping in the recliner in Jax's room or in the lobby outside the surgery room.

Sunday night, Jax returned to his room after the reconstructive surgery. The doctor's prognosis was good. In the initial assessment, the bone in the shoulder had been damaged beyond repair. He would live, but it would be difficult for him to lift heavy objects for a while. After the surgery, the prognosis had improved. His shoulder would mend completely, Jax would regain 100 percent use of the shoulder, but he would have to rest it for at least a year before he could use it again.

By Monday Jax had recovered enough to tell Annie every little detail about his trip. He didn't hold back. He told her everything, from the moment they'd left Dillon until they'd returned in the Husky bush plane.

He told her about the sulfuric smell of Pagosa Springs. He shared with her about Sven, the waiter at the restaurant. He told her how he'd borrowed a hotel robe to sneak into the resort to find Kris Dirkfield. He told her how depressed he'd felt when Mr. Dirkfield had rejected him. He shared with her his crazy idea of leaving the dirt at the hotel lobby with the clerk who spoke like a valley girl.

Jax sighed, "In the end, it was all a waste of time, like you'd said it would be."

"That doesn't matter. You're home and you're safe, that's what's important."

"What about the ranch?"

"Let's not worry about that right now. You just rest. When you get home, we can deal with that."

It took most of the morning to tell her about his meeting with Mr. Dirkfield. By noon, exhaustion overtook him. He needed a break. They stopped for lunch.

After lunch, Jax wanted to continue with his story until the end even though he was still tired. Annie knew Jax had tried calling her all night Wednesday and all Thursday morning, but he didn't mention anything about that. In his story he went straight from being rejected on Wednesday afternoon to Thursday morning when he'd left the dirt package with the clerk. From there he jumped to late Thursday morning when he'd loaded the plane with Zeren and Thomas's gear.

It seemed Jax had purposely skipped over the part where he had tried repeatedly to get ahold of her. Annie didn't ask why. If Jax didn't want to talk about it, then she didn't want to either. Right now she didn't want to be the one to bring up their argument. Not now, anyway.

Annie sat at the edge of his bed with eyes wide as Jax told the part about the plane's engine bursting into flames. Mayday calls had been made. Grand Junction had responded. The emergency transponder hadn't worked. It was all very exciting. Then came the meadow, the landing, the stream, and the flipping of the plane. Jax told about his twisted leg.

He pulled back the covers, showing Annie the torn skin and the bruise that covered 90 percent of his right thigh.

"I can't believe Zeren left you hanging there," Annie said.

"Yeah," Jax said, covering his leg with the blanket. "The moment Zeren kicked the door open, he took off. I actually thought he wasn't going to come back."

"What if he hadn't?"

"I'd probably still be hanging there."

"What happened next?"

While still unconscious, Thomas had been removed from the plane. Zeren's friends had come in a helicopter. Lots of shooting. Jax held up his left hand in front of him, as if he were sighting down his Colt .45.

"Six quick shots and one was lucky. I'd hit the helicopter." He pulled up his covers to show his bandaged side. "That's when I got hit in the side.

More shooting.

Jax told Annie how he'd shot one of them in the shoulder and how another one had run off. That left only one guy.

Jax went into detail about his argument with Zeren and how Zeren had wanted to leave Thomas. If it hadn't been for Zeren, the last tall guy wouldn't have been able to sneak up on them.

"Nobody knew it, but Thomas had woken up while Zeren and I were arguing."

Sitting partially up in bed, the bandage on his right shoulder was clearly visible.

"I was able to spin enough to avoid a direct hit, but one of the bullets nicked me in the shoulder, skipping off my scapula and tearing off the top part of my shoulder."

"It was a good thing Thomas was there to stop the bleeding, or we'd be having a funeral for you right now," Annie said.

"Thomas definitely was the hero. He didn't want to leave me, but there was no other way. He just never gave up."

"Who would've thought quiet Thomas would be the hero of the day. I'm going to have to give that man a hug the next time I see him."

A knock sounded on the partially open hospital door. Annie stood, rising off the bed. She turned toward the door as Mr. Windsor stepped in.

"Hello Annie, Jax." Dressed in a stylish, blue, pin-striped suit, he wore a bright red tie and a matching silk pocket square. Metal taps on the bottom of his shoes clicked on the hard vinyl floor as he entered.

Mr. Windsor stiffly walked into the room. He stopped at the end of the bed. He glanced out the window. He shuffled his feet. He turned back to Jax, folded his arms on his chest. He seemed uncomfortable. He finally said, "The board met this morning. They won't wait any longer."

No small talk. Straight to the business at hand.

Annie stepped in. "Honestly, you can't expect under the circumstances . . ."

"I've tried to explain all that," Mr. Windsor said. "I feel the same way. I've tried to reason with the board, but they won't listen. They feel horrible about what happened, but they have a business to run."

"You mean *you* have a business to run," Annie said.

"Annie," Mr. Windsor's head lowered slightly, his folded arms dropping to his side, "you know it's not like that. You know I don't want you to leave. I'm only a part of the bank. I may be the president, but I have to answer to the board, and right now I'm outnumbered. I've done all I can to hold off foreclosure proceedings this past year. There is nothing else I can do."

Another knock sounded on the door. Mr. Windsor, interrupted and forgotten, stepped back from the bed, practically disappearing behind the door as it swung open.

A woman with beautiful, long blond hair stepped into the room. She carried with her an air of confidence, stepping in as if she owned the place. It wasn't arrogance, Annie guessed. It was poise that came from an inner strength—a self-awareness.

She wore a sporty athletic outfit like she was heading to the gym. But she wasn't, not with the hair and the jewels.

The hair, masterfully crafted with large bouncy curls, cascaded over both shoulders and down the woman's back. She looked like she'd just stepped out of a fashion magazine. A diamond-studded tiara held the masterpiece in place. A solitary diamond that must have been five carats hung around her neck. She stepped in, wearing bedazzled three-inch high heels. The woman sparkled.

Fashionably sporty, Annie thought.

"Mr. Tagget?" The woman had a heavy German accent. As she scanned Jax's face, recognition dawned in her eyes. "I finally found you."

Annie recognized the woman from the website. Kris Dirkfield, *the other woman*, was in their hospital room. Annie's brow furrowed. *Do we have to do this right now?*

Chapter 64

Jaxon

Bad News

A world of emotion flooded over Jax as he remembered the last argument he'd had with Annie. The word *cheater* flashed through his mind. And now, Mrs. Dirkfield, the woman on the website, was in their hospital room. Even he'd been fooled by the tricky but effective advertising.

Annie stepped to the side of Jax's bed and placed her hand on his arm, gently making her way down it until she found his hand. Their fingers intertwined.

"Jax?" Annie said. Uneasiness readily apparent in her voice. She clutched on to his hand, cutting off the circulation in his fingers.

"Sophia Dirkfield," Jax said, overemphasizing her first name, "this is my wife Annie."

Mrs. Dirkfield stepped around the end of the bed with her hand extended. Annie let go of Jax's hand and shook hands with Mrs. Dirkfield.

"Nice to meet you," Mrs. Dirkfield said.

"Sophia?" Annie said. She glanced back at Jax. "Who is Kris Dirkfield?"

"That would be me." Mr. Dirkfield stepped through the door, sporting an Armani blue blazer over khaki slacks, a yellow button down opened at the collar, and loafers. Professional but casual.

A happy smile crossed Annie's face. She'd already picked up Jax's hand. She gave it a squeeze. She bent down and gave him a kiss on the lips. She whispered, "I love you." She gazed into his eyes. Her eyes twinkled as she smiled. A sweet and silent understanding passed between the two of them. *Everything was going to be okay*, Jax thought.

Jax glanced back at the couple standing at the end of his bed. "Mr. and Mrs. Dirkfield, why are you here?"

"I've been trying to get ahold of you for the past three days," Mr. Dirkfield said.

"You have? Why?"

"Because," Mrs. Dirkfield stepped forward, "when the clerk at the resort delivered your package of dirt to our room on Thursday morning, I told Kris, 'We are leaving today'."

"That's what she told me," Mr. Dirkfield said, a big smile crossing his face as he glanced at his wife. "She said, 'We are leaving today.' And I said, 'Where are we going?' And she said, 'We are going to Dallas to have this dirt tested today.' And I said, 'Why?' And, do you know what she said to me?"

"No," Jax said, excitement growing in his eyes. He figured this story was going somewhere and he hoped he knew where.

"She said, 'Because I like that boy. I could see it in his eyes, the desperation, the hope, and the faith. He is desperate for our help. He came all the way to Pagosa hoping we could help him. He had faith that if he had the chance to meet us we would listen to him and help him.' She said, 'He has guts. It took courage to come here to meet you, and because of that, we are going to Dallas today.' That's what she said, and that's why I've been trying to call you for the past three days."

"Well," Jax dropped his eyes, scanning his body covered by the hospital bed sheet, "as you can see, I've been kind of busy with my own little adventure. Sorry you couldn't get ahold of me."

"No matter," Mr. Dirkfield waved a dismissive hand. "We've come in person, but I'm afraid the news we have isn't good."

"You come all this way to Dillon to give me bad news."

"Just tell him," Mrs. Dirkfield said. "Can't you see that you're making this too painful for him?"

"Very well." Mr. Dirkfield pulled a legal-sized envelope from the left interior pocket of his blazer. "This is the test results of your dirt sample. At my request, the lab did a full workup on the sample, covering, not only gold, silver, and other precious metals, but also other valuable minerals. They performed a full-scale analysis. But, I'm truly sorry to say, there are only traces of gold and silver."

Mr. Dirkfield stopped talking, the words *only traces* hung heavily in the air.

Jax's chest sank.

Mr. Dirkfield continued. "There should be enough gold and silver to cover our digging expenses, but it won't be our primary target."

Jax's brow furrowed. "Not your primary target?" Jax hesitated for a moment as he thought about it. "What would be your primary target?"

"Talc." Mr. Dirkfield gently waved the envelope back and forth out in front of him. "According to this report, your mine is loaded with talc, a literal gold mine of talc."

"Talc?" Jax asked.

"Yes, you know, that white powdery stuff used in . . .

"Baby powder, paint, makeup."

"Even chewing gum." Mr. Dirkfield waved the report again. "The report estimates initial production levels of approximately 150,000 to 200,000 tons per year. I believe there could be more."

"Really?" That was all Jax could say. *Talc?* He knew what it was. He'd been blinded by the thought of gold that he'd missed what was right in front of him. Who would have ever thought Western Pleasure, an old abandoned gold mine, was a talc mine?

Jax's mind focused, and he saw the undetected Mr. Windsor standing back in the shadow of the door.

"So, what does this all mean?" Jax asked.

"It means we would like to—"

"It means," Mrs. Dirkfield cut in, "that you are a very wealthy man."

"What Sophia is saying is that we want to invest, with an initial signing bonus of two million dollars that will go directly to you. We would also like to hire you as a director of operations to run the mine."

Mr. Windsor's face lit up with a toothy grin that spanned from ear to ear. He'd obviously heard what he needed to hear. He gave Annie and Jax a slight nod with his head, acknowledging what he'd heard and silently communicating that the issue with the board about the mortgage would be taken care of. He quietly slipped around the door and disappeared out of the room undetected.

Jax turned to Annie, "We've done it."

"No, Jax," she smiled. She leaned down and kissed him gently on the lips. "You did it, like you always said you would."

Chapter 65

Annie

Good News

Mr. and Mrs. Dirkfield left after discussing the details of the necessary documents, which they said would be sent over by the end of the week. Once the documents were signed and everything was in order, the initial investment would be wired to their account. If all things went as planned, they would start moving equipment to the mine by the end of next month.

Jax was still in his hospital bed. Annie was sitting in a chair next to the bed, holding Jax's hand. The reality of what had just happened still hadn't set in.

"Thanks, Jax," Annie said.

"Thanks for what?"

"Thanks for being patient with me." Jax gave her a puzzled look.

"I know I've got baggage. My past isn't squeaky clean. I'm sorry you have to deal with all that's going on inside my head. My father and mother and their messed up lives have really got me screwed up." Annie stared down. "I mean, I shouldn't have allowed my past to cloud our relationship." Annie paused for a moment, gathering her thoughts. She wanted to say this just right without making it worse. Jax stayed silent, letting Annie talk, which was what she needed.

It was hard for her to say it, to admit that she'd had been wrong, but it needed to be said.

"I'm sorry. I'm truly sorry. I was wrong to jump to conclusions. I didn't trust you. I thought you'd run off to Colorado to cheat on me with another woman. I was wrong. Totally wrong. All you've ever done is take care of me. And the moment you ran off to Colorado, I jumped to conclusions, allowing my past to cloud my thinking. My imagination ran wild, which made the situation worse. Trust, that's what I need to work on. I know it sounds like I'm rambling all over the place, but let me say it again, I'm sorry."

Jax reached over and drew the chain visible around Annie's neck from under her blouse. On the end of the chain was the two hearts pendant he'd made for her. He held it in his hand.

"Two hearts. Yours and mine forever, never to part. When I said I do, I meant forever. I'm yours, and only yours. There is no one else. It has always been you and only you."

Suddenly, there was a knock on the door. Annie and Jax both turned as Annie's mother, Patricia Bradley, stepped into the room holding a vase of flowers. There were vibrant yellow chrysanthemums, red snapdragons, pink carnations, yellow daffodils, and violet gerbera. It was a stunning bouquet, guaranteed to brighten anyone's day.

"You're here?" Jax said.

"After you called me, Jax," Annie said, "I called her driving from the ranch to the airport and told her you'd been shot. I asked her to come."

"These are for those that have returned from the dead," Mrs. Bradley said. She held up the vase of flowers.

"Oh, Mother. They're beautiful." Annie stood and took the vase and placed them on the windowsill with the other flowers and cards Jax had received from family and friends.

Jax shook his head slightly. "I'm so sorry. I totally forgot."

Mrs. Bradley gave him a wink. "Under the circumstances it's understandable. If I'd have gone through the same ordeal as you, I would have forgotten as well."

"Forgot what?" Annie asked as she stepped back to the bed side.

"Before I left for Pagosa Springs," Jax said, "I'd arranged to pick up your mother in Denver on my return flight. But, after all that had happened, I forgot to stop.

"It's a good thing you forgot; what you went through didn't sound like much fun," Mrs. Bradley said.

"Why were you going to pick her up?" Annie asked.

"I wanted her to be here when I told you the news."

"About the mine? You were pretty optimistic, arranging to pick up my mother before you even knew."

"Not about the mine," Jax said. "Remember on Tuesday before I left for Pagosa, I went into Dillon to run some errands?"

"Yeah," Annie said, "that's when you brought Zeren and Thomas back to the ranch with you."

"Yeah, exactly. Before I ran into them, I saw Dr. Goodman on the street. Do you remember him running several tests after you'd fainted in the grocery store?"

"Yes. But, I've been fine since." Annie didn't mention how she'd been sick practically every morning for the past two weeks since those tests.

"Well, he gave me the results of those tests, and I wanted your mother to be here when I shared them with you."

He had her attention now. Her mother was here all the way from Denver. This was serious. Maybe she was dying and that's why she'd been so sick lately. At the thought of dying, she needed to sit down. She dropped into the chair.

"How much time do I have left?" she asked.

"About eight months," Jax said.

Eight months, that wasn't a long time. Annie's hand started to tremble on the armrest. "What do I have?"

"Do you have room in your heart for one more?"

"Yes?" Annie said. "Why?"

"You're having a baby."

Author Bio

James Eric Richey was born and raised in California. He attended Brigham Young University, studying English with an emphasis in Literature.

After graduating from BYU he returned home to California to further his education by attending law school. After passing the bar, James practiced in California for several years, but he quickly learned that he did not have a passion for the law.

In 1998 James obtained his real estate appraiser license, which has given him a flexible work schedule and allowed him to pursue his true passion, writing books. Besides his writing, he also enjoys reading, running, and sailing. James currently lives in Cheyenne, Wyoming, with his wife, Heather Dawn Richey, and their two daughters.

Made in the USA
Charleston, SC
11 June 2015